THE COMPLETE SHORT STORIES
OF D. H. LAWRENCE
VOL. III

D. H. LAWRENCE

The Complete
Short Stories
VOL. III

VIKING PRESS · NEW YORK

The Complete Short Stories of D. H. Lawrence

in Three Volumes

VIKING COMPASS EDITION

Issued in 1961 by The Viking Press, Inc.

625 Madison Avenue, New York, N.Y. 10022

Distributed in Canada by

The Macmillan Company of Canada Limited

Stories from *The Woman Who Rode Away* are reprinted by arrangement with Alfred A. Knopf, Inc.

SBN 670-00097-3
Library of Congress catalog card number: 71-101368

Tenth printing September 1972

Printed in the U.S.A. by The Murray Printing Company

CONTENTS

Volume III

Volume I

THE BORDER LINE

KATHERINE FARQUHAR was a handsome woman of forty, no longer slim, but attractive in her soft, full feminine way. The French porters ran round her, getting a voluptuous pleasure from merely carrying her bags. And she gave them ridiculously high tips, because, in the first place, she had never really known the value of money, and secondly, she had a morbid fear of underpaying anyone, but particularly a man who was eager to serve her.

It was really a joke to her, how eagerly these Frenchmen—all sorts of Frenchmen—ran round her, and *Madame'd* her. Their voluptuous obsequiousness. Because, after all, she was Boche. Fifteen years of marriage to an Englishman—or rather to two Englishmen—had not altered her racially. Daughter of a German baron she was, and remained in her own mind and body, although England had become her life-home. And surely she looked German, with her fresh complexion and her strong, full figure. But, like most people in the world, she was a mixture, with Russian blood and French blood also in her veins. And she had lived in one country and another, till she was somewhat indifferent to her surroundings. So that perhaps the Parisian men might be excused for running round her so eagerly, and getting a voluptuous pleasure from calling a taxi for her, or giving up a place in the omnibus to her, or carrying her bags, or holding the menu card before her. Nevertheless, it amused her. And she had to confess she liked them, these Parisians. They had their own kind of manliness, even if it wasn't an English sort; and if a woman looked pleasant and soft-fleshed, and a wee bit helpless, they were ardent and generous. Katherine understood so well that Frenchmen were rude to the dry, hard-seeming, competent Englishwoman or American. She sympathised with the Frenchman's point of view; too much obvious capacity to help herself is a disagreeable trait in a woman.

At the Gare de l'Est, of course, everybody was expected to be Boche, and it was almost a convention, with the porters, to assume a certain small-boyish superciliousness. Nevertheless, there was the same voluptuous scramble to escort

Katherine Farquhar to her seat in the first-class carriage. *Madame* was travelling alone.

She was going to Germany via Strasburg, meeting her sister in Baden-Baden. Philip, her husband, was in Germany, collecting some sort of evidence for his newspaper. Katherine felt a little weary of newspapers, and of the sort of 'evidence' that is extracted out of nowhere to feed them. However, Philip was quite clever, he was a little somebody in the world.

Her world, she had realised, consisted almost entirely of little somebodies. She was outside the sphere of the nobodies, always had been. And the Somebodies with a capital 'S' were all safely dead. She knew enough of the world to-day to know that it is not going to put up with any great Somebody; but many little nobodies and a sufficient number of little somebodies. Which, after all, is as it should be, she felt.

Sometimes she had vague misgivings.

Paris, for example, with its Louvre and its Luxembourg and its cathedral, seemed intended for Somebody. In a ghostly way it called for some supreme Somebody. But all its little men, nobodies and somebodies, were as sparrows twittering for crumbs, and dropping their little droppings on the palace cornices.

To Katherine, Paris brought back again her first husband, Alan Anstruther, that red-haired fighting Celt, father of her two grown-up children. Alan had had a weird innate conviction that he was beyond ordinary judgment. Katherine could never quite see where it came in. Son of a Scottish baronet, and captain in a Highland regiment did not seem to her stupendous. As for Alan himself, he was handsome in uniform, with his kilt swinging and his blue eye glaring. Even stark naked and without any trimmings, he had a bony, dauntless, overbearing manliness of his own. The one thing Katherine could *not quite* appreciate was his silent, indomitable assumption that he was actually first-born, a born lord. He was a clever man, too, ready to assume that General This or Colonel That might really be his superior. Until he actually came into contact with General This or Colonel That. Whereupon his over-weening blue eye arched in his bony face, and a faint tinge of contempt infused itself into his homage.

Lordly or not, he wasn't much of a success in the worldly sense. Katherine had loved him, and he had loved her: that was indisputable. But when it came to innate conviction of lordliness, it was a question which of them was worse. For she, in her amiable, queen-bee self, thought that ultimately hers was the right to the last homage.

Alan had been too unyielding and haughty to say much. But sometimes he would stand and look at her in silent rage, wonder, and indignation. The wondering indignation had been *almost* too much for her. What did the man think he was?

He was one of the hard, clever Scotsmen, with a philosophic tendency, but without sentimentality. His contempt of Nietzsche, whom she adored, was intolerable. Alan just asserted himself like a pillar of rock, and expected the tides of the modern world to recede around him. They didn't.

So he concerned himself with astronomy, gazing through a telescope and watching the worlds beyond worlds. Which seemed to give him relief.

After ten years they had ceased to live together, passionate as they both were. They were too proud and unforgiving to yield to one another, and much too haughty to yield to any outsider.

Alan had a friend, Philip, also a Scotsman, and a university friend. Philip, trained for the Bar, had gone into journalism, and had made himself a name. He was a little black High-lander of the insidious sort, clever and *knowing*. This look of knowing in his dark eyes, and the feeling of secrecy that went with his dark little body, made him interesting to women. Another thing he could do was to give off a great sense of warmth and offering, like a dog when it loves you. He seemed to be able to do this at will. And Katherine, after feeling cool about him and rather despising him for years, at last fell under the spell of the dark, insidious fellow.

"You!" she said to Alan, whose over-weening masterful-ness drove her wild. "You don't even know that a woman exists. And that's where Philip Farquhar is more than you are. He *does* know something of what a woman *is*."

"Bah! the little——" said Alan, using an obscene word of contempt.

Nevertheless, the friendship endured, kept up by Philip, who had an almost uncanny love for Alan. Alan was mostly indifferent. But he was used to Philip, and habit meant a great deal to him.

"Alan really is an amazing man!" Philip would say to

Katherine. "He is the only real man, what I call a real man, that I have ever met."

"But why is he the only real man?" she asked. "Don't you call yourself a real man?"

"Oh, I—I'm different! My strength lies in giving in—and then recovering myself. I do let myself be swept away. But, so far, I've always managed to get myself back again. Alan——" and Philip even had a half-reverential, half-envious way of uttering the word—"Alan *never* lets himself be swept away. And he's the only man I know who doesn't."

"Yah!" she said. "He is fooled by plenty of things. You can fool him through his vanity."

"No," said Philip. "Never altogether. You *can't* deceive him right through. When a thing really touches Alan, it is tested once and for all. You know if it's false or not. He's the only man I ever met who *can't help* being real."

"Ha! You over-rate his reality," said Katherine, rather scornfully.

And later, when Alan shrugged his shoulders with that mere indifferent tolerance, at the mention of Philip, she got angry.

"You are a poor friend," she said.

"Friend!" he answered. "I never was Farquhar's friend! If he asserts that he's mine, that's his side of the question. I never positively cared for the man. He's too much over the wrong side of the border for me."

"Then," she answered, "you've no business to let him *consider* he is your friend. You've no right to let him think so much of you. You should tell him you don't like him."

"I've told him a dozen times. He seems to enjoy it. It seems part of his game."

And he went away to his astronomy.

Came the war, and the departure of Alan's regiment for France.

"There!" he said. "Now you have to pay the penalty of having married a soldier. You find him fighting your own people. So it is."

She was too much struck by this blow even to weep.

"Good-bye!" he said, kissing her gently, lingeringly. After all, he had been a husband to her.

And as he looked back at her, with the gentle, protective husband knowledge in his blue eyes, and at the same time that other quiet realisation of destiny, her consciousness

fluttered into incoherence. She only wanted to alter everything, to alter the past, to alter all the flow of history—the
terrible flow of history. Secretly somewhere inside herself
she felt that with her queen-bee love, and queen-bee will, she
could divert the whole flow of history—nay, even reverse it.

But in the remote, realising look that lay at the back of his
eyes, behind all his changeless husband-care, she saw that it
could never be so. That the whole of her womanly, motherly
concentration could never put back the great flow of human
destiny. That, as he said, only the cold strength of a man,
accepting the destiny of destruction, could see the human
flow through the chaos and beyond to a new outlet. But the
chaos first, and the long rage of destruction.

For an instant her will broke. Almost her soul seemed
broken. And then he was gone. And as soon as he was gone
she recovered the core of her assurance.

Philip was a great consolation to her. He asserted that the
war was monstrous, that it should never have been, and that
men should refuse to consider it as anything but a colossal,
disgraceful accident.

She, in her German soul, knew that it was no accident. It
was inevitable, and even necessary. But Philip's attitude
soothed her enormously, restored her to herself.

Alan never came back. In the spring of 1915 he was missing. She had never mourned for him. She had never really
considered him dead. In a certain sense she had triumphed.
The queen-bee had recovered her sway, as queen of the earth;
the woman, the mother, the female with the ear of corn in
her hand, as against the man with the sword.

Philip had gone through the war as a journalist, always
throwing his weight on the side of humanity, and human
truth and peace. He had been an inexpressible consolation.
And in 1921 she had married him.

The thread of fate might be spun, it might even be
measured out, but the hand of Lachesis had been stayed
from cutting it through.

At first it was wonderfully pleasant and restful and
voluptuous, especially for a woman of thirty-eight, to be
married to Philip. Katherine felt he caressed her senses, and
soothed her, and gave her what she wanted.

Then, gradually, a curious sense of degradation started in
her spirit. She felt unsure, uncertain. It was almost like

having a disease. Life became dull and unreal to her, as it had never been before. She did not even struggle and suffer. In the numbness of her flesh she could feel no reactions. Everything was turning into mud.

Then again, she would recover, and *enjoy* herself wonderfully. And after a while, the suffocating sense of nullity and degradation once more. Why, why, why did she feel degraded, in her secret soul? *Never*, of course, outwardly.

The memory of Alan came back into her. She still thought of him and his relentlessness with an arrested heart, but without the angry hostility she used to feel. A little awe of him, of his memory, stole back into her spirit. She resisted it. She was not used to feeling awe.

She realised, however, the difference between being married to a soldier, a ceaseless born fighter, a sword not to be sheathed, and this other man, this cunning civilian, this subtle equivocator, this adjuster of the scales of truth.

Philip was cleverer than she was. He set her up, the queen-bee, the mother, the woman, the female judgment, and he served her with subtle, cunning homage. He put the scales, the balance in her hand. But also, cunningly, he blindfolded her, and manipulated the scales when she was sightless.

Dimly she had realised all this. But only dimly, confusedly, because she was blindfolded. Philip had the subtle, fawning power that could keep her always blindfolded.

Sometimes she gasped and gasped from her oppressed lungs. And sometimes the bony, hard, masterful, but honest face of Alan would come back, and suddenly it would seem to her that she was all right again, that the strange, voluptuous suffocation, which left her soul in mud, was gone, and she could breathe the air of the open heavens once more. Even fighting air.

It came to her on the boat crossing the Channel. Suddenly she seemed to feel Alan at her side again, as if Philip had never existed. As if Philip had never meant anything more to her than the shop assistant measuring off her orders. And escaping, as it were, by herself across the cold, wintry Channel, she suddenly deluded herself into feeling as if Philip had never existed, only Alan had ever been her husband. He was her husband still. And she was going to meet him.

This gave her her blitheness in Paris, and made the Frenchmen so nice to her. For the Latins love to feel a woman is really enveloped in the spell of some man. Beyond all race is the problem of man and woman.

Katherine now sat dimly, vaguely excited and almost happy in the railway carriage on the East railway. It was like the old days when she was going home to Germany. Or even more like the old days when she was coming back to Alan. Because, in the past, when he was her husband, feel as she might towards him, she could never get over the sensation that the wheels of the railway carriage had wings, when they were taking her back to him. Even when she knew that he was going to be awful to her, hard and relentless and destructive, still the motion went on wings.

Whereas towards Philip she moved with a strange, disintegrating reluctance. She decided not to think of him.

As she looked unseeing out of the carriage window, suddenly, with a jolt, the wintry landscape realised itself in her consciousness. The flat, grey, wintry landscape, ploughed fields of greyish earth that looked as if they were compounded of the clay of dead men. Pallid, stark, thin trees stood like wire beside straight, abstract roads. A ruined farm between a few more trees. And a dismal village filed past, with smashed houses like rotten teeth between the straight rows of the village street.

With sudden horror she realised that she must be in the Marne country, the ghastly Marne country, century after century digging the corpses of frustrated men into its soil. The border country, where the Latin races and the Germanic neutralise one another into horrid ash.

Perhaps even the corpse of her own man among that grey clay.

It was too much for her. She sat ashy herself with horror, wanting to escape.

"If I had only known," she said. "If only I had known, I would have gone by Basle."

The train drew up at Soissons; name ghastly to her. She simply tried to make herself unreceptive to everything. And mercifully luncheon was served. She went down to the restaurant-car, and sat opposite to a little French officer in horizon-blue uniform, who suggested anything but war. He looked so naïve, rather child-like and nice, with the certain innocence that so many French people preserve under their so-called wickedness, that she felt really relieved. He bowed to her with an odd, shy little bow when she returned him his half-bottle of red wine, which had slowly jigged its way the length of the table, owing to the motion of the train. How nice he was! And how he would give himself to a woman, if she would only find real pleasure in the male that he was.

Nevertheless, she herself felt very remote from this business of male and female, and giving and taking.

After luncheon, in the heat of the train and the flush of her half-bottle of white wine, she went to sleep again, her feet grilling uncomfortably on the iron plate of the carriage floor. And as she slept, life, as she had known it, seemed all to turn artificial to her, the sunshine of the world an artificial light, with smoke above, like the light of torches, and things artificially growing, in a night that was lit up artificially with such intensity that it gave the illusion of day. It had been an illusion, her life-day, as a ballroom evening is an illusion. Her love and her emotions, her very panic of love, had been an illusion. She realised how love had become panic-stricken inside her during the war.

And now even this panic of love was an illusion. She had run to Philip to be saved. And now, both her panic-love and Philip's salvation were an illusion.

What remained then? Even panic-stricken love, the intensest thing, perhaps, she had ever felt, was only an illusion. What was left? The grey shadows of death?

When she looked out again it was growing dark, and they were at Nancy. She used to know this country as a girl. At half-past seven she was in Strasburg, where she must stay the night as there was no train over the Rhine till morning.

The porter, a blond, hefty fellow, addressed her at once in Alsatian German. He insisted on escorting her safely to her hotel—a German hotel—keeping guard over her like an appointed sentinel, very faithful and competent, so different from Frenchmen.

It was a cold, wintry night, but she wanted to go out after dinner to see the minster. She remembered it all so well, in that other life.

The wind blew icily in the street. The town seemed empty, as if its spirit had left it. The few squat, hefty foot-passengers were all talking the harsh Alsatian German. Shop-signs were in French, often with a little concession to German underneath. And the shops were full of goods, glutted with goods from the once-German factories of Mulhausen and other cities.

She crossed the night-dark river, where the wash-houses of the washerwomen were anchored along the stream, a few odd women still kneeling over the water's edge, in the dim electric light, rinsing their clothes in the grim, cold water. In the big square the icy wind was blowing, and the place seemed a desert. A city once more conquered.

After all she could not remember her way to the cathedral. She saw a French policeman in his blue cape and peaked cap, looking a lonely, vulnerable, silky specimen in this harsh Alsatian city. Crossing over to him, she asked him in French where was the cathedral.

He pointed out to her, the first turning on the left. He did not seem hostile; nobody seemed really hostile. Only the great frozen weariness of winter in a conquered city, on a weary everlasting border-line.

And the Frenchmen seemed far more weary, and also more sensitive, than the crude Alsatians.

She remembered the little street, the old, overhanging houses with black timbers and high gables. And like a great ghost, a reddish flush in its darkness, the uncanny cathedral breasting the oncomer, standing gigantic, looking down in darkness out of darkness, on the pigmy humanness of the city. It was built of reddish stone, that had a flush in the night, like dark flesh. And vast, an incomprehensibly tall, strange thing, it looked down out of the night. The great rose window, poised high, seemed like a breast of the vast Thing, and prisms and needles of stone shot up, as if it were plumage, dimly, half visible in heaven.

There it was, in the upper darkness of the ponderous winter night, like a menace. She remembered her spirit used in the past to soar aloft with it. But now, looming with a faint rust of blood out of the upper black heavens, the Thing stood suspended, looking down with vast, demonish menace, calm and implacable.

Mystery and dim, ancient fear came over the woman's soul. The cathedral looked so strange and demonish-heathen. And an ancient, indomitable blood seemed to stir in it. It stood there like some vast silent beast with teeth of stone, waiting, and wondering when to stoop against this pallid humanity.

And dimly she realised that behind all the ashy pallor and sulphur of our civilisation, lurks the great blood-creature waiting, implacable and eternal, ready at last to crush our white brittleness and let the shadowy blood move erect once more, in a new implacable pride and strength. Even out of the lower heavens looms the great blood-dusky Thing, blotting out the Cross it was supposed to exalt.

The scroll of the night sky seemed to roll back, showing a huge, blood-dusky presence looming enormous, stooping, looking down, awaiting its moment.

As she turned to go away, to move away from the closed wings of the minster, she noticed a man standing on the pavement, in the direction of the post office which functions obscurely in the Cathedral Square. Immediately, she knew that that man, standing dark and motionless, was Alan. He was alone, motionless, remote.

He did not move towards her. She hesitated, then went in his direction, as if going to the post office. He stood perfectly motionless, and her heart died as she drew near. Then, as she passed, he turned suddenly, looking down on her.

It was he, though she could hardly see his face, it was so dark, with a dusky glow in the shadow.

"Alan!" she said.

He did not speak, but laid his hand detainingly on her arm, as he used in the early days, with strange, silent authority. And turning her with a faint pressure on her arm, he went along with her, leisurely, through the main street of the city, under the arcade where the shops were still lighted up.

She glanced at his face; it seemed much more dusky, and duskily ruddy, than she had known him. He was a stranger: and yet it was he, no other. He said nothing at all. But that was also in keeping. His mouth was closed, his watchful eyes seemed changeless, and there was a shadow of silence around him, impenetrable, but not cold. Rather aloof and gentle, like the silence that surrounds a wild animal.

She knew that she was walking with his spirit. But that even did not trouble her. It seemed natural. And there came over her again the feeling she had forgotten, the restful, thoughtless pleasure of a woman who moves in the aura of the man to whom she belongs. As a young woman she had had this unremarkable, yet very precious feeling, when she was with her husband. It had been a full contentment; and perhaps the fullness of it had made her unconscious of it. Later, it seemed to her she had almost wilfully destroyed it, this soft flow of contentment which she, a woman, had from him as a man.

Now, afterwards, she realised it. And as she walked at his side through the conquered city, she realised that it was the one enduring thing a woman can have, the intangible soft flood of contentment that carries her along at the side of the man she is married to. It is her perfection and her highest attainment.

Now, in the afterwards, she knew it. Now the strife was gone. And dimly she wondered why, why, why she had ever fought against it. No matter what the man does or is, as a person, if a woman can move at his side in this dim, full flood of contentment, she has the highest of him, and her scratching efforts at getting more than this, are her ignominious efforts at self-nullity.

Now she knew it, and she submitted. Now that she was walking with a man who came from the halls of death, to her, for her relief. The strong, silent kindliness of him towards her, even now, was able to wipe out the ashy, nervous horror of the world from her body. She went at his side, still and released, like one newly unbound, walking in the dimness of her own contentment.

At the bridge-head he came to a standstill, and drew his hand from her arm. She knew he was going to leave her. But he looked at her from under his peaked cap, darkly but kindly, and he waved his hand with a slight, kindly gesture of farewell, and of promise, as if in farewell he promised never to leave her, never to let the kindliness go out in his heart, to let it stay here always.

She hurried over the bridge with tears running down her cheeks, and on to her hotel. Hastily she climbed to her room. And as she undressed, she avoided the sight of her own face in the mirror. She must not rupture the spell of his presence.

Now, in the afterwards she realised *how* careful she must be, not to break the mystery that enveloped her. Now that she knew he had come back to her from the dead, she was aware how precious and how fragile the coming was. He had come back with his heart dark and kind, wanting her even in the afterwards. And not in any sense must she go against him. The warm, powerful, silent ghost had come back to her.

It was he. She must not even try to think about him definitely, not to realise him or to understand. Only in her own woman's soul could she silently ponder him, darkly, and know him present in her, without ever staring at him or trying to find him out. Once she tried to lay hands on him, to *have* him, to *realise* him, he would be gone for ever, and gone for ever this last precious flood of her woman's peace.

"Ah, no!" she said to herself. "If he leaves his peace with me, I must ask no questions whatsoever."

And she repented, silently, of the way she had questioned and demanded answers, in the past. What were the answers, when she had got them? Terrible ash in the mouth.

She now knew the supreme modern terror, of a world all ashy and nerve-dead. If a man could come back out of death to save her from this, she would not ask questions of him, but be humble, and beyond tears grateful.

In the morning, she went out into the icy wind, under the grey sky, to see if he would be there again. Not that she *needed* him: his presence was still about her. But he might be waiting.

The town was stony and cold. The people looked pale, chilled through, and doomed in some way. Very far from her they were. She felt a sort of pity for them, but knew she could do nothing, nothing in time or eternity. And they looked at her, and looked quickly away again, as if they were uneasy in themselves.

The cathedral reared its great reddish-grey façade in the stark light; but it did not loom as in the night. The cathedral square was hard and cold. Inside, the church was cold and repellent, in spite of the glow of stained glass. And he was nowhere to be found.

So she hastened away to her hotel and to the station, to catch the 10.30 train into Germany.

It was a lonely, dismal train, with a few forlorn souls waiting to cross the Rhine. Her Alsatian porter looked after her with the same dogged care as before. She got into the first-class carriage that was going through to Prague—she was the only passenger travelling first. A real French porter, in blouse and moustache, and swagger, tried to say something a bit jeering to her, in his few words of German. But she only looked at him, and he subsided. He didn't really want to be rude. There was a certain hopelessness even about that.

The train crept slowly, disheartened, out of town. She saw the weird humped-up creature of the cathedral in the distance, pointing its one finger above the city. Why, oh, why had the old Germanic races put it there like that!

Slowly the country disintegrated into the Rhine flats and marshes, the canals, the willow trees, the overflow streams, the wet places frozen but not flooded. Weary the place all seemed. And old Father Rhine flowing in greenish volume, implacable, separating the races now weary of race struggle, but locked in the toils as in the coils of a great snake, unable to escape. Cold, full, green, and utterly disheartening the river came along under the wintry sky, passing beneath the bridge of iron.

There was a long wait in Kehl, where the German officials and the French observed a numb, dreary kind of neutrality. Passport and customs examination was soon over. But the train waited and waited, as if unable to get away from that point of pure negation, where the two races neutralised one another, and no polarity was felt, no life—no principle dominated.

Katherine Farquhar just sat still in the suspended silence of her husband's return. She heeded neither French nor German, spoke one language or the other at need, hardly knowing. She waited while the hot train steamed and hissed, arrested at the perfect neutral point of the new border-line, just across the Rhine.

And at last a little sun came out, and the train silently drew away, nervously, from the neutrality.

In the great flat field of the Rhine plain, the shallow flood water was frozen, the furrows ran straight towards nowhere, the air seemed frozen, too, but the earth felt strong and barbaric, it seemed to vibrate, with its straight furrows, in a deep, savage undertone. There was the frozen, savage thrill in the air also, something wild and unsubdued, pre-Roman.

This part of the Rhine Valley, even on the right bank in Germany, was occupied by the French; hence the curious vacancy, the suspense, as if no men lived there, but some spirit was watching, watching over the vast, empty, straight-furrowed fields and the water-meadows. Stillness, emptiness, suspense, and a sense of something still impending.

A long wait in the station of Appenweier, on the main line of the Right-bank railway. The station was empty. Katherine remembered its excited, thrilling bustle in pre-war days.

"Yes," said the German guard to the stationmaster, "what do they hurry us out of Strasburg for, if they are only going to keep us so long here?"

The heavy Badisch German! The sense of resentful impotence in the Germans! Katherine smiled to herself. She realised that here the train left the occupied territory.

At last they set off, northwards, free for the moment, in Germany. It was the land beyond the Rhine, Germany of the pine forests. The very earth seemed strong and unsubdued, bristling with a few reeds and bushes, like savage hair. There was the same silence, and waiting, and the old barbaric undertone of the white-skinned north, under the waning civilisation. The audible overtone of our civilisation seemed to be wearing thin, the old, low, pine forest hum and roar of the ancient north seemed to be sounding through. At least, in Katherine's inner ear.

And there were the ponderous hills of the Black Forest, heaped and waiting sullenly, as if guarding the inner Germany. Black round hills, black with forest, save where white snow-patches of field had been cut out. Black and white, waiting there in the near distance, in sullen guard.

She knew the country so well. But not in this present mood, the emptiness, the sullenness, the heavy, recoiled waiting.

Steinbach! Then she was nearly there! She would have to change in Oos for Baden-Baden, her destination. Probably Philip would be there to meet her, in Oos; he would have come down from Heidelberg.

Yes, there he was! And at once she thought he looked ill, yellowish. His figure hollow and defeated.

"Aren't you well?" she asked, as she stepped out of the train on to the empty station.

"I'm so frightfully cold," he said. "I can't get warm."

"And the train was so hot," she said.

At last a porter came to carry her bags across to the little connecting train.

"How are you?" he said, looking at her with a certain pinched look in his face, and fear in his eyes.

"All right! It all feels very queer," she said.

"I don't know how it is," he said, "but Germany freezes my inside, and does something to my chest."

"We needn't stay long," she said easily.

He was watching the bright look in her face. And she was thinking how queer and *chétif* he looked! Extraordinary! As she looked at him she felt for the first time, with curious clarity, that it was humiliating to be married to him, even in name. She was humiliated even by the fact that her name was Katherine Farquhar. Yet she used to think it a nice name!

"Just think of me married to that little man!" she thought to herself. "Think of my having his name!"

It didn't fit. She thought of her own name: Katherine von Todtnau; or of her married name: Katherine Anstruther. The first seemed most fitting. But the second was her second nature. The third, Katherine Farquhar, wasn't her at all.

"Have you seen Marianne?" she asked.

"Oh yes!"

He was very brief. What was the matter with him?

"You'll have to be careful with your cold," she said politely.

"I *am* careful!" he cried petulantly.

Marianne, her sister, was at the station, and in two minutes they were rattling away in German, and laughing and crying and exploding with laughter again. Philip quite ignored. In these days of frozen economy, there was no taxi. A porter would wheel up the luggage on a trolley, the new arrivals walked to their little hotel, through the half-deserted town.

"But the little one is quite nice!" said Marianne deprecatingly.

"Isn't he!" cried Katherine in the same tone.

And both sisters stood still and laughed in the middle of the street. 'The little one' was Philip.

"The other was more a man," said Marianne. "But I'm sure this one is easier. *The little one!* Yes, he *should* be easier," and she laughed in her mocking way.

"The stand-up-mannikin!" said Katherine, referring to those little toy men weighed at the base with lead, that always stand up again.

Philip was very unhappy in this atmosphere. His strength was in his weakness, his appeal, his clinging dependence. He quite cunningly got his own way almost every time: but always by seeming to give in. In every emergency he bowed as low as need be and let the storm pass over him. Then he

rose again, the same as ever, sentimental, on the side of the
angels, offering defiance to nobody. The defiant men had been
killed off during the war. He had seen it and secretly smiled.
When the lion is shot, the dog gets the spoil. So he had come
in for Katherine, Alan's lioness. A live dog is better than a
dead lion. And so the little semi-angelic journalist exulted in
the triumph of his weakness.

But in Germany, in weird post-war Germany, he seemed
snuffed out again. The air was so cold and vacant, all feeling
seemed to have gone out of the country. Emotion, even sentiment, was numbed quite dead, as in a frost-bitten limb. And
if the sentiment were numbed out of him, he was truly dead.

"I'm most frightfully glad you've come, Kathy," he said.
"I could hardly have held out another day here, without you.
I feel you're the only thing on earth that remains real."

"You don't seem very real to me," she said.

"I'm not real! I'm *not!*—not when I'm alone. But when
I'm with you I'm the most real man alive. I know it!"

This was the sort of thing that had fetched her in the past,
thrilled her through and through in her womanly conceit,
even made her fall in love with the little creature who could
so generously admit such pertinent truths. So different from
the lordly Alan, who expected a woman to bow down to
him!

Now, however, some of the coldness of numbed Germany
seemed to have got into her breast too. She felt a cruel
derision of the whimpering little beast who claimed reality
only through a woman. She did not answer him, but looked
out at the snow falling between her and the dark trees.
Another world! When the snow left off, how bristling and
ghostly the cold fir trees looked, tall, conical creatures crowd-
ing darkly and half whitened with snow! So tall, so wolfish!

Philip shivered and looked yellower. There was shortage of
fuel, shortage of food, shortage of everything. He wanted
Katherine to go to Paris with him. But she would stay at
least two weeks near her people. The shortage she would put
up with. She saw at evening the string of decent townsfolk
waiting in the dark—the town was not half lighted—to fill
their hot-water bottles at the hot spring outside the Kurhaus,
silent, spectral, unable to afford fire to heat their own water.
And she felt quite cold about Philip's shivering. Let him
shiver.

The snow was crisp and dry, she walked out in the forest, up the steep slopes. The world was curiously vacant, gone wild again. She realised how very quickly the world would go wild if catastrophes overtook mankind. Philip, yellow and hollow, would trudge stumbling and reeling beside her: ludicrous. He was a man who never would walk firm on his legs. Now he just flopped. She could feel Alan among the trees, the thrill and vibration of him. And sometimes she would glance with beating heart at a great round fir-trunk that stood so alive and potent, so physical, bristling all its vast drooping greenness above the snow. She could feel him, Alan, in the trees' potent presence. She wanted to go and press herself against the trunk. But Philip would sit down on the snow, saying:

"Look here, Kathy, I can't go any farther. I've simply got no strength left!"

She stood on the path, proud, contemptuous, but silent, looking away towards where the dull, reddish rocks cropped out. And there, among the rocks, she was sure, Alan was waiting for her. She felt fierce and overbearing. Yet she took the stumbling Philip home.

He was really ill. She put him to bed, and he stayed in bed. The doctor came. But Philip was in a state of panic, afraid of everything. Katherine would walk out by herself, into the forest. She was expecting Alan, and was tingling to meet him. Then Philip would lie in bed half-conscious, and when she came back he would say, his big eyes glowing:

"You must have been *very far*!" And on the last two words he would show his large front teeth in a kind of snarl.

"Not very far," she said.

One day Alan came to her from out of the dull reddish rocks in the forest. He was wearing a kilt that suited him so: but a khaki tunic. And he had no cap on. He came walking towards her, his knees throwing the kilt in the way she knew so well. He came triumphantly, rather splendid, and she waited trembling. He was always utterly silent. But he led her away with his arm round her, and she yielded in a complete yielding she had never known before. And among the rocks he made love to her, and took her in the silent passion of a husband, took a complete possession of her.

Afterwards she walked home in a muse, to find Philip seriously ill. She could see, he really might die. And she didn't care a bit. But she tended him, and stayed with him, and he seemed to be better.

The next day, however, she wanted to go out in the afternoon, she *must*! She could feel her husband waiting, and the call was imperative. She must go. But Philip became almost hysterical when she wanted to leave him.

"I assure you I shall die while you are out! I assure you I shall die if you leave me now!" He rolled his eyes wildly, and looked so queer, she felt it was true. So she stayed, sullen and full of resentment, her consciousness away among the rocks.

The afternoon grew colder and colder. Philip shivered in bed, under the greast bolster.

"But it's a murderous cold! It's murdering me!" he said.

She did not mind it. She sat abstracted, remote from him, her spirit going out into the frozen evening. A very powerful flow seemed to envelop her in another reality. It was Alan calling to her, holding her. And the hold seemed to grow stronger every hour.

She slept in the same room as Philip. But she had decided not to go to bed. He was really very weak. She would sit up with him. Towards midnight he roused, and said faintly:

"Katherine, I can't bear it!"—and his eyes rolled up showing only the whites.

"What? What can't you bear?" she said, bending over him.

"I can't bear it! I can't bear it! Hold me in your arms. Hold me! Hold me!" he whispered in pure terror of death.

Curiously reluctant, she began to push her hands under his shoulders, to raise him. As she did so, the door opened, and Alan came in, bareheaded, and a frown on his face. Philip lifted feeble hands, and put them round Katherine's neck, moaning faintly. Silent, bareheaded, Alan came over to the bed and loosened the sick man's hands from his wife's neck, and put them down on the sick man's own breast.

Philip unfurled his lips and showed his big teeth in a ghastly grin of death. Katherine felt his body convulse in strange throes under the hand, then go inert. He was dead. And on his face was a sickly grin of a thief caught in the very act.

But Alan drew her away, drew her to the other bed, in the silent passion of a husband come back from a very long journey.

JIMMY AND THE DESPERATE WOMAN

"HE is very fine and strong somewhere, but he does need a level-headed woman to look after him."

That was the *friendly* feminine verdict upon him. It flattered him, it pleased him, it galled him.

Having divorced a very charming and clever wife, who had held this opinion for ten years, and at last had got tired of the level-headed protective game, his gall was uppermost.

"I want to throw Jimmy out on the world, but I know the poor little man will go and fall on some woman's bosom. That's the worst of him. If he could only stand alone for ten minutes. But he can't. At the same time, there *is* something fine about him, something rare."

This had been Clarissa's summing-up as she floated away in the arms of the rich young American. The rich young American got rather angry when Jimmy's name was mentioned. Clarissa was now *his* wife. But she did sometimes talk as if she were still married to Jimmy.

Not in Jimmy's estimation, however. That worm had turned. Gall was uppermost. Gall and wormwood. He knew exactly what Clarissa thought—and said—about him. And the "something fine, something rare, something strong" which he was supposed to have "about him" was utterly outbalanced, in his feelings at least, by the "poor little man" nestled upon "some woman's bosom," which he was supposed to *be*.

"I am not," he said to himself, "a poor little man nestled upon some woman's bosom. If I could only find the right sort of woman, she should nestle on mine."

Jimmy was now thirty-five, and this point, to nestle or to be nestled, was the emotional crux and turning-point.

He imagined to himself some really *womanly* woman, to whom he should be *only* "fine and strong," and not for one moment "the poor little man." Why not some simple uneducated girl, some Tess of the D'Urbervilles, some wistful Gretchen, some humble Ruth gleaning an aftermath? Why not? Surely the world was full of such!

The trouble was he never met them. He only met sophisti-
cated women. He really never had a chance of meeting "real"
people. So few of us ever do. Only the people we *don't* meet
are the "real" people, the simple, genuine, direct, spontaneous,
unspoilt souls. All, the simple, genuine, unspoilt people we
don't meet! What a tragedy it is!

Because, of course, they must be there! Somewhere! Only
we never come across them.

Jimmy was terribly handicapped by his position. It brought
him into contact with so many people. Only never the right
sort. Never the "real" people: the simple, genuine, unspoilt,
etc., etc.

He was editor of a high-class, rather high-brow, rather
successful magazine, and his rather personal, very candid
editorials brought him shoals, swarms, hosts of admiring
acquaintances. Realise that he was handsome, and could be
extraordinarily "nice", when he liked, and was really very
clever, in his own critical way, and you see how many
chances he had of being adored and protected.

In the first place his good looks: the fine, clean lines of his
face, like the face of the laughing faun in one of the faun's
unlaughing, moody moments. The long, clean, lines of the
cheeks, the strong chin and the slightly arched, full nose, the
beautiful dark-grey eyes with long lashes, and the thick black
brows. In his mocking moments, when he seemed most himself, it was a pure Pan face, with thick black eyebrows cocked
up, and grey eyes with a sardonic goaty gleam, and nose and
mouth curling with satire. A good-looking, smooth-skinned
satyr. That was Jimmy at his best. In the opinion of his men
friends.

In his own opinion, he was a sort of Martyred Saint
Sebastian, at whom the wicked world shot arrow after arrow
—Mater Dolorosa nothing to him—and he counted the drops
of blood as they fell: when he could keep count. Sometimes
—as for instance when Clarissa said she was really departing
with the rich young American, and should she divorce Jimmy,
or was Jimmy going to divorce her?—then the arrows assailed
him like a flight of starlings, flying straight at him, jabbing at
him, and the drops of martyred blood simple spattered down,
he couldn't keep count.

So, naturally, he divorced Clarissa.

In the opinion of his men friends, he was, or should be, a

consistently grinning faun, satyr, or Pan-person. In his own opinion, he was a Martyred Saint Sebastian with the mind of a Plato. In the opinion of his woman friends, he was fascinating little man with a profound understanding of life and the capacity really to understand a woman and to make a woman feel a queen; which of course was to make a woman feel her *real* self. . . .

He might, naturally, have made rich and resounding marriages, especially after the divorce. He didn't. The reason was, secretly, his resolve never to make any woman feel a queen any more. It was the turn of the women to make him feel a king.

Some unspoilt, unsophisticated, wild-blooded woman, to whom he would be a sort of Solomon of wisdom, beauty, and wealth. She would need to be in reduced circumstances to appreciate his wealth, which amounted to the noble sum of three thousand pounds and a little week-ending cottage in Hampshire. And to be unsophisticated she would have to be a woman of the people. Absolutely.

At the same time, not just the "obscure vulgar simplican".

He received many letters, many, many, many, enclosing poems, stories, articles, or more personal unbosomings. He read them all: like a solemn rook pecking and scratching among the litter.

And one—not one letter, but one correspondent—might be *the* one—Mrs. Emilia Pinnegar, who wrote from a mining village in Yorkshire. She was, of course, unhappily married.

Now Jimmy had always had a mysterious feeling about these dark and rather dreadful mining villages in the north. He himself had scarcely set foot north of Oxford. He felt that these miners up there must be the real stuff. And Pinnegar was a name, surely! And Emilia!

She wrote a poem, with a brief little note, that, if the editor of the *Commentator* thought the verses of no value, would he simply destroy them. Jimmy, as editor of the *Commentator*, thought the verses quite good and admired the brevity of the note. But he wasn't sure about printing the poem. He wrote back: Had Mrs. Pennegar nothing else to submit?

Then followed a correspondence. And at length, upon request, this from Mrs. Pinnegar:

"You ask me about myself, but what shall I say? I am a woman of thirty-one, with one child, a girl of eight, and I am married to a man who lives in the same house with me, but goes to another woman. I try to write poetry, if it is poetry, because I have no other way of expressing myself at all, and even if it doesn't matter to anybody besides myself, I feel I must and will express myself, if only to save myself from developing cancer or some disease that women have. I was a schoolteacher before I was married, and I got my certificates at Rotherham College. If I could, I would teach again, and live alone. But married women teachers can't get jobs any more, they aren't allowed——"

THE COAL-MINER
BY HIS WIFE

The donkey-engine's beating noise
And the rattle, rattle of the sorting screens
Come down on me like the beat of his heart,
And mean the same as his breathing means.

The burning big pit-hill with fumes
Fills the air like the presence of that fair-haired man.
And the burning fire burning deeper and deeper
Is his will insisting since time began.

As he breaths the chair goes up and down
In the pit-shaft; he lusts as the wheel-fans spin
The sucking air: he lives in the coal
Underground: and his soul is a strange engine.

That is the manner of man he is.
I married him and I should know.
The mother earth from bowels of coal
Brought him forth for the overhead woe.

This was the poem that the editor of the *Commentator* hesitated about. He reflected, also, that Mrs. Pinnegar didn't sound like one of the nestling, unsophisticated rustic type. It was something else that still attracted him: something desperate in a woman, something tragic.

THE NEXT EVENT

If at evening, when the twilight comes,
  You ask me what the day has been,
I shall not know. The distant drums
  Of some newcomer intervene

Between me and the day that's been
  Some strange man leading long columns
Of unseen soldiers through the green
  Sad twilight of these smoky slums.

And as the darkness slowly numbs
  My senses, everything I've seen
Or heard the daylight through, becomes
  Rubbish behind an opaque screen.

Instead, the sound of muffled drums
  Inside myself: I have to lean
And listen as my strength succumbs,
  To hear what these oncomings mean.

Perhaps the Death-God striking his thumbs
  On the drums in a deadly rat-ta-ta-plan.
Or a strange man marching slow as he strums
  The tune of a new weird hope in Man.

What does it matter! The day that began
  In coal-dust is ending the same, in crumbs
Of darkness like coal. I live if I can;
  If I can't then I welcome whatever comes.

This poem sounded so splendidly desperate, the editor of the *Commentator* decided to print it, and, moreover, to see the authoress. He wrote: Would she care to see him, if he happened to be in her neighbourhood? He was going to lecture in Sheffield. She replied: Certainly.

He gave his afternoon lecture, on *Men in Books and Men in Life*. Naturally, men in books came first. Then he caught a train to reach the mining village where the Pinnegars lived.

It was February, with gruesome patches of snow. It was dark when he arrived at Mill Valley, a sort of thick, turgid darkness full of menace, where men speaking in a weird accent went past like ghosts, dragging their heavy feet and emitting the weird scent of the coal-mine underworld. Weird and a bit gruesome it was.

He knew he had to walk uphill to the little market-place. As he went, he looked back and saw the black valleys with bunches of light, like camps of demons it seemed to him. And the demonish smell of sulphur and coal in the air, in the heavy, pregnant, clammy darkness.

They directed him to New London Lane, and down he went down another hill. His skin crept a little. The place felt uncanny and hostile, hard, as if iron and minerals breathed into the black air. Thank goodness he couldn't see much, or be seen. When he had to ask his way the people treated him in a "heave-half-a-brick-at-him" fashion.

After much weary walking and asking, he entered a lane between trees, in the cold slushy mud of the unfrozen February. The mines, apparently, were on the outskirts of the town, in some mud-sunk country. He could see the red, sore fires of the burning pit-hill through the trees, and he smelt the sulphur. He felt like some modern Ulysses wandering in the realms of Hecate. How much more dismal and horrible, a modern Odyssey among mines and factories, than any Sirens, Scyllas or Charybdises.

So he mused to himself as he waded through icy black mud, in a black lane, under black trees that moaned an accompaniment to the sound of the coal-mine's occasional hissing and chuffing, under a black sky that quenched even the electric sparkle of the colliery. And the place seemed uninhabited like a cold black jungle.

At last he came in sight of a glimmer. Apparently, there were dwellings. Yes, a new little street, with one street-lamp, and the houses all apparently dark. He paused. Absolute desertion. Then three children.

They told him the house, and he stumbled up a dark passage. There was light on the little back-yard. He knocked, in some trepidation. A rather tall woman, looking down at him with a "Who are you?" look, from the step above.

"Mrs. Pinnegar?"

"Oh, is it you, Mr. Firth? Come in."

He stumbled up the step into the glaring light of the kitchen. There stood Mrs. Pinnegar, a tall woman with a face like a mask of passive anger, looking at him coldly. Immediately he felt his own shabbiness and smallness. In utter confusion, he stuck out his hand.

"I had an awful time getting here," he said. "I'm afraid I shall make a frightful mess of your house." He looked down at his boots.

"That's all right," she said. "Have you had your tea?"

"No—but don't you bother about me."

There was a little girl with fair hair in a fringe over her forehead, troubled blue eyes under the fringe, and two dolls. He felt easier.

"Is this your little girl?" he asked. "She's awfully nice. What is her name?"

"Jane."

"How are you, Jane?" he said. But the child only stared at him with the baffled, bewildered, pained eyes of a child who lives with hostile parents.

Mrs. Pinnegar set his tea, bread, and butter, jam, and buns. Then she sat opposite him. She was handsome, dark, straight brows and grey eyes with yellow grains in them, and a way of looking straight at you as if she were used to holding her own. Her eyes were the nicest part of her. They had a certain kindliness, mingled, like the yellow grains among the grey, with a relentless, unyielding feminine will. Her nose and mouth were straight, like a Greek mask, and the expression was fixed. She gave him at once the impression of a woman who has made a mistake, who knows it, but who will not change: who cannot now change.

He felt very uneasy. Being a rather small, shambling man, she made him aware of his physical inconspicuousness. And she said not a word, only looked down on him, as he drank his tea, with that changeless look of a woman who is holding her own against Man and Fate. While, from the corner across the kitchen, the little girl with her fair hair and her dolls, watched him also in absolute silence, from her hot blue eyes.

"This seems a pretty awful place," he said to her.

"It is. It's absolutely awful," the woman said.

"You ought to get away from it," he said.

But she received this in dead silence.

It was exceedingly difficult to make any headway. He asked about Mr. Pinnegar. She glanced at the clock.

"He comes up at nine," she said.

"Is he down the mine?"

"Yes. He's on the afternoon shift."

There was never a sound from the little girl.

"Doesn't Jane ever talk?" he asked.

"Not much," said the mother, glancing round.

He talked a little about his lectures, about Sheffield, about London. But she was not really interested. She sat there rather distant, very laconic, looking at him with those curious unyielding eyes. She looked to him like a woman who has had her revenge, and is left stranded on the reefs where she wrecked her opponent. Still unrelenting, unregretting, unyielding, she seemed rather undecided as to what her revenge had been, and what it had all been about.

"You ought to get away from here," he said to her.

"Where to?" she asked.

"Oh"—he made a vague gesture—"anywhere, so long as it is *quite* away."

She seemed to ponder this, under her portentous brow.

"I don't see what difference it would make," she said. Then glancing round at her child: "I don't see what difference anything would make, except getting out of the world altogether. But there's *her* to consider." And she jerked her head in the direction of the child.

Jimmy felt definitely frightened. He wasn't used to this sort of grimness. At the same time he was excited. This handsome, laconic woman, with her soft brown hair and her unflinching eyes with their gold flecks, seemed to be challenging him to something. There was a touch of challenge in her remaining gold-flecked kindness. Somewhere, she had a heart. But what had happened to it? And why?

What had gone wrong with her? In some way, she must have gone against herself.

"Why don't you come and live with me?" he said, like the little gambler he was.

The queer, conflicting smile was on his face. He had taken up her challenge, like a gambler. The very sense of a gamble, in which he could not lose desperately, excited him. At the same time, he was scared of her, and determined to get beyond his scare.

She sat and watched him, with the faintest touch of a grim smile on her handsome mouth.

"How do you mean, live with you?" she said.

"Oh—I mean what it usually means," he said, with a little puff of self-conscious laughter.

"You're evidently not happy here. You're evidently in the wrong circumstances altogether. You're obviously *not* just an ordinary woman. Well, then, break away. When I say, Come and live with me, I mean just what I say. Come to London and live with me as my wife, if you like, and then if we want to marry, when you get a divorce, why, we can do it."

Jimmy made this speech more to himself than to the woman. That was how he was. He worked out all his things inside himself, as if it were all merely an interior problem of his own. And while he did so, he had an odd way of squinting his left eye and wagging his head loosely, like a man talking absolutely to himself, and turning his eyes inwards.

The woman watched him in a sort of wonder. This was something she was *not* used to. His extraordinary manner, and his extraordinary bald proposition, roused her from her own tense apathy.

"Well!" she said. "That's got to be thought about. What about *her*?"—and again she jerked her head towards the round-eyed child in the corner. Jane sat with a completely expressionless face, her little red mouth fallen a little open. She seemed in a sort of trance: as if she understood like a grown-up person, but, as a child, sat in a trance, unconscious.

The mother wheeled round in her chair and stared at her child. The little girl stared back at her mother, with hot, troubled, almost guilty blue eyes. And neither said a word. Yet they seemed to exchange worlds of meaning.

"Why, of course," said Jimmy, twisting his head again; "she'd come, too."

The woman gave a last look at her child, then turned to him, and started watching *him* with that slow, straight stare.

"It's not"—he began, stuttering—"it's not anything *sudden* and unconsidered on my part. I've been considering it for quite a long time—ever since I had the first poem, and your letter."

He spoke still with his eyes turned inwards, talking to himself. And the woman watched him unflinchingly.

"Before you ever saw me?" she asked, with a queer irony.

"Oh, of course. Of course before I ever saw you. Or else I never *should* have seen you. From the very first, I had a definite feeling——"

He made odd, sharp gestures, like a drunken man, and he spoke like a drunken man, his eyes turned inward, talking to himself. The woman was no more than a ghost moving inside his own consciousness, and he was addressing her there.

The actual woman sat outside looking on in a sort of wonder. This was really something new to her.

"And now you see me, do you want me, really, to come to London?"

She spoke in a dull tone of incredulity. The thing was just a little preposterous to her. But why not? It would have to be something a little preposterous, to get her out of the tomb she was in.

"Of course I do!" he cried, with another scoop of his head and scoop of his hand. "*Now* I do *actually* want you, now I actually see you." He never looked at her. His eyes were still turned in. He was still talking to himself in a sort of drunkenness with himself.

To her, it was something extraordinary. But it roused her from apathy.

He became aware of the hot blue eyes of the hot-cheeked little girl fixed upon him from the distant corner. And he gave a queer litle giggle.

"Why, it's more than I could ever have hoped for," he said, "to have you and Jane to live with me! Why, it will mean *life* to me." He spoke in an odd, strained voice, slightly delirious. And for the first time he looked up at the woman and, apparently, *straight* at her. But, even as he seemed to look straight at her, the curious cast was in his eye, and he was only looking at himself, inside himself, at the shadows inside his own consciousness.

"And when would you like me to come?" she asked, rather coldly.

"Why, as soon as possible. Come back with me to-morrow, if you will. I've got a little house in St. John's Wood, *waiting* for you. Come with me to-morrow. That's the simplest."

She watched him for some time, as he sat with ducked head. He looked like a man who is drunk—drunk with himself. He was going bald at the crown, his rather curly black hair was thin.

"I couldn't come to-morrow, I should need a few days," she said.

She wanted to see his face again. It was as if she could not remember what his face was like, this strange man who had appeared out of nowhere, with such a strange proposition.

He lifted his face, his eyes still cast in that inturned, blind look. He looked now like a Mephistopheles who has gone blind. With his black brows cocked up, Mephistopheles, Mephistopheles blind and begging in the street.

"Why, of course it's wonderful that it's happened like this for me," he said, with odd, pouting emphasis, pushing out his lips. "I was finished, absolutely finished. I was finished while Clarissa was with me. But after she'd gone, I was *absolutely* finished. And I thought there was no chance for me in the world again. It seems to me perfectly marvellous that this has happened—that I've come across you——" he lifted his face sightlessly—"and Jane—Jane—why, she's *really* too good to be true." He gave a slight hysterical laugh. "She really is."

The woman, and Jane, watched him with some embarrassment.

"I shall have to settle up here with Mr. Pinnegar," she said, rather coldly musing. "Do you want to see him?"

"Oh, I——" he said, with a deprecating gesture, "I don't *care*. But if you think I'd better—why, certainly——"

"I do think you'd better," she said.

"Very well, then, I *will*. I'll see him whenever you like."

"He comes in soon after nine," she said.

"All right, I'll see him then. Much better. But I suppose I'd better see about finding a place to sleep first. Better not leave it too late."

"I'll come with you and ask for you."

"Oh, you'd better not, really. If you tell me where to go——"

He had taken on a protective tone: he was protecting her against herself and against scandal. It was his manner, his rather Oxfordy manner, more than anything else, that went beyond her. She wasn't used to it.

Jimmy plunged out into the gulfing blackness of the Northern night, feeling how horrible it was, but pressing his hat on his brow in a sense of strong adventure. He was going through with it.

At the baker's shop, where she had suggested he should ask for a bed, they would have none of him. Absolutely they didn't like the looks of him. At the Pub, too, they shook their heads: didn't want to have anything to do with him. But, in a voice more expostulatingly Oxford than ever, he said:

"But look here—you can't ask a man to sleep under one of these hedges. Can't I see the landlady?"

He persuaded the landlady to promise to let him sleep on the big, soft settee in the parlour, where the fire was burning brightly. Then, saying he would be back about ten, he returned through mud and drizzle up New London Lane.

The child was in bed, a saucepan was boiling by the fire. Already the lines had softened a little in the woman's face.

She spread a cloth on the table. Jimmy sat in silence, feeling that she was hardly aware of his presence. She was absorbed, no doubt, in the coming of her husband. The stranger merely sat on the sofa, and waited. He felt himself wound up tight. And once he was really wound up, he could go through with anything.

They heard the nine o'clock whistle at the mine. The woman then took the saucepan from the fire and went into the scullery. Jimmy could smell the smell of potatoes being strained. He sat quite still. There was nothing for him to do or to say. He was wearing his big black-rimmed spectacles, and his face, blank and expressionless in the suspense of waiting, looked like the death-mask of some sceptical philosopher, who could wait through the ages, and who could hardly distinguish life from death at any time.

Came the heavy-shod tread up the house entry, and the man entered, rather like a blast of wind. The fair moustache stuck out from the blackish, mottled face, and the fierce blue eyes rolled their whites in the coal-blackened sockets.

"This gentleman is Mr. Frith," said Emily Pinnegar.

Jimmy got up, with a bit of an Oxford wriggle, and held out his hand, saying: "How do you do?"

His grey eyes, behind the spectacles, had an uncanny whitish gleam.

"My hand's not fit to shake hands," said the miner. "Take a seat."

"Oh, nobody minds coal-dust," said Jimmy, subsiding on to the sofa. "It's clean dirt."

"They say so," said Pinnegar.

He was a man of medium height, thin, but energetic in build.

Mrs. Pinnegar was running hot water into a pail from the bright brass tap of the stove, which had a boiler to balance the oven. Pinnegar dropped heavily into a wooden arm-chair, and stooped to pull off his ponderous grey pit-boots. He smelled of the strange, stale underground. In silence he pulled on his slipper, then rose, taking his boots into the scullery. His wife followed with the pail of hot water. She returned and spread a coarse roller-towel on the steel fender. The man could be heard washing in the scullery in the semi-dark. Nobody said anything. Mrs. Pinnegar attended to her husband's dinner.

After a while, Pinnegar came running in, naked to the waist, and squatted plumb in front of the big red fire, on his heels. His head and face and the front part of his body were all wet. His back was grey and unwashed. He seized the towel from the fender and began to rub his face and head with a sort of brutal vigour, while his wife brought a bowl, and with a soapy flannel silently washed his back, right down to the loins, where the trousers were rolled back. The man was entirely oblivious of the stranger—this washing was part of the collier's ritual, and nobody existed for the moment. The woman, washing her husband's back, stooping there as he kneeled with knees wide apart, squatting on his heels on the rag hearth-rug, had a peculiar look on her strong, hand-some face, a look sinister and derisive. She was deriding some-thing or somebody; but Jimmy could not make out whom or what.

It was a new experience for him to sit completely and brutally excluded from a personal ritual. The collier vigor-ously rubbed his own fair short hair, till it all stood on end, then he stared into the red-hot fire, oblivious, while the red colour burned in his cheeks. Then again he rubbed his breast and his body with the rough towel, brutally, as if his body were some machine he was cleaning, while his wife, with a peculiar slow movement, dried his back with another towel.

She took away the towel and bowl. The man was dry. He still squatted with his hands on his knees, gazing abstractedly, blankly into the fire. That, too, seemed part of his daily ritual. The colour flushed in his cheeks, his fair moustache was rubbed on end. But his hot blue eyes stared hot and vague into the red coals, while the red glare of the coal fell on his breast and naked body.

He was a man of about thirty-five, in his prime, with a pure smooth skin and no fat on his body. His muscles were not large, but quick, alive with energy. And as he squatted bathing abstractedly in the glow of the fire, he seemed like some pure-moulded engine that sleeps between its motions, with incomprehensible eyes of dark iron-blue.

He looked round, always averting his face from the stranger on the sofa, shutting him out of consciousness. The wife took out a bundle from the dresser cupboard, and handed it to the outstretched, work-scarred hand of the man on the hearth. Curious, that big, horny, work-battered clean hand, at the end of the suave, thin, naked arm.

Pinnegar unrolled his shirt and undervest in front of the fire, warmed them for a moment in the glow, vaguely, sleepily, then pulled them over his head. And then at last he rose, with his shirt hanging over his trousers, and in the same abstract, sleepy way, shutting the world out of his consciousness, he went out again to the scullery, pausing at the same dresser cupboard to take out his rolled-up day trousers.

Mrs. Pinnegar took away the towels and set the dinner on the table—rich, oniony stew out of a hissing brown stew-jar, boiled potatoes, and a cup of tea. The man returned from the scullery in his clean flannelette shirt and black trousers, his fair hair neatly brushed. He planked his wooden arm-chair beside the table, and sat heavily down, to eat.

Then he looked at Jimmy, as one wary, probably hostile man looks at another.

"You're a stranger in these parts, I gather?" he said. There was something slightly formal, even a bit pompous, in his speech.

"An absolute stranger," replied Jimmy, with a slight aside grin.

The man dabbed some mustard on his plate, and glanced at his food to see if he would like it.

"Come from a distance, do you?" he asked, as he began to eat. As he ate, he seemed to become oblivious again of Jimmy, bent his head over his plate, and ate. But probably he was ruminating something all the time, with barbaric wariness.

"From London," said Jimmy warily.

"London!" said Pinnegar, without looking from his plate.

Mrs. Pinnegar came and sat, in ritualistic silence, in her tall-backed rocking-chair under the light.

"What brings you this way, then?" asked Pinnegar, stirring his tea.

"Oh!" Jimmy writhed a little on the sofa. "I came to see Mrs. Pinnegar."

The miner took a hasty gulp of tea.

"You're acquainted then, are you?" he said, still without looking round. He sat with his side face to Jimmy.

"Yes, we are *now*," explained Jimmy. "I didn't know Mrs. Pinnegar till this evening. As a matter of fact, she sent me some poems for the *Commentator*—I'm the editor—and I thought they were good, so I wrote and told her so. Then I felt I wanted to come and see her, and she was willing, so I came."

The man reached out, cut himself a piece of bread, and swallowed a large mouthful.

"You thought her poetry was good?" he said, turning at last to Jimmy and looking straight at him, with a stare something like the child's, but aggressive. "Are you going to put it in your magazine?"

"Yes, I think I am," said Jimmy.

"I never read but one of her poems—something about a collier she knew all about, because she'd married him," he said, in his peculiar harsh voice, that had a certain jeering clang in it, and a certain indomitableness.

Jimmy was silent. The other man's harsh, fighting voice made him shrink.

"I could never get on with the *Commentator* myself," said Pinnegar, looking round for his pudding, pushing his meat-plate aside. "Seems to me to go a long way round to get nowhere."

"Well, probably it *does*," said Jimmy, squirming a little. "But so long as the *way* is interesting! I don't see that anything gets anywhere at present—certainly no periodical."

"I don't know," said Pinnegar. "There's some facts in the *Liberator*—and there's some ideas in the *Janus*. I can't see the use myself of all these feelings folk say they have. They get you nowhere."

"But," said Jimmy, with a slight pouf of laughter, "where do you *want* to get? It's all very well talking about getting somewhere, but where, where in the world to-day do you *want* to get? In general, I mean. If you want a better job in the mine—all right, go ahead and get it. But when you begin to talk about getting somewhere in *life*—why, you've got to know what you're talking about."

"I'm a man, aren't I?" said the miner, going very still and hard.

"But what do you *mean* when you say you're a man?" snarled Jimmy, really exasperated. "What do you mean? Yes, you *are* a man. But what about it?"

"Haven't I the right to say I won't be made use of?" said the collier, slow, harsh, and heavy.

"You've got a right to *say* it," retorted Jimmy, with a pouf of laughter. "But it doesn't *mean* anything. We're all made use of, from King George downwards. We have to be. When you eat your pudding you're making use of hundreds of people—including your wife."

"I know it. I know it. It makes no difference, though. I'm not going to be made use of."

Jimmy shrugged his shoulders.

"Oh, all right!" he said. "That's just a phrase, like any other."

The miner sat very still in his chair, his face going hard and remote. He was evidently thinking over something that was stuck like a barb in his consciousness, something he was trying to harden over, as the skin sometimes hardens over a steel splinter in the flesh.

"I'm nothing but made use of," he said, now talking hard and final to himself, and staring out into space. "Down the pit, I'm made use of, and they give me a wage, such as it is. At the house, I'm made use of, and my wife sets the dinner on the table as if I was a customer in a shop."

"But what do you *expect*?" cried Jimmy, writhing in his chair.

"Me? What do I expect? I expect nothing. But I tell you what——" he turned and looked straight and hard into Jimmy's eyes—"I'm not going to put up with anything, either."

Jimmy saw the hard finality in the other man's eyes, and squirmed away from it.

"If you *know* what you're not going to put up with——" he said.

"I don't want my wife writing poetry! And sending it to a parcel of men she's never seen. *I* don't want my wife sitting like Queen Boadicea, when I come home, and a face like a stone wall with holes in it. I don't know what's wrong with her. She doesn't know herself. But she does as she likes. Only, mark you, I do the same."

"Of course!" cried Jimmy, though there was no of course about it.

"She's told you I've got another woman?"

"Yes."

"And I'll tell you for why. If I give in to the coal face, and go down the mine every day to eight hours' slavery, more or less, somebody's got to give in to me."

"Then," said Jimmy, after a pause, "if you mean you want your wife to submit to you—well, that's the problem. You have to marry the woman who *will* submit."

It was amazing, this from Jimmy. He sat there and lectured the collier like a Puritan Father, completely forgetting the disintegrating flutter of Clarissa, in his own background.

"I want a wife who'll please me, who'll want to please me," said the collier.

"Why should *you* be pleased, any more than anybody else?" asked the wife coldly.

"My child, my little girl wants to please me—if her mother would let her. But the women hang together. I tell you"— and here he turned to Jimmy, with a blaze in his dark blue eyes—"I want a woman to please me, a woman who's anxious to please me. And if I can't find her in my own home, I'll find her out of it."

"I hope she pleases you," said the wife, rocking slightly.

"Well," said the man, "she does."

"Then why don't you go and live with her altogether?" she said.

He turned and looked at her.

"Why don't I?" he said. "Because I've got my home. I've got my house, I've got my wife, let her be what she may, as a woman to live with. And I've got my child. Why should I break it all up?"

"And what about me?" she asked, coldly and fiercely.

"You? You've got a home. You've got a child. You've got a man who works for you. You've got what you want. You do as you like——"

"Do I?" she asked, with intolerable sarcasm.

"Yes. Apart from the bit of work in the house, you do as you like. If you want to go, you can go. But while you live in my house, you must respect it. You bring no men here, you see."

"Do *you* respect your home?" she said.

"Yes! I do! If I get another woman—who pleases me— I deprive you of nothing. All I ask of you is to do your duty as a housewife."

"Down to washing your back!" she said, heavily sarcastic; and, Jimmy thought, a trifle vulgar.

"Down to washing my back, since it's got to be washed," he said.

"What about the other woman? Let her do it."

"This is my home."

The wife gave a strange movement, like a mad woman.

Jimmy sat rather pale and frightened. Behind the collier's quietness he felt the concentration of almost cold anger and an unchanging will. In the man's lean face he could see the bones, the fixity of the male bones, and it was as if the human soul, or spirit, had gone into the living skull and skeleton, almost invulnerable.

Jimmy, for some strange reason, felt a wild anger against this bony and logical man. It was the hard-driven coldness, fixity, that he could not bear.

"Look here!" he cried in a resonant Oxford voice, his eyes glaring and casting inwards behind his spectacles. "You say Mrs. Pinnegar is *free*—free to do as she pleases. In that case, you have no objection if she comes with me right away from here."

The collier looked at the pale, strange face of the editor in wonder. Jimmy kept his face slightly averted, and sightless, seeing nobody. There was a Mephistophelian tilt about the eyebrows, and a Martyred Sebastian straightness about the mouth.

"Does she *want* to?" asked Pinnegar, with devastating incredulity. The wife smiled faintly, grimly. She could see the vanity of her husband in his utter inability to believe that she could prefer the other man to him.

"That," said Jimmy, "you must ask her yourself. But it's what I came here for: to ask her to come and live with me, and bring the child."

"You came without having seen her, to ask her that?" said the husband, in growing wonder.

"Yes," said Jimmy vehemently, nodding his head with drunken emphasis. "Yes! Without ever having seen her!"

"You've caught a funny fish this time, with your poetry," he said, turning with curious husband-familiarity to his wife. She hated this off-hand husband-familiarity.

"What sort of fish have *you* caught?" she retorted. "And what did you catch *her* with?"

"Bird-lime!" he said, with a faint, quick grin.

Jimmy was sitting in suspense. They all three sat in suspense for some time.

"And what are you saying to him?" said the collier at length.

Jimmy looked up, and the malevolent half-smile on his face made him rather handsome again, a mixture of faun and Mephisto. He glanced curiously, invitingly, at the woman who was watching him from afar.

"I say yes!" she replied, in a cool voice.

The husband became very still, sitting erect in his wooden arm-chair and staring into space. It was as if he were fixedly watching something fly away from him, out of his own soul. But he was not going to yield at all to any emotion.

He could not now believe that this woman should *want* to leave him. Yet she did.

"I'm sure it's all for the best," said Jimmy, in his Puritan Father voice. "You don't mind, really"—he drawled uneasily—"if she brings the child. I give you my word I'll do my very best for it."

The collier looked at him as if he were very far away. Jimmy quailed under the look. He could see that the other man was relentlessly killing the emotion in himself, stripping himself, as it were, of his own flesh, stripping himself to the hard unemotional bone of the human male.

"I give her a blank cheque," said Pinnegar, with numb lips. "She does as she pleases."

"So much for fatherly love, compared with selfishness," she said.

He turned and looked at her with that curious power of remote anger. And immediately she became still, quenched.

"I give you a blank cheque, as far as I'm concerned," he repeated abstractedly.

"It *is* blank indeed!" she said, with her first touch of bitterness.

Jimmy looked at the clock. It was growing late: he might be shut out of the public-house. He rose to go, saying he would return in the morning. He was leaving the next day, at noon, for London.

He plunged into the darkness and mud of that black, night-ridden country. There was a curious elation in his spirits, mingled with fear. But then he always needed an element of fear, really, to elate him. He thought with terror of those two human beings left in that house together. The frightening state of tension! He himself could never bear an extreme tension. He always had to compromise, to become apologetic and pathetic. He would be able to manage Mrs. Pinnegar that way. Emily! He must get used to saying it. Emily! The Emilia was absurd. He had never known an Emily.

He felt really scared, and really elated. He was doing something big. It was not that he was in *love* with the woman. But, my God, he wanted to take her away from that man. And he wanted the adventure of her. Absolutely the adventure of her. He felt really elated, really himself, really manly.

But in the morning he returned rather sheepishly to the collier's house. It was another dark, drizzling day, with black trees, black road, black hedges, blackish brick houses, and the smell of the sound of collieries under a skyless day. Like living in some weird underground.

Unwillingly he went up that passage-entry again, and knocked at the back door, glancing at the miserable little back garden with its cabbage-stalks and its ugly sanitary arrangements.

The child opened the door to him: with her fair hair, flushed cheeks, and hot, dark-blue eyes.

"Hello, Jane!" he said.

The mother stood tall and square by the table, watching him with portentous eyes as he entered. She was handsome, but her skin was not very good: as if the battle had been too much for her health. Jimmy glanced up at her smiling his slow, ingratiating smile, that always brought a glow of success into a woman's spirit. And as he saw her gold-flecked eyes searching in his eyes, without a bit of kindliness, he thought to himself: "My God, however am I going to sleep with that woman!" His will was ready, however, and he would manage it somehow.

And when he glanced at the motionless, bony head and lean figure of the collier seated in the wooden arm-chair by the fire, he was the more ready. He must triumph over that man.

"What train are you going by?" asked Mrs. Pinnegar.

"By the 12.30." He looked up at her as he spoke, with the wide, shining, childlike, almost coy eyes that were his peculiar asset. She looked down at him in a sort of interested wonder. She seemed almost fascinated by his childlike, shining, inviting dark-grey eyes, with their long lashes: such an absolute change from that resentful unyielding that looked out always from the back of her husband's blue eyes. Her husband always seemed like a menace to her, in his thinness, his concentration, his eternal unyielding. And this man looked at one with the wide, shining, fascinating eyes of a young Persian kitten, something at once bold and shy and coy and strangely inviting. She fell at once under their spell.

"You'll have dinner before you go," she said.

"No!" he cried in panic, unwilling indeed to eat before that other man. "No, I ate a fabulous breakfast. I will get a sandwich when I change in Sheffield: *really!*"

She had to go out shopping. She said she would go out to the station with him when she got back. It was just after eleven.

"But look here," he said, addressing also the thin abstracted man who sat unnoticing, with a newspaper, "we've got to get this thing settled. I *want* Mrs. Pinnegar to come and live with me, her and the child. And she's coming! So don't you think, now, it would be better if she came right along with me to-day! Just put a few things in a bag and come along. Why drag the thing out?"

"I tell you," replied the husband, "she has a blank cheque from me to do as she likes."

"All right, then! Won't you do that? Won't you come along with me now?" said Jimmy, looking up at her exposedly, but casting his eyes a bit inwards. Throwing himself with deliberate impulsiveness on her mercy.

"I can't!" she said decisively. "I can't come to-day."

"But why not—really? Why not, while I'm here? You have that blank cheque, you can do as you please——"

"The blank cheque won't get me far," she said rudely. "I can't come to-day, anyhow."

"When can you come, then?" he said, with that queer, petulant pleading. "The sooner the better, surely."

"I can come on Monday," she said abruptly.

"Monday!" He gazed up at her in a kind of panic, through his spectacles. Then he set his teeth again, and nodded his head up and down. "All right, then! To-day is Saturday. Then Monday!"

"If you'll excuse me," she said, "I've got to go out for a few things. I'll walk to the station with you when I get back."

She bundled Jane into a little sky-blue coat and bonnet, put on a heavy black coat and black hat herself, and went out.

Jimmy sat very uneasily opposite the collier, who also wore spectacles to read. Pinnegar put down the newspaper and pulled the spectacles off his nose, saying something about a Labour Government.

"Yes," said Jimmy. "After all, best be logical. If you *are* democratic, the only logical thing is a Labour Government. Though, personally, one government is as good as another to me."

"Maybe so!" said the collier. "But *something's* got to come to an end, sooner or later."

"Oh, a great deal!" said Jimmy, and they lapsed into silence.

"Have you been married before?" asked Pinnegar, at length.

"Yes. My wife and I are divorced."

"I suppose you want me to divorce *my* wife?" said the collier.

"Why—yes!—that would be best——"

"It's the same to me," said Pinnegar; "divorce or no divorce. I'll *live* with another woman, but I'll never *marry* another. Enough is as good as a feast. But if she wants a divorce, she can have it."

"It would certainly be best," said Jimmy.

There was a long pause. Jimmy wished the woman would come back.

"I look on you as an instrument," said the miner. "Something had to break. You are the instrument that breaks it."

It was strange to sit in the room with this thin, remote, wilful man. Jimmy was a bit fascinated by him. But, at the same time, he hated him because he could not be in the same room with him without being under his spell. He felt himself dominated. And he hated it.

"My wife," said Pinnegar, looking up at Jimmy with a peculiar, almost humorous, teasing grin, "expects to see me go to the dogs when she leaves me. It is her last hope."

Jimmy ducked his head and was silent, not knowing what to say. The other man sat still in his chair, like a sort of infinitely patient prisoner, looking away out of the window and waiting.

"She thinks," he said again, "that she has some wonderful future awaiting her somewhere, and you're going to open the door."

And again the same amused grin was in his eyes.

And again Jimmy was fascinated by the man. And again he hated the spell of this fascination. For Jimmy wanted to be, in his own mind, the strongest man among men, but particularly among women. And this thin, peculiar man could dominate him. He knew it. The very silent unconsciousness of Pinnegar dominated the room, wherever he was.

Jimmy hated this.

At last Mrs. Pinnegar came back, and Jimmy set off with her. He shook hands with the collier.

"Good-bye!" he said.

"Good-bye!" said Pinnegar, looking down at him with those amused blue eyes, which Jimmy knew he would never be able to get beyond.

And the walk to the station was almost a walk of conspiracy against the man left behind, between the man in spectacles and the tall woman. They arranged the details for Monday. Emily was to come by the nine o'clock train: Jimmy would meet her at Marylebone, and install her in his house in St. John's Wood. Then, with the child, they would begin a new life. Pinnegar would divorce his wife, or she would divorce him: and then, another marriage.

Jimmy got a tremendous kick out of it all on the journey home. He felt he had really done something desperate and adventurous. But he was in too wild a flutter to analyse any results. Only, as he drew near London, a sinking feeling came over him. He was desperately tired after all, almost too tired to keep up.

Nevertheless, he went after dinner and sprang it all on Severn.

"You damn fool!" said Severn, in consternation. "What did you do it for?"

"Well," said Jimmy, writhing. "Because I *wanted* to."

"Good God! The woman sounds like the head of Medusa. You're a hero of some stomach, I must say! Remember Clarissa?"

"Oh," writhed Jimmy. "But this is different."

"Ay, her name's Emma, or something of that sort, isn't it?"

"Emily!" said Jimmy briefly.

"Well, you're a fool, anyway, so you may as well keep on acting in character. I've no doubt, by playing weeping-willow, you'll outlive all the female storms you ever prepare for yourself. I never yet did see a weeping-willow uprooted by a gale, so keep on hanging your harp on it, and you'll be all right. Here's luck! But for a man who was looking for a little Gretchen to adore him, you're a corker!"

Which was all that Severn had to say. But Jimmy went home with his knees shaking. On Sunday morning he wrote an anxious letter. He didn't know how to begin it: *Dear Mrs. Pinnegar* and *Dear Emily* seemed either too late in the day or too early. So he just plunged in, without dear anything.

"I want you to have this before you come. Perhaps we have been precipitate. I only beg you to decide *finally*, for yourself, before you come. Don't come, please, unless you are absolutely sure of yourself. If you are *in the least* unsure, wait a while, wait till you are quite certain, one way or the other.

"For myself, if you don't come I shall understand. But please send me a telegram. If you do come, I shall welcome both you and the child. Yours ever—J.F."

He paid a man his return fare, and three pounds extra, to go on the Sunday and deliver this letter.

The man came back in the evening. He had delivered the letter. There was no answer.

Awful Sunday night: tense Monday morning!

A telegram: *"Arrive Marylebone 12.50 with Jane. Yours ever. Emily."*

Jimmy set his teeth and went to the station. But when he felt her looking at him, and so met her eyes: and after that saw her coming slowly down the platform, holding the child by the hand, her slow cat's eyes smouldering under her straight brows, smouldering at him: he almost swooned. A sickly grin came over him as he held out his hand. Nevertheless, he said:

"I'm *awfully* glad you came."

And as he sat in the taxi, a perverse but intense desire for her came over him, making him almost helpless. He could feel, so strongly, the presence of that other man about her, and this went to his head like neat spirits. That other man! In some subtle, inexplicable way, he was actually bodily present, the husband. The woman moved in his aura. She was hopelessly married to him.

And this went to Jimmy's head like neat whisky. Which of the two would fall before him with a greater fall—the woman or the man, her husband?

THE LAST LAUGH

THERE was a little snow on the ground, and the church clock had just struck midnight. Hampstead in the night of winter for once was looking pretty, with clean white earth and lamps for moon, and dark sky above the lamps.

A confused little sound of voices, a gleam of hidden yellow light. And then the garden door of a tall, dark Georgian house suddenly opened, and three people confusedly emerged. A girl in a dark blue coat and fur turban, very erect: a fellow with a little dispatch-case, slouching: a thin man with a red beard, bareheaded, peering out of the gateway down the hill that swung in a curve downwards towards London.

"Look at it! A new world!" cried the man in the beard, ironically, as he stood on the step and peered out.

"No, Lorenzo! It's only white-wash!" cried the young man in the overcoat. His voice was handsome, resonant, plangent, with a weary sardonic touch. As he turned back his face was dark in shadow.

The girl with the erect, alert head, like a bird, turned back to the two men.

"What was that?" she asked, in her quick, quiet voice.

"Lorenzo says it's a new world. I say it's only white-wash," cried the man in the street.

She stood still and lifted her woolly, gloved finger. She was deaf and was taking it in.

Yes, she had got it. She gave a quick, chuckling laugh, glanced very quickly at the man in the bowler hat, then back at the man in the stucco gateway, who was grinning like a satyr and waving good-bye.

"Good-bye, Lorenzo!" came the resonant, weary cry of the man in the bowler hat.

"Good-bye!" came the sharp, night-bird call of the girl.

The green gate slammed, then the inner door. The two were alone in the street, save for the policeman at the corner. The road curved steeply downhill.

"You'd better mind how you *step*!" shouted the man in the

bowler hat, leaning near the erect, sharp girl, and slouching in his walk. She paused a moment, to make sure what he had said.

"Don't mind me, I'm quite all right. Mind yourself!" she said quickly. At that very moment he gave a wild lurch on the slippery snow, but managed to save himself from falling. She watched him, on tiptoes of alertness. His bowler hat bounced away in the thin snow. They were under a lamp near the curve. As he ducked for his hat he showed a bald spot, just like a tonsure, among his dark, thin, rather curly hair. And when he looked up at her, with his thick black brows sardonically arched, and his rather hooked nose self-derisive, jamming his hat on again, he seemed like a satanic young priest. His face had beautiful lines, like a faun, and a doubtful martyred expression. A sort of faun on the Cross, with all the malice of the complication.

"Did you hurt yourself?" she asked in her quick, cool, un-emotional way.

"No!" he shouted derisively.

"Give me the machine, won't you?" she said, holding out her woolly hand. "I believe I'm safer."

"Do you *want* it?" he shouted.

"Yes, I'm sure I'm safer."

He handed her the little brown dispatch-case, which was really a Marconi listening machine for her deafness. She marched erect as ever. He shoved his hands deep in his overcoat pockets and slouched along beside her, as if he wouldn't make his legs firm. The road curved down in front of them, clean and pale with snow under the lamps. A motor-car came churning up. A few dark figures slipped away into the dark recesses of the houses, like fishes among rocks above a sea-bed of white sand. On the left was a tuft of trees sloping upwards into the dark.

He kept looking around, pushing out his finely shaped chin and his hooked nose as if he were listening for something. He could still hear the motor-car climbing on to the Heath. Below was the yellow, foul-smelling glare of the Hampstead Tube Station. On the right the trees.

The girl, with her alert pink-and-white face, looked at him sharply, inquisitively. She had an odd nymph-like inquisitive-ness, sometimes like a bird, sometimes a squirrel, sometimes a rabbit: never quite like a woman. At last he stood still, as if he would go no farther. There was a curious, baffled grin on his smooth, cream-coloured face.

"James," he said loudly to her, leaning towards her ear. "Do you hear somebody *laughing?*"

"Laughing?" she retorted quickly. "Who's laughing?"

"I don't know. *Somebody!*" he shouted, showing his teeth at her in a very odd way.

"No, I hear nobody," she announced.

"But it's most *extraordinary!*" he cried, his voice slurring up and down. "Put on your machine."

"Put it on?" she retorted. "What for?"

"To see if you can *hear* it," he cried.

"Hear what?"

"The *laughing*. Somebody laughing. It's most *extraordinary.*"

She gave her odd little chuckle and handed him her machine. He held it while she opened the lid and attached the wires, putting the band over her head and the receivers at her ears, like a wireless operator. Crumbs of snow fell down the cold darkness. She switched on: little yellow lights in glass tubes shone in the machine. She was connected, she was listening. He stood with his head ducked, his hands shoved down in his overcoat pockets.

Suddenly he lifted his face and gave the weirdest, slightly neighing laugh, uncovering his strong, spaced teeth, and arching his black brows, and watching her with queer, gleaming, goat-like eyes.

She seemed a little dismayed.

"There!" he said. "Didn't you hear it?"

"I heard *you!*" she said, in a tone which conveyed that *that* was enough.

"But didn't you hear *it!*" he cried, unfurling his lips oddly again.

"No!" she said.

He looked at her vindictively, and stood again with ducked head. She remained erect, her fur hat in her hand, her fine bobbed hair banded with the machine-band and catching crumbs of snow, her odd, bright-eyed, deaf nymph's face lifted with blank listening.

"There!" he cried, suddenly jerking up his gleaming face. "You mean to tell me you can't——" He was looking at her almost diabolically. But something else was too strong for him. His face wreathed with a startling, peculiar smile, seeming to gleam, and suddenly the most extraordinary laugh came bursting out of him, like an animal laughing. It was a strange, neighing sound, amazing in her ears. She was startled, and switched her machine quieter.

A large form loomed up: a tall, clean-shaven young policeman.

"A radio?" he asked laconically.

"No, it's my machine. I'm deaf!" said Miss James quickly and distinctly. She was not the daughter of a peer for nothing.

The man in the bowler hat lifted his face and glared at the fresh-faced young policeman with a peculiar white glare in his eyes.

"Look here!" he said distinctly. "Did you hear someone laughing?"

"Laughing? I heard you, sir."

"No, *not* me." He gave an impatient jerk of his arm, and lifted his face again. His smooth, creamy face seemed to gleam, there were subtle curves of derisive triumph in all its lines. He was careful not to look directly at the young policeman. "The most extraordinary laughter I ever heard," he added, and the same touch of derisive exultation sounded in his tones.

The policeman looked down on him cogitatingly.

"It's perfectly all right," said Miss James coolly. "He's not drunk. He just hears something that we don't hear."

"Drunk!" echoed the man in the bowler hat, in profoundly amused derision. "If I were merely drunk——" And off he went again in the wild, neighing, animal laughter, while his averted face seemed to flash.

At the sound of the laughter something roused in the blood of the girl and of the policeman. They stood nearer to one another, so that their sleeves touched and they looked wonderingly across at the man in the bowler hat. He lifted his black brows at them.

"Do you mean to say you heard nothing?" he asked.

"Only you," said Miss James.

"Only you, sir!" echoed the policeman.

"What was it like?" asked Miss James.

"Ask me to *describe* it!" retorted the young man, in extreme contempt. "It's the most marvellous sound in the world."

And truly he seemed wrapped up in a new mystery.

"Where does it come from?" asked Miss James, very practical.

"Apparently," it answered in contempt, "from over there." And he pointed to the trees and bushes inside the railings over the road.

"Well, let's go and see!" she said. "I can carry my machine and go on listening."

The man seemed relieved to get rid of the burden. He shoved his hands in his pockets again and sloped off across the road. The policeman, a queer look flickering on his fresh young face, put his hand round the girl's arm carefull and subtly, to help her. She did not lean at all on the support of the big hand, but she was interested, so she did not resent it. Having held herself all her life intensely aloof from physical contact, and never having let any man touch her, she now, with a certain nymph-like voluptuousness, allowed the large hand of the young policeman to support her as they followed the quick wolf-like figure of the other man across the road uphill. And she could feel the presence of the young policeman, through all the thickness of his dark-blue uniform, as something young and alert and bright.

When they came up to the man in the bowler hat, he was standing with his head ducked, his ears pricked, listening beside the iron rail inside which grew big black holly trees tufted with snow, and old, ribbed, silent English elms.

The policeman and the girl stood waiting. She was peering into the bushes with the sharp eyes of a deaf nymph, deaf to the world's noises. The man in the bowler hat listened intensely. A lorry rolled downhill, making the earth tremble.

"There!" cried the girl, as the lorry rumbled darkly past. And she glanced round with flashing eyes at her policeman, her fresh soft face gleaming with startled life. She glanced straight into the puzzled, amused eyes of the young policeman. He was just enjoying himself.

"Don't you see?" she said, rather imperiously.

"What is it, Miss?" answered the policeman.

"I mustn't point," she said. "Look where I look."

And she looked away with brilliant eyes, into the dark holly bushes. She must see something, for she smiled faintly, with subtle satisfaction, and she tossed her erect head in all the pride of vindication. The policeman looked at her instead of into the bushes. There was a certain brilliance of triumph and vindication in all the poise of her slim body.

"I always knew I should see him," she said triumphantly to herself.

"Whom do you see?" shouted the man in the bowler hat.

"Don't you see him too?" she asked, turning round her soft, arch, nymph-like face anxiously. She was anxious for the little man to see.

"No, I see nothing. What do you see, James?" cried the man in the bowler hat, insisting.

"A man."

"Where?"

"There. Among the holly bushes.

"Is he there now?"

"No! He's gone."

"What sort of a man?"

"I don't know."

"What did he look like?"

"I can't tell you."

But at that instant the man in the bowler hat turned suddenly, and the arch, triumphant look flew to his face.

"Why, he must be *there*!" he cried, pointing up the grove. "Don't you hear him laughing? He must be behind those trees."

And his voice, with curious delight, broke into a laugh again, as he stood and stamped his feet on the snow, and danced to his own laughter, ducking his head. Then he turned away and ran swiftly up the avenue lined with old trees.

He slowed down as a door at the end of a garden path, white with untouched snow, suddenly opened, and a woman in a long-fringed black shawl stood in the light. She peered out into the night. Then she came down to the low garden gate. Crumbs of snow still fell. She had dark hair and a tall dark comb.

"Did you knock at my door?" she asked of the man in the bowler hat.

"I? No!"

"Somebody knocked at my door."

"Did they? Are you sure? They can't have done. There are no footmarks in the snow."

"Nor are there!" she said. "But somebody knocked and called something."

"That's very curious," said the man. "Were you expecting someone?"

"No. Not exactly expecting anyone. Except that one is always expecting Somebody, you know." In the dimness of the snow-lit night he could see her making big, dark eyes at him.

"Was it someone laughing?" he said.

"No. It was no one laughing, exactly. Someone knocked, and I ran to open, hoping as one always hopes, you know——"

"What?"

"Oh—that something wonderful is going to happen."

He was standing close to the low gate. She stood on the opposite side. Her hair was dark, her face seemed dusky, as she looked up at him with her dark, meaningful eyes.

"Did you wish someone would come?" he asked.

"Very much," she replied, in her plangent Jewish voice. She must be a Jewess.

"No matter who?" he said, laughing.

"So long as it was a man I could like," she said, in a low, meaningful, falsely shy voice.

"Really!" he said. "Perhaps after all it was I who knocked —without knowing."

"I think it was," she said. "It must have been."

"Shall I come in?" he asked, putting his hand on the little gate.

"Don't you think you'd better?" she replied.

He bent down, unlatching the gate. As he did so the woman in the black shawl turned, and, glancing over her shoulder, hurried back to the house, walking unevenly in the snow, on her high-heeled shoes. The man hurried after her, hastening like a hound to catch up.

Meanwhile the girl and the policeman had come up. The girl stood still when she saw the man in the bowler hat going up the garden walk after the woman in the black shawl with the fringe.

"Is he going in?" she asked quickly.

"Looks like it, doesn't it?" said the policeman.

"Does he know that woman?"

"I can't say. I should say he soon will," replied the policeman.

"But who is she?"

"I couldn't say who she is."

The two dark, confused figures entered the lighted doorway, then the door closed on them.

"He's gone," said the girl outside on the snow. She hastily began to pull off the band of her telephone receiver, and switched off her machine. The tubes of secret light disappeared, she packed up the little leather case. Then, pulling on her soft fur cap, she stood once more ready.

The slightly martial look which her long, dark-blue military-seeming coat gave her was intensified, while the slightly anxious, bewildered look of her face had gone. She seemed to stretch herself, to stretch her limbs free. And the inert look had left her full soft cheeks. Her cheeks were alive with the glimmer of pride and a new dangerous surety.

She looked quickly at the tall young policeman. He was clean-shaven, fresh-faced, smiling oddly under his helmet, waiting in subtle patience, a few yards away. She saw that he was a decent young man, one of the waiting sort.

The second of ancient fear was followed at once in her by a blithe, unaccustomed sense of power.

"Well!" she said. "I should say it's no use waiting." She spoke decisively.

"You don't have to wait for him, do you?" asked the policeman.

"Not at all. He's much better where he is." She laughed an odd, brief laugh. Then glancing over her shoulder, she set off down the hill, carrying her little case. Her feet felt light, her legs felt long and strong. She glanced over her shoulder again. The young policeman was following her, and she laughed to herself. Her limbs felt so lithe and so strong, if she wished she could easily run faster than he. If she wished she could easily kill him, even with her hands.

So it seemed to her. But why kill him? He was a decent young fellow. She had in front of her eyes the dark face among the holly bushes, with the brilliant, mocking eyes. Her breast felt full of power, and her legs felt long and strong and wild. She was surprised herself at the strong, bright, throbbing sensation beneath her breasts, a sensation of triumph and rosy anger. Her hands felt keen on her wrists. She who had always declared she had not a muscle in her body! Even now, it was not muscle, it was a sort of flame.

Suddenly it began to snow heavily, with fierce frozen puffs

of wind. The snow was small, in frozen grains, and hit sharp on her face. It seemed to whirl round her as if she herself were whirling in a cloud. But she did not mind. There was a flame in her, her limbs felt flamey and strong, amid the whirl.

And the whirling snowy air seemed full of presences, full of strange unheard voices. She was used to the sensation of noises taking place which she could not hear. This sensation became very strong. She felt something was happening in the wild air.

The London air was no longer heavy and clammy, saturated with ghosts of the unwilling dead. A new, clean tempest swept down from the Pole, and there were noises.

Voices were calling. In spite of her deafness she could hear someone, several voices, calling and whistling, as if many people were hallooing through the air:

"He's come back! Aha! He's come back!"

There was a wild, whistling, jubilant sound of voices in the storm of snow. Then obscured lightning winked through the snow in the air.

"Is that thunder and lightning?" she asked of the young policeman, as she stood still, waiting for his form to emerge through the veil of whirling snow.

"Seems like it to me," he said.

And at that very moment the lightning blinked again, and the dark, laughing face was near her face, it almost touched her cheek.

She started back, but a flame of delight went over her.

"There!" she said. "Did you see that?"

"It lightened," said the policeman.

She was looking at him almost angrily. But then the clean, fresh animal look of his skin, and the tame-animal look in his frightened eyes amused her, she laughed her low, triumphant laugh. He was obviously afraid, like a frightened dog that sees something uncanny.

The storm suddenly whistled louder, more violently, and, with a strange noise like castanets, she seemed to hear voices clapping and crying:

"He is here! He's come back!"

She nodded her head gravely.

The policeman and she moved on side by side. She lived alone in a little stucco house in a side street down the hill.

There was a church and a grove of trees and then the little old row of houses. The wind blew fiercely, thick with snow. Now and again a taxi went by, with its lights showing weirdly. But the world seemed empty, uninhabited save by snow and voices.

As the girl and the policeman turned past the grove of trees near the church, a great whirl of wind and snow made them stand still, and in the wild confusion they heard a whirling of sharp, delighted voices, something like seagulls, crying:

"He's here! He's here!"

"Well, I'm jolly glad he's back," said the girl calmly.

"What's that?" said the nervous policeman, hovering near the girl.

The wind let them move forward. As they passed along the railings it seemed to them the doors of the church were open, and the windows were out, and the snow and the voices were blowing in a wild career all through the church.

"How extraordinary that they left the church open!" said the girl.

The policeman stood still. He could not reply.

And as they stood they listened to the wind and the church full of whirling voices all calling confusedly.

"*Now* I hear the laughing," she said suddenly.

It came from the church: a sound of low, subtle, endless laughter, a strange, naked sound.

"Now I hear it!" she said.

But the policeman did not speak. He stood cowed, with his tail between his legs, listening to the strange noises in the church.

The wind must have blown out one of the windows, for they could see the snow whirling in volleys through the black gap, and whirling inside the church like a dim light. There came a sudden crash, followed by a burst of chuckling, naked laughter. The snow seemed to make a queer light inside the building, like ghosts moving, big and tall.

There was more laughter, and a tearing sound. On the wind, pieces of paper, leaves of books, came whirling among the snow through the dark window. Then a white thing, soaring like a crazy bird, rose up on the wind as if it had wings, and lodged on a black tree outside, struggling. It was the altar-cloth.

There came a bit of gay, trilling music. The wind was running over the organ-pipes like pan-pipes, quickly up and down. Snatches of wild, gay, trilling music, and bursts of the naked low laughter.

"Really!" said the girl. "This is most extraordinary. Do you hear the music and the people laughing?"

"Yes, I hear somebody on the organ!" said the policeman.

"And do you get the puff of warm wind? Smelling of spring. Almond blossom, that's what it is! A most marvellous scent of almond blossom. *Isn't* it an extraordinary thing!"

She went on triumphantly past the church, and came to the row of little old houses. She entered her own gate in the little railed entrance.

"Here I am!" she said finally. "I'm home now. Thank you very much for coming with me."

She looked at the young policeman. His whole body was white as a wall with snow, and in the vague light of the arc-lamp from the street his face was humble and frightened.

"Can I come in and warm myself a bit?" he asked humbly. She knew it was fear rather than cold that froze him. He was in mortal fear.

"Well!" she said. "Stay down in the sitting-room if you like. But don't come upstairs, because I am alone in the house. You can make up the fire in the sitting-room, and you can go when you are warm."

She left him on the big, low couch before the fire, his face bluish and blank with fear. He rolled his blue eyes after her as she left the room. But she went up to her bedroom and fastened her door.

In the morning she was in her studio upstairs in her little house, looking at her own paintings and laughing to herself. Her canaries were talking and shrilly whistling in the sunshine that followed the storm. The cold snow outside was still clean, and the white glare in the air gave the effect of much stronger sunshine than actually existed.

She was looking at her own paintings, and chuckling to herself over their comicalness. Suddenly they struck her as absolutely absurd. She quite enjoyed looking at them, they seemed to her so grotesque. Especially her self-portrait, with its nice brown hair and its slightly opened rabbit-mouth and its baffled, uncertain rabbit-eyes. She looked at the painted face and laughed in a long, rippling laugh, till the yellow canaries like faded daffodils almost went mad in an effort to sing louder. The girl's long, rippling laugh sounded through the house uncannily.

The housekeeper, a rather sad-faded young woman of a superior sort—nearly all people in England are of the superior sort, superiority being an English ailment—came in with an inquiring and rather disapproving look.

"Did you call, Miss James?" she asked loudly.

"No. No, I didn't call. Don't shout, I can hear quite well," replied the girl.

The housekeeper looked at her again.

"You knew there was a young man in the sitting-room?" she said.

"No. Really!" cried the girl. "What, the young policeman? I'd forgotten all about him. He came in in the storm to warm himself. Hasn't he gone?"

"No, Miss James."

"How extraordinary of him! What time is it? Quarter to nine! Why didn't he go when he was warm? I must go and see him, I suppose."

"He says he's lame," said the housekeeper censoriously and loudly.

"Lame! That's extraordinary. He certainly wasn't last night. But don't shout. I can hear quite well."

"Is Mr. Marchbanks coming in to breakfast, Miss James?" said the housekeeper, more and more censorious.

"I couldn't say. But I'll come down as soon as mine is ready. I'll be down in a minute, anyhow, to see the policeman. Extraordinary that he is still here."

She sat down before her window, in the sun, to think a while. She could see the snow outside, the bare, purplish trees. The air all seemed rare and different. Suddenly the world had become quite different: as if some skin or integument had broken, as if the old, mouldering London sky had crackled and rolled back, like an old skin, shrivelled, leaving an absolutely new blue heaven.

"It really is extraordinary!" she said to herself. "I certainly saw that man's face. What a wonderful face it was! I shall never forget it. Such laughter! He laughs longest who laughs last. He certainly will have the last laugh. I like him for that: he will laugh last. Must be someone really extraordinary! How very nice to be the one to laugh last. He certainly will. What a wonderful being! I suppose I must call him a being. He's not a person exactly.

"But how wonderful of him to come back and alter all the world immediately! *Isn't* that extraordinary. I wonder if he'll have altered Marchbanks. Of course Marchbanks never *saw* him. But he heard him. Wouldn't that do as well, I wonder!—I *wonder!*"

She went off into a muse about Marchbanks. She and he were *such* friends. They had been friends like that for almost two years. Never lovers. Never that at all. But *friends*.

And after all, she had been in love with him: in her head. This seemed now so funny to her: that she had been, in her head, so much in love with him. After all, life was too absurd.

Because now she saw herself and him as such a funny pair. He so funnily taking life terribly seriously, especially his own life. And she so ridiculously *determined* to save him from himself. Oh, how absurd! *Determined* to save him from himself, and wildly in love with him in the effort. The determination to save him from himself.

Absurd! Absurd! Absurd! Since she had seen the man laughing among the holly bushes—*such* extraordinary, wonderful laughter—she had seen her own ridiculousness. Really, what fantastic silliness, saving a man from himself! Saving anybody. What fantastic silliness! How much more amusing and lively to let a man go to perdition in his own way. Perdition was more amusing than salvation anyhow, and a much better place for most men to go to.

She had never been in love with any man, and only spuriously in love with Marchbanks. She saw it quite plainly now. After all, what nonsense it all was, this being-in-love business. Thank goodness she had never made the humiliating mistake.

No, the man among the holly bushes had made her see it all so plainly: the ridiculousness of being in love, the *infra dig.* business of chasing a man or being chased by a man.

"Is love *really* so absurd and *infra dig.?*" she said aloud to herself.

"Why, of course!" came a deep, laughing voice.

She started round, but nobody was to be seen.

"I expect it's that man again!" she said to herself. "It really *is* remarkable, you know. I consider it's a remarkable thing that I never really wanted a man, *any* man. And there I am over thirty. It *is* curious. Whether it's something wrong with me, or right with me, I can't say. I don't know till I've proved it. But I believe, if that man kept on laughing something would happen to me."

She smelt the curious smell of almond blossom in the room, and heard the distant laugh again.

"I do wonder why Marchbanks went with that woman last night—that Jewish-looking woman. Whatever could he want of her?—or she him? So strange, as if they both had made up their minds to something! How extraordinarily puzzling life is! So messy, it all seems.

"Why does nobody ever laugh in life like that man? He *did* seem so wonderful. So scornful! And so proud! And so real! With those laughing, scornful, amazing eyes, just laughing and disappearing again. I can't imagine him chasing a Jewish-looking woman. Or chasing any woman, thank goodness. It's all *so* messy. My policeman would be messy if one would let him: like a dog. I do dislike dogs, really I do. And men do seem so doggy!——"

But even while she mused, she began to laugh again to herself with a long, low chuckle. How wonderful of that man to come and laugh like that and make the sky crack and shrivel like an old skin! Wasn't he wonderful! Wouldn't it be wonderful if he just touched her. Even touched her. She felt, if he touched her, she herself would emerge new and tender out of an old, hard skin. She was gazing abstractedly out of the window.

"There he comes, just now," she said abruptly. But she meant Marchbanks, not the laughing man.

There he came, his hands still shoved down in his overcoat pockets, his head still rather furtively ducked in the bowler hat, and his legs still rather shambling. He came hurrying across the road, not looking up, deep in thought, no doubt. Thinking profoundly, with agonies of agitation, no doubt about his last night's experience. It made her laugh.

She, watching from the window above, burst into a long laugh, and the canaries went off their heads again.

He was in the hall below. His resonant voice was calling, rather imperiously:

"James! Are you coming down?"

"No," she called. "You come up."

He came up two at a time, as if his feet were a bit savage with the stairs for obstructing him.

In the doorway he stood staring at her with a vacant, sardonic look, his grey eyes moving with a queer light. And she looked back at him with a curious, rather haughty carelessness.

"Don't you want your breakfast?" she asked. It was his custom to come and take breakfast with her each morning.

"No," he answered loudly. "I went to a tea-shop."

"Don't shout," she said. "I can hear you quite well."

He looked at her with mockery and a touch of malice.

"I believe you always could," he said, still loudly.

"Well, anyway, I can now, so you needn't shout," she replied.

And again his grey eyes, with the queer, greyish phosphorescent gleam in them, lingered malignantly on her face.

"Don't look at me," she said calmly. "I know all about everything."

He burst into a pouf of malicious laughter.

"Who taught you—the policeman?" he cried.

"Oh, by the way, he must be downstairs! No, he was only incidental. So, I suppose, was the woman in the shawl. Did you stay all night?"

"Not entirely. I came away before dawn. What did you do?"

"Don't shout. I came home long before dawn." And she seemed to hear the long, low laughter.

"Why, what's the matter?" he said curiously. "What have you been doing?"

"I don't quite know. Why?—are you going to call me to account?"

"Did you hear that laughing?"

"Oh yes. And many more things. And saw things too."

"Have you seen the paper?"

"No. Don't shout, I can hear."

"There's been a great storm, blew out the windows and doors of the church outside here, and pretty well wrecked the place."

"I saw it. A leaf of the church Bible blew right in my face: from the Book of Job——" She gave a low laugh.

"But what else did you see?" he cried loudly.

"I saw *him*."

"Who?"

"Ah, that I can't say."

"But, what was he like?"

"That I can't tell you. I don't really know."

"But you must know. Did your policeman see him too?"

"No, I don't suppose he did. My policeman!" And she went off into a long ripple of laughter. "He is by no means mine. But I *must* go downstairs and see him."

"It's certainly made you very strange," Marchbanks said. "You've got no *soul*, you know."

"Oh, thank goodness for that!" she cried. "My policeman has one, I'm sure. *My policeman!*" And she went off again into a long peal of laughter, the canaries pealing shrill accompaniment.

"What's the matter with you?" he said.

"Having no soul. I never had one really. It was always fobbed off on me. Soul was the only thing there was between you and me. Thank goodness it's gone. Haven't you lost yours? The one that seemed to worry you, like a decayed tooth?"

"But what are you *talking* about?" he cried.

"I don't know," she said. "It's all so extraordinary. But look here, I *must* go down and see my policeman. He's downstairs in the sitting-room. You'd better come with me."

They went down together. The policeman, in his waistcoat and shirt-sleeves, was lying on the sofa, with a very long face.

"Look here!" said Miss James to him. "Is it true you're lame?"

"It is true. That's why I'm here. I can't walk," said the fair-haired young man as tears came to his eyes.

"But how did it happen? You weren't lame last night," she said.

"I don't know how it happened—but when I woke up and tried to stand up, I couldn't do it." The tears ran down his distressed face.

"How very extraordinary!" she said. "What can we do about it?"

"Which foot is it?" asked Marchbanks. "Let us have a look at it."

"I don't like to," said the poor devil.

"You'd better," said Miss James.

He slowly pulled off his stocking, and showed his white left foot curiously clubbed, like the weird paw of some animal. When he looked at it himself, he sobbed.

And as he sobbed, the girl heard again the low, exulting laughter. But she paid no heed to it, gazing curiously at the weeping young policeman.

"Does it hurt?" she asked.

"It does if I try to walk on it," wept the young man.

"I'll tell you what," she said. "We'll telephone for a doctor, and he can take you home in a taxi."

The young fellow shamefacedly wiped his eyes.

"But have you no idea how it happened?" asked Marchbanks anxiously.

"I haven't myself," said the young fellow.

At that moment the girl heard the low, eternal laugh right in her ear. She started, but could see nothing.

She started round again as Marchbanks gave a strange, yelping cry, like a shot animal. His white face was drawn, distorted in a curious grin, that was chiefly agony but partly wild recognition. He was staring with fixed eyes at something. And in the rolling agony of his eyes was the horrible grin of a man who realises he has made a final, and this time fatal, fool of himself.

"Why," he yelped in a high voice, "I knew it was he!" And with a queer shuddering laugh he pitched forward on the carpet and lay writhing for a moment on the floor. Then he lay still, in a weird, distorted position, like a man struck by lightning.

Miss James stared with round, staring brown eyes.

"Is he dead?" she asked quickly.

The young policeman was trembling so that he could hardly speak. She could hear his teeth chattering.

"Seems like it," he stammered.

There was a faint smell of almond blossom in the air.

IN LOVE

"WELL, my dear!" said Henrietta. "If I had such a worried look on my face, when I was going down to spend the week-end with the man I was engaged to—and going to be married to in a month—well! I should either try and change my face, or hide my feelings, or something."

"You shut up!" said Hester curtly. "Don't look at my face, if it doesn't please you."

"Now, my dear Hester, don't go into one of your tempers! Just look in the mirror, and you'll see what I mean."

"Who cares what you mean! You're not responsible for my face," said Hester desperately, showing no intention of looking in the mirror, or of otherwise following her sister's kind advice.

Henrietta, being the younger sister, and mercifully un-engaged, hummed a tune lightly. She was only twenty-one, and had not the faintest intention of jeopardising her peace of mind by accepting any sort of fatal ring. Nevertheless, it *was* nice to see Hester 'getting off', as they say; for Hester was nearly twenty-five, which is serious.

The worst of it was, lately Hester had had her famous 'worried' look on her face, when it was a question of the faith-ful Joe: dark shadows under the eyes, drawn lines down the cheeks. And when Hester looked like that, Henrietta couldn't help feeling the most horrid jangled echo of worry and appre-hension in her own heart, and she hated it. She simply couldn't stand that sudden feeling of fear.

"What I mean to say," she continued, "*is*—that it's jolly unfair to Joe, if you go down looking like that. Either put a better face on it, or——" But she checked herself. She was going to say "don't go". But really, she did hope that Hester would go through with this marriage. Such a weight off her, Henrietta's, mind.

"Oh, hang!" cried Hester. "Shut up!" And her dark eyes flashed a spark of fury and misgiving at the young Henrietta.

Henrietta sat down on the bed, lifted her chin, and com-posed her face like a meditating angel. She really was intensely fond of Hester, and the worried look was such a terribly bad sign.

"Look here, Hester!" she said. "Shall I come down to Markbury with you? *I* don't mind, if you'd like me to."

"My dear girl," cried Hester in desperation, "what earthly use do you think that would be?"

"Well, I thought it might take the edge off the intimacy, if that's what worries you."

Hester re-echoed with a hollow, mocking laugh.

"Don't be such a *child*, Henrietta, really!" she said.

And Hester set off alone, down to Wiltshire, where her Joe had just started a little farm, to get married on. After being in the artillery, he had got sick and tired of business: besides, Hester would never have gone into a little surburban villa. Every woman sees her home through a wedding ring. Hester had only taken a squint through her engagement ring, so far. But Ye Gods! not Golders Green, not even Harrow!

So Joe had built a little brown wooden bungalow—largely with his own hands: and at the back was a small stream with two willows, old ones. At the sides were brown sheds, and chicken-runs. There were pigs in a hog-proof wire fence, and two cows in a field, and a horse. Joe had thirty-odd acres, with only a youth to help him. But of course, there would be Hester.

It all looked very new and tidy. Joe was a worker. He too looked rather new and tidy, very healthy and pleased with himself. He didn't even see the 'worried look'. Or if he did, he only said:

"You're looking a bit fagged, Hester. Going up to the City takes it out of you, more than you know. You'll be another girl down here."

"Shan't I just!" cried Hester.

She did like it, too!—the lots of white and yellow hens, and the pigs so full of pep! And the yellow thin blades of willow leaves showering softly down at the back of her house from the leaning old trees. She liked it awfully: especially the yellow leaves on the earth.

She told Joe she thought it was all lovely, topping, fine! And he was awfully pleased. Certainly *he* looked fit enough.

The mother of the helping youth gave them dinner at half-past twelve. The afternoon was all sunshine and little jobs to do, after she had dried the dishes for the mother of the youth.

"Not long now, miss, before you'll be cooking at this range: and a good little range it is."

"Not long now, no!" echoed Hester, in the hot little wooden kitchen, that was over-heated from the range.

The woman departed. After tea, the youth also departed and Joe and Hester shut up the chickens and the pigs. It was nightfall. Hester went in and made the supper, feeling somehow a bit of a fool, and Joe made a fire in the living-room, he feeling rather important and luscious.

He and Hester would be alone in the bungalow, till the youth appeared next morning. Six months ago, Hester would have enjoyed it. They were so perfectly comfortable together, he and she. They had been friends, and his family and hers had been friends for years, donkey's years. He was a perfectly decent boy, and there would never have been anything messy to fear from him. Nor from herself. Ye Gods, no!

But now, alas, since she had promised to marry him, he had made the wretched mistake of falling 'in love' with her. He had never been that way before. And if she had known he would get this way now, she would have said decidedly: Let us remain friends, Joe, for this sort of thing is a come-down. Once he started cuddling and petting, she couldn't stand him. Yet she felt she ought to. She imagined she even ought to like it. Though where the *ought* came from, she could not see.

"I'm afraid, Hester," he said sadly, "you're not in love with me as I am with you."

"Hang it all!" she cried. "If I'm not, you ought to be jolly well thankful, that's all I've got to say."

Which double-barrelled remark he heard, but did not register. He never liked looking anything in the very pin-point middle of the eye. He just left it, and left all her feelings comfortably in the dark. Comfortably for him, that is.

He was extremely competent at motor-cars and farming and all that sort of thing. And surely she, Hester, was as complicated as a motor-car! Surely she had as many subtle little valves and magnetos and accelerators and all the rest of it, to her make-up! If only he would try to handle *her* as carefully as he handled his car! She needed starting, as badly as ever any automobile did. Even if a car had a self-starter, the man had to give it the right twist. Hester felt she would need a lot of cranking up, if ever she was to start off on the matrimonial road with Joe. And he, the fool, just sat in a motionless car and pretended he was making heaven knows how many miles an hour.

This evening she felt really desperate. She had been quite all right doing things with him, during the afternoon, about the place. Then she liked being with him. But now that it was evening and they were alone, the stupid little room, the cosy fire, Joe, Joe's pipe, and Joe's smug sort of hypocritical face, all was just too much for her.

"Come and sit here, dear," said Joe persuasively, patting the sofa at his side. And she, because she believed a *nice* girl would have been only too delighted to go and sit 'there', went and sat beside him. But she was boiling. What cheek! What cheek of him even to have a sofa! She loathed the vulgarity of sofas.

She endured his arm round her waist, and a certain pressure of his biceps which she presumed was cuddling. He had carefully knocked his pipe out. But she thought how smug and silly his face looked, all its natural frankness and straightforwardness had gone. How ridiculous of him to stroke the back of her neck! How idiotic he was, trying to be lovey-dovey! She wondered what sort of sweet nothings Lord Byron, for example, had murmured to his various ladies. Surely not so blithering, not so incompetent! And how monstrous of him, to kiss her like that.

"I'd infinitely rather you'd play to me, Joe," she snapped.

"You don't want me to play to you to-night, do you, dear?" he said.

"Why not to-night? I'd love to hear some Tchaikowsky, something to stir me up a bit."

He rose obediently and went to the piano. He played quite well. She listened. And Tchaikowsky might have stirred her up all right. The music itself, that is. If she hadn't been so desperately aware that Joe's love-making, if you can call it such, became more absolutely impossible after the sound of the music.

"That was fine!" she said. "Now do me my favourite nocturne."

While he concentrated on the fingering, she slipped out of the house.

Oh! she gasped a sigh of relief to be in the cool October

air. The darkness was dim. In the west was a half moon freshly shining, and all the air was motionless, dimness lay like a haze on the earth.

Hester shook her hair, and strode away from the bungalow, which was a perfect little drum, re-echoing to her favourite nocturne. She simply rushed to get out of ear-shot.

Ah! the lovely night! She tossed her short hair again, and felt like Mazeppa's horse, about to dash away into the infinite. Though the infinite was only a field belonging to the next farm. But Hester felt herself seething in the soft moonlight. Oh! to rush away over the edge of the beyond! if the beyond, like Joe's bread-knife, did have an edge to it. "I know I'm an idiot," she said to herself. But that didn't take away the wild surge of her limbs. Oh! If there were only some other solution, instead of Joe and his spooning. Yes, SPOONING! The word made her lose the last shred of her self-respect, but she said it aloud.

There was, however, a bunch of strange horses in this field, so she made her way cautiously back through Joe's fence. It was just like him, to have such a little place that you couldn't get away from the sound of his piano, without trespassing on somebody else's ground.

As she drew near the bungalow, however, the drumming of Joe's piano suddenly ceased. Oh, Heaven! She looked wildly round. An old willow leaned over the stream. She stretched, crouching, and with the quickness of a long cat, climbed up into the net of cool-bladed foliage.

She had scarcely shuffled and settled into a tolerable position when he came round the corner of the house and into the moonlight, looking for her. How dare he look for her! She kept as still as a bat among the leaves, watching him as he sauntered with erect, tiresomely manly figure and lifted head, staring round in the darkness. He looked for once very ineffectual, insignificant, and at a loss. Where was his supposed male magic? Why was he so slow and unequal to the situation?

There! He was calling softly and self-consciously: "Hester! Hester! Where have you put yourself?"

He was angry really. Hester kept still in her tree, trying not to fidget. She had not the faintest intention of answering him. He might as well have been on another planet. He sauntered vaguely and unhappily out of sight.

Then she had a qualm. "Really, my girl, it's a bit thick, the way you treat him! Poor old Joe!"

Immediately something began to hum inside her: "I hear those tender voices calling Poor Old Joe!"

Nevertheless, she didn't want to go indoors to spend the evening *tête-à-tête*—my word!—with him.

"Of course it's absurd to think I could possibly fall in love like that. I would rather fall into one of his pig-troughs. It's so frightfully common. As a matter of fact, it's just a proof that he doesn't love me."

This thought went through her like a bullet. "The very fact of his being in love with me proves that he doesn't love me. No man that loved a woman could be in love with her like that. It's so insulting to her."

She immediately began to cry, and fumbling in her sleeve for her hanky, she nearly fell out of the tree. Which brought her to her senses.

In the obscure distance she saw him returning to the house, and she felt bitter. "Why did he start all this mess? I never wanted to marry anybody, and I certainly never bargained for anybody falling in love with me. Now I'm miserable, and I feel abnormal. Because the majority of girls must like this in-love business, or men wouldn't do it. And the majority must be normal. So I'm abnormal, and I'm up a tree. I loathe myself. As for Joe, he's spoilt all there was between us, and he expects me to marry him on the strength of it. It's perfectly sickening! What a mess life is. How I loathe messes!"

She immediately shed a few more tears, in the course of which she heard the door of the bungalow shut with something of a bang. He had gone indoors, and he was going to be righteously offended. A new misgiving came over her.

The willow tree was uncomfortable. The air was cold and damp. If she caught another chill she'd probably snuffle all winter long. She saw the lamplight coming warm from the window of the bungalow, and she said "Damn!" which meant, in her case, that she was feeling bad.

She slid down out of the tree, and scratched her arm and probably damaged one of her nicest pair of stockings. "Oh, hang!" she said with emphasis, preparing to go into the bungalow and have it out with poor old Joe. "I will *not* call him Poor Old Joe!"

At that moment she heard a motor-car slow down in the

lane, and there came a low, cautious toot from a hooter. Headlights shone at a standstill near Joe's new iron gate.

"The cheek of it! The unbearable cheek of it! There's that young Henrietta come down on me!"

She flew along Joe's cinder-drive like a Mænad.

"Hello, Hester!" came Henrietta's young voice, coolly floating from the obscurity of the car. "How's everything?"

"What cheek!" cried Hester. "What amazing cheek!" She leaned on Joe's iron gate and panted.

"How's everything?" repeated Henrietta's voice blandly.

"What do you mean by it?" demanded Hester, still panting.

"Now, my girl, don't go off at a tangent! We weren't coming in unless you came out. You needn't think we want to put our noses in your affairs. We're going down to camp on Bonamy. Isn't the weather too divine!"

Bonamy was Joe's pal, also an old artillery man, who had set up a 'farm' about a mile farther along the land. Joe was by no means a Robinson Crusoe in his bungalow.

"Who are you, anyway?" demanded Hester.

"Same old birds," said Donald, from the driver's seat. Donald was Joe's brother. Henrietta was sitting in front, next to him.

"Same as ever," said Teddy, poking his head out of the car. Teddy was a second cousin.

"Well," said Hester, sort of climbing down. "I suppose you may as well come in, now you *are* here. Have you eaten?"

"Eaten, yes," said Donald. "But we aren't coming in this trip, Hester; don't you fret."

"Why not?" flashed Hester, up in arms.

" 'Fraid of brother Joe," said Donald.

"Besides, Hester," said Henrietta anxiously, "you know you don't want us."

"Henrietta, don't be a fool!" flashed Hester.

"*Well*, Hester——!" remonstrated the pained Henrietta.

"Come on in, and no more nonsense!" said Hester.

"Not this trip, Hester," said Donny.

"No, sir!" said Teddy.

"But what idiots you all are! Why not?" cried Hester.

" 'Fraid of our elder brother," said Donald.

"All right," said Hester. "Then I'll come along with you." She hastily opened the gate.

"Shall I just have a peep? I'm pining to see the house,"

said Henrietta, climbing with a long leg over the door of
the car.

The night was now dark, the moon had sunk. The two girls
crunched in silence along the cinder track to the house.

"You'd say, if you'd rather I didn't come in—or if Joe'd
rather," said Henrietta anxiously. She was very much dis-
turbed in her young mind, and hoped for a clue. Hester
walked on without answering. Henrietta laid her hand on
her sister's arm. Hester shook it off, saying:

"My dear Henrietta, do be normal!"

And she rushed up the three steps to the door, which she
flung open, displaying the lamp-lit living-room, Joe in an arm-
chair by the low fire, his back to the door. He did not turn
round.

"Here's Henrietta!" cried Hester, in a tone which meant:
"*How's that?*"

He got up and faced round, his brown eyes in his stiff face
very angry.

"How did *you* get here?" he asked rudely.

"Came in a car," said young Henrietta, from her Age of
Innocence.

"With Donald and Teddy—they're there just outside the
gate," said Hester. "The old gang!"

"Coming in?" asked Joe, with greater anger in his voice.

"I suppose you'll go out and invite them," said Hester.

Joe said nothing, just stood like a block.

"I expect you'll think it's awful of me to come intruding,"
said Henrietta meekly. "We're just going on to Bonamy's."
She gazed innocently round the room. "But it's an adorable
little place, awfully good taste in a cottagey sort of way. I
like it awfully. Can I warm my hands?"

Joe moved from in front of the fire. He was in his slippers.
Henrietta dangled her long red hands, red from the night air,
before the grate.

"I'll rush right away again," she said.

"Oh-h," drawled Hester curiously. "Don't do that!"

"Yes, I must. Donald and Teddy are waiting."

The door stood wide open, the headlights of the car could
be seen in the lane.

"Oh-h!" Again that curious drawl from Hester. "I'll tell
them you're staying the night with me. I can do with a bit of
company."

Joe looked at her.

"What's the game?" he said.

"No game at all! Only now Tatty's come, she may as well stay."

'Tatty' was the rather infrequent abbreviation of 'Henrietta'.

"Oh, but Hester!" said Henrietta. "I'm going on to Bonamy's with Donald and Teddy."

"Not if I want you to stay here!" said Hester.

Henrietta looked all surprised, resigned helplessness.

"What's the game?" repeated Joe. "Had you fixed up to come down here to-night?"

"No, Joe, really!" said Henrietta, with earnest innocence. "I hadn't the faintest idea of such a thing, till Donald suggested it, at four o'clock this afternoon. Only the weather was too perfectly divine, we had to go out somewhere, so we thought we'd descend on Bonamy. I hope *he* won't be frightfully put out as well."

"And if we had arranged it, it wouldn't have been a crime," struck in Hester. "And, anyway, now you're here you might as well all camp here."

"Oh no, Hester! I know Donald will never come inside the gate. He was angry with me for making him stop, and it was I who tooted. It wasn't him, it was me. The curiosity of Eve, I suppose. Anyhow, I've put my foot in it, as usual. So now I'd better clear out as fast as I can. Good night!"

She gathered her coat round her with one arm and moved vaguely to the door.

"In that case, I'll come along with you," said Hester.

"But Hester!" cried Henrietta. And she looked inquiringly at Joe.

"I know as little as you do," he said, "what's going on."

His face was wooden and angry, Henrietta could make nothing of him.

"Hester!" cried Henrietta. "Do be sensible! What's gone wrong! Why don't you at least *explain*, and give everybody a chance! Talk about being normal!—you're always flinging it at *me!*"

There was a dramatic silence.

"What's happened?" Henrietta insisted, her eyes very bright and distressed, her manner showing that she was determined to be sensible.

"Nothing, of course!" mocked Hester.

"Do *you* know, Joe?" said Henrietta, like another Portia, turning very sympathetically to the man.

For a moment Joe thought how much nicer Henrietta was than her sister.

"I only know she asked me to play the piano, and then she dodged out of the house. Since then, her steering-gear's been out of order."

"Ha-ha-ha!" laughed Hester falsely and melodramatically. "I like that. I like my dodging out of the house! I went out for a breath of fresh air. I should like to know whose steering-gear is out of order, talking about my dodging out of the house!"

"You dodged out of the house," said Joe.

"Oh, did I? And why should I, pray?"

"I suppose you have your own reasons."

"I have too. And very good reasons."

There was a moment of stupefied amazement. . . . Joe and Hester had known each other so well, for such a long time. And now look at them!

"But why did you, Hester?" asked Henrietta, in her most breathless, naïve fashion.

"Why did I what?"

There was a low toot from the motor-car in the lane.

"They're calling me! Good-bye!" cried Henrietta, wrapping her coat round her and turning decisively to the door.

"If you go, my girl, I'm coming with you," said Hester.

"But why?" cried Henrietta in amazement. The horn tooted again. She opened the door and called into the night: "Half a minute!" Then she closed the door again, softly, and turned once more in her amazement to Hester.

"But why, Hester?"

Hester's eyes almost squinted with exasperation. She could hardly bear even to glance at the wooden and angry Joe.

"Why?"

"Why?" came the soft reiteration of Henrietta's question. All the attention focused on Hester, but Hester was a sealed book.

"Why?"

"She doesn't know herself," said Joe, seeing a loop-hole.

Out rang Hester's crazy and melodramatic laugh.

"Oh, doesn't she!" Her face flew into sudden strange fury. "Well, if you want to know, I absolutely *can't stand* your making love to me, if that's what you call the business,"

Henrietta let go the door-handle and sank weakly into a chair.

The worst had come to the worst. Joe's face became purple, then slowly paled to yellow.

"Then," said Henrietta in a hollow voice, "you can't marry him."

"I couldn't possibly marry him if he kept on being *in love* with me." She spoke the two words with almost snarling emphasis.

"And you couldn't possibly marry him if he *wasn't*," said the guardian angel, Henrietta.

"Why not," cried Hester. "I could stand him all right till he started being in love with me. Now, he's simply out of the question."

There was a pause, out of which came Henrietta's:

"After all, Hester, a man's *supposed* to be in love with the woman he wants to marry."

"Then he'd better keep it to himself, that's all I've got to say."

There was a pause. Joe, silent as ever, looked more wooden and sheepishly angry.

"But Hester! Hasn't a man *got* to be in love with you——?"

"Not with me! You've not had it to put up with, my girl."

Henrietta sighed helplessly.

"Then you can't marry him, that's obvious. What an awful pity!"

A pause.

"Nothing can be so perfectly humiliating as a man making love to you," said Hester. "I *loathe* it."

"Perhaps it's because it's the wrong man," said Henrietta sadly, with a glance at the wooden and sheepish Joe.

"I don't believe I could stand that sort of thing, with *any* man. Henrietta, do you know what it is, being stroked and cuddled? It's too perfectly awful and ridiculous."

"Yes!" said Henrietta, musing sadly. "As if one were a perfectly priceless meat-pie, and the dog licked it tenderly before he gobbled it up. It *is* rather sickening, I agree."

"And what's so awful, a perfectly decent man will go and get that way. Nothing is so awful as a man who has fallen in love," said Hester.

"I know what you mean, Hester. So doggy!" said Henrietta sadly.

The motor-horn tooted exasperatedly. Henrietta rose like a Portia who has been a failure. She opened the door and suddenly yelled fiercely into the night:

"Go on without me. I'll walk. Don't wait."

"How long will you be?" came a voice.

"I don't know. If I want to come, I'll walk," she yelled.

"Come back for you in an hour."

"Right," she shrieked, and slammed the door in their distant faces. Then she sat down dejectedly, in the silence. She was going to stand by Hester. That *fool*, Joe, standing there like a mutton-head!

They heard the car start, and retreat down the lane.

"Men are awful!" said Henrietta dejectedly.

"Anyhow, you're mistaken," said Joe with sudden venom to Hester. "I'm not in love with you, Miss Clever."

The two women looked at him as if he were Lazarus risen.

"And I never was in love with you, that way," he added, his brown eyes burning with a strange fire of self-conscious shame and anger, and naked passion.

"Well, what a liar you must be then. That's all I can say!" replied Hester coldly.

"Do you mean," said young Henrietta acidly, "that you put it all on?"

"I thought she expected it of me," he said, with a nasty little smile that simply paralysed the two young women. If he had turned into a boa-constrictor, they would not have been more amazed. That sneering little smile! Their good-natured Joe!

"I thought it was expected of me," he repeated, jeering.

Hester was horrified.

"Oh, but how beastly of you to do it!" cried Henrietta to him.

"And what a lie!" cried Hester. "He liked it."

"Do you think he did, Hester?" said Henrietta.

"I liked it in a way," he said impudently. "But I shouldn't have liked it, if I thought she didn't."

Hester flung out her arms.

"Henrietta," she cried, "why can't we kill him?"

"I wish we could," said Henrietta.

"What are you to do when you know a girl's rather strict,

and you like her for it—and you're not going to be married
for a month—and—and you—and you've got to get over the
interval somehow—and what else does Rudolf Valentino do
for you?—you like *him*——"

"He's dead, poor dear. But I loathed him, *really*," said
Hester.

"You didn't seem to," said he.

"Well, anyhow, you aren't Rudolf Valentino, and I loathe
you in the rôle."

"You won't get a chance again. I loathe *you* altogether."

"And I'm extremely relieved to hear it, my boy."

There was a lengthy pause, after which Henrietta said with
decision:

"Well, that's that! Will you come along to Bonamy's with
me, Hester, or shall I stay here with you?"

"*I* don't care, my girl," said Hester with bravado.

"Neither do I care what you do," said he. "But I call it
pretty rotten of you, not to tell me right out, at first."

"I thought it was real with you then, and I didn't want to
hurt you," said Hester.

"You look as if you didn't want to hurt me," he said.

"Oh, now," she said, "since it was all pretence, it doesn't
matter."

"I should say it doesn't," he retorted.

There was a silence. The clock, which was intended to be
their family clock, ticked rather hastily.

"Anyway," he said, "I consider you've let me down."

"I like that!" she cried, "considering what you've played
off on me!"

He looked her straight in the eye. They knew each other
so well.

Why had he tried that silly love-making game on her? It
was a betrayal of their simple intimacy. He saw it plainly,
and repented.

And she saw the honest, patient love for her in his eyes,
and the queer, quiet central desire. It was the first time she
had seen it, that quiet, patient, central desire of a young man
who has suffered during his youth, and seeks now almost with
the slowness of age. A hot flush went over her heart. She
felt herself responding to him.

"What have you decided, Hester?" said Henrietta.

"I'll stay with Joe, after all," said Hester.

"Very well," said Henrietta. "And I'll go along to Bonamy's." She opened the door quietly, and was gone.

Joe and Hester looked at one another from a distance.

"I'm sorry, Hester," said he.

"You know, Joe," she said, "I don't mind what you do, if you love me *really*."

GLAD GHOSTS

I KNEW Carlotta Fell in the early days before the war. Then she was escaping into art, and was just "Fell". That was at our famous but uninspired school of art, the Thwaite, where I myself was diligently murdering my talent. At the Thwaite they always gave Carlotta the Still-life prizes. She accepted them calmly, as one of our conquerors, but the rest. of the students felt vicious about it. They called it buttering the laurels, because Carlotta was Hon., and her father a well-known peer.

She was by way of being a beauty, too. Her family was not rich, yet she had come into five hundred a year of her own, when she was eighteen; and that, to us, was an enormity. Then she appeared in the fashionable papers, affecting to be wistful, with pearls, slanting her eyes. Then she went and did another of her beastly still-lives, a cactus-in-a-pot.

At the Thwaite, being snobs, we were proud of her too. She showed off a bit, it is true, playing bird of paradise among the pigeons. At the same time, she *was* thrilled to be with us, and out of her own set. Her wistfulness and yearning "for something else" was absolutely genuine. Yet she was not going to hobnob with us either, at least not indiscriminately.

She was ambitious, in a vague way. She wanted to coruscate, somehow or other. She had a family of clever and "distinguished" uncles, who had flattered her. What then?

Her cactuses-in-a-pot were admirable. But even she didn't expect them to start a revolution. Perhaps she would rather glow in the wide if dirty skies of life, than in the somewhat remote and unsatisfactory ether of Art.

She and I were "friends" in a bare, stark, but real sense. I was poor, but I didn't really care. She didn't really care either. Whereas I did care about some passionate vision which, I could feel, lay embedded in the half-dead body of this life. The quick body within the dead. I could *feel* it. And I wanted to get at it, if only for myself.

She didn't know what I was after. Yet she could feel that I was It, and, being an aristocrat of the Kingdom of It, as well as the realm of Great Britain, she was loyal—loyal to me because of It, the quick body which I imagined within the dead.

Still, we never had much to do with one another. I had no money. She never wanted to introduce me to her own people. I didn't want it either. Sometimes we had lunch together, sometimes we went to a theatre, or we drove in the country, in some car that belonged to neither of us. We never flirted or talked love. I don't think she wanted it, any more than I did. She wanted to marry into her own surroundings, and I knew she was of too frail a paste to face my future.

Now I come to think of it, she was always a bit sad when we were together. Perhaps she looked over seas she would never cross. She belonged finally, fatally, to her own class. Yet I think she hated them. When she was in a group of people who talked "smart", titles and *beau monde* and all that, her rather short nose would turn up, her wide mouth press into discontent, and a languor of bored irritation come even over her broad shoulders. Bored irritation, and a loathing of climbers, a loathing of the ladder altogether. She hated her own class: yet it was also sacrosanct to her. She disliked, even to me, mentioning the titles of her friends. Yet the very hurried resentment with which she said, when I asked her: Who is it——?

"Lady Nithsdale, Lord Staines—old friends of my mother," proved that the coronet was wedged into her brow, like a ring of iron grown into a tree.

She had another kind of reverence for a true artist: perhaps more genuine, perhaps not; anyhow, more free and easy.

She and I had a curious understanding in common: an inkling, perhaps, of the unborn body of life hidden within the body of this half-death which we call life: and hence a tacit hostility to the commonplace world, its inert laws. We were rather like two soldiers on a secret mission into enemy country. Life, and people, was an enemy country to us both. But she would never declare herself.

She always came to me to find out what I thought, particularly in a moral issue. Profoundly, fretfully discontented with the conventional moral standards, she didn't know how to take a stand of her own. So she came to me. She had to try to get her own feelings straightened out. In that she showed her old British fibre. I told her what, as a young man, I thought: and usually she was resentful. She did so want to be conventional. She would even act quite perversely, in her determination to be conventional. But she always had to come back to me, to ask me again. She depended on me morally. Even when she disagreed with me, it soothed her, and restored her to know my point of view. Yet she disagreed with me.

We had then a curious abstract intimacy, that went very deep, yet showed no obvious contact. Perhaps I was the only person in the world with whom she felt, in her uneasy self, at home, at peace. And to me, she was always of my own *intrinsic* sort, of my own species. Most people are just another species to me. They might as well be turkeys.

But she would always *act* according to the conventions of her class, even perversely. And I knew it.

So, just before the war she married Lord Lathkill. She was twenty-one. I did not see her till war was declared; then she asked me to lunch with her and her husband, in town. He was an officer in a Guards regiment, and happened to be in uniform, looking very handsome and well set-up, as if he expected to find the best of life served up to him for ever. He was very dark, with dark eyes and fine black hair, and a very beautiful, diffident voice, almost womanish in its slow, delicate inflections. He seemed pleased and flattered at having Carlotta for a wife.

To me he was beautifully attentive, almost deferential, because I was poor, and of the other world, those poor devils of outsiders. I laughed at him a little, and laughed at Carlotta, who was a bit irritated by the gentle delicacy with which he treated me.

She was elated too. I remember her saying:

"We need war, don't you think? Don't you think men need the fight, to keep life chivalrous and put martial glamour into it?"

And I remember saying: "I think we need some sort of fight; but my sort isn't the war sort." It was August, we could take it lightly.

"What's your sort?" she asked quickly.

"I don't know: single-handed, anyhow," I said, with a grin. Lord Lathkill made me feel like a lonely sansculotte, he was so completely unostentatious, so very willing to pay all the attention to me, and yet so subtly complacent, so unquestionably sure of his position. Whereas I was not a very sound

earthenware pitcher which had already gone many time to
the well.

He was not conceited, not half as *conceited* as I was. He
was willing to leave me all the front of the stage, even with
Carlotta. He felt so sure of some things, like a tortoise in a
glittering, polished tortoise-shell that mirrors eternity. Yet he
was not quite easy with me.

"You are Derbyshire?" I said to him, looking into his face.
"So am I! I was born in Derbyshire."

He asked me with a gentle, uneasy sort of politeness,
where? But he was a bit taken aback. And his dark eyes,
brooding over me, had a sort of fear in them. At the centre
they were hollow with a certain misgiving. He was so sure of
circumstances, and not by any means sure of the man in the
middle of the circumstances. Himself! Himself! That was
already a ghost.

I felt that he saw in me something crude but real, and saw
himself as something in its own way perfect, but quite unreal.
Even his love for Carlotta, and his marriage, was a circumstance that was inwardly unreal to him. One could tell by
the curious way in which he waited, before he spoke. And
by the hollow look, almost a touch of madness, in his dark
eyes, and in his soft, melancholy voice.

I could understand that she was fascinated by him. But God
help him if ever circumstances went against him!

She had to see me again, a week later, to talk about him.
So she asked me to the opera. She had a box, and we were
alone, and the notorious Lady Perth was two boxes away.
But this was one of Carlotta's conventional perverse little
acts, with her husband in France. She only wanted to talk to
me about him.

So she sat in the front of her box, leaning a little to the
audience and talking sideways to me. Anyone would have
known at once there was a *liaison* between us, how *danger-
euse* they would never have guessed. For there, in the full
view of the world—her world at least, not mine—she was
talking sideways to me, saying in a hurried, yet stony voice:

"What do you think of Luke?"

She looked up at me heavily, with her sea-coloured eyes,
waiting for my answer.

"He's tremendously charming," I said, above the theatreful
of faces.

"Yes, he's that!" she replied, in the flat, plangent voice she had when she was serious, like metal ringing flat, with a strange far-reaching vibration. "Do you think he'll be happy?"

"*Be* happy!" I ejaculated. "When, *be* happy?"

"With me," she said, giving a sudden little snirt of laughter, like a schoolgirl, and looking up me shyly, mischievously, anxiously.

"If you make him," I said, still casual.

"How can I make him?"

She said it with flat plangent earnestness. She was always like that, pushing me deeper in than I wanted to go.

"Be happy yourself, I suppose: and quite sure about it. And then *tell* him you're happy, and tell him he is, too, and he'll be it."

"Must I do all that?" she said rapidly. "Not otherwise?"

I knew I was frowning at her, and she was watching my frown.

"Probably not," I said roughly. "He'll never make up his mind about it himself."

"How did you know?" she asked, as if it had been a mystery.

"I didn't. It only seems to me like that."

"Seems to you like that," she re-echoed, in that sad, clean monotone of finality, always like metal. I appreciate it in her, that she does not murmur or whisper. But I wished she left me alone, in that beastly theatre.

She was wearing emeralds, on her snow-white skin, and leaning forward gazing fixedly down into the auditorium, as a crystal-gazer into a crystal. Heaven knows if she saw all those little facets of faces and plastrons. As for me, I knew that, like a sansculotte, I should never be king till breeches were off.

"I had terrible work to make him marry me," she said, in her swift, clear, low tones.

"Why?"

"He was frightfully in love with me. *He is!* But he thinks he's unlucky. . . ."

"Unlucky, how? In cards or in love?" I mocked.

"In both," she said briefly, with sudden cold resentment at my flippancy. There was over her eyes a glaze of fear. "It's in their family."

"What did you say to him?" I asked, rather laboured feeling the dead weight.

"I promised to have luck for two," she said. "And war was declared a fortnight later."

"Ah, well!" I said. "That's the world's luck, not yours."

"Quite!" she said.

There was a pause.

"Is his family supposed to be unlucky?" I asked.

"The Worths? Terribly! They really are!"

It was interval, and the box door had opened. Carlotta always had her eye, a good half of it at least, on the external happenings. She rose, like a reigning beauty—which she wasn't, and never became—to speak to Lady Perth, and out of spite, did not introduce me.

Carlotta and Lord Lathkill came, perhaps a year later, to visit us when we were in a cottage in Derbyshire, and he was home on leave. She was going to have a child, and was slow, and seemed depressed. He was vague, charming, talking about the country and the history of the lead-mines. But the two of them seemed vague, as if they never got anywhere.

The last time I saw them was when the war was over, and I was leaving England. They were alone at dinner, save for me. He was still haggard, with a wound in the throat. But he said he would soon be well. His slow, beautiful voice was a bit husky now. And his velvety eyes were hardened, haggard, but there was weariness, emptiness in the hardness.

I was poorer than ever, and felt a little weary myself. Carlotta was struggling with his silent emptiness. Since the war, the melancholy fixity of his eyes was more noticeable, the fear at the centre was almost monomania. She was wilting and losing her beauty.

There were twins in the house. After dinner, we went straight up to look at them, to the night nursery. They were two boys, with their father's fine dark hair, both of them.

He had put out his cigar, and leaned over the cots, gazing in silence. The nurse, dark-faced and faithful, drew back. Carlotta glanced at her children; but more helplessly, she gazed at him.

"Bonny children! Bonny boys, aren't they, nurse?" I said softly.

"Yes, sir!" she said quickly. "They are!"

"Ever think I'd have twins, roistering twins?" said Carlotta, looking at me.

"I never did," said I.

"Ask Luke whether it's bad luck or bad management," she said, with that schoolgirl's snirt of laughter, looking up apprehensively at her husband.

"Oh, I!" he said, turning suddenly and speaking loud, in his wounded voice. "I call it amazing good luck, myself! Don't know what other people think about it." Yet he had the fine, wincing fear in his body, of an injured dog.

After that, for years I did not see her again. I heard she had a baby girl. Then a catastrophe happened: both the twins were killed in a motor-car accident in America, motoring with their aunt.

I learned the news late, and did not write to Carlotta. What could I say?

A few months later, crowning disaster, the baby girl died of some sudden illness. The Lathkill ill-luck seemed to be working surely.

Poor Carlotta! I had no further news of her, only I heard that she and Lord Lathkill were both living in seclusion, with his mother, at the place in Derbyshire.

When circumstances brought me to England, I debated within myself, whether I should write or not to Carlotta. At last I sent a note to the London address.

I had a reply from the country: "So glad you are within reach again! When will you come and see us?"

I was not very keen on going to Riddings. After all, it was Lord Lathkill's place, and Lady Lathkill, his mother, was old and of the old school. And I always something of a sans-culotte, who will only be king when breeches are off.

"Come to town," I wrote, "and let us have lunch together."

She came. She looked older, and pain had drawn horizontal lines across her face.

"You're not a bit different," she said to me.

"And you're only a little bit," I said.

"Am I!" she replied, in a deadened, melancholic voice. "Perhaps! I suppose while we live we've got to live. What do you think?"

"Yes, I think it. To be the living dead, that's awful."

"Quite!" she said, with terrible finality.

"How is Lord Lathkill?" I asked.

"Oh," she said. "It's finished him, as far as living is concerned. But he's very willing for *me* to live."

"And you, are you willing?" I said.

She looked up into my eyes, strangely.

"I'm not sure," she said. "I need help. What do you think about it?"

"Oh, God, live if you can!"

"Even take help?" she said, with her strange involved simplicity.

"Ah, certainly."

"Would you recommend it?"

"Why, yes! You are a young thing——" I began.

"Won't you come down to Riddings?" she said quickly.

"And Lord Lathkill—and his mother?" I asked.

"They want you."

"Do you want me to come?"

"I want you to, yes! Will you?"

"Why, yes, if you want me."

"When, then?"

"When you wish."

"Do you mean it?"

"Why, of course."

"You're not afraid of the Lathkill ill-luck?"

"*I!*" I exclaimed in amazement; such amazement, that she gave her schoolgirl snirt of laughter.

"Very well, then," she said. "Monday? Does that suit you?"

We made arrangements, and I saw her off at the station.

I knew Riddings, Lord Lathkill's place, from the outside. It was an old Derbyshire stone house, at the end of the village of Middleton: a house with three sharp gables, set back not very far from the high road, but with a gloomy moor for a park behind.

Monday was a dark day over the Derbyshire hills. The green hills were dark, dark green, the stone fences seemed almost black. Even the little railway station, deep in the green, cleft hollow, was of stone, and dark and cold, and seemed in the underworld.

Lord Lathkill was at the station. He was wearing spectacles, and his brown eyes stared strangely. His black hair fell lank over his forehead.

"I'm so awfully glad you've come," he said. "It is cheering Carlotta up immensely."

Me, as a man myself, he hardly seemed to notice. I was something which had arrived, and was expected. Otherwise he had an odd, unnatural briskness of manner.

"I hope I shan't disturb your mother, Lady Lathkill," I said as he tucked me up in the car.

"On the contrary," he sang, in his slow voice, "she is looking forward to your coming as much as we both are. Oh no, don't look on mother as too old-fashioned, she's not so at all. She's tremendously up to date in art and literature and that kind of thing. She has her leaning towards the uncanny—spiritualism, and that kind of thing—nowadays, but Carlotta and I think that if it gives her an interest, all well and good."

He tucked me up most carefully in the rugs, and the servant put a foot-warmer at my feet.

"Derbyshire, you know, is a cold county," continued Lord Lathkill, "especially among the hills."

"It's a very dark county," I said.

"Yes, I suppose it is, to one coming from the tropics. We, of course, don't notice it; we rather like it."

He seemed curiously smaller, shrunken, and his rather long cheeks were sallow. His manner, however, was much more cheerful, almost communicative. But he talked, as it were, to the faceless air, not really to me. I wasn't really there at all. He was talking to himself. And when once he looked at me, his brown eyes had a hollow look, like gaps with nothing in them except a haggard, hollow fear. He was gazing through the windows of nothingness, to see if I were really there.

It was dark when we got to Riddings. The house had no door in the front, and only two windows upstairs were lit. It did not seem very hospitable. We entered at the side, and a very silent manservant took my things.

We went upstairs in silence, in the dead-seeming house. Carlotta had heard us, and was at the top of the stairs. She was already dressed; her long white arms were bare; she had something glittering on a dull green dress.

"I was so afraid you wouldn't come," she said, in a dulled voice, as she gave me her hand. She seemed as if she would begin to cry. But of course she wouldn't. The corridor, dark-panelled and with blue carpet on the floor, receded dimly, with a certain dreary gloom. A servant was diminishing in the distance, with my bags, silently. There was a curious, unpleasant sense of the fixity of the materials of the house, the obscene triumph of dead matter. Yet the place was warm, central-heated.

Carlotta pulled herself together and said, dulled:

"Would you care to speak to my mother-in-law before you go to your room? She would like it."

We entered a small drawing-room abruptly. I saw the water-colours on the walls and a white-haired lady in black bending round to look at the door as she rose cautiously.

"This is Mr. Morier, Mother-in-law," said Carlotta, in her dull, rather quick way, "on his way to his room."

The dowager Lady Lathkill came a few steps forward, lean- ing from heavy hips, and gave me her hand. Her crest of hair was snow white, and she had curious blue eyes, fixed, with a tiny dot of a pupil, peering from her pink, soft-skinned face of an old and well-preserved woman. She wore a lace fichu. The upper part of her body was moderately slim, leaning for- ward slightly from her heavy black-silk hips.

She murmured something to me, staring at me fixedly for a long time, but as a bird does, with shrewd, cold, far-distant sight. As a hawk, perhaps, looks shrewdly far down, in his search. Then, muttering, she presented to me the other two people in the room: a tall, short-faced, swarthy young woman with the hint of a black moustache; and a plump man in a dinner-jacket, rather bald and ruddy, with a little grey moustache, but yellow under the eyes. He was Colonel Hale.

They all seemed awkward, as if I had interrupted them at a séance. I didn't know what to say: they were utter strangers to me.

"Better come and choose your room, then," said Carlotta, and I bowed dumbly, following her out of the room. The old Lady Lathkill still stood planted on her heavy hips, looking half round after us with her ferret's blue eyes. She had hardly any eyebrows, but they were arched high up on her pink, soft forehead, under the crest of icily white hair. She had never emerged for a second from the remote place where she un- yieldingly kept herself.

Carlotta, Lord Lathkill and I tramped in silence down the corridor and round a bend. We could none of us get a word out. As he suddenly, rather violently flung open a door at the end of the wing, he said, turning round to me with a resentful, hang-dog air:

"We did you the honour of offering you our ghost room.

It doesn't look much, but it's our equivalent for a royal apartment."

It was a good-sized room with faded, red-painted panelling showing remains of gilt, and the usual big, old mahogany furniture, and a big pinky-faded carpet with big, whitish, faded roses. A bright fire was burning in the stone fire-place.

"Why?" said I, looking at the stretches of the faded, once handsome carpet.

"Why what?" said Lord Lathkill. "Why did we offer you this room?"

"Yes! No! Why is it your equivalent for a royal apartment?"

"Oh, because our ghost is as rare as sovereignty in her visits, and twice as welcome. Her gifts are infinitely more worth having."

"What sort of gifts?"

"The family fortune. She invariably restores the family fortune. That's why we put you here, to tempt her."

"What temptation should *I* be?—especially to restoring your family fortunes. I didn't think they needed it, anyhow."

"Well!" he hesitated. "Not exactly in money: we can manage modestly that way; but in everything else but money——"

There was a pause. I was thinking of Carlotta's 'luck for two'. Poor Carlotta! She looked worn now. Especially her chin looked worn, showing the edge of the jaw. She had sat herself down in a chair by the fire, and put her feet on the stone fender, and was leaning forward, screening her face with her hand, still careful of her complexion. I could see her broad, white shoulders, showing the shoulder-blades, as she leaned forward, beneath her dress. But it was as if some bitterness had soaked all the life out of her, and she was only weary, or inert, drained off her feelings. It grieved me, and the thought passed through my mind that a man should take her in his arms and cherish her body, and start her flame again. If she would let him, which was doubtful.

Her courage was fallen, in her body; only her spirit fought on. She would have to restore the body of her life, and only a living body could do it.

"What *about* your ghost?" I said to him. "Is she really ghastly?"

"Not at all!" he said. "She's supposed to be lovely. But I

have no experience, and I don't know anybody who has. We hoped you'd come, though, and tempt her. Mother had a message about you, you know."

"No, I didn't know."

"Oh yes! When you were still in Africa.. The medium said: 'There is a man in Africa. I can only see M, a double M. He is thinking of your family. It would be good if he entered your family.' Mother was awfully puzzled, but Carlotta said 'Mark Morier' at once."

"That's not why I asked you down," said Carlotta quickly, looking round, shading her eyes with her hand as she looked at me.

I laughed, saying nothing.

"But, of course," continued Lord Lathkill, "you *needn't* have this room. We have another one ready as well. Would you like to see it?"

"How does your ghost manifest herself?" I said, parrying.

"Well, I hardly knew. She seems to be a very grateful *presence*, and that's about all I do know. She was apparently quite *persona grata* to everyone she visited. *Gratissima*, apparently!"

"*Benissimo!*" said I.

A servant appeared in the doorway, murmuring something I could not hear. Everybody in the house, except Carlotta and Lord Lathkill, seemed to murmur under their breath.

"What's she say?" I asked.

"If you will stay in this room? I told her you might like a room on the front. And if you'll take a bath?" said Carlotta.

"Yes!" said I. And Carlotta repeated to the maidservant.

"And for heaven's sake speak to me loudly," said I to that elderly correct female in her starched collar, in the doorway.

"Very good, sir!" she piped up. "And shall I make the bath hot or medium?"

"Hot!" said I, like a cannon-shot.

"Very good, sir!" she piped up again, and her elderly eyes twinkled as she turned and disappeared.

Carlotta laughed, and I sighed.

We were six at table. The pink Colonel with the yellow creases under his blue eyes sat opposite me, like an old boy with a liver. Next him sat Lady Lathkill, watching from her distance. Her pink, soft old face, naked-seeming, with its pinpoint blue eyes, was a real modern witch-face.

Next me, on my left, was the dark young woman, whose slim, swarthy arms had an indiscernible down on them. She had a blackish neck, and her expressionless yellow-brown eyes said nothing, under level black brows. She was inaccessible. I made some remarks, without result. Then I said:

"I didn't hear your name when Lady Lathkill introduced me to you."

Her yellow-brown eyes stared into mine for some moments before she said:

"Mrs. Hale!" Then she glanced across the table. "Colonel Hale is my husband."

My face must have signalled my surprise. She stared into my eyes very curiously, with a significance I could not grasp, a long, hard stare. I looked at the bald, pink head of the Colonel bent over his soup, and I returned to my own soup.

"Did you have a good time in London?" said Carlotta.

"No," said I. "It was dismal."

"Not a good word to say for it?"

"Not one."

"No nice people?"

"Not my sort of nice."

"What's your sort of nice?" she asked, with a little laugh.

The other people were stone. It was like talking into a chasm.

"Ah! If I knew myself, I'd look for them! But not sentimental, with a lot of soppy emotions on top, and nasty ones underneath."

"Who are you thinking of?" Carlotta looked up at me as the man brought the fish. She had a crushed sort of roguishness. The other diners were images.

"I? Nobody. Just everybody. No, I think I was thinking of the Obelisk Memorial Service."

"Did you go to it?"

"No, but I fell into it."

"Wasn't it moving?"

"Rhubarb, senna, that kind of moving!"

She gave a little laugh, looking up into my face, from the fish.

"What was wrong with it?"

I noticed that the Colonel and Lady Lathkill each had a little dish of rice, no fish, and that they were served second—

oh, humility!—and that neither took the white wine. No, they had no wine-glasses. The remoteness gathered about them, like the snows on Everest. The dowager peered across at me occasionally, like a white ermine out of the snow, and she had that cold air about her, of being good, and containing a secret of goodness: remotely, ponderously, fixedly knowing better. And I, with my chatter, was one of those fabulous fleas that are said to hop upon glaciers.

"Wrong with it? *It* was wrong, all wrong. In the rain, a soppy crowd, with soppy bare heads, soppy emotions, soppy chrysanthemums and prickly laurestinus! A steam of wet mob-emotions! Ah, no, it shouldn't be allowed."

Carlotta's face had fallen. She again could feel death in her bowels, the kind of death the war signifies.

"Wouldn't you have us honour the dead?" came Lady Lathkill's secretive voice across at me, as if a white ermine had barked.

"Honour the dead!" My mind opened in amazement. "Do you think they'd be honoured?"

I put the question in all sincerity.

"They would understand the *intention* was to honour them," came her reply.

I felt astounded.

"If I were dead, would I be honoured if a great, steamy wet crowd came after me with soppy chrysanthemums and prickly laurestinus? Ugh! I'd run to the nethermost ends of Hades. Lord, how I'd run from them!"

The manservant gave us roast mutton, and Lady Lathkill and the Colonel chestnuts in sauce. Then he poured the burgundy. It was good wine. The pseudo-conversation was interrupted.

Lady Lathkill ate in silence, like an ermine in the snow, feeding on his prey. Sometimes she looked round the table, her blue eyes peering fixedly, completely uncommunicative. She was very watchful to see that we were all properly attended to; "The currant jelly for Mr. Morier," she would murmur, as if it were her table. Lord Lathkill, next her, ate in complete absence. Sometimes she murmured to him, and he murmured back, but I never could hear what they said. The Colonel swallowed the chestnuts in dejection, as if all were weary duty to him now. I put it down to his liver.

It was an awful dinner-party. I never could hear a word

anybody said, except Carlotta. They all let their words die in their throats, as if the larynx were the coffin of sound.

Carlotta tried to keep her end up, the cheerful hostess sort of thing. But Lady Lathkill somehow, in silence and apparent humility, had stolen the authority that goes with the hostess, and she hung on to it grimly, like a white ermine sucking a rabbit. Carlotta kept glancing miserably at me, to see what I thought. I didn't think anything. I just felt frozen within the tomb. And I drank the good, good warm burgundy.

"Mr. Morier's glass!" murmured Lady Lathkill, and her blue eyes with their black pin-points rested on mine a moment.

"Awfully nice to drink good burgundy!" said I pleasantly.

She bowed her head slightly, and murmured something inaudible.

"I beg your pardon?"

"Very glad you like it!" she repeated, with distaste at having to say it again, out loud.

"Yes, I do. It's good."

Mrs. Hale, who had sat tall and erect and alert, like a black she-fox, never making a sound, looked round at me to see what sort of specimen I was. She was just a bit intrigued.

"Yes, thanks," came a musical murmur from Lord Lathkill. "I think I *will* take some more."

The man, who had hesitated, filled his glass.

"I'm awfully sorry I can't drink wine," said Carlotta absently. "It has the wrong effect on me."

"I should say it has the wrong effect on everybody," said the Colonel, with an uneasy attempt to be there. "But some people like the effect, and some don't."

I looked at him in wonder. Why was he chipping in? He looked as if he'd liked the effect well enough, in his day.

"Oh no!" retorted Carlotta coldly. "The effect on different people is quite different."

She closed with finality, and a further frost fell on the table.

"Quite so," began the Colonel, trying, since he'd gone off the deep end, to keep afloat.

But Carlotta turned abruptly to me.

"Why is it, do you think, that the effect is so different on different people?"

"And on different occasions," said I, grinning through my burgundy. "Do you know what they say? They say that alcohol, if it has an effect on your psyche, takes you back to

old states of consciousness, and old reactions. But some
people it doesn't stimulate at all, there is only a nervous reaction of repulsion."

"There's certainly a nervous reaction of repulsion in me,"
said Carlotta.

"As there is in all higher natures," murmured Lady Lathkill.

"Dogs hate whisky," said I.

"That's quite right," said the Colonel. "Scared of it!"

"I've often thought," said I, "about those old states of
consciousness. It's supposed to be an awful retrogression,
reverting back to them. Myself, my desire to go onwards
takes me back a little."

"Where to?" said Carlotta.

"Oh, I don't know! To where you feel it a bit warm, and
like smashing the glasses, don't you know?

> *"J'avons bien bu et nous boirons!*
> *Cassons les verres nous les payerons!*
> *Compagnons! Voyez vous bien!*
> *Voyez vous bien!*
> *Voyez! voyez! voyez vous bien*
> *Que les d'moiselles sont belles*
> *Où nous allons!"*

I had the effrontery to sing this verse of an old soldier's
song while Lady Lathkill was finishing her celery and nut
salad. I sang it quite nicely, in a natty, well-balanced little
voice, smiling all over my face meanwhile. The servant, as
he went round for Lady Lathkill's plate, furtively fetched a
look at me. *Look!* thought I. *You chicken that's come un-
trussed!*

The partridges had gone, we had swallowed the *flan*, and
were at dessert. They had accepted my song in complete
silence. Even Carlotta! My *flan* had gone down in one gulp,
like an oyster.

"You're quite right!" said Lord Lathkill, amid the squash-
ing of walnuts. "I mean the state of mind of a Viking, shall
we say, or of a Catiline conspirator, might be frightfully good
for us, if we could recapture it."

"A Viking!" said I, stupefied. And Carlotta gave a wild
snirt of laughter.

"Why not a Viking?" he asked in all innocence.

"A Viking!" I repeated, and swallowed my port. Then I looked round at my black-browed neighbour.

"Why do you never say anything?" I asked.

"What should I say?" she replied, frightened at the thought.

I was finished. I gazed into my port as if expecting the ultimate revelation.

Lady Lathkill rustled her finger-tips in the finger-bowl, and laid down her napkin decisively. The Colonel, old buck, rose at once to draw back her chair. *Place aux hommes!* I bowed to my neighbour, Mrs. Hale, a most disconcerting bow, and she made a circuit to get by me.

"You won't be awfully long?" said Carlotta, looking at me with her slow, hazel-green eyes, between mischief and wistfulness and utter depression.

Lady Lathkill steered heavily past me as if I didn't exist, perching rather forward, with her crest of white hair, from her big hips. She seemed abstracted, concentrated on something, as she went.

I closed the door, and turned to the men.

> *"Dans la première auberge*
> *J'eus b'en bu!*

sang I in a little voice.

"Quite right," said Lord Lathkill. "You're quite right."

And we sent the port round.

"This house," I said, "needs a sort of spring-cleaning."

"You're quite right," said Lord Lathkill.

"There's a bit of a dead smell!" said I. "We need Bacchus, and Eros, to sweeten it up, to freshen it."

"You think Bacchus and Eros?" said Lord Lathkill, with complete seriousness; as if one might have telephoned for them.

"In the best sense," said I. As if we were going to get them from Fortnum and Mason's, at least.

"What exactly is the best sense?" asked Lord Lathkill.

"Ah! The flame of life! There's a dead smell here."

The Colonel fingered his glass with thick, inert fingers uneasily.

"Do you think so?" he said, looking up at me heavily.

"Don't you?"

He gazed at me with blank, glazed blue eyes, that had

deathly yellow stains underneath. Something was wrong
with him, some sort of breakdown. He should have been a
fat, healthy, jolly old boy. Not very old either: probably not
quite sixty. But with this collapse on him, he seemed, somehow, to smell.

"You know," he said, staring at me with a sort of gruesome
challenge, then looking down at his wine, "there's more things
than we're aware of happening to us!" He looked up at me
again, shutting his full lips under his little grey moustache,
and gazing with a glazed defiance.

"Quite!" said I.

He continued to gaze at me with glazed, gruesome defiance.

"Ha!" He made a sudden movement, and seemed to break
up, collapse and become brokenly natural. "There, you've
said it. I married my wife when I was a kid of twenty."

"Mrs. Hale?" I exclaimed.

"Not this one"—he jerked his head towards the door—"my
first wife." There was a pause; he looked at me with shamed
eyes, then turned his wine-glass round and his head dropped.
Staring at his twisting glass, he continued: "I married her
when I was twenty, and she was twenty-eight. You might
say, she married me. Well, there it was! We had three
children—I've got three married daughters—and we got on
all right. I suppose she mothered me, in a way. And I never
thought a thing. I was content enough, wasn't tied to her
apron-strings, and she never asked questions. She was always
fond of me, and I took it for granted. I took it for granted.
Even when she died—I was away in Salonika—I took it for
granted, if you understand me. It was part of the rest of
things—war—life—death. I knew I should feel lonely when
I got back. Well, then I got buried—shell dropped, and the
dug-out caved in—and that queered me. They sent me home.
And the minute I saw the Lizard light—it was evening when
we got up out of the Bay—I realised that Lucy had been waiting for me. I could feel her there, at my side, more plainly
than I feel you now. And do you know, at that moment I
woke up to her, and she made an awful impression on me.
She seemed, if you get me, tremendously powerful, important;
everything else dwindled away. There was the Lizard light
blinking a long way off, and that meant home. And all the
rest was my wife, Lucy: as if her skirts filled all the darkness. In a way, I was frightened; but that was because I

couldn't quite get myself into line. I felt: *Good God! I never knew her!* And she was this tremendous thing! I felt like a child, and as weak as a kitten. And, believe me or not, from that day to this she's never left me. I know quite well she can hear what I'm saying. But she'll let me tell you. I knew that at dinner-time."

"But what made you marry again?" I said.

"She made me!" He went a trifle yellow on his cheekbones. "I could feel her telling me: '*Marry! Marry!*' Lady Lathkill had messages from her too; she was her great friend in life. I didn't think of marrying. But Lady Lathkill had the same message, that I must marry. Then a medium described the girl in detail: my present wife. I knew her at once, friend of my daughters. After that the messages became more insistent, waking me three and four times in the night. Lady Lathkill urged me to propose, and I did it, and was accepted. My present wife was just twenty-eight, the age Lucy had been——"

"How long ago did you marry the present Mrs. Hale?"

"A little over a year ago. Well, I thought I had done what was required of me. But directly after the wedding, such a state of terror came over me—perfectly unreasonable—I became almost unconscious. My present wife asked me if I was ill, and I said I was. We got ot Paris. I felt I was dying. But I said I was going out to see a doctor, and I found myself kneeling in a church. Then I found peace—and Lucy. She had her arms round me, and I was like a child at peace. I must have knelt there for a couple of hours in Lucy's arms. I *never* felt like that when I was alive: why, I couldn't stand that sort of thing! It's all come on after—after—— And now, I daren't offend Lucy's spirit. If I do, I suffer tortures till I've made peace again, till she folds me in her arms. Then I can live. But she won't let me go near the present Mrs. Hale. I—I—I daren't go near her."

He looked up at me with fear, and shame, and shameful secrecy, and a sort of gloating showing in his unmanned blue eyes. He had been talking as if in his sleep.

"Why did your dead wife urge you to marry again?" I said.

"I don't know," he replied. "I don't know. She was older than I was, and all the cleverness was on her side. She was a very clever woman, and I was never much in the intellectual line myself. I just took it for granted she liked me. She never showed jealousy, but I think now, perhaps she was jealous all the time, and kept it under. I don't know. I think she never felt quite straight about having married me. It seems like that. As if she had something on her mind. Do you know, while she was alive, I never gave it a thought. And now I'm aware of nothing else but her. It's as if her spirit wanted to live in my body, or at any rate—I don't know——"

His blue eyes were glazed, almost fishy, with fear and gloating shame. He had a short nose, and full, self-indulgent lips, and a once-comedy chin. Eternally a careless boy of thirteen. But now, care had got him in decay.

"And what does your present wife say?" I asked.

He poured himself some more wine.

"Why," he replied, "except for her, I shouldn't mind so much. She says nothing. Lady Lathkill has explained everything to her, and she agrees that—that—a spirit from the other side is more important than mere pleasure—you know what I mean. Lady Lathkill says that this is a preparation for my next incarnation, when I am going to serve Woman, and help Her to take Her place."

He looked up again, trying to be proud in his shame.

"Well, what a damned curious story!" exclaimed Lord Lathkill. "Mother's idea for herself—she had it in a message too—is that she is coming on earth the next time to save the animals from the cruelty of man. That's why she hates meat at table, or anything that has to be killed."

"And does Lady Lathkill encourage you in this business with your dead wife?" said I.

"Yes. She helps me. When I get as you might say at cross-purposes with Lucy—with Lucy's spirit, that is—Lady Lathkill helps to put it right between us. Then I'm all right, when I know I'm loved."

He looked at me stealthily, cunningly.

"Then you're all wrong," said I, "surely."

"And do you mean to say," put in Lord Lathkill, "that you don't live with the present Mrs. Hale at all? Do you mean to say you never *have* lived with her?"

"I've got a higher claim on me," said the unhappy Colonel.

"My God!" said Lord Lathkill.

I looked in amazement: the sort of chap who picks up a woman and has a good time with her for a week, then goes home as nice as pie, and now look at him! It was obvious

that he had a terror of his black-browed new wife, as well
as of Lucy's spirit. A devil and a deep sea with a vengeance!

"A damned curious story!" mused Lord Lathkill. "I'm not
so sure I like. Something's wrong somewhere. We shall have
to go upstairs."

"Wrong!" said I. "Why, Colonel, don't you turn round
and quarrel with the spirit of your first wife, fatally and
finally, and get rid of her?"

The Colonel looked at me, still diminished and afraid, but
perking up a bit, as we rose from table.

"How would you go about it?" he said.

"I'd just face her, wherever she seemed to be, and say:
'Lucy, go to blazes!'"

Lord Lathkill burst into a loud laugh, then was suddenly
silent as the door noiselessly opened, and the dowager's white
hair and pointed, uncanny eyes peered in, then entered.

"I think I left my papers in here, Luke," she murmured.

"Yes, mother. There they are. We're just coming up."

"Take your time."

He held the door, and ducking forward, she went out again,
clutching some papers. The Colonel had blenched yellow on
his cheek-bones.

We went upstairs to the small drawing-room.

"You were a long time," said Carlotta, looking in all our
faces. "Hope the coffee's not cold. We'll have fresh if it is."

She poured out, and Mrs. Hale carried the cups. The dark
young woman thrust out her straight, dusky arm, offering me
sugar, and gazing at me with her unchanging, yellow-brown
eyes. I looked back at her, and being clairvoyant in this house,
was conscious of the curves of her erect body, the sparse
black hairs there would be on her strong-skinned dusky thighs.
She was a woman of thirty, and she had had a great dread
lest she should never marry. Now she was as if mesmerised.

"What do you do usually in the evenings?" I said.

She turned to me as if startled, as she nearly always did
when addressed.

"We do nothing," she replied. "Talk; and sometimes Lady
Lathkill reads."

"What does she read?"

"About spiritualism."

"Sounds pretty dull."

She looked at me again, but she did not answer. It was diffi-

cult to get anything out of her. She put up no fight, only remained in the same swarthy, passive, negative resistance. For
a moment I wondered that no men made love to her: it
was obvious they didn't. But then, modern young men are
accustomed to being attracted, flattered, impressed: they
expect an effort to please. And Mrs. Hale made none: didn't
know how. Which for me was her mystery. She was passive,
static, locked up in a resistant passivity that had fire beneath
it.

Lord Lathkill came and sat by us. The Colonel's confession
had had an effect on him.

"I'm afraid," he said to Mrs. Hale, "you have a thin time
here."

"Why?" she asked.

"Oh, there is so little to amuse you. Do you like to dance?"

"Yes," she said.

"Well, then," he said, "let us go downstairs and dance to
the Victrola. There are four of us. You'll come, of course?"
he said to me.

Then he turned to his mother.

"Mother, we shall go down to the morning-room and
dance. Will you come? Will you, Colonel?"

The dowager gazed at her son.

"I will come and look on," she said.

"And I will play the pianola, if you like," volunteered the
Colonel. We went down and pushed aside the chintz chairs
and the rugs. Lady Lathkill sat in a chair, the Colonel worked
away at the pianola. I danced with Carlotta, Lord Lathkill
with Mrs. Hale.

A quiet soothing came over me, dancing with Carlotta. She
was very still and remote, and she hardly looked at me. Yet
the touch of her was wonderful, like a flower that yields itself
to the morning. Her warm, silken shoulder was soft and grateful under my hand, as if it knew me with that second knowledge which is part of one's childhood, and which so rarely
blossoms again in manhood and womanhood. It was as if we
had known each other perfectly, as children, and now, as
man and woman met in the full, further sympathy. Perhaps,
in modern people, only after long suffering and defeat, can
the naked intuition break free between woman and man.

She, I knew, let the strain and the tension of all her life
depart from her then, leaving her nakedly still, within my

arm. And I only wanted to be with her, to have her in my touch.

Yet after the second dance she looked at me, and suggested that she should dance with her husband. So I found myself with the strong, passive shoulder of Mrs. Hale under my hand, and her inert hand in mine, as I looked down at her dusky, dirty-looking neck—she wisely avoided powder. The duskiness of her mesmerised body made me see the faint dark sheen of her thighs, with intermittent black hairs. It was as if they shone through the silk of her mauve dress, like the limbs of a half-wild animal that is locked up in its own helpless dumb winter, a prisoner.

She knew, with the heavy intuition of her sort, that I glimpsed her crude among the bushes, and felt her attraction. But she kept looking away over my shoulder, with her yellow eyes, towards Lord Lathkill.

Myself or him, it was a question of which got there first. But she preferred him. Only for some things she would rather it were me.

Luke had changed curiously. His body seemed to have come alive, in the dark cloth of his evening suit; his eyes had a devil-may-care light in them, his long cheeks a touch of scarlet, and his black hair fell loose over his forehead. He had again some of that Guardsman's sense of well-being and claim to the best in life, which I had noticed the first time I saw him. But now it was a little more florid, defiant, with a touch of madness.

He looked down at Carlotta with uncanny kindness and affection. Yet he was glad to hand her over to me. He, too, was afraid of her: as if with her his bad luck had worked. Whereas, in a throb of crude brutality, he felt it would not work with the dark young woman. So, he handed Carlotta over to me with relief, as if, with me, she would be safe from the doom of his bad luck. And he, with the other woman, would be safe from it too. For the other woman was outside the circle.

I was glad to have Carlotta again: to have that inexpressible delicate and complete quiet of the two of us, resting my heart in a balance now at last physical as well as spiritual. Till now, it had always been a fragmentary thing. Now, for this hour at least, it was whole, a soft, complete, physical flow, and a unison deeper even than childhood.

As she danced she shivered slightly, and I seemed to smell

frost in the air. The Colonel, too, was not keeping the rhythm.

"Has it turned colder?" I said.

"I wonder?" she answered, looking up at me with a slow beseeching. Why, and for what was she beseeching me? I pressed my hand a little closer, and her small breasts seemed to speak to me. The Colonel recovered the rhythm again.

But at the end of the dance she shivered again, and it seemed to me I too was chilled.

"Has it suddenly turned colder?" I said, going to the radiator. It was quite hot.

"It seems to me it has," said Lord Lathkill in a queer voice.

The Colonel was sitting abjectly on the music-stool, as if broken.

"Shall we have another? Shall we try a tango?" said Lord Lathkill. "As much of it as we can manage?"

"I—I——" the Colonel began, turning round on the seat, his face yellow. "I'm not sure——"

Carlotta shivered. The frost seemed to touch my vitals. Mrs. Hale stood stiff, like a pillar of brown rock-salt, staring at her husband.

"We had better leave off," murmured Lady Lathkill, rising.

Then she did an extraordinary thing. She lifted her face, staring to the other side, and said suddenly, in a clear, cruel sort of voice:

"Are you here, Lucy?"

She was speaking across to the spirits. Deep inside me leaped a jump of laughter. I wanted to howl with laughter. Then instantly I went inert again. The chill gloom seemed to deepen suddenly in the room, everybody was overcome. On the piano-seat the Colonel sat yellow and huddled, with a terrible hang-dog look of guilt on his face. There was a silence, in which the cold seemed to creak. Then came again the peculiar bell-like ringing of Lady Lathkill's voice:

"Are you here? What do you wish us to do?"

A dead and ghastly silence, in which we all remained transfixed. Then from somewhere came two slow thuds, and a sound of drapery moving. The Colonel, with mad fear in his eyes, looked round at the uncurtained windows, and crouched on his seat.

"We must leave this room," said Lady Lathkill.

"I'll tell you what, mother," said Lord Lathkill curiously;

"you and the Colonel go up, and we'll just turn on the Victrola."

That was almost uncanny of him. For myself, the cold effluence of these people had paralysed me. Now I began to rally. I felt that Lord Lathkill was sane, it was these other people who were mad.

Again from somewhere indefinite came two slow thuds.

"We must leave this room," repeated Lady Lathkill in monotony.

"All right, mother. You go. I'll just turn on the Victrola."

And Lord Lathkill strode across the room. In another moment the monstrous barking howl of the opening of a jazz tune, an event far more extraordinary than thuds, poured from the unmoving bit of furniture called a Victrola.

Lady Lathkill silently departed. The Colonel got to his feet.

"I wouldn't go if I were you, Colonel," said I. "Why not dance? I'll look on this time."

I felt as if I were resisting a rushing, cold, dark current.

Lord Lathkill was already dancing with Mrs. Hale, skating delicately along, with a certain smile of obstinacy, secrecy, and excitement kindled on his face. Carlotta went up quietly to the Colonel, and put her hand on his broad shoulder. He let himself be moved into the dance, but he had no heart in it.

There came a heavy crash, out of the distance. The Colonel stopped as if shot: in another moment he would go down on his knees. And his face was terrible. It was obvious he really felt another presence, other than ours, blotting us out. The room seemed dree and cold. It was heavy work, bearing up.

The Colonel's lips were moving, but no sound came forth. Then, absolutely oblivious of us, he went out of the room.

The Victrola had run down. Lord Lathkill went to wind it up again, saying:

"I suppose mother knocked over a piece of furniture."

But we were all of us depressed, in abject depression.

"Isn't it awful!" Carlotta said to me, looking up beseechingly.

"Abominable!" said I.

"What do you think there is in it?"

"God knows. The only thing is to stop it, as one does hysteria. It's on a par with hysteria."

"Quite," she said.

Lord Lathkill was dancing, and smiling very curiously down

into his partner's face. The Victrola was at its loudest.

Carlotta and I looked at one another, with hardly the heart to start again. The house felt hollow and gruesome. One wanted to get out, to get away from the cold, uncanny blight which filled the air.

"Oh, I say, keep the ball rolling," called Lord Lathkill.

"Come," I said to Carlotta.

Even then she hung back a little. If she had not suffered, and lost so much, she would have gone upstairs at once to struggle in the silent wrestling of wills with her mother-in-law. Even now, *that* particular fight drew her, almost the strongest. But I took her hand.

"Come," I said. "Let us dance it down. We'll roll the ball the opposite way."

She danced with me, but she was absent, unwilling. The empty gloom of the house, the sense of cold, and of deadening opposition, pressed us down. I was looking back over my life, and thinking how the cold weight of an unliving spirit was slowly crushing all warmth and vitality out of everything. Even Carlotta herself had gone numb again, cold and resistant even to me. The thing seemed to happen wholesale in her.

"One has to choose to live," I said, dancing on.

But I was powerless. With a woman, when her spirit goes inert in opposition, a man can do nothing. I felt my life-flow sinking in my body.

"This house is awfully depressing," I said to her, as we mechanically danced. "Why don't you *do* something? Why don't you get out of this tangle? Why don't you break it?"

"How?" she said.

I looked down at her, wondering why she was suddenly hostile.

"You needn't fight," I said. "You needn't fight it. Don't get tangled up in it. Just side-step, on to another ground."

She made a pause of impatience before she replied:

"I don't see where I am to side-step to, precisely."

"You do," said I. "A little while ago, you were warm and unfolded and good. Now you are shut up and prickly, in the cold. You needn't be. Why not stay warm?"

"It's nothing I do," she said coldly.

"It is. Stay warm to me. I am here. Why clutch in a tug-of-war with Lady Lathkill?"

"Do I clutch in a tug-of-war with my mother-in-law?"

"You know you do."

She looked up at me, with a faint little shadow of guilt and beseeching, but with a *moue* of cold obstinacy dominant.

"Let's have done," said I.

And in cold silence we sat side by side on the lounge. The other two danced on. They at any rate were in unison. One could see from the swing of their limbs. Mrs. Hale's yellow-brown eyes looked at me every time she came round.

"Why does she look at me?" I said.

"I can't imagine," said Carlotta, with a cold grimace.

"I'd better go upstairs and see what's happening," she said, suddenly rising and disappearing in a breath.

Why should she go? Why should she rush off to the battle of wills with her mother-in-law? In such a battle, while one has any life to lose, one can only lose it. There is nothing positively to be done, but to withdraw out of the hateful tension.

The music ran down. Lord Lathkill stopped the Victrola.

"Carlotta gone?" he said.

"Apparently."

"Why didn't you stop her?"

"Wild horses wouldn't stop her."

He lifted his hand with a mocking gesture of helplessness.

"The lady loves her will," he said. "Would you like to dance?"

I looked at Mrs. Hale.

"No," I said. "I won't butt in. I'll play the pianola. The Victrola's a brute."

I hardly noticed the passage of time. Whether the others danced or not, I played, and was unconscious of almost everything. In the midst of one rattling piece, Lord Lathkill touched my arm.

"Listen to Carlotta. She says closing time," he said, in his old musical voice, but with the sardonic ring of war in it now.

Carlotta stood with her arms dangling, looking like a penitent schoolgirl.

"The Colonel has gone to bed. He hasn't been able to manage a reconciliation with Lucy," she said. "My mother-in-law thinks we ought to let him try to sleep."

Carlotta's slow eyes rested on mine, questioning, penitent —or so I imagined—and somewhat sphinx-like.

"Why, of course," said Lord Lathkill. "I wish him all the sleep in the world."

Mrs. Hale said never a word.

"Is mother retiring too?" asked Luke.

"I think so."

"Ah! then supposing we up and look at the supper-tray."

We found Lady Lathkill mixing herself some nightcap brew over a spirit-lamp: something milky and excessively harmless. She stood at the sideboard stirring her potations, and hardly noticed us. When she had finished she sat down with her steaming cup.

"Colonel Hale all right, mother?" said Luke, looking across at her.

The dowager, under her uplift of white hair, stared back at her son. There was an eye-battle for some moments, during which he maintained his arch, debonair ease, just a bit crazy.

"No," said Lady Lathkill, "he is in great trouble."

"Ah!" replied her son. "Awful pity we can't do anything for him. But if flesh and blood can't help him, I'm afraid I'm a dud. Suppose he didn't mind our dancing? Frightfully good for *us*! We've been forgetting that we're flesh and blood, mother."

He took another whisky and soda, and gave me one. And in a paralysing silence Lady Lathkill sipped her hot brew, Luke and I sipped our whiskies, the young woman ate a little sandwich. We all preserved an extraordinary aplomb, and an obstinate silence.

It was Lady Lathkill who broke it. She seemed to be sinking downwards, crouching into herself like a skulking animal.

"I suppose," she said, "we shall all go to bed?"

"You go, mother. We'll come along in a moment."

She went, and for some time we four sat silent. The room seemed to become pleasanter, the air was more grateful.

"Look here," said Lord Lathkill at last. "What do you think of this ghost business?"

"I?" said I. "I don't like the atmosphere it produces. There may be ghosts, and spirits, and all that. The dead must be somewhere; there's no such place as nowhere. But they don't affect me particularly. Do they you?"

"Well," he said, "no, not directly. Indirectly I suppose it does."

"I think it makes a horribly depressing atmosphere, spirit-ualism," said I. "I want to kick."

"Exactly! And ought one?" he asked in his terribly sane-seeming way.

This made me laugh. I knew what he was up to.

"I don't know what you mean by *ought*," said I. "If I really want to kick, if I know I can't stand a thing, I kick. Who's going to authorise me, if my own genuine feeling doesn't?"

"Quite," he said, staring at me like an owl, with a fixed, meditative stare.

"Do you know," he said, "I suddenly thought at dinner-time, what corpses we all were, sitting eating our dinners. I thought it when I saw you look at those little Jerusalem arti-choke things in a white sauce. Suddenly it struck me, you were alive and twinkling, and we were all bodily dead. Bodily dead, if you understand. Quite alive in other directions, but bodily dead. And whether we ate vegetarian or meat made no difference. We were bodily dead."

"Ah, with a slap in the face," said I, "we come to life! You or I or anybody."

"I *do* understand poor Lucy," said Luke. "Don't you? She forgot to be flesh and blood while she was alive, and now she can't forgive herself, nor the Colonel. That must be pretty rough, you know, not to realise it till you're dead, and you haven't, so to speak, anything left to go on. I mean, it's awfully important to be flesh and blood."

He looked so solemnly at us, we three broke simultaneously into an uneasy laugh.

"Oh, but I *do* mean it," he said. "I've only realised how very extraordinary it is to be a man of flesh and blood, alive. It seems so ordinary, in comparison, to be dead, and merely spirit. That seems so commonplace. But fancy having a living face, and arms, and thighs. Oh, my God, I'm glad I've realised in time!"

He caught Mrs. Hale's hand, and pressed her dusky arm against his body.

"Oh, but if one had died without realising it!" he cried. "Think how ghastly for Jesus, when He was risen and wasn't touchable! How very awful, to have to say *Noli me tangere!* Ah, touch me, touch me *alive!*"

He pressed Mrs. Hale's hand convulsively against his breast.

The tears had already slowly gathered in Carlotta's eyes and were dropping on to her hands in her lap.

"Don't cry, Carlotta," he said. "Really, don't. We haven't killed one another. We're too decent, after all. We've almost become two spirits side by side. We've almost become two ghosts to one another, wrestling. Oh, but I want you to get back your body, even if I can't give it you. I want my flesh and blood, Carlotta, and I want you to have yours. We've suffered so much the other way. And the children, it is as well they are dead. They were born of our will and our disembodiment. Oh, I feel like the Bible. Clothe me with flesh again, and wrap my bones with sinew, and let the fountain of blood cover me. My spirit is like a naked nerve on the air."

Carlotta had ceased to weep. She sat with her head dropped, as if asleep. The rise and fall of her small, slack breasts was still heavy, but they were lifting on a heaving sea of rest. It was as if a slow, restful dawn were rising in her body, while she slept. So slack, so broken she sat, it occurred to me that in this crucifixion business the crucified does not put himself alone on the cross. The woman is nailed even more inexorably up, and crucified in the body even more cruelly.

It is a monstrous thought. But the deed is even more monstrous. Oh, Jesus, didn't you know that you couldn't be crucified alone?—that the two thieves crucified along with you were the two women, your wife and your mother! You called them two thieves. But what would they call you, who had their women's bodies on the cross? The abominable trinity on Calvary!

I felt an infinite tenderness for my dear Carlotta. She could not yet be touched. But my soul streamed to her like warm blood. So she sat slack and drooped, as if broken. But she was not broken. It was only the great release.

Luke sat with the hand of the dark young woman pressed against his breast. His face was warm and fresh, but he too breathed heavily, and stared unseeing. Mrs. Hale sat at his side erect and mute. But she loved him, with erect, black-faced, remote power.

"Morier!" said Luke to me. "If you can help Carlotta, you will, won't you? I can't do any more for her now. We are in mortal fear of each other."

"As much as she'll let me," said I, looking at her drooping figure, that was built on such a strong frame.

The fire rustled on the hearth as we sat in complete silence. How long it lasted I cannot say. Yet we were none of us startled when the door opened.

It was the Colonel, in a handsome brocade dressing-gown, looking worried.

Luke still held the dark young woman's hand clasped against his thigh. Mrs. Hale did not move.

"I thought you fellows might help me," said the Colonel, in a worried voice, as he closed the door.

"What is wrong, Colonel?" said Luke.

The Colonel looked at him, looked at the clasped hands of Luke and the dark young woman, looked at me, looked at Carlotta, without changing his expression of anxiety, fear, and misery. He didn't care about us.

"I can't sleep," he said. "It's gone wrong again. My head feels as if there was a cold vacuum in it, and my heart beats, and something screws up inside me. I know it's Lucy. She hates me again. I can't stand it."

He looked at us with eyes half-glazed, obsessed. His face seemed as if the flesh were breaking under the skin, decomposing.

"Perhaps, poor thing," said Luke, whose madness seemed really sane this night, "perhaps you hate *her*."

Luke's strange concentration instantly made us feel a tension, as of hate, in the Colonel's body.

"I?" The Colonel looked up sharply, like a culprit. "I! I wouldn't say that, if I were you."

"Perhaps that's what's the matter," said Luke, with mad, beautiful calm. "Why can't you feel kindly towards her, poor thing! She must have been done out of a lot while she lived."

It was as if he had one foot in life and one in death, and knew both sides. To us it was like madness.

"I—I!" stammered the Colonel; and his face was a study. Expression after expression moved across it: of fear, repudiation, dismay, anger, repulsion, bewilderment, guilt. "I was good to her."

"Ah, yes," said Luke. "Perhaps *you* were good to her. But was your body good to poor Lucy's body, poor dead thing!"

He seemed to be better acquainted with the ghost than with us.

The Colonel gazed blankly at Luke, and his eyes went up and down, up and down, up and down, up and down.

"My body!" he said blankly.

And he looked down amazedly at his little round stomach, under the silk gown, and his stout knee, in its blue-and-white pyjama.

"My body!" he repeated blankly.

"Yes," said Luke. "Don't you see, you may have been awfully good to her. But her poor woman's body, were you ever good to that?"

"She had everything she wanted. She had three of my children," said the Colonel dazedly.

"Ah yes, that may easily be. But your body of a man, was it ever good to her body of a woman? That's the point. If you understand the marriage service: with my body I thee worship. That's the point. No getting away from it."

The queerest of all accusing angels did Lord Lathkill make, as he sat there with the hand of the other man's wife clasped against his thigh. His face was fresh and naïve, and the dark eyes were bright with a clairvoyant candour, that was like madness, and perhaps was supreme sanity.

The Colonel was thinking back, and over his face a slow understanding was coming.

"It may be," he said. "It may be. Perhaps, that way, I despised her. It may be, it may be."

"I know," said Luke. "As if she weren't worth noticing, what you did to her. Haven't I done it myself? And don't I know now, it's a horrible thing to do, to oneself as much as to her? Her poor ghost, that ached, and never had a real body! It's not so easy to worship with the body. Ah, if the Church taught us *that* sacrament: *with my body I thee worship!* that would easily make up for any honouring and obeying the woman might do. But that's why she haunts you. You ignored and disliked her body, and she was only a living ghost. Now she wails in the afterworld, like a still-wincing nerve."

The Colonel hung his head, slowly pondering. Pondering with all his body. His young wife watched the sunken, bald head in a kind of stupor. His day seemed so far from her day. Carlotta had lifted her face; she was beautiful again, with the tender before-dawn freshness of a new understanding.

She was watching Luke, and it was obvious he was another

man to her. The man she knew, the Luke who was her husband, was gone, and this other strange, uncanny creature had taken his place. She was filled with wonder. Could one so change, as to become another creature entirely? Ah, if it were so! If she herself, as she knew herself, could cease to be! If that woman who was married to Luke, married to him in an intimacy of misfortune that was like a horror, could only cease to be, and let a new, delicately-wild Carlotta take her place!

"It may be," said the Colonel, lifting his head. "It may be." There seemed to come a relief over his soul, as he realised. "I didn't worship her with my body. I think maybe I worshipped other women that way; but maybe I never did. But I thought I was good to her. And I thought she didn't want it."

"It's no good thinking. We all want it," asserted Luke. "And before we die, we know it. I say, before we die. It may be after. But everybody wants it, let them say and do what they will. Don't you agree, Morier?"

I was startled when he spoke to me. I had been thinking of Carlotta: how she was looking like a girl again, as she used to look at the Thwaite, when she painted cactuses-in-a-pot. Only now, a certain rigidity of the will had left her, so that she looked even younger than when I first knew her, having now a virginal, flower-like *stillness* which she had not had then. I had always believed that people could be born again: if they would only let themselves.

"I'm sure they do," I said to Luke.

But I was thinking, if people were born again, the old circumstances would not fit the new body.

"What about yourself, Luke?" said Carlotta abruptly.

"I!" he exclaimed, and the scarlet showed in his cheek. "I! I'm not fit to be spoken about. I've been moaning like the ghost of disembodiment myself, ever since I became a man."

The Colonel said never a word. He hardly listened. He was pondering, pondering. In this way, he, too, was a brave man.

"I have an idea what you mean," he said. "There's no denying it, I didn't like her body. And now, I suppose it's too late."

He looked up bleakly: in a way, willing to be condemned, since he knew vaguely that something was wrong. Anything better than the blind torture

"Oh, I don't know," said Luke. "Why don't you, even now, love her a little with your real heart? Poor disembodied thing! Why don't you take her to your warm heart, even now, and comfort her inside there? Why don't you be kind to her poor ghost, bodily?"

The Colonel did not answer. He was gazing fixedly at Luke. Then he turned, and dropped his head, alone in a deep silence. Then, deliberately, but not lifting his head, he pulled open his dressing-gown at the breast, unbuttoned the top of his pyjama jacket, and sat perfectly still, his breast showing white and very pure, so much younger and purer than his averted face. He breathed with difficulty, his white breast rising irregularly. But in the deep isolation where he was, slowly a gentleness of compassion came over him, moulding his elderly features with strange freshness, and softening his blue eye with a look it had never had before. Something of the tremulous gentleness of a young bridegroom had come upon him, in spite of his baldness, his silvery little moustache, the weary marks of his face.

The passionate, compassionate soul stirred in him and was pure, his youth flowered over his face and eyes.

We sat very still, moved also in the spirit of compassion. There seemed a presence in the air, almost a smell of blossom, as if time had opened and gave off the perfume of spring. The Colonel gazed in silence into space, his smooth white chest, with the few dark hairs, open and rising and sinking with life.

Meanwhile his dark-faced young wife watched as if from afar. The youngness that was on him was not for her.

I knew that Lady Lathkill would come. I could feel her far off in her room, stirring and sending forth her rays. Swiftly I steeled myself to be in readiness. When the door opened, I rose and walked across the room.

She entered with characteristic noiselessness, peering in round the door, with her crest of white hair, before she ventured bodily in. The Colonel looked at her swiftly, and swiftly covered his breast, holding his hand at his bosom, clutching the silk of his robe.

"I was afraid," she murmured, "that Colonel Hale might be in trouble."

"No," said I. "We are all sitting very peacefully. There is no trouble."

Lord Lathkill also rose.

"No trouble at all, I assure you, mother!" he said.

Lady Lathkill glanced at us both, then turned heavily to the Colonel.

"She is unhappy to-night?" she asked.

The Colonel winced.

"No," he said hurriedly. "No, I don't think so." He looked up at her with shy, wincing eyes.

"Tell me what I can do," she said in a very low tone, bending towards him.

"Our ghost is walking to-night, mother," said Lord Lathkill. "Haven't you felt the air of spring, and smelt the plum-blossom? Don't you feel us all young? Our ghost is walking, to bring Lucy home. The Colonel's breast is quite extra-ordinary, white as plum-blossom, mother, younger-looking than mine, and he's already taken Lucy into his bosom, in his breast, where he breathes like the wind among trees. The Colonel's breast is white and extraordinarily beautiful, mother, I don't wonder poor Lucy yearned for it, to go home into it at last. It's like going into an orchard of plum-blossom for a ghost."

His mother looked round at him, then back at the Colonel, who was still clutching his hand over his chest, as if protecting something.

"You see, I didn't understand where I'd been wrong," he said, looking up at her imploringly. "I never realised that it was my body which had not been good to her."

Lady Lathkill curved sideways to watch him. But her power was gone. His face had come smooth with the tender glow of compassionate life, that flowers again. She could not get at him.

"It's no good, mother. You know our ghost is walking She's supposed to be absolutely like a crocus, if you know what I mean: harbinger of spring in the earth. So it says in my great-grandfather's diary: for she rises with silence like a crocus at the feet, and violets in the hollows of the heart come out. For she is of the feet and the hands, the thighs and breast, the face and the all-concealing belly, and her name is silent, but her odour is of spring, and her contact is the all-in-all."

He was quoting from his great-grandfather's diary, which only the sons of the family read. And as he quoted he rose curiously on his toes, and spread his fingers, bringing his hands together

till the finger-tips touched. His father had done that before
him, when he was deeply moved.

Lady Lathkill sat down heavily in the chair next the
Colonel.

"How do you feel?" she asked him, in a secretive mutter.

He looked round at her, with the large blue eyes of candour.

"I never knew what was wrong," he said, a little nervously.
"She only wanted to be looked after a bit, not to be a homeless, houseless ghost. It's all right! She's all right here." He
pressed his clutched hand on his breast. "It's all right; it's all
right. She'll be all right now."

He rose, a little fantastic in his brocade gown, but once
more manly, candid and sober.

"With your permission," he said, "I will retire."—He made
a little bow.—"I am glad you helped me. I didn't know—
didn't know."

But the change in him, and his secret wondering were so
strong in him, he went out of the room scarcely being aware
of us.

Lord Lathkill threw up his arms, and stretched quivering.

"Oh, pardon, pardon," he said, seeming, as he stretched,
quivering, to grow bigger and almost splendid, sending out
rays of fire to the dark young woman. "Oh, mother, thank
you for my limbs, and my body! Oh, mother, thank you for
my knees and my shoulders at this moment! Oh, mother,
thank you that my body is straight and alive! Oh, mother,
torrents of spring, torrents of spring, whoever said that?"

"Don't you forget yourself, my boy?" said his mother.

"Oh no, dear no! Oh, mother dear, a man has to be in love
in his thighs, the way you ride a horse. Why don't we stay
in love that way all our lives? Why do we turn into corpses
with consciousness? Oh, mother of my body, thank you for
my body, you strange woman with white hair! I don't know
much about you, but my body came from you, so thank you,
my dear. I shall think of you to-night!"

"Hadn't we better go?" she said, beginning to tremble.

"Why, yes," he said, turning and looking strangely at the
dark young woman. "Yes, let us go; let us go!"

Carlotta gazed at him, then, with strange, heavy, searching
look, at me. I smiled to her, and she looked away. The dark
young woman looked over her shoulder as she went out.
Lady Lathkill hurried past her son, with head ducked. But

still he laid his hand on her shoulder, and she stopped dead.

"Good night, mother; mother of my face and my thighs. Thank you for the night to come, dear mother of my body."

She glanced up at him rapidly, nervously, then hurried away. He stared after her, then switched off the light.

"Funny old mother!" he said. "I never realised before that she was the mother of my shoulders and my hips, as well as my brain. Mother of my thighs!"

He switched off some of the lights as we went, accompanying me to my room.

"You know," he said, "I can understand that the Colonel is happy, now the forlorn ghost of Lucy is comforted in his heart. After all, he married her! And she must be content at last: he has a beautiful chest, don't you think? Together they will sleep well. And then he will begin to live the life of the living again. How friendly the house feels to-night! But, after all, it is my old home. And the smell of plum-blossom—don't you notice it? It is our ghost, in silence like a crocus. There, your fire has died down! But it's a nice room! I hope our ghost will come to you. I think she will. Don't speak to her. It makes her go away. She, too, is a ghost of silence. We talk far too much. But now I am going to be silent, too, and a ghost of silence. Good night!"

He closed the door softly and was gone. And softly, in silence, I took off my things. I was thinking of Carlotta, and a little sadly, perhaps, because of the power of circumstance over us. This night I could have worshipped her with my body, and she, perhaps, was stripped in the body to be worshipped. But it was not for me, at this hour, to fight against circumstances.

I had fought too much, even against the most imposing circumstances, to use any more violence for love. Desire is a sacred thing, and should not be violated.

"Hush!" I said to myself. "I will sleep, and the ghost of my silence can go forth, in the subtle body of desire, to meet that which is coming to meet it. Let my ghost go forth, and let me not interfere. There are many intangible meetings, and unknown fulfilments of desire."

So I went softly to sleep, as I wished to, without interfering with the warm, crocus-like ghost of my body.

And I must have gone far, far down the intricate galleries of sleep, to the very heart of the world. For I know I passed

on beyond the strata of images and words, beyond the iron
veins of memory, and even the jewels of rest, to sink in the
final dark like a fish, dumb, soundless, and imageless, yet alive
and swimming.

And at the very core of the deep night the ghost came to
me, at the heart of the ocean of oblivion, which is also the
heart of life. Beyond hearing, or even knowledge of contact,
I met her and knew her. How I know it I don't know. Yet
I know it with eyeless, wingless knowledge.

For man in the body is formed through countless ages, and
at the centre is the speck, or spark, upon which all his forma-
tion has taken place. It is even not himself, deep beyond his
many depths. Deep from him calls to deep. And according
as deep answers deep, man glistens and surpasses himself.

Beyond all the pearly mufflings of consciousness, of age
upon age of consciousness, deep calls yet to deep, and sometimes is answered. It is calling and answering, new-awakened
God calling within the deep of man, and new God calling
answer from the other deep. And sometimes the other deep
is a woman, as it was with me, when my ghost came.

Women were not unknown to me. But never before had
woman come, in the depths of night, to answer my deep
with her deep. As the ghost came, came as a ghost of silence,
still in the depth of sleep.

I know she came. I know she came even as a woman, to
my man. But the knowledge is darkly naked as the event. I
only know, it was so. In the deep of sleep a call was called
from the deeps of me, and answered in the deeps, by a woman
among women. Breasts or thighs or face, I remember not a
touch, no, nor a movement of my own. It is all complete in
the profundity of darkness. Yet I know it was so.

I awoke towards dawn, from far, far away. I was vaguely
conscious of drawing nearer and nearer, as the sun must have
been drawing towards the horizon, from the complete beyond.
Till at last the faint pallor of mental consciousness coloured
my waking.

And then I was aware of a pervading scent, as of plum-
blossom, and a sense of extraordinary silkiness—though
where, and in what contact, I could not say. It was as the
first blemish of dawn.

And even with so slight a conscious registering, *it* seemed
to disappear. Like a whale that has sounded to the bottom-

less seas. That knowledge of *it*, which was the mating of the ghost and me, disappeared from me, in its rich weight of certainty, as the scent of the plum-blossom moved down the lanes of my consciousness, and my limbs stirred in a silkiness for which I have no comparison.

As I became aware, I also became uncertain. I wanted to be certain of *it*, to have definite evidence. And as I sought for evidence, *it* disappeared, my perfect knowledge was gone. I no longer knew in full.

Now as the daylight slowly amassed, in the windows from which I had put back the shutters, I sought in myself for evidence, and in the room.

But I shall never know. I shall never know if it was a ghost, some sweet spirit from the innermost of the ever-deepening cosmos; or a woman, a very woman, as the silkiness of my limbs seems to attest; or a dream, a hallucination! I shall never know. Because I went away from Riddings in the morning, on account of the sudden illness of Lady Lathkill.

"You will come again," Luke said to me. "And in any case, you will never really go away from us."

"Good-bye," she said to me. "At last it was perfect!"

She seemed so beautiful, when I left her, as if it were the ghost again, and I was far down the deeps of consciousnes.

The following autumn, when I was overseas once more, I had a letter from Lord Lathkill. He wrote very rarely.

"Carlotta has a son," he said, "and I an heir. He has yellow hair, like a little crocus, and one of the young plum trees in the orchard has come out of all season into blossom. To me he is flesh and blood of our ghost itself. Even mother doesn't look over the wall, to the other side, any more. It's all this side for her now.

"So our family refuses to die out, by the grace of our ghost. We are calling him Gabriel.

"Dorothy Hale also is a mother, three days before Carlotta. She has a black lamb of a daughter, called Gabrielle. By the bleat of the little thing, I know its father. Our own is a blue eyed one, with the dangerous repose of a pugilist. I have no fears of our family misfortune for him, ghost-begotten and ready-fisted.

"The Colonel is very well, quiet, and self-possessed. He is farming in Wiltshire, raising pigs. It is a passion with him, the *crême de la crême* of swine. I admit, he has golden sows as elegant as a young Diane de Poictiers, and young hogs like Perseus in the first red-gold flush of youth. He looks me in the eye, and I look him back, and we understand. He is quiet, and proud now, and very hale and hearty, raising swine *ad maiorem gloriam Dei*. A good sport!

"I am in love with this house and its inmates, including the plum-blossom-scented one, she who visited you, in all the peace. I cannot understand why you wander in uneasy and distant parts of the earth. For me, when I am at home, I am there. I have peace upon my bones, and if the world is going to come to a violent and untimely end, as prophets aver, I feel the house of Lathkill will survive, built upon our ghost. So come back, and you'll find we shall not have gone away. . . ."

NONE OF THAT

I MET Luis Colmenares in Venice, not having seen him for years. He is a Mexican exile living on the scanty remains of what was once wealth, and eking out a poor and lonely existence by being a painter. But his art is only a sedative to him. He wanders about like a lost soul, mostly in Paris or in Italy, where he can live cheaply. He is rather short, rather fat, pale, with black eyes, which are always looking the other way, and a spirit the same, always averted.

"Do you know who is in Venice?" he said to me. "Cuesta! He is in the Hôtel Romano. I saw him bathing yesterday on the Lido."

There was a world of gloomy mockery in this last sentence.

"Do you mean Cuesta, the bull-fighter?" I asked.

"Yes. Don't you know, he retired? Do you remember? An American woman left him a lot of money. Did you ever see him?"

"Once," said I.

"Was it before the revolution? Do you remember, he retired and bought a *hacienda* very cheap from one of Madero's generals, up in Chihuahua? It was after the Carranzista, and I was already in Europe."

"How does he look now?" I said.

"Enormously fat, like a yellow, round, small whale in the sea. You saw him? You know he was rather short and rather fat always. I think his mother was a Mixtec Indian woman. Did you ever know him?"

"No," said I. "Did you?"

"Yes. I knew him in the old days, when I was rich, and thought I should be rich for ever."

He was silent, and I was afraid he had shut up for good. It was unusual for him to be even as communicative as he had been. But it was evident that having seen Cuesta, the toreador whose fame once rang through Spain and through Latin America, had moved him deeply. He was in a ferment, and could not quite contain himself.

"But he wasn't interesting, was he?" I said. "Wasn't he just a—a bull-fighter—a brute?"

Colmenares looked at me out of his own blackness. He didn't want to talk. Yet he had to.

"He was a brute, yes," he admitted grudgingly. "But not just a brute. Have you seen him when he was at his best? Where did you see him? I never liked him in Spain, he was too vain. But in Mexico he was very good. Have you seen him play with the bull, and play with death? He was marvellous. Do you remember him, what he looked like?"

"Not very well," said I.

"Short, and broad, and rather fat, with rather a yellow colour, and a pressed-in nose. But his eyes, they were marvellous, also rather small, and yellow, and when he looked at you, so strange and cool, you felt your inside melting. Do you know that feeling? He looked into the last little place of you, where you keep your courage. Do you understand? And so you felt yourself melting. Do you know what I mean?"

"More or less, perhaps," said I.

Colmenares' black eyes were fixed on my face, dilated and gleaming, but not really seeing me at all. He was seeing the past. Yet a curious force streamed out of his face; one understood him by the telepathy of passion, inverted passion.

"And in the bull-ring he was marvellous. He would stand with his back to the bull, and pretend to be adjusting his stockings, while the bull came charging on him. And with a little glance over his shoulder, he would make a small movement, and the bull had passed him without getting him. Then he would smile a little, and walk after it. It is marvellous that he was not killed hundreds of times, but I saw him bathing on the Lido to-day, like a fat, yellow, small whale. It is extraordinary! But I did not see his eyes. . . . ."

A queer look of abstracted passion was on Colmenares' fat, pale, clean-shaven face. Perhaps the toreador had cast a spell over him, as over so many people in the old and the new world.

"It is strange that I have never seen eyes anywhere else like his. Did I tell you, they were yellow, and not like human eyes at all? They didn't look at you. I don't think they ever looked at anybody. He only looked at the little bit inside your body where you keep your courage. I don't think he could

see people, any more than an animal can: I mean see them
personally, as I see you and you see me. He was an animal,
a marvellous animal. I have often thought, if human beings
had not developed minds and speech, they would have become marvellous animals like Cuesta, with those marvellous
eyes, much more marvellous than a lion's or a tiger's. Have
you noticed a lion or a tiger never sees you personally? It
never really looks at you. But also it is afraid to look at the
last little bit of you, where your courage lives inside you.
But Cuesta was not afraid. He looked straight at it, and it
melted."

"And what was he like, in ordinary life?" said I.

"He did not talk, was very silent. He was not clever at all.
He was not even clever enough to be a general. And he could
be very brutal and disgusting. But usually he was quiet. But
he was always *something*. If you were in the room with him,
you always noticed him more than anybody, more than
women or men, even very clever people. He was stupid, but
he made you physically aware of him; like a cat in the room.
I tell you, that litle bit of you where you keep your courage
was enchanted by him; he put over you an enchantment."

"Did he do it on purpose?"

"Well! It is hard to say. But he knew he could do it. To
some people, perhaps, he could not do it. But he never saw
such people. He only saw people who were in his enchantment. And of course, in the bull-ring, he mesmerised everybody. He could draw the natural magnetism of everybody to
him—everybody. And then he was marvellous, he played
with death as if it were a kitten, so quick, quick as a star.
and calm as a flower, and all the time, laughing at death. It
is marvellous he was never killed. But he retired very young.
And then suddenly it was he who killed the bull, with one
hand, one stroke. He was very strong. And the bull sank
down at his feet, heavy with death. The people went mad!
And he just glanced at them, with his yellow eyes, in a cool,
beautiful contempt, as if he were an animal that wrapped the
skin of death round him. Ah, he was wonderful! And to-day
I saw him bathing on the Lido, in an American bathing-suit,
with a woman. His bathing-suit was just a little more yellow
than he is. I have held the towel when he was being rubbed
down and massaged often. He had the body of an Indian, very
smooth, with hardly any hair, and creamy-yellow. I always

thought it had something childish about it, so soft. But also, it had the same mystery as his eyes, as if you could never touch it, as if, when you touched it, still it was not he. When he had no clothes on, he was naked. But it seemed he would have many, many more nakednesses before you really came to *him*. Do you understand me at all? Or does it seem to you foolish?"

"It interests me," I said. "And women, of course, fell for him by the thousand?"

"By the million! And they were mad because of him. Women went mad, once they felt him. It was not like Rudolf Valentino, sentimental. It was madness, like cats in the night which howl, no longer knowing whether they are on earth or in hell or in paradise. So were the women. He could have had forty beautiful women every night, and different ones each night, from the beginning of the year to the end."

"But he didn't, naturally?"

"Oh no! At first, I think, he took many women. But later, when I knew him, he took none of those that besieged him. He had two Mexican women whom he lived with, humble women, Indians. And all the others he spat at, and spoke of them with terrible, obscene language. I think he would have liked to whip them, or kill them, for pursuing him."

"Only he must enchant them when he was in the bull-ring," said I.

"Yes. But that was like sharpening his knife on them."

"And when he retired—he had plenty of money—how did he amuse himself?"

"He was rich, he had a big *hacienda*, and many people like slaves to work for him. He raised cattle. I think he was very proud to be *hacendado* and *padròn* of so many people, with a little army of his own. I think he was proud, living like a king. I had not heard of him for years. Now, suddenly, he is in Venice with a Frenchwoman, a Frenchwoman who talks bad Spanish——"

"How old is he?"

"How old? He is about fifty, or a little less."

"So young! And will you speak to him?"

"I don't know. I can't make up my mind. If I speak to him, he will think I want money."

There was a certain note of hatred now in Colmenares' voice.

"Well, why shouldn't he give you money? He is still rich, I suppose?"

"Rich, yes! He must always be rich. He has got American money. An American woman left him half a million dollars. Did you never hear of it?"

"No. Then why shouldn't he give you money? I suppose you often gave him some, in the past?"

"Oh, that—that is *quite* the past. He will never give me anything—or a hundred francs, something like that! Because he is mean. Did you never hear of the American woman who left him half a million dollars, and committed suicide?"

"No. When was it?"

"It was a long time ago—about 1914 or 1913. I had already lost all my money. Her name was Ethel Cane. Did you never hear of her?"

"I don't think I did," I said, feeling it remiss not to have heard of the lady.

"Ah! You should have known her. She was extraordinary. I had known her in Paris, even before I came back to Mexico and knew Cuesta well. She was almost as extraordinary as Cuesta: one of those American women, born rich, but what we should call provincial. She didn't come from New York or Boston, but somewhere else. Omaha or something. She was blonde, with thick, straight, blonde hair, and she was one of the very first to wear it short, like a Florentine page-boy. Her skin was white, and her eyes very blue, and she was not thin. At first, there seemed something childish about her— do you know that look, rather round cheeks and clear eyes, so false-innocent? Her eyes especially were warm and naïve and false-innocent, but full of light. Only sometimes they were bloodshot. Oh, she was extraordinary! It was only when I knew her better I noticed how her blonde eyebrows gathered together above her nose, in a diabolic manner. She was much too much a personality to be a lady, and she had all that terrible American energy! Ah, energy! She was a dynamo. In Paris she was married to a dapper little pink-faced American who got yellow at the gills, bilious, running after her when she would not have him. He painted pictures and wanted to be modern. She knew all the people, and had all sorts come to her, as if she kept a human menagerie. And she bought old furniture and brocades; she would go mad if she saw someone get a piece of velvet brocade with the misty bloom of years on it, that she coveted. She coveted such things with lust, and would go into a strange sensual trance, looking at some old worm-eaten chair. And she would go mad if someone else got it, and not she: that nasty old wormy chair of the quattrocento! Things! She was mad about 'things'. But it was only for a time. She always got tired, especially of her own enthusiasms.

"That was when I knew her in Paris. Then I think she divorced that husband, and, when the revolutions in Mexico became quieter, she came to Mexico. I think she was fascinated by the idea of Carranza. If ever she heard of a man who seemed to have a dramatic sort of power in him, she must know that man. It was like her lust for brocade and old chairs and a perfect æsthetic setting. Now it was to know the most dangerous man, especially if he looked like a prophet or a reformer. She was a socialist also, at this time. She no longer was in love with chairs.

"She found me again in Mexico: she knew thousands of people, and whenever one of them might be useful to her, she remembered him. So she remembered me, and it was nothing to her that I was now poor. I know she thought of me as 'that little Luis Something', but she had a certain use for me, and found, perhaps, a certain little flavour in me. At least she asked me often to dinner, or to drive with her. She was curious, quite reckless and a dare-devil, yet shy and awkward out of her own *milieu*. It was only in intimacy that she was unscrupulous and dauntless as a devil incarnate. In public, and in strange places, she was very uneasy, like one who has a bad conscience towards society, and is afraid of it. And for that reason she could never go out without a man to stand between her and all the others.

"While she was in Mexico, I was that man. She soon discovered that I was satisfactory. I would perform all the duties of a husband without demanding any of the rights. Which was what she wanted. I think she was looking round for a remarkable and epoch-making husband. But, of course, it would have to be a husband who would be a fitting instrument for her remarkable and epoch-making energy and character. She was extraordinary, but she could only work through individuals, through others. By herself she could accomplish nothing. She lay on a sofa and mused and schemed, with the energy boiling inside her. Only when she had a group, or a few real individuals, or just one man, then she could start something, and make them all dance in a tragi-comedy, like marionettes.

"But in Mexico, men do not care for women who will make them dance like puppets. In Mexico, women must run in the dust like the Indian women, with meek little heads. American women are not very popular. Their energy, and their power to make other people do things, are not in request. The men would rather go to the devil in their own way than be sent there by the women, with a little basket in which to bring home the goods.

"So Ethel found not a cold shoulder, but a number of square, fat backs turned to her. They didn't want her. The revolutionaries would not take any notice of her at all. They wanted no woman interfering. General Isidor Garabay danced with her, and expected her immediately to become his mistress. But, as she said, she was having *none of that*. She had a terrible way of saying 'I'm having none of that!'—like hitting a mirror with a hammer. And as nobody wanted to get into trouble over her, they were having none of her.

"At first, of course, when the generals saw her white shoulders and blonde hair and innocent face, they thought at once: 'Here is a *type* for us!' They were not deceived by her innocent look. But they were deceived by what looked like her helplessness. The blood would come swelling into her neck and face, her eyes would go hot, her whole figure would swell with repellant energy, and she would say something very American and very crushing, in French, or in American. None of *that!* Stop *that!*

"She, too, had a lot of power. She could send out of her body a repelling energy, to compel people to submit to her will. Men in Europe or the United States nearly always crumpled up before her. But in Mexico she had come to the wrong shop. The men were a law to themselves. While she was winning and rather lovely, with her blue eyes so full of light and her white skin glistening with energetic health, they expected her to become at once their mistress. And when they saw, very quickly, that she was having *none of that*, they turned on their heels and showed her their fat backs. Because she was clever, and remarkable, and had wonderful energy and a wonderful power for making people dance while she pulled the strings, they didn't care a bit. They, too, wanted *none of that*. They would, perhaps, have carried her off and shared her as a mistress, except for the fear of trouble with the American Government.

"So, soon, she began to be bored, and to think of returning to New York. She said that Mexico was a place without a soul and without a culture, and it had not even brain enough to be mechanically efficient. It was a city and a land of naughty little boys doing obscene little things, and one day it would learn its lesson. I told her that history is the account of a lesson which nobody ever learns, and she told me the world certainly *had* progressed. Only not in Mexico, she supposed. I asked her why she had come, then, to Mexico. And she said she had thought there was something doing, and she would like to be in it. But she found it was only naughty and mostly cowardly little boys letting off guns and doing mediocre obscenities, so she would leave them to it. I told her I supposed it was life. And she replied that since it was not good enough for her, it was not life to her.

"She said all she wanted was to live the life of the imagination and get it acted on. At the time, I thought this ridiculous. I thought she was just trying to find somebody to fall in love with. Later, I saw she was right. She had an imaginary picture of herself as an extraordinary and potent woman who would make a stupendous change in the history of man. Like Catherine of Russia, only cosmopolitan, not merely Russian. And it is true, she *was* an extraordinary woman, with tremendous power of will, and truly amazing energy, even for an American woman. She was like a locomotive-engine stoked up inside and bursting with steam, which it has to let off by rolling a lot of trucks about. But I did not see how this was to cause a change in the tide of mortal affairs. It was only a part of the hubbub of traffic. She sent the trucks bouncing against one another with a clash of buffers, and sometimes she derailed some unfortunate item of the rolling-stock. But I did not see how this was to change the history of mankind. She seemed to have arrived just a little late, as some heroes, and heroines also, to-day, always do.

"I wondered always, why she did not take a lover. She was a woman between thirty and forty, very healthy and full of this extraordinary energy. She saw many men, and was always drawing them out, always on the *qui vive* to start them rolling down some incline. She attracted men, in a certain way. Yet she had no lover.

"I wondered even with regard to myself. We were friends, and a great deal together. Certainly I was under her spell. I came running as soon as I thought she wanted me. I did the things she suggested I should do. Even among my own acquaintances, when I found everybody laughing at me and disliking me for being at the service of an American woman, and I tried to rebel against her, and put her in her place, as the Mexicans say—which means, to them, in bed with no clothes on—still, the moment I saw her, with a look and a word she won me round. She was very clever. She flattered me, of course. She made me feel intelligent. She drew me out. There was her cleverness. She made *me* clever. I told her all about Mexico: all my life: all my ideas of history, philosophy. I sounded awfully clever and original, to myself. And she listened with such attention, which I thought was deep interest in what I was saying. But she was waiting for something she could fasten on, so that she could 'start something'. That was her constant craving, to 'start something'. But, of course, I thought she was interested in *me*.

"She would lie on a large couch that was covered with old sarapes—she began to buy them as soon as she came to Mexico—herself wrapped in a wonderful black shawl that glittered all over with brilliant birds and flowers in vivid colour, a very fine specimen of the embroidered shawls our Mexican ladies used to wear at a bull-fight or in an open-air *fiesta*: and there, with her white arms glistening through the long fringe of the shawl, the old Italian jewellery rising on her white, dauntless breast, and her short, thick, blonde hair falling like yellow metal, she would draw me out, draw me out. I never talked so much in my life before or since. Always talk! And I believe I talked very well, really, really very clever. But nothing besides talk! Sometimes I stayed till after midnight. And sometimes she would snort with impatience or boredom, rather like a horse, flinging back her head and shaking that heavy blonde hair. And I think some part of her wanted me to make love to her.

"But I didn't. I couldn't. I was there, under her influence, in her power. She could draw me out in talk, marvellously. I'm sure I was very clever indeed. But any other part of me was stiff, petrified. I couldn't even touch her. I couldn't even

take her hand in mine. It was a physical impossibility. When
I was away from her, I could think of her white, healthy
body with a voluptuous shiver. I could even run to her apartment, intending to kiss her, and make her my mistress that
very night. But the moment I was in her presence, it left me.
I could not touch her. I was averse from touching her.
Physically, for some reason, I hated her.

"And I felt within myself, it was because she was repelling
me and because she was always hating men, hating all active
maleness in a man. She only wanted passive maleness, and
then this 'talk', this life of the imagination, as she called it.
Inside herself she seethed, and she thought it was because she
wanted to be made love to, very much made love to. But it
wasn't so. She seethed against all men, with repulsion. She
was cruel to the body of a man. But she excited his mind,
his spirit. She loved to do that. She loved to have a man
hanging round, like a servant. She loved to stimulate him,
especially his mind. And she, too, when the man was not
there, she thought she wanted him to be her lover. But when
he was there, and he wanted to gather for himself that
mysterious fruit of her body, she revolted against him with
a fearful hate. A man must be *absolutely* her servant, and
only that. That was what she meant by the life of the
imagination.

"And I was her servant. Everybody jeered at me. But I
said to myself, I would make her my mistress. I almost set
my teeth to do it. That was when I was away from her. When
I came to her, I could not even touch her. When I tried to
make myself touch her, something inside me began to
shudder. It was impossible. And I knew it was because,
with her inner body, she was repelling me, always really
repelling me.

"Yet she wanted me too. She was lonely: lonesome, she
said. She was lonesome, and she would have liked to get me
making love to her external self. She would even, I think,
have become my mistress, and allowed me to take her sometimes for a little, miserable, humiliating moment, then quickly
have got rid of me again. But I couldn't do it. Her inner body
never wanted me. And I couldn't just be her prostitute. Because immediately she would have despised me, and insulted
me if I had persisted in trying to get some satisfaction of her.
I knew it. She had already had two husbands, and she was a

woman who always ached to tell *all*, everything. She had told me too much. I had seen one of her American husbands. I did not choose to see myself in a similar light: or plight.

"No, she wanted to live the life of the imagination. She said the imagination could master everything; so long, of course, as one was not shot in the head, or had an eye put out. Talking of the Mexican atrocities, and of the famous case of raped nuns, she said it was all nonsense that a woman was broken because she had been raped. She could rise above it. The imagination could rise above *anything*, that was not real organic damage. If one lived the life of the imagination, one could rise above any experience that ever happened to one. One could even commit murder, and rise above that. By using the imagination, and by using cunning, a woman can justify herself in anything, even the meanest and most bad things. A woman uses her imagination on her own behalf, and she becomes more innocent to herself than an innocent child, no matter what bad things she has done."

"Men do that, too," I interrupted. "It's the modern dodge. That's why everybody to-day is innocent. To the imagination all things are pure, if you did them yourself."

Colmenares looked at me with quick, black eyes, to see if I were mocking him. He did not care about me and my interruptions. He was utterly absorbed in his recollections of that woman, who had made him so clever, and who had made him her servant, and from whom he had never had any satisfaction.

"And then what?" I asked him. "Then did she try her hand on Cuesta?"

"Ah!" said Colmenares, rousing, and glancing at me suspiciously again. "Yes! That was what she did. And I was jealous. Though I couldn't bring myself to touch her, yet I was excruciated with jealousy, because she was interested in someone else. She was interested in someone besides myself, and my vanity suffered tortures of jealousy. Why was I such a fool? Why, even now, could I kill that fat, yellow pig Cuesta? A man is always a fool."

"How did she meet the bull-fighter?" I asked. "Did you introduce him to her?"

"She went once to the bull-fight, because everyone was talking about Cuesta. She did not care for such things as the bull-ring; she preferred the modern theatre, Duse and Rein-

hardt, and 'things of the imagination'. But now she was going
back to New York, and she had never seen a bull-fight, so she
must see one. I got seats in the shade—high up, you know—
and went with her.

"At first she was very disgusted, and very contemptuous,
and a little bit frightened, you know, because a Mexican
crowd in a bull-ring is not very charming. She was afraid of
people. But she sat stubborn and sulky, like a sulky child,
saying: 'Can't they do anything more subtle than this, to get
a thrill? It's on such a low level!'

"But when Cuesta at last began to play with a bull, she
began to get excited. He was in pink and silver, very gorgeous,
and looking very ridiculous, as usual. Till he began to play;
and then there really was something marvellous in him, you
know, so quick and so light and so playful—do you know?
When he was playing with a bull and playing with death in
the ring, he was the most playful thing I have ever seen:
more playful than kittens or leopard cubs: and you know
how they play; do you? Oh, marvellous! More gay and
light than if they had lots of wings all over them, all wings
of playing! Well, he was like that, playing with death in the
ring, as if he had all kinds of gay little wings to spin him with
the quickest, tiniest, most beautiful little movements, quite
unexpected, like a soft leopard cub. And then at the end,
when he killed the bull and the blood squirted past him, ugh!
it was as if all his body laughed, and still the same soft, surprised laughter like a young thing, but more cruel than anything you can imagine. He fascinated me, but I always hated
him. I would have liked to stick him as he stuck the bulls.

"I could see that Ethel was trying not to be caught by his
spell. He had the most curious charm, quick and unexpected
like play, you know, like leopard kittens, or slow sometimes,
like tiny little bears. And yet the perfect cruelty. It was the
joy in cruelty! She hated the blood and messiness and dead
animals. Ethel hated all that. It was not the life of the
imagination. She was very pale, and very silent. She leaned
forward and hardly moved, looking white and obstinate and
subdued. And Cuesta had killed three bulls before she made
any sign of any sort. I did not speak to her. The fourth bull
was a beauty, full of life, curling and prancing like a narcissus-
flower in January. He was a very special bull, brought from
Spain, and not so stupid as the others. He pawed the ground

and blew the breath on the ground, lowering his head. And Cuesta opened his arms to him with a little smile, but endearing, lovingly endearing, as a man might open his arms to a little maiden he really loves, but, really, for her to come to his body, his warm, open body, to come softly. So he held his arms out to the bull, with love. And that was what fascinated the women. They screamed and they fainted, longing to go into the arms of Cuesta, against his soft, round body, that was more yearning than a fico. But the bull, of course, rushed past him, and only got two darts sticking in his shoulder. That was the love.

"Then Ethel shouted, *Bravo! Bravo!* and I saw that she, too, had gone mad. Even Cuesta heard her, and he stopped a moment and looked at her. He saw her leaning forward, with her short, thick hair hanging like yellow metal, and her face dead-white, and her eyes glaring to his, like a challenge. They looked at one another, for a second, and he gave a little bow, then turned away. But he was changed. He didn't play so unconsciously any more: he seemed to be thinking of something, and forgetting himself. I was afraid he would be killed; but so afraid! He seemed absent-minded, and taking risks too great. When the bull came after him over the gangway barrier, he even put his hand on its head as he vaulted back, and one horn caught his sleeve and tore it just a little. Then he seemed to be absent-mindedly looking at the tear, while the bull was almost touching him again. And the bull was mad. Cuesta was a dead man it seemed, for sure: yet he seemed to wake up and *waked* himself just out of reach. It was like an awful dream, and it seemed to last for hours. I think it must have been a long time, before the bull was killed. He killed him at last, as a man takes his mistress at last because he is almost tired of playing with her. But he liked to kill his own bull.

"Ethel was looking like death, with beads of perspiration on her face. And she called to him: 'That's enough! That's enough now! *Ya es bastante! Basta!*' He looked at her, and heard what she said. They were both alike there, they heard and saw in a flash. And he lifted his face, with the rather squashed nose and the yellow eyes, and he looked at her, and though he was so far away, he seemed quite near. And he was smiling like a small boy. But I could see he was looking at the little place in her body, where she kept her courage. And she was trying to catch his look on her imagination, not on her naked inside body. And they both found it difficult. When he tried to look at her, she set her imagination in front of him, like a mirror they put in front of a wild dog. And when she tried to catch him in her imagination, he seemed to melt away, and was gone. So neither really had caught the other.

"But he played with two more bulls, and killed them, without ever looking at her. And she went away when the people were applauding him, and did not look at him. Neither did she speak to me of him. Neither did she go to any more bull-fights.

"It was Cuesta who spoke to me of her, when I met him at Clavel's house. He said to me, in his very coarse Spanish: 'And what about your American skirt?' I told him, there was nothing to say about her. She was leaving for New York. So he told me to ask her if she would like to come and say good-bye to Cuesta, before she went. I said to him: 'But why should I mention your name to her? She has never mentioned yours to me.' He made an obscene joke to me.

"And it must have been because I was thinking of him that she said that evening: 'Do you know Cuesta?' I told her I did, and she asked me what I thought of him. I told her I thought he was a marvellous beast, but he wasn't really a man. 'But he is a beast with imagination,' she said to me. 'Couldn't one get a response out of him?' I told her I didn't know, but I didn't want to try. I would leave Cuesta to the bull-ring. I would never dream of trying my imagination on him. She said, always ready with an answer: 'But wasn't there a marvellous *thing* in him, something quite exceptional?' I said, maybe! But so has a rattlesnake a marvellous thing in him: two things, one in his mouth, one in his tail. But I didn't want to try to get response out of a rattlesnake. She wasn't satisfied, though. She was tortured. I said to her: 'Anyhow, you are leaving on Thursday.' 'No, I've put it off,' she said. 'Till when?' 'Indefinite,' she said.

"I could tell she was tormented. She had been tormented ever since she had been to the bull-fight, because she couldn't get past Cuesta. She couldn't get past him, as the Americans say. He seemed like a fat, squat, yellow-eyed demon just smiling at her, and dancing ahead of her. 'Why don't you bring him here?' she said at last, though she didn't want to say it.—'But why? What it the good of bringing him here? Would you bring a criminal here, or a yellow scorpion?'—'I would if I wanted to find out about it.'—'But what is there to find out about Cuesta? He is just a sort of beast. He is less than a man.'—'Maybe he's a *schwarze Bestie*,' she said, 'and I'm a *blonde Bestie*. Anyway, bring him.'

"I always did what she wanted me, though I never wanted to myself. So it was now. I went to a place where I knew Cuesta would be, and he asked me: 'How is the blonde skirt? Has she gone yet?' I said, 'No. Would you like to see her?' He looked at me with his yellow eyes, and that pleasant look which was really hate undreaming. 'Did she tell you to ask me?' he said. 'No,' I said. 'We were talking of you, and she said, bring the fabulous animal along and let us see what he really is.'—'He is the animal for her meat, this one,' he said, in his vulgar way. Then he pretended he wouldn't come. But I knew he would. So I said I would call for him.

"We were going in the evening, after tea, and he was dressed to kill, in a light French suit. We went in his car. But he didn't take flowers or anything. Ethel was nervous and awkward, offering us cocktails and cigarettes, and speaking French, though Cuesta didn't understand any French at all. There was another old American woman there, for chaperon.

"Cuesta just sat on a chair, with his knees apart and his hands between his thighs, like an Indian. Only his hair, which was done up in his little pigtail, and taken back from his forehead, made him look like a woman, or a Chinaman; and his flat nose and little yellow eyes made him look like a Chinese idol, maybe a god or a demon, as you please. He just sat and said nothing, and had that look on his face which wasn't a smile, and wasn't a grimace, it was nothing. But to me it meant rhapsodic hate.

"She asked him in French if he liked his profession, and how long he had been doing it, and if he got a great kick out of it, and was he a pure-blood Indian?—all that kind of thing. I translated to him as short as possible, Ethel flushing with embarrassment. He replied just as short, to me, in his coarse, flat sort of voice, as if he knew it was mere pretence. But he looked at her, straight into her face, with that strange, far-off sort of stare, yet very vivid, taking no notice of her, yet staring right into her: as if all that she was putting forward to him was merely window-dressing, and he was just looking way in, to the marshes and the jungle in her, where she didn't even look herself. It made one feel as if there was a mountain behind her, Popocatepetl, that he was staring at, expecting a mountain-lion to spring down off a tree on the slopes of the mountain, or a snake to lean down from a bough. But the mountain was all she stood for, and the mountain-lion or the snake was her own animal self, that he was watching for, like a hunter.

"We didn't stay long, but when we left she asked him to come in whenever he liked. He wasn't really the person to have calling on one: and he knew it, as she did. But he thanked her, and hoped he would one day be able to receive her at her—meaning his—humble house in the Guadalupe Road, where everything was her own. She said: 'Why, sure, I'll come one day. I should love to.' Which he understood, and bowed himself out like some quick but lurking animal: quick as a scorpion, with silence of venom the same.

"After that he would call fairly often, at about five o'clock, but never alone, always with some other man. And he never said anything, always responded to her questions in the same short way, and always looked at her when he was speaking to the other man. He never once *spoke* to her—always spoke to his interpreter, in his flat, coarse Spanish. And he always looked at her when he was speaking to someone else.

"She tried every possible manner in which to touch his imagination: but never with any success. She tried the Indians, the Aztecs, the history of Mexico, politics, Don Porfirio, the bull-ring, love, women, Europe, America—and all in vain. All she got out of him was *Verdad!* He was utterly uninterested. He actually *had* no mental imagination. Talk was just noise to him. The only spark she roused was when she talked of money. Then the queer half-smile deepened on his face, and he asked his interpreter if the Señora was very rich. To which Ethel replied she didn't really know what he meant by rich: he must be rich himself. At which, he asked the interpreter friend if she had more than a million American dollars. To which she replied that perhaps she had—but she wasn't sure. And he looked at her so strangly, even more like a yellow scorpion about to sting.

"I asked him later, what made him put such a crude question? Did he think of offering to marry her? 'Marry a ——?' he replied, using an obscene expression. But I didn't know even then what he really intended. Yet I saw he had her on his mind.

"Ethel was gradually getting into a state of tension. It was as if something tortured her. She seemed like a woman who would go insane. I asked her: 'Why, whatever's wrong with you?' 'I'll tell you, Luis,' she said, 'but don't you say anything to anybody, mind. It's Cuesta! I don't know whether I want him or not.'—'You don't know whether he wants *you* or not,' said I.—'I can handle that,' she said. 'if I know about myself: if I know my own mind. But I don't. My mind says he's a nada-nada, a dumb-bell, no brain, no imagination, no anything. But my body says he's marvellous, and he's got something I haven't got, and he's stronger than I am, and he's more an angel or a devil than a man, and I'm too merely human to get him—and all that, till I feel I shall just go crazy, and take an overdose of drugs. What am I to *do* with my body, I tell you? What am I to *do* with it? I've got to master it. I've got to be *more* than that man. I've got to get all round him, and past him. I've *got* to.'—'Then just take the train to New York to-night, and forget him,' I said.—'I can't! That's side-tracking. I *won't* side-track my body. I've got to get the best of it. I've got to.'—'Well,' I said, 'you're a point or two beyond me. If it's a question of getting all round Cuesta, and getting past him, why, take the train, and you'll forget him in a fortnight. Don't fool yourself you're in love with the fellow.'—'I'm afraid he's stronger than I am,' she cried out.—'And what then? He's stronger than I am, but that doesn't prevent me sleeping. A jaguar even is stronger than I am, and an anaconda could swallow me whole. I tell you, it's all in a day's march. There's a kind of animal called Cuesta. Well, what of it?'

"She looked at me, and I could tell I made no impression on her. She despised me. She sort of wanted to go off the deep end about something. I said to her: 'God's love, Ethel, cut out the Cuesta caprice! It's not even good acting.' But I might just as well have mewed, for all the notice she took of me.

"It was as if some dormant Popocatepetl inside her had begun to erupt. She didn't love the fellow. Yet she was in a blind kill-me-quick sort of state, neither here nor there, nor hot or cold, nor desirous nor undesirous, but just simply *insane.* In a certain kind of way, she seemed to want him. And in a very definite kind of way she seemed *not* to want him. She was in a kind of hysterics, lost her feet altogether. I tried might and main to get her away to the United States. She'd have come sane enough, once she was there. But I thought she'd kill me, when she found I'd been trying to interfere. Oh, she was not quite in her mind, that's sure.

" 'If my body is stronger than my imagination, I shall kill myself,' she said.—'Ethel,' I said, 'people who talk of killing themselves always call a doctor if they cut their finger. What's the quarrel between your body and your imagination? Aren't they the same thing?'—'No!' she said. 'If the imagination has the body under control, you can do anything, it doesn't matter what you do, physically. If my body was under the control of my imagination, I could take Cuesta for my lover, and it would be an imaginative act. But if my body acted without my imagination, I—I'd kill myself.'— 'But what do you mean by your body acting without your imagination?' I said. 'You are not a child. You've been married twice. You know what it means. You even have two children. You must have had at least several lovers. If Cuesta is to be another of your lovers, I think it is deplorable, but I think it only shows you are very much like the other women who fall in love with him. If you've fallen in love with him, your imagination has nothing to do but to accept the fact and put as many roses on the ass's head as you like.' She looked at me very solemnly, and seemed to think about it. Then she said: 'But my imagination has not fallen in love with him. He wouldn't meet me imaginatively. He's a brute. And once I start, where's it going to end? I'm afraid my body has fallen—not fallen in love with him, but fallen *for* him. It's abject! And if I can't get my body on its feet again, and either forget him or else get him to make it an imaginative act with me—I—I shall kill myself'.—'All right,' said I. 'I don't know what you are talking about, imaginative acts and unimaginative acts. The act is always the same.'—'It isn't!' she cried, furious with me. 'It is either imaginative or else it's *impossible*—to me.' Well, I just spread my hands. What could I say, or do? I simply hated her way of putting it. Imaginative act! Why, I would hate performing an imaginative act with a woman. Damn it, the act is either real, or let it alone. But now I knew why I had never even touched her, or kissed her, not once: because I couldn't stand that imaginative sort of bullying from her. It is death to a man.

"I said to Cuesta: 'Why do you go to Ethel? Why don't you stay away, and make her go back to the United States? Are you in love with her?' He was obscene, as usual. 'Am I in love with a cuttlefish, that is all arms and eyes, and no legs or tail! That blonde is a cuttlefish. She is an octopus, all arms and eyes and beak, and a lump of jelly.'—'Then why don't you leave her alone?'—'Even cuttlefish is good when it's cooked in sauce,' he said. 'You had much better leave her alone,' I said.—'Leave her alone yourself, my esteemed Señor,' he said to me. And I knew I had better go no further.

She said to him one evening, when only I was there—and she said it in Spanish, direct to him: 'Why do you never come alone to see me? Why do you always come with another person? Are you afraid?' He looked at her, and his eyes never changed. But he said, in his usual flat, meaningless voice: 'It is because I cannot speak, except Spanish.'—'But we could understand one another,' she said, giving one of her little violent snorts of impatience and embarrassed rage. 'Who knows!' he replied, imperturbably.

"Afterwards, he said to me: 'What does she want? She hates a man as she hates a red-hot iron. A white devil, as sacred as the communion wafer!'—'Then why don't you leave her alone?' I said.—'She is so rich,' he smiled. 'She has all the world in her thousand arms. She is as rich as God. The Archangels are poor beside her, she is so rich and so white-skinned and white-souled.—'Then all the more, why don't you leave her alone?' But he did not answer me.

"He went alone, however, to see her. But always in the early evening. And he never stayed more than half an hour. His car, well-known everywhere, waited outside: till he came out in his French-grey suit and glistening brown shoes, his hat rather on the back of his head.

"What they said to one another, I don't know. But she became always more distraught and absorbed, as if she were brooding over a single idea. I said to her: 'Why take it so seriously? Dozens of women have slept with Cuesta, and think no more of it. Why take him seriously?'—'I don't,' she said. 'I take myself seriously, that's the point.'—'Let it be the point. Go on taking yourself seriously, and leave him out of the question altogether.'

"But she was tired of my playing the wise uncle, and I was tired of her taking herself seriously. She took herself so seriously, it seemed to me she would deserve what she got, playing the fool with Cuesta. Of course she did not love him at all. She only wanted to see if she could make an impression on him, make him yield to her will. But all the impression she made on him was to make him call her a squid and an octopus and other nice things. And I could see their 'love' did not go forward at all.

" 'Have you made love to her?' I asked him.—'I have not touched the zopilote,' he said. 'I hate her bare white neck.'

"But still he went to see her: always, for a very brief call, before sundown. She asked him to come to dinner with me. He said he could never come to dinner, nor after dinner, as he was always engaged from eight o'clock in the evening onwards. She looked at him as much as to tell him she knew it was a lie and a subterfuge, but he never turned a hair. He was, she put it, utterly unimaginative: an impervious animal.

" 'You, however, come one day to your poor house in the Guadalupe Road,' he said—meaning his house. He had said it, suggestively, several times.

" 'But you are always engaged in the evening,' she said.

" 'Come, then, at night—come at eleven, when I am free,' he said, with supreme animal impudence, looking into her eyes.

" 'Do you receive calls so late?' she said, flushing with anger and embarrassment and obstinacy.

" 'At times,' he said. 'When it is very special.'

"A few days later, when I called to see her as usual, I was told she was ill, and could see no one. The next day, she was still not to be seen. She had had a dangerous nervous collapse. The third day, a friend rang me up to say Ethel was dead.

"The thing was hushed up. But it was known she had poisoned herself. She left a note to me, in which she merely said: 'It is as I told you. Good-bye. But my testament holds good.'

"In her will, she had left half her fortune to Cuesta. The will had been made some ten days before her death—and it was allowed to stand. He took the money——"

Colmenares' voice tailed off into silence.

"Her body had got the better of her imagination, after all," I said.

"It was worse than that," he said.

"How?"

He was a long time before he answered. Then he said:

"She actually went to Cuesta's house that night, way down there beyond the Volador market. She went by appointment. And there in his bedroom he handed her over to half a dozen of his bull-ring gang, with orders not to bruise her. Yet at the inquest there were a few deep, strange bruises, and the doctors made reports. Then apparently the visit to Cuesta's house came to light, but no details were ever told. Then there was another revolution, and in the hubbub this affair was dropped. It was too shady, anyhow. Ethel had certainly encouraged Cuesta at her apartment."

"But how do you know he handed her over like that?"

"One of the men told me himself. He was shot afterwards."

THE MAN WHO LOVED ISLANDS

I

THERE was a man who loved islands. He was born on one, but it didn't suit him, as there were too many other people on it, besides himself. He wanted an island all of his own: not necessarily to be alone on it, but to make it a world of his own.

An island, if it is big enough, is no better than a continent. It has to be really quite small, before it *feels* like an island; and this story will show how tiny it has to be, before you can presume to fill it with your own personality.

Now circumstances so worked out that this lover of islands, by the time he was thirty-five, actually acquired an island of his own. He didn't own it as freehold property, but he had a ninety-nine years' lease of it, which, as far as a man and an island are concerned, is as good as everlasting. Since, if you are like Abraham, and want your offspring to be numberless as the sands of the sea-shore, you don't choose an island to start breeding on. Too soon there would be over-population, overcrowding, and slum conditions. Which is a horrid thought, for one who loves an island for its insulation. No, an island is a nest which holds one egg, and one only. This egg is the islander himself.

The island acquired by our potential islander was not in the remote oceans. It was quite near at home, no palm trees nor boom of surf on the reef, nor any of that kind of thing; but a good solid dwelling-house, rather gloomy, above the landing-place, and beyond, a small farmhouse with sheds, and a few outlying fields. Down on the little landing-bay were three cottages in a row, like coastguards' cottages, all neat and whitewashed.

What could be more cosy and home-like? It was four miles if you walked all round your island, through the gorse and the blackthorn bushes, above the steep rocks of the sea and down in the little glades where the primroses grew. If you walked straight over the two humps of hills, the length of it, through the rocky fields where the cows lay chewing, and through the rather sparse oats, on into the gorse again, and so to the low cliffs' edge, it took you only twenty minutes. And when you came to the edge, you could see another, bigger island lying beyond. But the sea was between you and it. And as you returned over the turf where the short, downland cowslips nodded, you saw to the east still another island, a tiny one this time, like the calf of the cow. This tiny island also belonged to the islander.

Thus it seems that even islands like to keep each other company.

Our islander loved his island very much. In early spring, the little ways and glades were a snow of blackthorn, a vivid white among the Celtic stillness of close green and grey rock, blackbirds calling out in the whiteness their first long, triumphant calls. After the blackthorn and the nestling primroses came the blue apparition of hyacinths, like elfin lakes and slipping sheets of blue, among the bushes and under the glade of trees. And many birds with nests you could peep into, on the island all your own. Wonderful what a great world it was!

Followed summer, and the cowslips gone, the wild roses faintly fragrant through the haze. There was a field of hay, the foxgloves stood looking down. In a little cove, the sun was on the pale granite where you bathed, and the shadow was in the rocks. Before the mist came stealing, you went home through the ripening oats, the glare of the sea fading from the high air as the fog-horn started to moo on the other island. And then the sea-fog went, it was autumn, the oatsheaves lying prone, the great moon, another island, rose golden out of the sea, and rising higher, the world of the sea was white.

So autumn ended with rain, and winter came, dark skies and dampness and rain, but rarely frost. The island, your island, cowered dark, holding away from you. You could feel, down in the wet, sombre hollows, the resentful spirit coiled upon itself, like a wet dog coiled in gloom, or a snake that is neither asleep nor awake. Then in the night, when the wind left off blowing in great gusts and volleys, as at sea, you felt that your island was a universe, infinite and old as the darkness; not an island at all, but an infinite dark world where all the souls from all the other bygone nights lived on, and the infinite distance was near.

Strangely, from your little island in space, you were gone forth into the dark, great realms of time, where all the souls that never die veer and swoop on their vast, strange errands. The little earthly island has dwindled, like a jumping-off place, into nothingness, for you have jumped off, you know not how, into the dark wide mystery of time, where the past is vastly alive, and the future is not separated off.

This is the danger of becoming an islander. When, in the city, you wear your white spats and dodge the traffic with the fear of death down your spine, then you are quite safe from the terrors of infinite time. The moment is your little islet in time, it is the spatial universe that careers round you.

But once isolate yourself on a little island in the sea of space, and the moment begins to heave and expand in great circles, the solid earth is gone, and your slippery, naked dark soul finds herself out in the timeless world, where the chariots of the so-called dead dash down the old streets of centuries, and souls crowd on the footways that we, in the moment, call bygone years. The souls of all the dead are alive again, and pulsating actively around you. You are out in the other infinity.

Something of this happened to our islander. Mysterious 'feelings' came upon him that he wasn't used to; strange awarenesses of old, far-gone men, and other influences; men of Gaul, with big moustaches, who had been on his island, and had vanished from the face of it, but not out of the air of night. They were there still, hurtling their big, violent, unseen bodies through the night. And there were priests, with golden knives and mistletoe; then other priests with a crucifix; then pirates with murder on the sea.

Our islander was uneasy. He didn't believe, in the day-time, in any of this nonsense. But at night it just was so. He had reduced himself to a single point in space, and, a point being that which has neither length nor breadth, he had to step off it into somewhere else. Just as you must step into the sea, if the waters wash your foothold away, so he had, at night, to step off into the other worlds of undying time.

He was uncannily aware, as he lay in the dark, that the blackthorn grove that seemed a bit uncanny even in the realm of space and day, at night was crying with old men of an invisible race, around the altar stone. What was a ruin under the hornbeam trees by day, was a moaning of blood-stained

priests with crucifixes, on the ineffable night. What was a
cave and a hidden beach between coarse rocks, became in the
invisible dark the purple-lipped imprecation of pirates.

To escape any more of this sort of awareness, our islander
daily concentrated upon his material island. Why should it
not be the Happy Isle at last? Why not the last small isle of
the Hesperides, the perfect place, all filled with his own
gracious, blossom-like spirit? A minute world of pure perfection, made by man himself.

He began, as we begin all our attempts to regain Paradise,
by spending money. The old, semi-feudal dwelling-house he
restored, let in more light, put clear lovely carpets on the
floor, clear, flower-petal curtains at the sullen windows, and
wines in the cellars of rock. He brought over a buxom housekeeper from the world, and a soft-spoken, much-experienced
butler. These two were to be islanders.

In the farmhouse he put a bailiff, with two farm-hands.
There were Jersey cows, tinkling a slow bell, among the gorse.
There was a call to meals at midday, and the peaceful smoking
of chimneys at evening, when rest descended.

A jaunty sailing-boat with a motor accessory rode in the
shelter in the bay, just below the row of three white cottages.
There was also a little yawl, and two row-boats drawn up on
the sand. A fishing-net was drying on its supports, a boat-
load of new white planks stood criss-cross, a woman was
going to the well with a bucket.

In the end cottage lived the skipper of the yacht, and his
wife and son. He was a man from the other, large island, at
home on this sea. Every fine day he went out fishing, with
his son, every fair day there was fresh fish in the island.

In the middle cottage lived an old man and wife, a very
faithful couple. The old man was a carpenter, and man of
many jobs. He was always working, always the sound of his
plane or his saw; lost in his work, he was another kind of
islander.

In the third cottage was a mason, a widower with a son and
two daughters. With the help of his boy, this man dug ditches
and built fences, raised buttresses and erected a new out-
building, and hewed stone from the little quarry. One
daughter worked at the big house.

It was a quiet, busy little world. When the islander brought
you over as his guest, you met first the dark-bearded, thin,

smiling skipper, Arnold, then his boy Charles. At the house, the smooth-lipped butler who had lived all over the world valeted you, and created that curious creamy-smooth, disarming sense of luxury around you which only a perfect and rather untrustworthy servant can create. He disarmed you and had you at his mercy. The buxom housekeeper smiled and treated you with the subtly respectful familiarity that is only dealt out to the true gentry. And the rosy maid threw a glance at you, as if you were very wonderful, coming from the great outer world. Then you met the smiling but watchful bailiff, who came from Cornwall, and the shy farm-hand from Berkshire, with his clean wife and two little children: then the rather sulky farm-hand from Suffolk. The mason, a Kent man, would talk to you by the yard if you let him. Only the old carpenter was gruff and elsewhere absorbed.

Well then, it was a little world to itself, and everybody feeling very safe, and being very nice to you, as if you were really something special. But it was the islander's world, not yours. He was the Master. The special smile, the special attention was to the Master. They all knew how well off they were. So the islander was no longer Mr. So-and-so. To everyone on the island, even to you yourself, he was 'the Master'.

Well, it was ideal. The Master was no tyrant. Ah, no! He was a delicate, sensitive, handsome Master, who wanted everything perfect and everybody happy. Himself, of course, to be the fount of this happiness and perfection.

But in his way, he was a poet. He treated his guests royally, his servants liberally. Yet he was shrewd, and very wise. He never came the boss over his people. Yet he kept his eye on everything, like a shrewd, blue-eyed young Hermes. And it was amazing what a lot of knowledge he had at hand. Amazing what he knew about Jersey cows, and cheese-making, ditching and fencing, flowers and gardening, ships and the sailing of ships. He was a fount of knowledge about everything, and this knowledge he imparted to his people in an odd, half-ironical, half-portentous fashion, as if he really belonged to the quaint, half-real world of the gods.

They listened to him with their hats in their hands. He loved white clothes; or creamy white; and cloaks, and broad hats. So, in fine weather, the bailiff would see the elegant tall figure in creamy-white serge coming like some bird over the fallow, to look at the weeding of the turnips. Then there would be a doffing of hats, and a few minutes of whimsical, shrewd, wise talk, to which the bailiff answered admiringly, and the farm-hands listened in silent wonder, leaning on their hoes. The bailiff was almost tender, to the Master.

Or, on a windy morning, he would stand with his cloak blowing in the sticky sea-wind, on the edge of the ditch that was being dug to drain a little swamp, talking in the teeth of the wind to the man below, who looked up at him with steady and inscrutable eyes.

Or at evening in the rain he would be seen hurrying across the yard, the broad hat turned against the rain. And the farm-wife would hurriedly exclaim: "The Master! Get up, John, and clear him a place on the sofa." And then the door opened, and it was a cry of: "Why, of all things, if it isn't the Master! Why, have ye turned out then, of a night like this, to come across to the like of we?" And the bailiff took his cloak, and the farm-wife his hat, the two farm-hands drew their chairs to the back, he sat on the sofa and took a child up near him. He was wonderful with children, talked to them simply wonderful, made you think of Our Saviour Himself, said the woman.

He was always greeted with smiles, and the same peculiar deference, as if he were a higher, but also frailer being. They handled him almost tenderly, and almost with adulation. But when he left, or when they spoke of him, they had often a subtle, mocking smile on their faces. There was no need to be afraid of 'the Master'. Just let him have his own way. Only the old carpenter was sometimes sincerely rude to him; so he didn't care for the old man.

It is doubtful whether any of them really liked him, man to man, or even woman to man. But then it is doubtful if he really liked any of them, as man to man, or man to woman. He wanted them to be happy, and the little world to be perfect. But anyone who wants the world to be perfect must be careful not to have real likes or dislikes. A general goodwill is all you can afford.

The sad fact is, alas, that general goodwill is always felt as something of an insult, by the mere object of it; and so it breeds a quite special brand of malice, Surely general good-will is a form of egoism, that it should have such a result!

Our islander, however, had his own resources. He spent

long hours in his library, for he was compiling a book of references to all the flowers mentioned in the Greek and Latin authors. He was not a great classical scholar; the usual public-school equipment. But there are such excellent translations nowadays. And it was so lovely, tracing flower after flower as it blossomed in the ancient world.

So the first year on the island passed by. A great deal had been done. Now the bills flooded in, and the Master, conscientious in all things, began to study them. The study left him pale and breathless. He was not a rich man. He knew he had been making a hole in his capital to get the island into running order. When he came to look, however, there was hardly anything left but hole. Thousands and thousands of pounds had the island swallowed into nothingness.

But surely the bulk of the spending was over! Surely the island would now begin to be self-supporting, even if it made no profit! Surely he was safe. He paid a good many of the bills, and took a little heart. But he had had a shock, and the next year, the coming year, there must be economy, frugality. He told his people so in simple and touching language. And they said: "Why, surely! Surely!"

So, while the wind blew and the rain lashed outside, he would sit in his library with the bailiff over a pipe and pot of beer, discussing farm projects. He lifted his narrow, handsome face, and his blue eyes became dreamy. "*What* a wind!" It blew like cannon-shots. He thought of his island, lashed with foam, and inaccessible, and he exulted. . . . No, he must not lose it. He turned back to the farm projects with the zest of genius, and his hands flicked white emphasis, while the bailiff intoned: "Yes, sir! Yes, sir! You're right, Master!"

But the man was hardly listening. He was looking at the Master's blue lawn shirt and curious pink tie with the fiery red stone, at the enamel sleeve-links, and at the ring with the peculiar scarab. The brown searching eyes of the man of the soil glanced repeatedly over the fine, immaculate figure of the Master, with a sort of slow, calculating wonder. But if he happened to catch the Master's bright, exalted glance, his own eye lit up with a careful cordiality and deference, as he bowed his head slightly.

Thus between them they decided what crops should be sown, what fertilizers should be used in different places, which breed of pigs should be imported, and which line of turkeys.

That is to say, the bailiff, by continually cautiously agreeing with the Master, kept out of it, and let the young man have his own way.

The Master knew what he was talking about. He was brilliant at grasping the gist of a book, and knowing how to apply his knowledge. On the whole, his ideas were sound. The bailiff even knew it. But in the man of the soil there was no answering enthusiasm. The brown eyes smiled their cordial deference, but the thin lips never changed. The Master pursed his own flexible mouth in a boyish versatility, as he cleverly sketched in his ideas to the other man, and the bailiff made eyes of admiration, but in his heart he was not attending, he was only watching the Master as he would have watched a queer, caged animal, quite without sympathy, not implicated.

So, it was settled, and the Master rang for Elvery, the butler, to bring a sandwich. He, the Master, was pleased. The butler saw it, and came back with anchovy and ham sandwiches, and a newly opened bottle of vermouth. There was always a newly opened bottle of something.

It was the same with the mason. The Master and he discussed the drainage of a bit of land, and more pipes were ordered, more special bricks, more this, more that.

Fine weather came at last; there was a little lull in the hard work on the island. The Master went for a short cruise in his yacht. It was not really a yacht, just a little bit of a thing. They sailed along the coast of the mainland, and put in at the ports. At every port some friend turned up, the butler made elegant little meals in the cabin. Then the Master was invited to villas and hotels, his people disembarked him as if he were a prince.

And oh, how expensive it turned out! He had to telegraph to the bank for money. And he went home again to economise.

The marsh-marigolds were blazing in the little swamp where the ditches were being dug for drainage. He almost regretted, now, the work in hand. The yellow beauties would not blaze again.

Harvest came, and a bumper crop. There must be a harvest-home supper. The long barn was now completely restored and added to. The carpenter had made long tables. Lanterns hung from the beams of the high-pitched roof. All the people of the island were assembled. The bailiff presided. It was a gay scene.

Towards the end of the supper the Master, in a velvet jacket, appeared with his guests. Then the bailiff rose and proposed "The Master! Long life and health to the Master!" All the people drank the health with great enthusiasm and cheering. The Master replied with a little speech: They were on an island in a little world of their own. It depended on them all to make this world a world of true happiness and content Each must do his part. He hoped he himself did what he could, for his heart was in his island, and with the people of his island.

The butler responded: As long as the island had such a Master, it could not help but be a little heaven for all the people on it. This was seconded with virile warmth by the bailiff and the mason, the skipper was beside himself. Then there was dancing, the old carpenter was fiddler.

But under all this, things were not well. The very next morning came the farm-boy to say that a cow had fallen over the cliff. The Master went to look. He peered over the not very high declivity, and saw her lying dead on a green ledge under a bit of late-flowering broom. A beautiful, expensive creature, already looking swollen. But what a fool, to fall so unnecessarily!

It was a question of getting several men to haul her up the bank, and then of skinning and burying her. No one would eat the meat. How repulsive it all was!

This was symbolic of the island. As sure as the spirits rose in the human breast, with a movement of joy, an invisible hand struck malevolently out of the silence. There must not be any joy, nor even any quiet peace. A man broke a leg, another was crippled with rheumatic fever. The pigs had some strange disease. A storm drove the yacht on a rock. The mason hated the butler, and refused to let his daughter serve at the house.

Out of the very air came a stony, heavy malevolence. The island itself seemed malicious. It would go on being hurtful and evil for weeks at a time. Then suddenly again one morning it would be fair, lovely as a morning in Paradise, everything beautiful and flowing. And everybody would begin to feel a great relief, and a hope for happiness.

Then as soon as the Master was opened out in spirit like an

open flower, some ugly blow would fall. Somebody would
send him an anonymous note, accusing some other person on
the island. Somebody else would come hinting things against
one of his servants.

"Some folks think they've got an easy job out here, with
all the pickings they make!" the mason's daughter screamed
at the suave butler, in the Master's hearing. He pretended not
to hear.

"My man says this island is surely one of the lean kine of
Egypt, it would swallow a sight of money, and you'd never
get anything back out of it," confided the farm-hand's wife
to one of the Master's visitors.

The people were not contented. They were not islanders.
"We feel we're not doing right by the children," said those
who had children. "We feel we're not doing right by our-
selves," said those who had no children. And the various
families fairly came to hate one another.

Yet the island was so lovely. When there was a scent of
honeysuckle and the moon brightly flickering down on the
sea, then even the grumblers felt a strange nostalgia for it. It
set you yearning, with a wild yearning; perhaps for the past,
to be far back in the mysterious past of the island, when the
blood had a different throb. Strange floods of passion came
over you, strange violent lusts and imaginations of cruelty.
The blood and the passion and the lust which the island
had known. Uncanny dreams, half-dreams, half-evocated
yearnings.

The Master himself began to be a little afraid of his island.
He felt here strange, violent feelings he had never felt before,
and lustful desires that he had been quite free from. He knew
quite well now that his people didn't love him at all. He
knew that their spirits were secretly against him, malicious,
jeering, envious, and lurking to down him. He became just
as wary and secretive with regard to them.

But it was too much. At the end of the second year, several
departures took place. The housekeeper went. The Master
always blamed self-important women most. The mason said
he wasn't going to be monkeyed about any more, so he took
his departure, with his family. The rheumatic farm-hand left.

And then the year's bills came in, the Master made up his
accounts. In spite of good crops, the assets were ridiculous,
against the spending. The island had again lost, not hundreds

but thousands of pounds. It was incredible. But you simply couldn't believe it! Where had it all gone?

The Master spent gloomy nights and days going through accounts in the library. He was thorough. It became evident, now the housekeeper had gone, that she had swindled him. Probably everybody was swindling him. But he hated to think it, so he put the thought away.

He emerged, however, pale and hollow-eyed from his balancing of unbalanceable accounts, looking as if something had kicked him in the stomach. It was pitiable. But the money had gone, and there was an end of it. Another great hole in his capital. How could people be so heartless?

It couldn't go on, that was evident. He would soon be bankrupt. He had to give regretful notice to his butler. He was afraid to find out how much his butler had swindled him. Because the man was such a wonderful butler, after all. And the farm bailiff had to go. The Master had no regrets in that quarter. The losses on the farm had almost embittered him.

The third year was spent in rigid cutting down of expenses. The island was still mysterious and fascinating. But it was also treacherous and cruel, secretly, fathomlessly malevolent. In spite of all its fair show of white blossom and bluebells, and the lovely dignity of foxgloves bending their rose-red bells, it was your implacable enemy.

With reduced staff, reduced wages, reduced splendour, the third year went by. But it was fighting against hope. The farm still lost a good deal. And once more there was a hole in that remnant of capital. Another hole in that which was already a mere remnant round the old holes. The island was mysterious in this also: it seemed to pick the very money out of your pocket, as if it were an octopus with invisible arms stealing from you in every direction.

Yet the Master still loved it. But with a touch of rancour now.

He spent, however, the second half of the fourth year intensely working on the mainland, to be rid of it. And it was amazing how difficult he found it, to dispose of an island. He had thought that everybody was pining for such an island as his; but not at all. Nobody would pay any price for it. And he wanted now to get rid of it, as a man who wants a divorce at any cost.

It was not till the middle of the fifth year that he transferred it, at a considerable loss to himself, to an hotel company who were willing to speculate in it. They were to turn it into a handy honeymoon-and-golf island.

There, take that, island which didn't know when it was well off. Now be a honeymoon-and-golf island!

II

THE SECOND ISLAND

The islander had to move. But he was not going to the mainland. Oh, no! He moved to the smaller island, which still belonged to him. And he took with him the faithful old carpenter and wife, the couple he never really cared for; also a widow and daughter, who had kept house for him the last year; also an orphan lad, to help the old man.

The small island was very small; but being a hump of rock in the sea, it was bigger than it looked. There was a little track among the rocks and bushes, winding and scrambling up and down around the islet, so that it took you twenty minutes to do the circuit. It was more than you would have expected.

Still, it was an island. The islander moved himself, with all his books, into the commonplace six-roomed house up to which you had to scramble from the rocky landing-place. There were also two joined-together cottages. The old carpenter lived in one, with his wife and the lad, the widow and daughter lived in the other.

At last all was in order. The Master's books filled two rooms. It was already autumn, Orion lifting out of the sea. And in the dark nights, the Master could see the lights on his late island, where the hotel company were entertaining guests who would advertise the new resort for honeymoon-golfers.

On his lump of rock, however, the Master was still master. He explored the crannies, the odd hand-breadths of grassy level, the steep little cliffs where the last harebells hung and the seeds of summer were brown above the sea, lonely and untouched. He peered down the old well. He examined the stone pen where the pig had been kept. Himself, he had a goat.

Yes, it was an island. Always, always underneath among

the rocks the Celtic sea sucked and washed and smote its feathery greyness. How many different noises of the sea! Deep explosions, rumblings, strange long sighs and whistling noises; then voices, real voices of people clamouring as if they were in a market, under the waters: and again, the far-off ringing of a bell, surely an actual bell! Then a tremendous trilling noise, very long and alarming, and an undertone of hoarse gasping.

On this island there were no human ghosts, no ghosts of any ancient race. The sea, and the spume and the weather, had washed them all out, washed them out so there was only the sound of the sea itself, its own ghost, myriad-voiced, communing and plotting and shouting all winter long. And only the smell of the sea, with a few bristly bushes of gorse and coarse tufts of heather, among the grey, pellucid rocks, in the grey, more-pellucid air. The coldness, the greyness, even the soft, creeping fog of the sea, and the islet of rock humped up in it all, like the last point in space.

Green star Sirius stood over the sea's rim. The island was a shadow. Out at sea a ship showed small lights. Below, in the rocky cove, the row-boat and the motor-boat were safe. A light shone in the carpenter's kitchen. That was all.

Save, of course, that the lamp was lit in the house, where the widow was preparing supper, her daughter helping. The islander went in to his meal. Here he was no longer the Master, he was an islander again and he had peace. The old carpenter, the widow and daughter were all faithfulness itself. The old man worked while ever there was light to see, because he had a passion for work. The widow and her quiet, rather delicate daughter of thirty-three worked for the Master, because they loved looking after him, and they were infinitely grateful for the haven he provided them. But they didn't call him 'the Master'. They gave him his name: 'Mr. Cathcart, sir!' softly and reverently. And he spoke back to them also softly, gently, like people far from the world, afraid to make a noise.

The island was no longer a 'world'. It was a sort of refuge. The islander no longer struggled for anything. He had no need. It was as if he and his few dependents were a small flock of sea-birds alighted on this rock, as they travelled through space, and keeping together without a word. The silent mystery of travelling birds.

He spent most of his day in his study. His book was coming along. The widow's daughter could type out his manuscript for him, she was not uneducated. It was the one strange sound on the island, the typewriter. But soon even its spattering fitted in with the sea's noises, and the wind's.

The months went by. The islander worked away in his study, the people of the island went quietly about their concerns. The goat had a little black kid with yellow eyes. There were mackerel in the sea. The old man went fishing in the row-boat with the lad, when the weather was calm enough; they went off in the motor-boat to the biggest island for the post. And they brought supplies, never a penny wasted. And the days went by, and the nights, without desire, without ennui.

The strange stillness from all desire was a kind of wonder to the islander. He didn't want anything. His soul at last was still in him, his spirit was like a dim-lit cave under water, where strange sea-foliage expands upon the watery atmosphere, and scarcely sways, and a mute fish shadowily slips in and slips away again. All still and soft and uncrying, yet alive as rooted seaweed is alive.

The islander said to himself: "Is this happiness?" He said to himself: "I am turned into a dream. I feel nothing, or I don't know what I feel. Yet it seems to me I am happy."

Only he had to have something upon which his mental activity could work. So he spent long, silent hours in his study, working not very fast, nor very importantly, letting the writing spin softly from him as if it were drowsy gossamer. He no longer fretted whether it were good or not, what he produced. He slowly, softly spun it like gossamer, and if it were to melt away as gossamer in autumn melts, he would not mind. It was only the soft evanescence of gossamy things which now seemed to him permanent. The very mist of eternity was in them. Whereas stone buildings, cathedrals for example, seemed to him to howl with temporary resistance, knowing they must fall at last; the tension of their long endurance seemed to howl forth from them all the time.

Sometimes he went to the mainland and to the city. Then he went elegantly, dressed in the latest style, to his club. He sat in a stall at the theatre, he shopped in Bond Street. He discussed terms for publishing his book. But over his face was that gossamy look of having dropped out of the race of progress, which made the vulgar city people feel they had won it over him, and made him glad to go back to his island.

He didn't mind if he never published his book. The years were blending into a soft mist, from which nothing obtruded. Spring came. There was never a primrose on his island, but he found a winter-aconite. There were two little sprayed bushes of blackthorn, and some wind-flowers. He began to make a list of the flowers of his islet, and that was absorbing. He noted a wild currant bush and watched for the elder flowers on a stunted little tree, then for the first yellow rags of the broom, and wild roses. Bladder campion, orchids stitchwort, celandine, he was prouder of them than if they had been people on his island. When he came across the golden saxifrage, so inconspicuous in a damp corner, he crouched over it in a trance, he knew not for how long, looking at it. Yet it was nothing to look at. As the widow's daughter found, when he showed it her.

He had said to her in real triumph:

"I found the golden saxifrage this morning."

The name sounded splendid. She looked at him with fascinated brown eyes, in which was a hollow ache that frightened him a little.

"Did you, sir? Is it a nice flower?"

He pursed his lips and tilted his brows.

"Well—not showy exactly. I'll show it you if you like."

"I should like to see it."

She was so quiet, so wistful. But he sensed in her a persistency which made him uneasy. She said she was so happy: really happy. She followed him quietly, like a shadow, on the rocky track where there was never room for two people to walk side by side. He went first, and could feel her there, immediately behind him, following so submissively, gloating on him from behind.

It was a kind of pity for her which made him become her lover: though he never realised the extent of the power she had gained over him, and how *she* willed it. But the moment he had fallen, a jangling feeling came upon him, that it was all wrong. He felt a nervous dislike of her. He had not wanted it. And it seemed to him, as far as her physical self went, she had not wanted it either. It was just her will. He went away, and climbed at the risk of his neck down to a ledge near the sea. There he sat for hours, gazing all jangled at the sea, and saying miserably to himself: "We didn't want it. We didn't really want it."

It was the automatism of sex that had caught him again. Not that he hated sex. He deemed it, as the Chinese do, one of the great life-mysteries. But it had become mechanical, automatic, and he wanted to escape that. Automatic sex shattered him, and filled him with a sort of death. He thought he had come through, to a new stillness of desire-lessness. Perhaps beyond that there was a new fresh delicacy of desire, an unentered frail communion of two people meeting on untrodden ground.

Be that as it might, this was not it. This was nothing new or fresh. It was automatic, and driven from the will. Even she, in her true self, hadn't wanted it. It was automatic in her.

When he came home, very late, and saw her face white with fear and apprehension of his feeling against her, he pitied her, and spoke to her delicately, reassuringly. But he kept himself remote from her.

She gave no sign. She served him with the same silence, the same hidden hunger to serve him, to be near where he was. He felt her love following him with strange, awful persistency. She claimed nothing. Yet now, when he met her bright, brown, curiously vacant eyes, he saw in them the mute question. The question came direct at him, with a force and a power of will he never realised.

So he succumbed, and asked her again.

"Not," she said, "if it will make you hate me."

"Why should it?" he replied, nettled. "Of course not."

"You know I would do anything on earth for you."

It was only afterwards, in his exasperation, he remembered what she said, and was more exasperated. Why should she pretend to do this *for him?* Why not herself? But in his exasperation, he drove himself deeper in. In order to achieve some sort of satisfaction, which he never did achieve, he abandoned himself to her. Everybody on the island knew. But he did not care.

Then even what desire he had left him, and he felt only shattered. He felt that only with her will had she wanted him. Now he was shattered and full of self-contempt. His island was smirched and spoiled. He had lost his place in the rare, desireless levels of Time to which he had at last arrived, and he had fallen right back. If only it had been true, delicate desire between them, and a delicate meeting on the third rare place where a man might meet a woman, when they were both true to the frail, sensitive, crocus-flame of desire in them. But it had been no such thing: automatic, an act of will, not of true desire, it left him feeling humiliated.

He went away from the islet, in spite of her mute reproach. And he wandered about the continent, vainly seeking a place where he could stay. He was out of key; he did not fit in the world any more.

There came a letter from Flora—her name was Flora—to say she was afraid she was going to have a child. He sat down as if he were shot, and he remained sitting. But he replied to her: "Why be afraid? If it is so, it is so, and we should rather be pleased than afraid."

At this very moment, it happened there was an auction of islands. He got the maps, and studied them. And at the auction he bought, for very little money, another island. It was just a few acres of rock away in the north, on the outer fringe of the isles. It was low, it rose low out of the great ocean. There was not a building, not even a tree on it. Only northern sea-turf, a pool of rain-water, a bit of sedge, rock, and sea-birds. Nothing else. Under the weeping wet western sky.

He made a trip to visit his new possession. For several days, owing to the seas, he could not approach it. Then, in a light sea-mist, he landed, and saw it hazy, low, stretching apparently a long way. But it was illusion. He walked over the wet, springy turf, and dark-grey sheep tossed away from him, spectral, bleating hoarsely. And he came to the dark pool, with the sedge. Then on in the dampness, to the grey sea sucking angrily among the rocks.

This was indeed an island.

So he went home to Flora. She looked at him with guilty fear, but also with a triumphant brightness in her uncanny eyes. And again he was gentle, he reassured her, even he wanted her again, with that curious desire that was almost like toothache. So he took her to the mainland, and they were married, since she was going to have his child.

They returned to the island. She still brought in his meals, her own along with then. She sat and ate with him. He would have it so. The widowed mother preferred to stay in the kitchen. And Flora slept in the guest-room of his house, mistress of his house.

His desire, whatever it was, died in him with nauseous finality. The child would still be months coming. His island was hateful to him, vulgar, a suburb. He himself had lost all his finer distinction. The weeks passed in a sort of prison, in humiliation. Yet he stuck it out, till the child was born. But he was meditating escape. Flora did not even know.

A nurse appeared, and ate at table with them. The doctor came sometimes, and, if the sea were rough, he too had to stay. He was cheery over his whisky.

They might have been a young couple in Golders Green.

The daughter was born at last. The father looked at the baby, and felt depressed, almost more than he could bear. The millstone was tied round his neck. But he tried not to show what he felt. And Flora did not know. She still smiled with a kind of half-witted triumph in her joy, as she got well again. Then she began again to look at him with those aching, suggestive, somehow impudent eyes. She adored him so.

This he could not stand. He told her that he had to go away for a time. She wept, but she thought she had got him. He told her he had settled the best part of his property on her, and wrote down for her what income it would produce. She hardly listened, only looked at him with those heavy, adoring, impudent eyes. He gave her a cheque-book, with the amount of her credit duly entered. This did arouse her interest. And he told her, if she got tired of the island, she could choose her home wherever she wished.

She followed him with those aching, persistent brown eyes, when he left, and he never even saw her weep.

He went straight north, to prepare his third island.

III

THE THIRD ISLAND

The third island was soon made habitable. With cement and the big pebbles from the shingle beach, two men built him a hut, and roofed it with corrugated iron. A boat brought over a bed and table, and three chairs, with a good cupboard, and a few books. He laid in a supply of coal and paraffin and food—he wanted so little.

The house stood near the flat shingle bay where he landed,

and where he pulled up his light boat. On a sunny day in August the men sailed away and left him. The sea was still and pale blue. On the horizon he saw the small mail-steamer slowly passing northwards, as if she were walking. She served the outer isles twice a week. He could row out to her if need be, in calm weather, and he could signal her from a flagstaff behind his cottage.

Half a dozen sheep still remained on the island, as company; and he had a cat to rub against his legs. While the sweet, sunny days of the northern autumn lasted, he would walk among the rocks, and over the springy turf of his small domain, always coming to the ceaseless, restless sea. He looked at every leaf, that might be different from another, and he watched the endless expansion and contraction of the water-tossed seaweed. He had never a tree, not even a bit of heather to guard. Only the turf, and tiny turf-plants, and the sedge by the pool, the seaweed in the ocean. He was glad. He didn't want trees or bushes. They stood up like people, too assertive. His bare, low-pitched island in the pale blue sea was all he wanted.

He no longer worked at his book. The interest had gone. He liked to sit on the low elevation of his island, and see the sea; nothing but the pale, quiet sea. And to feel his mind turn soft and hazy, like the hazy ocean. Sometimes, like a mirage, he would see the shadow of land rise hovering to northwards. It was a big island beyond. But quite without substance.

He was soon almost startled when he perceived the steamer on the near horizon, and his heart contracted with fear, lest it were going to pause and molest him. Anxiously he watched it go, and not till it was out of sight did he feel truly relieved, himself again. The tension of waiting for human approach was cruel. He did not want to be approached. He did not want to hear voices. He was shocked by the sound of his own voice, if he inadvertently spoke to his cat. He rebuked himself for having broken the great silence. And he was irritated when his cat would look up at him and mew faintly, plaintively. He frowned at her. And she knew. She was becoming wild, lurking in the rocks, perhaps fishing.

But what he disliked most was when one of the lumps of sheep opened its mouth and baa-ed its hoarse, raucous baa. He watched it, and it looked to him hideous and gross. He came to dislike the sheep very much.

He wanted only to hear the whispering sound of the sea, and

the sharp cries of the gulls, cries that came out of another world to him. And best of all, the great silence.

He decided to get rid of the sheep when the boat came. They were accustomed to him now, and stood and stared at him with yellow or colourless eyes, in an insolence that was almost cold ridicule. There was a suggestion of cold indecency about them. He disliked them very much. And when they jumped with staccato jumps off the rocks, and their hoofs made the dry, sharp hit, and the fleece flopped on their square backs, he found them repulsive, degrading.

The fine weather passed, and it rained all day. He lay a great deal on his bed, listening to the water trickling from his roof into the zinc water-butt, looking through the open door at the rain, the dark rocks, the hidden sea. Many gulls were on the island now: many sea-birds of all sorts. It was another world of life. Many of the birds he had never seen before. His old impulse came over him, to send for a book, to know their names. In a flicker of the old passion, to know the name of everything he saw, he even decided to row out to the steamer. The names of these birds! He must know their names, otherwise he had not got them, they were not quite alive to him.

But the desire left him, and he merely watched the birds as they wheeled or walked around him, watched them vaguely, without discrimination. All interest had left him. Only there was one gull, a big, handsome fellow, who would walk back and forth, back and forth in front of the open door of the cabin, as if he had some mission there. He was big, and pearl-grey, and his roundnesses were as smooth and lovely as a pearl. Only the folded wings had shut black pinions, and on the closed black feathers were three very distinct white dots, making a pattern. The islander wondered very much, why this bit of trimming on the bird out of the far, cold seas. And as the gull walked back and forth, back and forth in front of the cabin, strutting on pale-dusky gold feet, holding up his pale yellow beak, that was curved at the tip, with curious alien importance, the man wondered over him. He was portentous, he had a meaning.

Then the bird came no more. The island, which had been full of sea-birds, the flash of wings, the sound and cut of wings and sharp eerie cries in the air, began to be deserted again. No longer they sat like living eggs on the rocks and turf, moving their heads, but scarcely rising into flight round his feet. No longer they ran across the turf among the sheep, and lifted themselves upon low wings. The host had gone. But some remained, always.

The days shortened, and the world grew eerie. One day the boat came: as if suddenly, swooping down. The islander found it a violation. It was torture to talk to those two men, in their homely clumsy clothes. The air of familiarity around them was very repugnant to him. Himself, he was neatly dressed, his cabin was neat and tidy. He resented any intrusion, the clumsy homeliness, the heavy-footedness of the two fishermen was really repulsive to him.

The letters they had brought he left lying unopened in a little box. In one of them was his money. But he could not bear to open even that one. Any kind of contact was repulsive to him. Even to read his name on an envelope. He hid the letters away.

And the hustle and horror of getting the sheep caught and tied and put in the ship made him loathe with profound repulsion the whole of the animal creation. What repulsive god invented animals and evil-smelling men? To his nostrils, the fishermen and the sheep alike smelled foul; an uncleanness on the fresh earth.

He was still nerve-racked and tortured when the ship at last lifted sail and was drawing away, over the still sea. And sometimes, days after, he would start with repulsion, thinking he heard the munching of sheep.

The dark days of winter drew on. Sometimes there was no real day at all He felt ill, as if he were dissolving, as if dissolution had already set in inside him. Everything was twilight, outside, and in his mind and soul. Once, when he went to the door, he saw black heads of men swimming in his bay. For some moments he swooned unconscious. It was the shock, the horror of unexpected human approach. The horror in the twilight! And not till the shock had undermined him and left him disembodied, did he realise that the black heads were the heads of seals swimming in. A sick relief came over him. But he was barely conscious, after the shock. Later on, he sat and wept with gratitude, because they were not men. But he never realised that he wept. He was too dim. Like some strange, ethereal animal, he no longer realised what he was doing.

Only he still derived his single satisfaction from being

alone, absolutely alone, with the space soaking into him. The grey sea alone, and the footing of his sea-washed island. No other contact. Nothing human to bring its horror into contact with him. Only space, damp, twilit, sea-washed space! This was the bread of his soul.

For this reason, he was most glad when there was a storm, or when the sea was high. Then nothing could get at him. Nothing could come through to him from the outer world. True, the terrific violence of the wind made him suffer badly. At the same time, it swept the world utterly out of existence for him. He always liked the sea to be heavily rolling and tearing. Then no boat could get at him. It was like eternal ramparts round his island.

He kept no track of time, and no longer thought of opening a book. The print, the printed letters, so like the depravity of speech, looked obscene. He tore the brass label from his paraffin stove. He obliterated any bit of lettering in his cabin.

His cat had disappeared. He was rather glad. He shivered at her thin, obtrusive call. She had lived in the coal-shed. And each morning he had put her a dish of porridge, the same as he ate. He washed her saucer with repulsion. He did not like her writhing about. But he fed her scrupulously. Then one day she did not come for her porridge; she always mewed for it. She did not come again.

He prowled about his island in the rain, in a big oilskin coat, not knowing what he was looking at, nor what he went out to see. Time had ceased to pass. He stood for long spaces, gazing from a white, sharp face, with those keen, far-off blue eyes of his, gazing fiercely and almost cruelly at the dark sea under the dark sky. And if he saw the labouring sail of a fishing-boat away on the cold waters, a strange malevolent anger passed over his features.

Sometimes he was ill. He knew he was ill, because he staggered as he walked, and easily fell down. Then he paused to think what it was. And he went to his stores and took out dried milk and malt, and ate that. Then he forgot again. He ceased to register his own feelings.

The days were beginning to lengthen. All winter the weather had been comparatively mild, but with much rain, much rain. He had forgotten the sun. Suddenly, however, the air was very cold, and he began to shiver. A fear came over him. The sky was level and grey, and never a star appeared at night. It was very cold. More birds began to arrive. The island was freezing. With trembling hands he made a fire in his grate. The cold frightened him.

And now it continued, day after day, a dull, deathly cold. Occasional crumblings of snow were in the air. The days were greyly longer, but no change in the cold. Frozen grey daylight. The birds passed away, flying away. Some he saw lying frozen. It was as if all life were drawing away, contracting away from the north, contracting southwards. "Soon," he said to himself, "it will all be gone, and in all these regions nothing will be alive." He felt a cruel satisfaction in the thought.

Then one night there seemed to be a relief; he slept better, did not tremble half-awake, and writhe so much, half-conscious. He had become so used to the quaking and writhing of his body, he hardly noticed it. But when for once it slept deep, he noticed that.

He woke in the morning to a curious whiteness. His window was muffled. It had snowed. He got up and opened his door, and shuddered. Ugh! How cold! All white, with a dark leaden sea, and black rocks curiously speckled with white. The foam was no longer pure. It seemed dirty. And the sea ate at the whiteness of the corpse-like land. Crumbles of snow were silting down the dead air.

On the ground the snow was a foot deep, white and smooth and soft, windless. He took a shovel to clear round his house and shed. The pallor of morning darkened. There was a strange rumbling of far-off thunder in the frozen air, and through the newly-falling snow, a dim flash of lightning. Snow now fell steadily down in the motionless obscurity.

He went out for a few minutes. But it was difficult. He stumbled and fell in the snow, which burned his face. Weak, faint, he toiled home. And when he recovered, took the trouble to make hot milk.

It snowed all the time. In the afternoon again there was a muffled rumbling of thunder, and flashes of lightning blinking reddish through the falling snow. Uneasy, he went to bed and lay staring fixedly at nothingness.

Morning seemed never to come. An eternity long he lay and waited for one alleviating pallor on the night. And at last it seemed the air was paler. His house was a cell faintly

illuminated with white light. He realised the snow was walled
outside his window. He got up, in the dead cold. When he
opened his door, the motionless snow stopped him in a wall as
high as his breast. Looking over the top of it, he felt the dead
wind slowly driving, saw the snow-powder lift and travel like
a funeral train. The blackish sea churned and champed, seeming to bite at the snow, impotent. The sky was grey, but
luminous.

He began to work in a frenzy, to get at his boat. If he was
to be shut in, it must be by his own choice, not by the
mechanical power of the elements. He must get to the sea.
He must be able to get at his boat.

But he was weak, and at times the snow overcame him. It
fell on him, and he lay buried and lifeless. Yet every time he
struggled alive before it was too late, and fell upon the snow
with the energy of fever. Exhausted, he would not give in.
He crept indoors and made coffee and bacon. Long since he
had cooked so much. Then he went at the snow once more.
He must conquer the snow, this new, white brute force which
had accumulated against him.

He worked in the awful, dead wind, pushing the snow aside,
pressing it with his shovel. It was cold, freezing hard in the
wind, even when the sun came out for a while, and showed
him his white, lifeless surroundings, the black sea rolling
sullen, flecked with dull spume, away to the horizons. Yet
the sun had power on his face. It was March.

He reached the boat. He pushed the snow away, then sat
down under the lee of the boat, looking at the sea, which
swirled nearly to his feet, in the high tide. Curiously natural
the pebbles looked, in a world gone all uncanny. The sun
shone no more. Snow was falling in hard crumbs, that
vanished as if by a miracle as they touched the hard blackness of the sea. Hoarse waves rang in the shingle, rushing up
at the snow. The wet rocks were brutally black. And all the
time the myriad swooping crumbs of snow, demonish,
touched the dark sea and disappeared.

During the night there was a great storm. It seemed to him
he could hear the vast mass of snow striking all the world
with a ceaseless thud; and over it all, the wind roared in
strange hollow volleys, in between which came a jump of
blindfold lightning, then the low roll of thunder heavier than
the wind. When at last the dawn faintly discoloured the

dark, the storm had more or less subsided, but a steady wind drove on. The snow was up to the top of his door.

Sullenly, he worked to dig himself out. And he managed through sheer persistency to get out. He was in the tail of a great drift, many feet high. When he got through, the frozen snow was not more than two feet deep. But his island was gone. Its shape was all changed, great heaping white hills rose where no hills had been, inaccessible, and they fumed like volcanoes, but with snow powder. He was sickened and overcome.

His boat was in another, smaller drift. But he had not the strength to clear it. He looked at it helplessly. The shovel slipped from his hands, and he sank in the snow, to forget. In the snow itself, the sea resounded.

Something brought him to. He crept to his house. He was almost without feeling. Yet he managed to warm himself, just that part of him which leaned in snow-sleep over the coal fire. Then again he made hot milk. After which, carefully, he built up the fire.

The wind dropped. Was it night again? In the silence, it seemed he could hear the panther-like dropping of infinite snow. Thunder rumbled nearer, crackled quick after the bleared reddened lightning. He lay in bed in a kind of stupor. The elements! The elements! His mind repeated the word dumbly. You can't win against the elements.

How long it went on, he never knew. Once, like a wraith, he got out and climbed to the top of a white hill on his unrecognisable island. The sun was hot. "It is summer," he said to himself, "and the time of leaves." He looked stupidly over the whiteness of his foreign island, over the waste of the lifeless sea. He pretended to imagine he saw the wink of a sail. Because he knew too well there would never again be a sail on that stark sea.

As he looked, the sky mysteriously darkened and chilled. From far off came the mutter of the unsatisfied thunder, and he knew it was the signal of the snow rolling over the sea. He turned, and felt its breath on him.

THE OVERTONE

His wife was talking to two other women. He lay on the lounge pretending to read. The lamps shed a golden light, and, through the open door, the night was lustrous, and a white moon went like a woman, unashamed and naked across the sky. His wife, her dark hair tinged with grey looped low on her white neck, fingered as she talked the pearl that hung in a heavy, naked drop against the bosom of her dress. She was still a beautiful woman, and one who dressed like the night, for harmony. Her gown was of silk lace, all in flakes, as if the fallen, pressed petals of black and faded-red poppies were netted together with gossamer about her. She was fifty-one, and he was fifty-two. It seemed impossible. He felt his love cling round her like her dress, like a garment of dead leaves. She was talking to a quiet woman about the suffrage. The other girl, tall, rather aloof, sat listening in her chair, with the posture of one who neither accepts nor rejects, but who allows things to go on around her, and will know what she thinks only when she must act. She seemed to be looking away into the night. A scent of honeysuckle came through the open door. Then a large grey moth blundered into the light.

It was very still, almost too silent, inside the room. Mrs. Renshaw's quiet, musical voice continued:

"But think of a case like Mrs. Mann's now. She is a clever woman. If she had slept in my cradle, and I in hers, she would have looked a greater lady than I do at this minute. But she married Mann, and she has seven children by him, and goes out charring. Her children she can never leave. So she must stay with a dirty, drunken brute like Mann. If she had an income of two pounds a week, she could say to him: 'Sir, goodbye to you,' and she would be well rid. But no, she is tied to him for ever."

They were discussing the State-endowment of mothers. She and Mrs. Hankin were bitterly keen upon it. Elsa Laskell sat and accepted their talk as she did the scent of the honeysuckle or the blundering adventure of the moth round the silk: it came burdened, not with the meaning of the words, but with the feeling of the woman's heart as she spoke. Perhaps she heard a nightingale in the park outside—perhaps she did. And then this talk inside drifted also to the girl's heart, like a sort of inarticulate music. Then she was vaguely aware of the man sprawled in his homespun suit upon the lounge. He had not changed for dinner: he was called unconventional.

She knew he was old enough to be her father, and yet he looked young enough to be her lover. They all seemed young, the beautiful hostess, too, but with a meaningless youth that cannot ripen, like an unfertilised flower which lasts a long time. He was a man she classed as a Dane—with fair, almost sandy hair, blue eyes, long loose limbs, and a boyish activity. But he was fifty-two—and he lay looking out on the night, with one of his hands swollen from hanging so long inert, silent. The women bored him.

Elsa Laskell sat in a sort of dreamy state, and the feelings of her hostess, and the feeling of her host drifted like iridescence upon the quick of her soul, among the white touch of that moon out there, and the exotic heaviness of the honeysuckle, and the strange flapping of the moth. So still, it was, behind the murmur of talk: a silence of being. Of the third woman, Mrs. Hankin, the girl had no sensibility. But the night and the moon, the moth, Will Renshaw and Edith Renshaw and herself were all in full being, a harmony.

To him it was six months after his marriage, and the sky was the same, and the honeysuckle in the air. He was living again his crisis, as we all must, fretting and fretting against our failure, till we have worn away the thread of our life. It was six months after his marriage, and they were down at the little bungalow on the bank of the Soar. They were comparatively poor, though her father was rich, and his was well-to-do. And they were alone in the little two-roomed bungalow that stood on its wild bank over the river, among the honeysuckle bushes. He had cooked the evening meal, they had eaten the omelette and drank the coffee, and all was settling into stillness.

He sat outside, by the remnants of the fire, looking at the country lying level and lustrous grey opposite him. Trees hung like vapour in a perfect calm under the moonlight. And that was the moon so perfectly naked and unfaltering, going her errand simply through the night. And that was the river faintly rustling. And there, down the darkness, he saw a flashing of activity white betwixt black twigs. It was the water mingling and thrilling with the moon. So! It made him quiver, and reminded him of the starlit rush of a hare. There was vividness then in all this lucid night, things flashing and quivering with being, almost as the soul quivers in the darkness of the eye. He could feel it. The night's great circle was the pupil of an eye, full of the mystery, and the unknown fire of life, that does not burn away, but flickers unquenchable.

So he rose, and went to look for his wife. She sat with her dark head bent into the light of a reading-lamp, in the little hut. She wore a white dress, and he could see her shoulders' softness and curve through the lawn. Yet she did not look up when he moved. He stood in the doorway, knowing that she felt his presence. Yet she gave no sign.

"Will you come out?" he asked.

She looked up at him as if to find out what he wanted, and she was rather cold to him. But when he had repeated his request, she had risen slowly to acquiesce, and a tiny shiver had passed down her shoulders. So he unhung from its peg her beautiful Paisley shawl, with its tempered colours that looked as if they had faltered through the years and now were here in their essence, and put it round her. They sat again outside the little hut, under the moonlight. He held both her hands. They were heavy with rings. But one ring was his wedding ring. He had married her, and there was nothing more to own. He owned her, and the night was the pupil of her eye, in which was everything. He kissed her fingers, but she sat and made no sign. It was as he wished. He kissed her fingers again.

Then a corncrake began to call in the meadow across the river, a strange, dispassionate sound, that made him feel not quite satisfied, not quite sure. It was not all achieved. The moon, in her white and naked candour, was beyond him. He felt a little numbness, as one who has gloves on. He could not feel that clear, clean moon. There was something betwixt him and her, as if he had gloves on. Yet he ached for the clear touch, skin to skin—even of the moonlight. He wanted a further purity, a newer cleanness and nakedness. The corncrake cried too. And he watched the moon, and he watched her light on his hands. It was like a butterfly on his glove, that he could see, but not feel. And he wanted to unglove himself. Quite clear, quite, quite bare to the moon, the touch of everything, he wanted to be. And after all, his wife was everything—moon, vapour of trees, trickling water and drift of perfume—it was all his wife. The moon glistened on her finger-tips as he cherished them, and a flash came out of a diamond, among the darkness. So, even here in the quiet harmony, life was at a flash with itself.

"Come with me to the top of the red hill," he said to his wife quietly.

"But why?" she asked.

"Do come."

And dumbly she acquiesced, and her shawl hung gleaming above the white flash of her skirt. He wanted to hold her hand, but she was walking apart from him, in her long shawl. So he went to her side, humbly. And he was humble, but he felt it was great. He had looked into the whole of the night, as into the pupil of an eye. And now, he would come perfectly clear out of all his embarrassments of shame and darkness, clean as the moon who walked naked across the night, so that the whole night was as an effluence from her, the whole of it was hers, held in her effluence of moonlight, which was her perfect nakedness, uniting her to everything. Covering was barrier, like cloud across the moon.

The red hill was steep, but there was a tiny path from the bungalow, which he had worn himself. And in the effort of climbing, he felt he was struggling nearer and nearer to himself. Always he looked half round, where, just behind him, she followed, in the lustrous obscurity of her shawl. Her steps came with a little effort up the steep hill, and he loved her feet, he wanted to kiss them as they strove upwards in the gloom. He put aside the twigs and branches. There was a strong scent of honeysuckle like a thick strand of gossamer over his mouth.

He knew a place on the ledge of the hill, on the lip of the cliff, where the trees stood back and left a little dancing-green, high up above the water, there in the midst of miles of moonlit, lonely country. He parted the boughs, sure as a fox that runs to its lair. And they stood together on this little dancing-green presented towards the moon, with the red cliff cumbered with bushes going down to the river below, and the haze of moon-dust on the meadows, and the trees behind them, and only the moon could look straight into the place he had chosen.

She stood always a little way behind him. He saw her face all compounded of shadows and moonlight, and he dared not kiss her yet.

"Will you," he said, "will you take off your things and love me here?"

"I can't," she said.

He looked away to the moon. It was difficult to ask her again, yet it meant so much to him. There was not a sound in the night. He put his hand to his throat and began to unfasten his collar.

"Take off all your things and love me," he pleaded.

For a moment she was silent.

"I can't," she said.

Mechanically, he had taken off his flannel collar and pushed it into his pocket. Then he stood on the edge of the land, looking down into all that gleam, as into the living pupil of an eye. He was bareheaded to the moon. Not a breath of air ruffled his bare throat. Still, in the dropping folds of her shawl, she stood, a thing of dusk and moonlight, a little back. He ached with the earnestness of his desire. All he wanted was to give himself, clean and clear, into this night, this time. Of which she was all, she was everything. He could go to her now, under the white candour of the moon, without shame or shadow, but in his completeness loving her completeness, without a stain, without a shadow between them such as even a flower could cast. For this he yearned as never in his life he could yearn more deeply.

"Do take me," he said, gently parting the shawl on her breast. But she held it close, and her voice went hard.

"No—I can't," she said.

"Why?"

"I can't—let us go back."

He looked again over the countryside of dimness, saying in a low tone, his back towards her:

"But I love you—and I want you so much—like that, here and now. I'll never ask you anything again," he said quickly, passionately, as he turned to her. "Do this for me," he said. "I'll never trouble you for anything again. I promise."

"I can't," she said stubbornly, with some hopelessness in her voice.

"Yes," he said. "Yes. You trust me, don't you?"

"I don't want it. Not here—not now," she said.

"Do," he said. "Yes."

"You can have me in the bungalow. Why do you want me here?" she asked.

"But I do. Have me, Edith. Have me now."

"No," she said, turning away. "I want to go down."

"And you won't?"

"No—I can't."

There was something like fear in her voice. They went down the hill together. And he did not know how he hated her, as if she had kept him out of the promised land that was justly his. He thought he was too generous to bear her a grudge. So he had always held himself deferential to her. And later that evening he had loved her. But she hated it, it had been really his hate ravaging her. Why had he lied, calling it love? Ever since, it had seemed the same, more or less. So that he had ceased to come to her, gradually. For one night she had said: "I think a man's body is ugly—all in parts with mechanical joints." And now he had scarcely had her for some years. For she thought him an ugliness. And there were no children.

Now that everything was essentially over for both of them, they lived on the surface, and had good times. He drove to all kinds of unexpected places in his motor-car, bathed where he liked, said what he liked, and did what he liked. But nobody minded very much his often aggressive unconventionality. It was only fencing with the foils. There was no danger in his thrusts. He was a castrated bear. So he prided himself on being a bear, on being known as an uncouth bear.

It was not often he lay and let himself drift. But always when he did, he held it against her that on the night when they climbed the red bank, she refused to have him. There were perhaps many things he might have held against her, but this was the only one that remained: his real charge against her on the Judgment Day. Why had she done it? It had been, he might almost say, a holy desire on his part. It had been almost like taking off his shoes before God. Yet she refused him, she who was his religion to him. Perhaps she had been afraid, she who was so good—afraid of the big righteousness of it—as if she could not trust herself so near the Burning Bush, dared not go near for transfiguration, afraid of herself.

It was a thought he could not bear. Rising softly, because she was still talking, he went out into the night.

Elsa Laskell stirred uneasily in her chair. Mrs. Renshaw went on talking like a somnambule, not because she really had anything to say about the State-endowment of mothers, but because she had a weight on her heart that she wanted to talk away. The girl heard, and lifted her hand, and stirred her fingers uneasily in the dark-purple porphyry bowl, where pink rose-leaves and crimson, thrown this morning from the stem, lay gently shrivelling. There came a slight acrid scent of new rose-petals. And still the girl lifted her long white fingers among the red and pink in the dark bowl, as if they stirred in blood.

And she felt the nights behind like a purple bowl into which the woman's heart-beats were shed, like rose-leaves fallen and left to wither and go brown. For Mrs. Renshaw had waited for him. During happy days of stillness and blueness she had moved, while the sunshine glancing through her blood made flowers in her heart, like blossoms underground thrilling with expectancy, lovely fragrant things that would have delight to appear. And all day long she had gone secretly and quietly saying, saying: "To-night—to-night they will blossom for him. To-night I shall be a bed of blossom for him, all narcissi and fresh fragrant things shaking for joy, when he comes with his deeper sunshine, when he turns the darkness like mould, and brings them forth with his sunshine for spade. Yea, there are two suns; him in the sky and that other, warmer one whose beams are our radiant bodies. He is a sun to me, shining full on my heart when he comes, and everything stirs." But he had come like a bitter morning. He had never bared the sun of himself to her—a sullen day he had been on her heart, covered with cloud impenetrable. She had waited so heavy anxious, with such a wealth of possibility. And he in his blindness had never known. He could never let the real rays of his love through the cloud of fear and mistrust. For once she had denied him. And all her flowers had been shed inwards, so that her heart was like a heap of leaves, brown, withered, almost scentless petals that had never given joy to anyone. And yet again she had come to him pregnant with beauty and love, but he had been afraid. When she lifted her eyes to him, he had looked aside. The kisses she needed like warm raindrops he dared not give, till she was parched and gone hard, and did not want them. Then he gave kisses enough. But he never trusted himself. When she was open and eager to him, he was afraid. When she was shut, it was like playing at pride, to pull her petals apart, a game that gave him pleasure.

So they had been mutually afraid of each other, but he most often. Whenever she had needed him at some mystery of love, he had overturned her censers and her sacraments, and made profane love in her sacred place. Which was why, at last, she had hated his body; but perhaps she had hated it at first, or feared it so much that it was hate.

And he had said to her: "If we don't have children, you might have them by another man——" which was surely one of the cruellest things a woman ever heard from her husband. For so little was she his, that he would give her a caller and not mind. This was all the wife she was to him. He was a free and easy man, and brought home to dinner any man who pleased him, from a beggar upwards. And his wife was to be as public as his board.

Nay, to the very bowl of her heart, any man might put his lips and he would not mind. And so, she sadly set down the bowl from between her two hands of offering, and went always empty, and aloof.

Yet they were married, they were good friends. It was said they were the most friendly married couple in the county. And this was it. And all the while, like a ascent, the bitter psalm of the woman filled the room.

"Like a garden in winter, I was full of bulbs and roots, I was full of little flowers, all conceived inside me.

"And they were all shed away unborn, little abortions of flowers.

"Every day I went like a bee gathering honey from the sky and among the stars I rummaged for yellow honey, filling it in my comb.

"Then I broke the comb, and put it to your lips. But you turned your mouth aside and said: 'You have made my face unclean, and smeared my mouth.'

"And week after week my body was a vineyard, my veins were vines. And as the grapes, the purple drops grew full and sweet, I crushed them in a bowl, I treasured the wine.

"Then when the bowl was full I came with joy to you. But you in fear started away, and the bowl was thrown from my hands, and broke in pieces at my feet.

"Many times, and many times, I said: 'The hour is striking,' but he answered: 'Not yet.'

"Many times and many times he has heard the cock crow, and gone out and wept, he knew not why.

"I was a garden and he ran in me as in the grass.

"I was a stream, and he threw his waste in me.

"I held the rainbow balanced on my outspread hands, and he said: 'You open your hands and give me nothing.'

"What am I now but a bowl of withered leaves, but a kaleidoscope of broken beauties, but an empty bee-hive, yea, a rich garment rusted that no one has worn, a dumb singer, with the voice of a nightingale yet making discord.

"And it was over with me, and my hour is gone. And soon like a barren sea-shell on the strand, I shall be crushed underfoot to dust.

"But meanwhile I sing to those that listen with their ear against me, of the sea that gave me form and being, the everlasting sea, and in my song is nothing but bitterness, for of the fluid life of the sea I have no more, but I am to be dust, that powdery stuff the sea knows not. I am to be dead, who was born of life, silent who was made a mouth, formless who was all of beauty. Yea, I was a seed that held the heavens lapped up in bud, with a whirl of stars and a steady moon.

"And the seed is crushed that never sprouted, there is a heaven lost, and stars and a moon that never came forth.

"I was a bud that never was discovered, and in my shut chalice, skies and lake water and brooks lie crumbling, and stars and the sun are smeared out, and birds are a little powdery dust, and their singing is dry air, and I am a dark chalice."

And the girl, hearing the hostess talk, still talk, and yet her voice like the sound of a sea-shell whispering hoarsely of despair, rose and went out into the garden, timidly, beginning to cry. For what should she do for herself?

Renshaw, leaning on the wicket that led to the paddock, called:

"Come on, don't be alarmed—Pan is dead."

And then she bit back her tears. For when he said, 'Pan is dead,' he meant Pan was dead in his own long, loose Dane's body. Yet she was a nymph still, and if Pan were dead, she ought to die. So with tears she went up to him.

"It's all right out here," he said. "By Jove, when you see a night like this, how can you say that life's tragedy—or death either, for that matter?"

"What is it, then?" she asked.

"Nay, that's one too many—a joke, eh?"

"I think," she said, "one has no business to be irreverent."

"Who?" he asked.

"You," she said, "and me, and all of us."

Then he leaned on the wicket, thinking till he laughed.

"Life's a real good thing," he said.

"But why protest it?" she answered.

And again he was silent.

"If the moon came nearer and nearer," she said, "and were a naked woman, what would you do?"

"Fetch a wrap, probably," he said.

"Yes—you would do that," she answered.

"And if he were a man, ditto?" he teased.

"If a star came nearer and were a naked man, I should look at him."

"That is surely very improper," he mocked, with still a tinge of yearning.

"If he were a star come near——" she answered.

Again he was silent.

"You are a queer fish of a girl," he said.

They stood at the gate, facing the silver-grey paddock. Presently their hostess came out, a long shawl hanging from her shoulders.

"So you are here," she said. "Were you bored?"

"I was," he replied amiably. "But there, you know I always am."

"And I forgot," replied the girl.

"What were you talking about?" asked Mrs. Renshaw, simply curious. She was not afraid of her husband's running loose.

"We were just saying 'Pan is dead'," said the girl.

"Isn't that rather trite?" asked the hostess.

"Some of us miss him fearfully," said the girl.

"For what reason?" asked Mrs. Renshaw.

"Those of us who are nymphs—just lost nymphs among farm-lands and suburbs. I wish Pan were alive."

"Did he die of old age?" mocked the hostess.

"Don't they say, when Christ was born, a voice was heard

in the air saying: 'Pan is dead.' I wish Christ needn't have killed Pan."

"I wonder how He managed it," said Renshaw.

"By disapproving of him, I suppose," replied his wife. And her retort cut herself, and gave her a sort of fakir pleasure.

"The men are all women now," she said, "since the fauns died in a frost one night."

"A frost of disapproval," said the girl.

"A frost of fear," said Renshaw.

There was a silence.

"Why was Christ afraid of Pan?" said the girl suddenly.

"Why was Pan so much afraid of Christ that he died?" asked Mrs. Renshaw bitterly.

"And all his fauns in a frost one night," mocked Renshaw. Then a light dawned on him. "Christ was woman, and Pan was man," he said. It gave him real joy to say this bitterly, keenly—a thrust into himself, and into his wife. "But the fauns and satyrs are there—you have only to remove the surplices that all men wear nowadays."

"Nay," said Mrs. Renshaw, "it is not true—the surplices have grown into their limbs, like Hercules's garment."

"That his wife put on him," said Renshaw.

"Because she was afraid of him—not because she loved him," said the girl.

"She imagined that all her lonely wasted hours wove him a robe of love," said Mrs. Renshaw. "It was to her horror she was mistaken. You can't weave love out of waste."

"When I meet a man," said the girl, "I shall look down the pupil of his eye, for a faun. And after a while it will come, skipping——"

"Perhaps a satyr," said Mrs. Renshaw bitterly.

"No," said the girl, "because satyrs are old, and I have seen some fearfully young men."

"Will is young even now—quite a boy," said his wife.

"Oh no!" cried the girl. "He says that neither life nor death is a tragedy. Only somebody very old could say that."

There was a tension in the night. The man felt something give way inside him.

"Yes, Edith," he said, with a quiet, bitter joy of cruelty, "I am old."

The wife was frightened.

"You are always preposterous," she said quickly, crying inside herself. She knew she herself had been never young.

"I shall look in the eyes of my man for the faun," the girl continued in a sing-song, "and I shall find him. Then I shall pretend to run away from him. And both our surplices, and all the crucifix, will be outside the wood. Inside nymph and faun, Pan and his satyrs—ah, yes: for Christ and the Cross is only for day-time, and bargaining. Christ came to make us deal honourably.

"But love is no deal, nor merchant's bargaining, and Christ neither spoke of it nor forbade it. He was afraid of it. If once His faun, the faun of the young Jesus had run free, seen one white nymph's brief breast, He would not have been content to die on a Cross—and then the men would have gone on cheating the women in life's business, all the time. Christ made one bargain in mankind's business—and He made it for the women's sake—I suppose for His mother's, since He was fatherless. And Christ made a bargain for me, and I shall avail myself of it. I won't be cheated by my man. When between my still hands I weave silk out of the air, like a cocoon, He shall not take it to pelt me with. He shall draw it forth and weave it up. For I want to finger the sunshine I have drawn through my body, stroke it, and have joy of the fabric.

"And when I run wild on the hills with Dionysus, and shall come home like a bee that has rolled in floury crocuses, he must see the wonder on me, and make bread of it.

"And when I say to him, 'It is harvest in my soul', he shall look in my eyes and lower his nets where the shoal moves in a throng in the dark, and lift out the living blue silver for me to see, and know, and taste.

"All this, my faun in commerce, my faun at traffic with me.

"And if he cheat me, he must take his chance.

"But I will not cheat him, in his hour, when he runs like a faun after me. I shall flee, but only to be overtaken. I shall flee, but never out of the wood to the crucifix. For that is to deny I am a nymph; since how can a nymph cling at the crucifix? Nay, the cross is the sign I have on my money, for honesty.

"In the morning, when we come out of the wood, I shall say to him: 'Touch the cross, and prove you will deal fairly,' and if he will not, I will set the dogs of anger and judgment on him, and they shall chase him. But if, perchance, some night he contrive to crawl back into the wood, beyond the crucifix, he will be faun and I nymph, and I shall have no knowledge what happened outside, in the realm of the crucifix. But in the morning, I shall say: 'Touch the cross, and prove you will deal fairly.' And being renewed, he will touch the cross.

"Many a dead faun I have seen, like dead rabbits poisoned lying about the paths, and many a dead nymph, like swans that could not fly and the dogs destroyed.

"But I am a nymph and a woman, and Pan is for me, and Christ is for me.

"For Christ I cover myself in my robe, and weep, and vow my vow of honesty.

"For Pan I throw my coverings down and run headlong through the leaves, because of the joy of running.

"And Pan will give me my children and joy, and Christ will give me my pride.

"And Pan will give me my man, and Christ my husband.

"To Pan I am nymph, to Christ I am woman.

"And Pan is in the darkness, and Christ in the pale light.

"And night shall never be day, and day shall never be night.

"But side by side they shall go, day and night, night and day, for ever apart, for ever together.

"Pan and Christ, Christ and Pan.

"Both moving over me, so when in the sunshine I go in my robes among my neighbours, I am a Christian. But when I run robeless through the dark-scented woods alone, I am Pan's nymph.

"Now I must go, for I want to run away. Not run away from myself, but to myself.

"For neither am I a lamp that stands in the way in the sunshine.

"Now am I a sundial foolish at night.

"I am myself, running through light and shadow for ever, a nymph and a Christian; I, not two things, but an apple with a gold side and a red, a freckled deer, a stream that tinkles and a pool where light is drowned; I, no fragment, no half-thing like the day, but a blackbird with a white breast and underwings, a peewit, a wild thing, beyond understanding."

"I wonder if we shall hear the nightingale to-night," said Mrs. Renshaw.

"He's a gurgling fowl—I'd rather hear a linnet," said Renshaw. "Come a drive with me to-morrow, Miss Laskell."

And the three went walking back to the house. And Elsa Laskell was glad to get away from them.

THE LOVELY LADY

AT seventy-two, Pauline Attenborough could still sometimes be mistaken, in the half-light, for thirty. She really was a wonderfully preserved woman, of perfect *chic*. Of course, it helps a great deal to have the right frame. She would be an exquisite skeleton, and her skull would be an exquisite skull, like that of some Etruscan woman, with feminine charm still in the swerve of the bone and the pretty naïve teeth.

Mrs. Attenborough's face was of the perfect oval, and slightly flat type that wears best. There is no flesh to sag. Her nose rode serenely, in its finely bridged curve. Only her big grey eyes were a tiny bit prominent on the surface of her face, and they gave her away most. The bluish lids were heavy, as if they ached sometimes with the strain of keeping the eyes beneath them arch and bright; and at the corners of the eyes were fine little wrinkles which would slacken with haggardness, then be pulled up tense again, to that bright, gay look like a Leonardo woman who really could laugh outright.

Her niece Cecilia was perhaps the only person in the world who was aware of the invisible little wire which connected Pauline's eye-wrinkles with Pauline's will-power. Only Cecilia *consciously* watched the eyes go haggard and old and tired, and remain so, for hours; until Robert came home. Then ping!—the mysterious little wire that worked between Pauline's will and her face went taut, the weary, haggard, prominent eyes suddenly began to gleam, the eyelids arched, the queer curved eyebrows which floated in such frail arches on Pauline's forehead began to gather a mocking significance, and you had the *real* lovely lady, in all her charm.

She really had the secret of everlasting youth; that is to say, she could don her youth again like an eagle. But she was sparing of it. She was wise enough not to try being young for too many people. Her son Robert, in the evenings, and Sir Wilfred Knipe sometimes in the afternoon to tea: then occasional visitors on Sunday, when Robert was home: for these she was her lovely and changeless self, that age could not wither, nor custom stale: so bright and kindly and yet subtly mocking, like Mona Lisa, who knew a thing or two.

But Pauline knew more, so she needn't be smug at all, she could laugh that lovely mocking Bacchante laugh of hers, which was at the same time never malicious, always good-naturedly tolerant, both of virtues and vices. The former, of course, taking much more tolerating. So she suggested, roguishly.

Only with her niece Cecilia she did not trouble to keep up the glamour. Ciss was not very observant, anyhow: and more than that, she was plain: more still, she was in love with Robert: and most of all, she was thirty, and dependent on her Aunt Pauline. Oh, Cecilia! Why make music for her!

Cecilia, called by her aunt and by her cousin Robert just Ciss, like a cat spitting, was a big dark-complexioned, pug-faced young woman who very rarely spoke, and when she did, couldn't get it out. She was the daughter of a poor Congregational minister who had been, while he lived, brother to Ronald, Aunt Pauline's husband. Ronald and the Congregational minister were both well dead, and Aunt Pauline had had charge of Ciss for the last five years.

They lived all together in a quite exquisite though rather small Queen Anne house some twenty-five miles out of town, secluded in a little dale, and surrounded by small but very quaint and pleasant grounds. It was an ideal place and an ideal life for Aunt Pauline, at the age of seventy-two. When the kingfishers flashed up the little stream in the garden, going under the alders, something still flashed in her heart. She was that kind of woman.

Robert, who was two years older than Ciss, went every day to town, to his chambers in one of the Inns. He was a barrister, and, to his secret but very deep mortification, he earned about a hundred pounds a year. He simply *couldn't* get above that figure, though it was rather easy to get below it. Of course, it didn't matter. Pauline had money. But then what was Pauline's was Pauline's, and though she could give almost lavishly, still, one was always aware of having a *lovely* and *undeserved* present made to one: presents are so much nicer when they are undeserved, Aunt Pauline would say.

Robert too was plain, and almost speechless. He was medium-sized, rather broad and stout, though not fat. Only his creamy, clean-shaven face was rather fat, and sometimes suggestive of an Italian priest, in its silence and its secrecy. But he had grey eyes like his mother, but very shy and uneasy, not bold like hers. Perhaps Ciss was the only person who fathomed his awful shyness and *malaise*, his habitual feeling that he was in the wrong place: almost like a soul that has got into the wrong body. But he never did anything about it. He went up to his chambers and read law. It was, however, all the weird old processes that interested him. He had, unknown to everybody but his mother, a quite extraordinary collection of old Mexican legal documents, reports of processes and trials, pleas, accusations, the weird and awful mixture of ecclesiastical law and common law in seventeenth-century Mexico. He had started a study in this direction through coming across a report of a trial of two English sailors, for murder, in Mexico in 1620, and he had gone on, when the next document was an accusation against a Don Miguel Estrada for seducing one of the nuns of the Sacred Heart Convent in Oaxaca in 1680.

Pauline and her son Robert had wonderful evenings with these old papers. The lovely lady knew a little Spanish. She even looked a trifle Spanish herself, with a high comb and a marvellous dark brown shawl embroidered in thick silvery silk embroidery. So she would sit at the perfect old table, soft as velvet in its deep brown surface, a high comb in her hair, ear-rings with dropping pendants in her ears, her arms bare and still beautiful, a few strings of pearls round her throat, a puce velvet dress on and this or another beautiful shawl, and by candle-light she looked, yes, a Spanish high-bred beauty of thirty-two or three. She set the candles to give her face just the chiaroscuro she knew suited her; her high chair that rose behind her face was done in old green brocade, against which her face emerged like a Christmas rose.

They were always three at table; and they always drank a bottle of champagne: Pauline two glasses, Ciss two glasses, Robert the rest. The lovely lady sparkled and was radiant. Ciss, her black hair bobbed, her broad shoulders in a very nice and becoming dress that Aunt Pauline had helped her to make, stared from her aunt to her cousin and back again, with rather confused, mute, hazel eyes, and played the part of an audience suitably impressed. She *was* impressed, somewhere, all the time. And even rendered speechless by Pauline's brilliancy, even after five years. But at the bottom of her consciousness were the data of as weird a document as Robert ever studied: all the things she knew about her aunt and cousin.

Robert was always a gentleman, with an old-fashioned punctilious courtesy that covered his shyness quite completely. He was, and Ciss knew it, more confused than shy. He was worse than she was. Cecilia's own confusion dated from only five years back—Robert's must have started before he was born. In the lovely lady's womb he must have felt *very* confused.

He paid all his attention to his mother, drawn to her as a humble flower to the sun. And yet, priest-like, he was all the time aware, with the tail of his consciousness, that Ciss was there, and that she was a bit shut out of it, and that something wasn't right. He was aware of the third consciousness in the room. Whereas to Pauline, her niece Cecilia was an appropriate part of her own setting, rather than a distinct consciousness.

Robert took coffee with his mother and Ciss in the warm drawing-room, where all the furniture was so lovely, all collectors' pieces—Mrs. Attenborough had made her own money, dealing privately in pictures and furniture and rare things from barbaric countries—and the three talked desultorily till about eight or half-past. It was very pleasant, very cosy, very homely even: Pauline made a real home cosiness out of so much elegant material. The chat was simple, and nearly always bright. Pauline was her *real* self, emanating a friendly mockery and an odd, ironic gaiety. Till there came a little pause.

At which Ciss always rose and said good night and carried out the coffee-tray, to prevent Burnett from intruding any more.

And then! Oh, then, the lovely glowing intimacy of the evening, between mother and son, when they deciphered manuscripts and discussed points, Pauline with that eagerness of a girl, for which she was famous. And it was quite genuine. In some mysterious way she had *saved up* her power for being thrilled, in connection with a man. Robert, solid, rather quiet and subdued, seemed like the elder of the two: almost like a priest with a young girl pupil. And that was rather how he felt.

Ciss had a flat for herself just across the courtyard, over the old coach-house and stables. There were no horses. Robert kept his car in the coach-house. Ciss had three very nice rooms up there, stretching along in a row one after another, and she had got used to the ticking of the stable clock.

But sometimes she did not go up to her rooms. In the summer she would sit on the lawn, and from the open window of the drawing-room upstairs she would hear Pauline's wonderful heart-searching laugh. And in the winter the young woman would put on a thick coat and walk slowly to the little balustraded bridge over the stream, and then look back at the three lighted windows of that drawing-room where mother and son were so happy together.

Ciss loved Robert, and she believed that Pauline intended the two of them to marry: when she was dead. But poor Robert, he was so convulsed with shyness already, with man or woman. What would he be when his mother was dead—in a dozen more years? He would be just a shell, the shell of a man who had never lived.

The strange unspoken sympathy of the young with one another, when they are overshadowed by the old, was one of the bonds between Robert and Ciss. But another bond, which Ciss did not know how to draw tight, was the bond of passion. Poor Robert was by nature a passionate man. His silence and his agonised, though hidden, shyness were both the result of a secret physical passionateness. And how Pauline could play on this! Ah, Ciss was not blind to the eyes which he fixed on his mother, eyes fascinated yet humiliated, full of shame. He was ashamed that he was not a man. And he did not love his mother. He was fascinated by her. Completely fascinated. And for the rest, paralysed in a life-long confusion.

Ciss stayed in the garden till the lights leapt up in Pauline's bedroom—about ten o'cock. The lovely lady had retired. Robert would now stay another hour or so, alone. Then he too would retire. Ciss, in the dark outside, sometimes wished she could creep up to him and say: "Oh, Robert! It's all wrong!" But Aunt Pauline would hear. And, anyhow, Ciss couldn't do it. She went off to her own rooms once more, and so for ever.

In the morning coffee was brought up on a tray to each of the three relatives. Ciss had to be at Sir Wilfred Knipe's at nine o'clock, to give two hours' lessons to his little granddaughter. It was her sole serious occupation, except that she played the piano for the love of it. Robert set off to town about nine. And, as a rule, Aunt Pauline appeared at lunch, though sometimes not until tea-time. When she appeared, she looked fresh and young. But she was inclined to fade rather quickly, like a flower without water, in the day-time. Her hour was the candle hour.

So she always rested in the afternoon. When the sun shone, if possible she took a sun-bath. This was one of her secrets. Her lunch was very light, she could take her sun-and-air-bath before noon or after, as it pleased her. Often it was in the afternoon, when the sun shone very warmly into a queer little yew-walled square just behind the stables. Here Ciss stretched out the lying-chair and rugs, and put the light parasol in the silent little enclosure of thick dark yew hedges beyond the red walls of the unused stables. And hither came the lovely lady with her book. Ciss then had to be on guard in one of her own rooms, should her aunt, who was very keen-eared, hear a footstep.

One afternoon it occurred to Cecilia that she herself might while away this rather long afternoon by taking a sun-bath. She was growing restive. The thought of the flat roof of the stable buildings, to which she could climb from a loft at the end, started her on a new adventure. She often went on to the roof: she had to, to wind up the stable clock, which was a job she had assumed to herself. Now she took a rug, climbed out under the heavens, looked at the sky and the great elm-tops, looked at the sun, then took off her things and lay down perfectly serenely, in a corner of the roof under the parapet, full in the sun.

It was rather lovely, to bask all one's length like this in warm sun and air. Yes, it was very lovely! It even seemed to melt some of the hard bitterness of her heart, some of that core of unspoken resentment which never dissolved. Luxuriously, she spread herself, so that the sun should touch her limbs fully, fully. If she had no other lover, she should have the sun! She rolled voluptuously. And suddenly her heart stood still in her body, and her hair almost rose on end as a voice said very softly, musingly in her ear:

"No, Henry dear! It was not my fault you died instead of marrying that Claudia. No, darling. I was quite, quite willing for you to marry her, unsuitable though she was."

Cecilia sank down on her rug powerless and perspiring with dread. That awful voice, so soft, so musing, yet so unnatural. Not a human voice at all. Yet there must, there must be someone on the roof! Oh! how unspeakably awful!

She lifted her weak head and peeped across the sloping leads. Nobody! The chimneys were far too narrow to shelter anybody. There was nobody on the roof. Then it must be someone in the trees, in the elms. Either that, or terror unspeakable, a bodiless voice! She reared her head a little higher.

And as she did so, came the voice again:

"No, darling! I told you you would tire of her in six months. And you see, it was true, dear. It was true, true, true! I wanted to spare you that. So it wasn't I who made you feel weak and disabled, wanting that very silly Claudia; poor thing, she looked so woebegone afterwards! Wanting her and not wanting her, you got *yourself* into that perplexity, my dear. I only warned you. What else could I do? And you lost your spirit and died without ever knowing me again. It was bitter, bitter——"

The voice faded away. Cecilia subsided weakly on to her rug, after the anguished tension of listening. Oh, it was awful. The sun shone, the sky was blue, all seemed so lovely and afternoony and summery. And yet, oh, horror!—she was going to be forced to believe in the supernatural! And she loathed the supernatural, ghosts and voices and rappings and all the rest.

But that awful creepy bodiless voice, with its rusty sort of whisper of an overtone! It had something so fearfully familiar in it too! and yet was so utterly uncanny. Poor Cecilia could only lie there unclothed, and so all the more agonisingly helpless, inert, collapsed in sheer dread.

And then she heard the thing sigh! A deep sigh that seemed weirdly familiar, yet was not human. "Ah, well; ah, well, the heart must bleed! Better it should bleed than break. It is grief, grief! But it wasn't my fault, dear. And Robert could marry our poor dull Ciss to-morrow, if he wanted her. But he doesn't care about it, so why force him into anything!" The sounds were very uneven, sometimes only a husky sort of whisper. Listen! Listen!

Cecilia was about to give vent to loud and piercing screams

of hysteria, when the last two sentences arrested her. All her
caution and her cunning sprang alert. It was Aunt Pauline!
It must be Aunt Pauline, practising ventriloquism or something like that! What a devil she was!

Where was she? She must be lying down there, right below
where Cecilia herself was lying. And it was either some
fiend's trick of ventriloquism, or else thought transference
that conveyed itself like sound. The sounds were very uneven. Sometimes quite inaudible, sometimes only a brushing sort of noise. Ciss listened intently. No, it could not be
ventriloquism. It was worse, some form of thought transference. Some horror of that sort. Cecilia still lay weak and
inert, terrified to move, but she was growing calmer with
suspicion. It was some diabolic trick of that unnatural
woman.

But *what a devil* of a woman! She even knew that she,
Cecilia, had mentally accused her of killing her son Henry.
Poor Henry was Robert's elder brother, twelve years older
than Robert. He had died suddenly when he was twenty-
two, after an awful struggle with himself, because he was
passionately in love with a young and very good-looking
actress, and his mother had humorously despised him for the
attachment. So he had caught some sudden ordinary disease,
but the poison had gone to his brain and killed him before
he ever regained consciousness. Ciss knew the few facts from
her own father. And lately she had been thinking that
Pauline was going to kill Robert as she had killed Henry. It
was clear murder: a mother murdering her sensitive sons,
who were fascinated by her: the Circe!

"I suppose I may as well get up," murmured the dim, un-
breaking voice. "Too much sun is as bad as too little. Enough
sun, enough love thrill, enough proper food, and not too much
of any of them, and a woman might live for ever. I verily
believe for ever. If she absorbs as much vitality as she
expends! Or perhaps a trifle more!"

It was certainly Aunt Pauline! How, how horrible! She,
Ciss, was hearing Aunt Pauline's thoughts. Oh, how ghastly!
Aunt Pauline was sending out her thoughts in a sort of radio,
and she, Ciss, had to *hear* what her aunt was thinking. How
ghastly! How insufferable! One of them would surely have
to die.

She twisted and she lay inert and crumpled, staring

vacantly in front of her. Vacantly! Vacantly! And her eyes were staring almost into a hole. She was staring into it unseeing, a hole going down in the corner from the lead gutter. It meant nothing to her. Only it frightened her a little more.

When suddenly out of the hole came a sigh and a last whisper. "Ah, well! Pauline! Get up, it's enough for to-day!" Good God! Out of the hole of the rain-pipe! The rain-pipe was acting as a speaking-tube! Impossible! No, quite possible. She had read of it even in some book. And Aunt Pauline, like the old and guilty woman she was, talked aloud to herself. That was it!

A sullen exultance sprang into Ciss's breast. *That* was why she would never have anybody, not even Robert, in her bed-room. That was why she never dozed in a chair, never sat absent-minded anywhere, but went to her room, and kept to her room, except when she roused herself to be alert. When she slackened off, she talked to herself! She talked in a soft little crazy voice to herself. But she was not crazy. It was only her thoughts murmuring themselves aloud.

So she had qualms about poor Henry! Well she might have! Ciss believed that Aunt Pauline had loved her big, handsome, brilliant first-born much more than she loved Robert, and that his death had been a terrible blow and a chagrin to her. Poor Robert had been only ten years old when Henry died. Since then he had been the substitute.

Ah, how awful!

But Aunt Pauline was a strange woman. She had left her husband when Henry was a small child, some years even before Robert was born. There was no quarrel. Sometimes she saw her husband again, quite amicably, but a little mock-ingly. And she even gave him money.

For Pauline earned all her own. Her father had been a consul in the East and in Naples: and a devoted collector of beautiful and exotic things. When he died, soon after his grandson Henry was born, he left his collection of treasures to his daughter. And Pauline, who had really a passion and a genius for loveliness, whether in texture or form or colour, had laid the basis of her fortune on her father's collection. She had gone on collecting, buying where she could, and selling to collectors and to museums. She was one of the first to sell old, weird African wooden figures to the museums, and ivory carvings from New Guinea. She bought Renoir as soon as she saw his pictures. But not Rousseau. And all by herself she made a fortune.

After her husband died, she had not married again. She was not even *known* to have had lovers. If she did have lovers, it was not among the men who admired her most and paid her devout and open attendance. To these she was a 'friend'.

Cecilia slipped on her clothes and caught up her rug, hastened carefully down the ladder to the loft. As she descended she heard the ringing musical call: "All right, Ciss!" which meant that the lovely lady was finished, and returning to the house. Even her voice was marvellously young and sonorous, beautifully balanced and self-possessed. So different from the little voice in which she talked to herself. *That* was much more the voice of an old woman.

Ciss hastened round to the yew enclosure, where lay the comfortable chaise-longue with the various delicate rugs. Everything Pauline had was choice, to the fine straw mat on the floor. The great yew walls were beginning to cast long shadows. Only in the corner, where the rugs tumbled their delicate colours, was there hot, still sunshine.

The rugs folded up, the chair lifted away, Cecilia stooped to look at the mouth of the rain-pipe. There it was, in the corner, under a little hood of masonry and just projecting from the thick leaves of the creeper on the wall. If Pauline, lying there, turned her face towards the wall, she would speak into the very mouth of the hole. Cecilia was reassured. She had heard her aunt's thoughts indeed, but by no uncanny agency.

That evening, as if aware of something, Pauline was a little quicker than usual, though she looked her own serene, rather mysterious self. And after coffee she said to Robert and Ciss: "I'm so sleepy. The sun has made me so sleepy. I feel full of sunshine like a bee. I shall go to bed, if you don't mind. You two sit and have a talk."

Cecilia looked quickly at her cousin.

"Perhaps you would rather be alone," she said to him.

"No, no," he replied. "Do keep me company for a while, if it doesn't bore you."

The windows were open, the scent of the honeysuckle wafted in with the sound of an owl. Robert smoked in silence. There was a sort of despair in the motionless, rather squat body. He looked like a caryatid bearing a weight.

"Do you remember Cousin Henry?" Cecilia asked him suddenly.

He looked up in surprise.

"Yes, very well," he said.

"What did he look like?" she said, glancing into her cousin's big, secret-troubled eyes, in which there was so much frustration.

"Oh, he was handsome: tall and fresh-coloured, with mother's soft brown hair." As a matter of fact, Pauline's hair was grey. "The ladies admired him very much; he was at all the dances."

"And what kind of character had he?"

"Oh, very good-natured and jolly. He liked to be amused. He was rather quick and clever, like mother, and very good company."

"And did he love your mother?"

"Very much. She loved him too—better than she does me, as a matter of fact. He was so much more nearly her idea of a man."

"Why was he more her idea of a man?"

"Tall—handsome—attractive, and very good company— and would, I believe, have been very successful at law. I'm afraid I am merely negative in all those respects."

Ciss looked at him attentively, with her slow-thinking hazel eyes. Under his impassive mask, she knew he suffered.

"Do you think you are so much more negative than he?" she said.

He did not lift his face. But after a few moments he replied:

"My life, certainly, is a negative affair."

She hesitated before she dared ask him:

"And do you mind?"

He did not answer her at all. Her heart sank.

"You see, I am afraid my life is as negative as yours is," she said. "And I'm beginning to mind bitterly. I'm thirsty."

She saw his creamy, well-bred hand tremble.

"I suppose," he said, without looking at her, "one will rebel when it is too late."

That was queer, from him.

"Robert," she said, "do you like me at all?"

She saw his dusky, creamy face, so changeless in its folds, go pale. "I am very fond of you," he murmured.

"Won't you kiss me? Nobody ever kisses me," she said pathetically.

He looked at her, his eyes strange with fear and a certain haughtiness Then he rose and came softly over to her and kissed her gently on the cheek.

"It's an awful shame, Ciss!" he said softly.

She caught his hand and pressed it to her breast.

"And sit with me some time in the garden," she said, murmuring with difficulty. "Won't you?"

He looked at her anxiously and searchingly.

"What about mother?" he said.

Ciss smiled a funny little smile, and looked into his eyes. He suddenly flushed crimson, turning aside his face. It was a painful sight.

"I know," he said, "I am no lover of women."

He spoke with sarcastic stoicism against himself, but even she did not know the shame it was to him.

"You never try to be!" she said.

Again his eyes changed uncannily.

"Does one have to try?" he said.

"Why, yes! One never does anything if one doesn't try."

He went pale again.

"Perhaps you are right," he said.

In a few minutes she left him and went to her room. At least, she had tried to take off the everlasting lid from things.

The weather continued sunny, Pauline continued her sun-baths, and Ciss lay on the roof eavesdropping in the literal sense of the word. But Pauline was not to be heard. No sound came up the pipe. She must be lying with her face away into the open. Ciss listened with all her might. She could just detect the faintest, faintest murmur away below, but no audible syllable.

And at night, under the stars, Cecilia sat and waited in silence, on the seat which kept in view the drawing-room windows and the side door into the garden. She saw the light go up in her aunt's room. She saw the lights at last go out in the drawing-room. And she waited. But he did not come. She stayed on in the darkness half the night, while the owl hooted. But she stayed alone.

Two days she heard nothing. her aunt's thoughts were not

revealed and at evening nothing happened. Then the second night, as she sat with heavy, helpless persistence in the garden, suddenly she started. He had come out. She rose and went softly over the grass to him.

"Don't speak," he murmured.

And in silence, in the dark, they walked down the garden and over the little bridge to the paddock, where the hay, cut very late, was in cock. There they stood disconsolate under the stars.

"You see," he said, "how can I ask for love, if I don't feel any love in myself. You know I have a real regard for you——"

"How can you feel any love, when you never feel anything?" she said.

"That is true," he replied.

And she waited for what next.

"And how can I marry?" he said. "I am a failure even at making money. I can't ask my mother for money."

She sighed deeply.

"Then don't bother yet about marrying," she said. "Only love me a little. Won't you?"

He gave a short laugh.

"It sounds so atrocious, to say it is hard to begin," he said.

She sighed again. He was so stiff to move.

"Shall we sit down a minute," she said. And then as they sat on the hay, she added: "May I touch you? Do you mind?"

"Yes, I mind! But do as you wish," he replied, with that mixture of shyness and queer candour which made him a little ridiculous, as he knew quite well. But in his heart there was almost murder.

She touched his black, always tidy hair with her fingers.

"I suppose I shall rebel one day," he said again, suddenly.

They sat some time, till it grew chilly. And he held her hand fast, but he never put his arms round her. At last she rose and went indoors, saying good night.

The next day, as Cecilia lay stunned and angry on the roof, taking her sun-bath, and becoming hot and fierce with sunshine, suddenly she started. A terror seized her in spite of herself. It was the voice.

"*Caro, caro, tu non l'hai visto!*" it was murmuring away, in a language Cecilia did not understand. She lay and writhed her limbs in the sun, listening intently to words she could not follow. Softly, whisperingly, with infinite caressiveness and yet with that subtle, insidious arrogance under its velvet, came the voice, murmuring in Italian: *"Bravo, si molto bravo, poverino, ma uomo come te non lo sara mai, mai, mai!"* Oh, especially in Italian Cecilia heard the poisonous charm of the voice, so caressive, so soft and flexible, yet so utterly egoistic. She hated it with intensity as it sighed and whispered out of nowhere. Why, why should it be so delicate, so subtle and flexible and beautifully controlled, while she herself was so clumsy! Oh, poor Cecilia, she writhed in the afternoon sun, knowing her own clownish clumsiness and lack of suavity, in comparison.

"No, Robert dear, you will never be the man your father was, though you have some of his looks. He was a marvellous lover, soft as a flower, yet piercing as a humming-bird. No, Robert dear, you will never know how to serve a woman as Monsignor Mauro did. *Cara, cara mia bellissima, ti ho aspettato come l'agonizzante aspetta la morte, morte deliziosa, quasi quasi troppo deliziosa per un' anima humana*—Soft as a flower, yet probing like a humming-bird. He gave himself to a woman as he gave himself to God. Mauro! Mauro! How you loved me!"

The voice ceased in reverie, and Cecilia knew what she had guessed before, that Robert was not the son of her Uncle Ronald, but of some Italian.

"I am disappointed in you, Robert. There is no poignancy in you. Your father was a Jesuit, but he was the most perfect and poignant lover in the world. You are a Jesuit like a fish in a tank. And that Ciss of yours is the cat fishing for you. It is less edifying even than poor Henry."

Cecilia suddenly bent her mouth down to the tube, and said in a deep voice:

"Leave Robert alone! Don't kill him as well."

There was a dead silence, in the hot July afternoon that was lowering for thunder. Cecilia lay prostrate, her heart beating in great thumps. She was listening as if her whole soul were an ear. At last she caught the whisper:

"Did someone speak?"

She leaned again to the mouth of the tube.

"Don't kill Robert as you killed me," she said with slow enunciation, and a deep but small voice.

"Ah!" came the sharp little cry. "Who is that speaking?"

"Henry!" said the deep voice.

There was a dead silence. Poor Cecilia lay with all the use gone out of her. And there was dead silence. Till at last came the whisper:

"I didn't kill Henry. No, NO! Henry, surely you can't blame me! I loved you, dearest. I only wanted to help you."

"You killed me!" came the deep, artificial, accusing voice. "Now, let Robert live. Let him go! Let him marry!"

There was a pause.

"How very, very awful!" mused the whispering voice. "Is it possible, Henry, you are a spirit, and you condemn me?"

"Yes! I condemn you!"

Cecilia felt all her pent-up rage going down that rain-pipe. At the same time, she almost laughed. It was awful.

She lay and listened and listened. No sound! As if time had ceased, she lay inert in the weakening sun. The sky was yellowing. Quickly she dressed herself, went down, and out to the corner of the stables.

"Aunt Pauline!" she called discreetly. "Did you hear thunder?"

"Yes! I am going in. Don't wait," came a feeble voice.

Cecilia retired, and from the loft watched, spying, as the figure of the lovely lady, wrapped in a lovely wrap of old blue silk, went rather totteringly to the house.

The sky gradually darkened, Cecilia hastened in with the rugs. Then the storm broke. Aunt Pauline did not appear to tea. She found the thunder trying. Robert also did not arrive till after tea, in the pouring rain. Cecilia went down the covered passage to her own house, and dressed carefully for dinner, putting some white columbines at her breast.

The drawing-room was lit with a softly-shaded lamp. Robert, dressed, was waiting, listening to the rain. He too seemed strangely cracking and on edge. Cecilia came in with the white flowers nodding at her breast. Robert was watching her curiously, a new look on his face. Cecilia went to the bookshelves near the door, and was peering for something, listening acutely. She heard a rustle, then the door softly opening. And as it opened, Ciss suddenly switched on the strong electric light by the door.

Her aunt, in a dress of black lace over ivory colour, stood in the doorway. Her face was made up, but haggard with a look of unspeakable irritability, as if years of suppressed exasperation and dislike of her fellow-men had suddenly crumpled her into an old witch.

"Oh, aunt!" cried Cecilia.

"Why, mother, you're a little old lady!" came the astounded voice of Robert: like an astonished boy: as if it were a joke.

"Have you only just found it out?" snapped the old woman venomously.

"Yes! Why, I thought——" his voice tailed out in misgiving.

The haggard, old Pauline, in a frenzy of exasperation, said: "Aren't we going down?"

She had never even noticed the excess of light, a thing she shunned. And she went downstairs almost tottering.

At table she sat with her face like a crumpled mask of unspeakable irritability. She looked old, very old, and like a witch. Robert and Cecilia fetched furtive glances at her. And Ciss, watching Robert, saw that he was so astonished and repelled by his mother's looks, that he was another man.

"What kind of a drive home did you have?" snapped Pauline, with an almost gibbering irritability.

"It rained, of course," he said.

"How clever of you to have found that out!" said his mother, with the grisly grin of malice that had succeeded her arch smirk.

"I don't understand," he said with quiet suavity.

"It's apparent," said his mother, rapidly and sloppily eating her food.

She rushed through the meal like a crazy dog, to the utter consternation of the servant. And the moment it was over, she darted in a queer, crab-like way upstairs. Robert and Cecilia followed her, thunderstruck, like two conspirators.

"You pour the coffee. I loathe it! I'm going! Good night!" said the old woman, in a succession of sharp shots. And she scrambled out of the room.

There was a dead silence. At last he said:

"I'm afraid mother isn't well. I must persuade her to see a doctor."

"Yes!" said Cecilia.

The evening passed in silence. Robert and Ciss stayed on in the drawing-room, having lit a fire. Outside was cold rain.

Each pretended to read. They did not want to separate. The evening passed with ominous mysteriousness, yet quickly.

At about ten o'clock, the door suddenly opened, and Pauline appeared in a blue wrap. She shut the door behind her, and came to the fire. Then she looked at the two young people in hate, real hate.

"You two had better get married quickly," she said in an ugly voice. "It would look more decent; such a passionate pair of lovers!"

Robert looked up at her quietly.

"I thought you believed that cousins should not marry, mother," he said.

"I do! But you're not cousins. Your father was an Italian priest." Pauline held her daintily-slippered foot to the fire, in an old coquettish gesture. Her body tried to repeat all the old graceful gestures. But the nerve had snapped, so it was a rather dreadful caricature.

"Is that really true, mother?" he asked.

"True! What do you think? He was a distinguished man, or he wouldn't have been my lover. He was far too distinguished a man to have had you for a son. But that joy fell to me."

"How unfortunate all round," he said slowly.

"Unfortunate for you? *You* were lucky. It was *my* misfortune," she said acidly to him.

She was really a dreadful sight, like a piece of lovely Venetian glass that has been dropped, and gathered up again in horrible, sharp-edged fragments.

Suddenly she left the room again.

For a week it went on. She did not recover. It was as if every nerve in her body had suddenly started screaming in an insanity of discordance. The doctor came, and gave her sedatives, for she never slept. Without drugs, she never slept at all, only paced back and forth in her room, looking hideous and evil, reeking with malevolence. She could not bear to see either her son or her niece. Only when either of them came, she asked in pure malice:

"Well! When's the wedding! Have you celebrated the nuptials yet?"

At first Cecilia was stunned by what she had done. She realised vaguely that her aunt, once a definite thrust of condemnation had penetrated her beautiful armour, had just

collapsed squirming inside her shell. It was too terrible. Ciss
was almost terrified into repentance. Then she thought: This
is what she always was. Now let her live the rest of her days
in her true colours.

But Pauline would not live long. She was literally shrivelling away. She kept to her room, and saw no one. She had her
mirrors taken away.

Robert and Cecilia sat a good deal together. The jeering of
the mad Pauline had not driven them apart, as she had hoped.
But Cecilia dared not confess to him what she had done.

"Do you think your mother ever loved anybody?" Ciss
asked him tentatively, rather wistfully, one evening.

He looked at her fixedly.

"Herself!" he said at last.

"She didn't even *love* herself," said Ciss. "It was something
else—what was it?" She lifted a troubled, utterly puzzled
face to him.

"Power!" he said curtly.

"But what power?" she asked. "I don't understand."

"Power to feed on other lives," he said bitterly. "She was
beautiful, and she fed on life. She has fed on me as she fed
on Henry. She put a sucker into one's soul and sucked up
one's essential life."

"And don't you forgive her?"

"No."

"Poor Aunt Pauline!"

But even Ciss did not mean it. She was only aghast.

"I *know* I've got a heart," he said, passionately striking his
breast. "But it's almost sucked dry. I *know* people who want
power over others."

Ciss was silent; what was there to say?

And two days later, Pauline was found dead in her bed,
having taken too much veronal, for her heart was weakened.
From the grave even she hit back at her son and her niece.
She left Robert the noble sum of one thousand pounds; and
Ciss one hundred. All the rest, with the nucleus of her
valuable antiques, went to form the 'Pauline Attenborough
Museum'.

RAWDON'S ROOF

RAWDON was the sort of man who said, privately, to his men friends, over a glass of wine after dinner: "No woman shall sleep again under my roof!"

He said it with pride, rather vaunting, pursing his lips. "Even my housekeeper goes home to sleep."

But the housekeeper was a gentle old thing of about sixty, so it seemed a little fantastic. Moreover, the man had a wife, of whom he was secretly rather proud, as a piece of fine property, and with whom he kept up a very witty correspondence, epistolary, and whom he treated with humorous gallantry when they occasionally met for half an hour. Also he had a love affair going on. At least, if it wasn't a love affair, what was it? However!

"No, I've come to the determination that no woman shall ever sleep under my roof again—not even a female cat!"

One looked at the roof, and wondered what it had done amiss. Besides, it wasn't his roof. He only rented the house. What does a man mean, anyhow, when he says "my roof"? My roof! The ony roof I am conscious of having, myself, is the top of my head. However, he hardly can have meant that no woman should sleep under the elegant dome of his skull. Though there's no telling. You see the top of a sleek head through a window, and you say: "By Jove, what a pretty girl's head!" And after all, when the individual comes out, it's in trousers.

The point, however, is that Rawdon said so emphatically— no, not emphatically, succinctly: "No woman shall ever again sleep under my roof." It was a case of futurity. No doubt he had had his ceilings whitewashed, and their memories put out. Or rather, repainted, for it was a handsome wooden ceiling. Anyhow, if ceilings have eyes, as walls have ears, then Rawdon had given his ceilings a new outlook, with a new coat of paint, and all memory of any woman's having slept under them—for after all, in decent circumstances we sleep under ceilings, not under roofs—was wiped out for ever.

"And will you neither sleep under any woman's roof?"

That pulled him up rather short. He was not prepared to

sauce his gander as he had sauced his goose. Even I could
see the thought flitting through his mind, that some of his
pleasantest holidays depended on the charm of his hostess.
Even some of the nicest hotels were run by women.

"Ah! Well! That's not quite the same thing, you know.
When one leaves one's own house one gives up the keys of
circumstance, so to speak. But, as far as possible, I make it
a rule not to sleep under a roof that is openly, and obviously,
and obtrusively a woman's roof!"

"Quite!" said I with a shudder. "So do I!"

Now I understood his mysterious love affair less than ever.
He was never known to speak of this love affair: he did not
even write about it to his wife. The lady—for she was a lady
—lived only five minutes' walk from Rawdon. She had a
husband, but he was in diplomatic service or something like
that, which kept him occupied in the sufficiently-far distance.
Yes, far enough. And, as a husband, he was a complete
diplomat. A balance of power. If he was entitled to occupy
the wide field of the world, she, the other and contrasting
power, might concentrate and consolidate her position at
home.

She was a charming woman, too, and even a beautiful
woman. She had two charming children, long-legged, stalky,
clove-pink-half-opened sort of children. But really charming.
And she was a woman with a certain mystery. She never
talked. She never said anything about herself. Perhaps she
suffered; perhaps she was frightfully happy, and made *that*
her cause for silence. Perhaps she was wise enough even to
be beautifully silent about her happiness. Certainly she
never mentioned her sufferings, or even her trials: and
certainly she must have a fair handful of the latter, for Alec
Drummond sometimes fled home in the teeth of a gale of
debts. He simply got through his own money and through
hers, and, third and fatal stride, through other people's as
well. Then something had to be done about it. And Janet,
dear soul, had to put her hat on and take journeys. But she
never said anything of it. At least, she did just hint that Alec
didn't *quite* make enough money to meet expenses. But
after all, we don't go about with our eyes shut, and Alec
Drummond, whatever else he did, didn't hide his prowess
under a bushel.

Rawdon and he were quite friendly, but really! None of

them ever talked. Drummond didn't talk, he just went off and behaved in his own way. And though Rawdon would chat away till the small hours, *he* never 'talked'. Not to his nearest male friend did he ever mention Janet save as a very pleasant woman and his neighbour: he admitted he adored her children. They often came to see him.

And one felt about Rawdon, he was making a mystery of something. And that was rather irritating. He went every day to see Janet, and of course we saw him going: going or coming. How can one help but see? But he always went in the morning, at about eleven, and did not stay for lunch: or he went in the afternoon, and came home to dinner. Apparently he was never there in the evening. Poor Janet, she lived like a widow.

Very well, if Rawdon wanted to make it so blatantly obvious that it was only platonic, purely platonic, why wasn't he natural? Why didn't he say simply: "I'm very fond of Janet Drummond, she is my very dear friend?" Why did he sort of curl up at the very mention of her name, and curdle into silence: or else say rather forcedly: "Yes, she is a charming woman. I see a good deal of her, but chiefly for the children's sake. I'm devoted to the children!" Then he would look at one in such a curious way, as if he were hiding something. And after all, what was there to hide? If he was the woman's friend, why not? It could be a charming friendship. And if he were her lover, why, heaven bless me, he ought to have been proud of it, and showed just a glint, just an honest man's glint.

But no, never a glint of pride or pleasure in the relation either way. Instead of that, this rather theatrical reserve. Janet, it is true, was just as reserved. If she could, she avoided mentioning his name. Yet one knew, sure as houses, she felt something. One suspected her of being more in love with Rawdon than ever she had been with Alec. And one felt that there was a hush put upon it all. She had had a hush put upon her. By whom? By both the men? Or by Rawdon only? Or by Drummond? Was it for her husband's sake? Impossible! For her children's? But why! Her children were devoted to Rawdon.

It now had become the custom for them to go to him three times a week, for music. I don't mean he taught them the piano. Rawdon was a very refined musical amateur. He had

them sing, in their delicate girlish voices, delicate little songs,
and really he succeeded wonderfully with them; he made
them so true, which children rarely are, musically, and so
pure and effortless, like little flamelets of sound. It really
was rather beautiful, and sweet of him. And he taught them
music, the delicacy of the feel of it. They had a regular
teacher for the practice.

Even the little girls, in their young little ways, were in love
with Rawdon! So if their mother were in love too, in her
ripened womanhood, why not?

Poor Janet! She was so still, and so elusive: the hush upon
her! She was rather like a half-opened rose that somebody
had tied a string round, so that it couldn't open any more
But why? Why? In her there was a real touch of mystery.
One could never *ask* her, because one knew her heart was too
keenly involved: or her pride.

Whereas there was, really, no mystery about Rawdon, refined and handsome and subtle as he was. He *had* no mystery:
at least, to a man. What *he* wrapped himself up in was a
certain amount of mystification.

Who wouldn't be irritated to hear a fellow saying, when
for months and months he has been paying a daily visit to
a lonely and very attractive woman—nay, lately even a twice-
daily visit, even if always before sundown—to hear him say,
pursing his lips after a sip of his own very moderate port:
"I've taken a vow that no woman shall sleep under my roof
again!"

I almost snapped out: "Oh, what the hell! And what
about your Janet?" But I remembered in time, it was not *my*
affair, and if he wanted to have his mystifications, let him
have them.

If he meant he wouldn't have his wife sleep under his roof
again, that one could understand. They were really very
witty with one another, he and she, but fatally and damn-
ably married.

Yet neither wanted a divorce. And neither put the slightest
claim to any control over the other's behaviour. He said:
"Women live on the moon, men on the earth." And she said:
"I don't mind in the least if he loves Janet Drummond, poor
thing. It would be a change for him, from loving himself.
And a change for her, if somebody loved her——"

Poor Janet! But he wouldn't have her sleep under his roof,

no, not for any money. And apparently he never slept under hers—if she could be said to have one. So what the deuce?

Of course, if they were friends, just friends, all right! But then in that case, why start talking about not having a woman sleep under your roof? Pure mystification!

The cat never came out of the bag. But one evening I distinctly heard it mewing inside its sack, and I even believe I saw a claw through the canvas.

It was in November—everything much as usual—myself pricking my ears to hear if the rain had stopped, and I could go home, because I was just a little bored about 'cornemuse' music. I had been having dinner with Rawdon, and listening to him ever since on his favourite topic: not, of course, women, and why they shouldn't sleep under his roof, but fourteenth-century melody and windbag accompaniment.

It was not late—not yet ten o'clock—but I was restless, and wanted to go home. There was no longer any sound of rain. And Rawdon was perhaps going to make a pause in his monologue.

Suddenly there was a tap at the door, and Rawdon's man, Hawken, edged in. Rawdon, who had been a major in some fantastic capacity during the war, had brought Hawken back with him. This fresh-faced man of about thirty-five appeared in the doorway with an intensely blank and bewildered look on his face. He was really an extraordinarily good actor.

"A lady, sir!" he said, with a look of utter blankness.

"A what?" snapped Rawdon.

"A lady!"—then with a most discreet drop in his voice: "Mrs. Drummond, sir!" He looked modestly down at his feet.

Rawdon went deathly white, and his lips quivered.

"Mrs. Drummond! Where?"

Hawken lifted his eyes to his master in a fleeting glance.

"I showed her into the dining-room, there being no fire in the drawing-room."

Rawdon got to his feet and took two or three agitated strides. He could not make up his mind. At last he said, his lips working with agitation:

"Bring her in here."

Then he turned with a theatrical gesture to me.

"What this is all about, I *don't* know," he said.

"Let me clear out," said I, making for the door.

He caught me by the arm.

"No, for God's sake! For God's sake, stop and see me through!"

He gripped my arm till it really hurt, and his eyes were quite wild. I did not know my Olympic Rawdon.

Hastily I backed away to the side of the fire—we were in Rawdon's room, where the books and piano were—and Mrs. Drummond appeared in the doorway. She was much paler than usual, being a rather warm-coloured woman, and she glanced at me with big reproachful eyes, as much as to say: You intruder! You interloper! For my part, I could do nothing but stare. She wore a black wrap, which I knew quite well, over her black dinner-dress.

"Rawdon!" she said, turning to him and blotting out my existence from her consciousness. Hawken softly closed the door, and I could *feel* him standing on the threshold outside, listening keen as a hawk.

"Sit down, Janet," said Rawdon, with a grimace of a sour smile, which he could not get rid of once he had started it, so that his face looked very odd indeed, like a mask which he was unable either to fit on or take off. He had several conflicting expressions all at once, and they had all stuck.

She let her wrap slip back on her shoulders, and knitted her white fingers against her skirt, pressing down her arms, and gazing at him with a terrible gaze. I began to creep to the door.

Rawdon started after me.

"No, don't go! Don't go! I specially want you not to go," he said in extreme agitation.

I looked at her. She was looking at him with a heavy, sombre kind of stare. Me she absolutely ignored. Not for a second could she forgive me for existing on the earth. I slunk back to my post behind the leather arm-chair, as if hiding.

"Do sit down, Janet," he said to her again. "And have a smoke. What will you drink?"

"No, thanks!" she said, as if it were one word slurred out. "No, thanks."

And she proceeded again to fix him with that heavy, portentous stare.

He offered her a cigarette, his hand trembling as he held out the silver box.

"Nothanks!" she slurred out again, not even looking at the box, but keeping him fixed with that dark and heavy stare.

He turned away, making a great delay lighting a cigarette, with his back to her, to get out of the stream of that stare. He carefully went for an ash-tray, and put it carefully within reach—all the time trying not to be swept away on that stare. And she stood with her fingers locked, her straight, plump, handsome arms pressed downwards against her skirt, and she gazed at him.

He leaned his elbow on the mantelpiece abstractedly for a moment—then he started suddenly, and rang the bell. She turned her eyes from him for a moment, to watch his middle finger pressing the bell-button. Then there was a tension of waiting, an interruption in the previous tension. We waited. Nobody came. Rawdon rang again.

"That's very curious!" he murmured to himself. Hawken was usually so prompt. Hawken, not being a woman, slept under the roof, so there was no excuse for his not answering the bell. The tension in the room had now changed quality, owing to this new suspense. Poor Janet's sombre stare became gradually loosened, so to speak. Attention was divided. Where was Hawken? Rawdon rang the bell a third time, a long peal. And now Janet was no longer the centre of suspense. Where was Hawken? The question loomed large over every other.

"I'll just look in the kitchen," said I, making for the door.

"No, no. I'll go," said Rawdon.

But I was in the passage—and Rawdon was on my heels.

The kitchen was very tidy and cheerful, but empty; only a bottle of beer and two glasses stood on the table. To Rawdon the kitchen was as strange a world as to me—he never entered the servants' quarters. But to me it was curious that the bottle of beer was empty, and both the glasses had been used. I knew Rawdon wouldn't notice.

"That's very curious!" said Rawdon: meaning the absence of his man.

At that moment we heard a step on the servants' stairs, and Rawdon opened the door, to reveal Hawken descending with an armful of sheets and things.

"What are you doing?"

"Why!——" and a pause. "I was airing the clean laundry, like—not to waste the fire last thing."

Hawken descended into the kitchen with a very flushed face and very bright eyes and rather ruffled hair, and proceeded to spread the linen on chairs before the fire.

"I hope I've not done wrong, sir," he said in his most winning manner. "Was you ringing?"

"Three times! Leave that linen and bring a bottle of the fizz."

"I'm sorry, sir. You can't hear the bell from the front, sir."

It was perfectly true. The house was small, but it had been built for a very nervous author, and the servants' quarters were shut off, padded off from the rest of the house.

Rawdon said no more about the sheets and things, but he looked more peaked than ever.

We went back to the music-room. Janet had gone to the hearth, and stood with her hand on the mantel. She looked round at us, baffled.

"We're having a bottle of fizz," said Rawdon. "Do let me take your wrap."

"And where was Hawken?" she asked satirically.

"Oh, busy somewhere upstairs."

"He's a busy young man, that!" she said sardonically. And she sat uncomfortably on the edge of the chair where I had been sitting.

When Hawken came with the tray, she said:

"I'm not going to drink."

Rawdon appealed to me, so I took a glass. She looked inquiringly at the flushed and bright-eyed Hawken, as if she understood something.

The manservant left the room. We drank our wine, and the awkwardness returned.

"Rawdon!" she said suddenly, as if she were firing a revolver at him. "Alec came home to-night in a bigger mess than ever, and wanted to make love to me to get it off his mind. I can't stand it any more. I'm in love with you, and I simply can't stand Alec getting too near to me. He's dangerous when he's crossed—and when he's worked up. So I just came here. I didn't see what else I could do."

She left off as suddenly as a machine-gun leaves off firing. We were just dazed.

"You are quite right," Rawdon began, in a vague and neutral tone. . . .

"I am, am I not?" she said eagerly.

"I'll tell you what I'll do," he said. "I'll go round to the hotel to-night, and you can stay here."

"Under the kindly protection of Hawken, you mean!" she said, with quiet sarcasm.

"Why!—I could send Mrs. Betts, I suppose," he said.

Mrs. Betts was his housekeeper.

"You couldn't stay and protect me yourself?" she said quietly.

"I! I! Why, I've made a vow—haven't I, Joe?"—he turned to me—"not to have any woman sleep under my roof again."—He got the mixed sour smile on his face.

She looked up at the ceiling for a moment, then lapsed into silence. Then she said:

"Sort of monastery, so to speak!"

And she rose and reached for her wrap, adding:

"I'd better go, then."

"Joe will see you home," he said.

She faced round on me.

"Do you mind *not* seeing me home, Mr. Bradley?" she said, gazing at me.

"Not if you don't want me," said I.

"Hawken will drive you," said Rawdon.

"Oh, no, he won't!" she said. "I'll walk. Good night."

"I'll get my hat," stammered Rawdon, in an agony. "Wait! Wait! The gate will be locked."

"It was open when I came," she said.

He rang for Hawken to unlock the iron doors at the end of the short drive, whilst he himself huddled into a greatcoat and scarf, fumbling for a flashlight.

"You won't go till I come back, will you?" he pleaded to me. "I'd be awfully glad if you'd stay the night. The sheets *will* be aired."

I had to promise—and he set off with an umbrella, in the rain, at the same time asking Hawken to take a flashlight and go in front. So that was how they went, in single file along the path over the fields to Mrs. Drummond's house, Hawken in front, with flashlight and umbrella, curving round to light up in front of Mrs. Drummond, who, with umbrella only, walked isolated between two lights, Rawdon shining his flashlight on her from the rear from under his umbrella. I turned indoors.

So that was over! At least, for the moment!

I thought I would go upstairs and see how damp the bed in the guest-chamber was before I actually stayed the night with Rawdon. He never had guests—preferred to go away himself.

The guest-chamber was a good room across a passage and round a corner from Rawdon's room—its door just opposite the padded service-door. This latter service-door stood open, and a light shone through. I went into the spare bedroom, switching on the light.

To my surprise, the bed looked as if it had just been left— the sheets tumbled, the pillows pressed. I put in my hands under the bedclothes, and it was warm. Very curious!

As I stood looking round in mild wonder, I heard a voice call softly: "Joe!"

"Yes!" said I instinctively, and, though startled, strode at once out of the room and through the servants' door, towards the voice. Light shone from the open doorway of one of the servants' rooms.

There was a muffled little shriek, and I was standing looking into what was probably Hawken's bedroom, and seeing a soft and pretty white leg and a very pretty feminine posterior very thinly dimmed in a rather short night-dress, just in the act of climbing into a narrow little bed, and, then arrested, the owner of the pretty posterior burying her face in the bedclothes, to be invisible, like the ostrich in the sand.

I discreetly withdrew, went downstairs and poured myself a glass of wine. And very shortly Rawdon returned looking like Hamlet in the last act.

He said nothing, neither did I. We sat and merely smoked. Only as he was seeing me upstairs to bed, in the now immaculate bedroom, he said pathetically:

"Why aren't women content to be what a man wants them to be?"

"Why aren't they!" said I wearily.

"I thought I had made everything clear," he said.

"You start at the wrong end," said I.

And as I said it, the picture came into my mind of the pretty feminine butt-end in Hawken's bedroom. Yes, Hawken made better starts, wherever he ended.

When he brought me my cup of tea in the morning, he was very soft and cat-like. I asked him what sort of day it was, and he asked me if I'd had a good night, and was I comfortable.

"Very comfortable!" said I. "But I turned you out, I'm afraid."

"Me, sir?" He turned on me a face of utter bewilderment. But I looked him in the eye.

"Is your name Joe?" I asked him.

"You're right, sir."

"So is mine," said I. "However, I didn't see her face, so it's all right. I suppose you *were* a bit tight, in that little bed!"

"Well, sir!" and he flashed me a smile of amazing impudence, and lowered his tone to utter confidence. "This is the best bed in the house, this is." And he touched it softly.

"You've not tried them all, surely?"

A look of indignant horror on his face!

"No, sir, indeed I haven't."

That day, Rawdon left for London, on his way to Tunis, and Hawken was to follow him. The roof of his house looked just the same.

The Drummonds moved too—went away somewhere, and left a lot of unsatisfied tradespeople behind.

THE ROCKING-HORSE WINNER

THERE was a woman who was beautiful, who started with all the advantages, yet she had no luck. She married for love, and the love turned to dust. She had bonny children, yet she felt they had been thrust upon her, and she could not love them. They looked at her coldly, as if they were finding fault with her. And hurriedly she felt she must cover up some fault in herself. Yet what it was that she must cover up she never knew. Nevertheless, when her children were present, she always felt the centre of her heart go hard. This troubled her, and in her manner she was all the more gentle and anxious for her children, as if she loved them very much. Only she herself knew that at the centre of her heart was a hard little place that could not feel love, no, not for anybody. Everybody else said of her: "She is such a good mother. She adores her children." Only she herself, and her children themselves, knew it was not so. They read it in each other's eyes.

There were a boy and two little girls. They lived in a pleasant house, with a garden, and they had discreet servants, and felt themselves superior to anyone in the neighbourhood.

Although they lived in style, they felt always an anxiety in the house. There was never enough money. The mother had a small income, and the father had a small income, but not nearly enough for the social position which they had to keep up. The father went into town to some office. But though he had good prospects, these prospects never materialised. There was always the grinding sense of the shortage of money, though the style was always kept up.

At last the mother said: "I will see if I can't make something." But she did not know where to begin. She racked her brains, and tried this thing and the other, but could not find anything successful. The failure made deep lines comes into her face. Her children were growing up, they would have to go to school. There must be more money, there must be more money. The father, who was always very handsome and expensive in his tastes, seemed as if he never *would* be able to do anything worth doing. And the mother, who had a great belief in herself, did not succeed any better, and her tastes were just as expensive.

And so the house came to be haunted by the unspoken phrase: *There must be more money! There must be more money!* The children could hear it all the time, though nobody said it aloud. They heard it at Christmas, when the expensive and splendid toys filled the nursery. Behind the shining modern rocking-horse, behind the smart doll's house, a voice would start whispering: "There *must* be more money! There *must* be more money!" And the children would stop playing, to listen for a moment. They would look into each other's eyes, to see if they had all heard. And each one saw in the eyes of the other two that they too had heard. "There *must* be more money! There *must* be more money!"

It came whispering from the springs of the still-swaying rocking-horse, and even the horse, bending his wooden, champing head, heard it. The big doll, sitting so pink and smirking in her new pram, could hear it quite plainly, and seemed to be smirking all the more self-consciously because of it. The foolish puppy, too, that took the place of the teddy-bear, he was looking so extraordinarily foolish for no other reason but that he heard the secret whisper all over the house: "There *must* be more money!"

Yet nobody ever said it aloud. The whisper was everywhere, and therefore no one spoke it. Just as no one ever says: "We are breathing!" in spite of the fact that breath is coming and going all the time.

"Mother," said the boy Paul one day, "why don't we keep a car of our own? Why do we always use uncle's, or else a taxi?"

"Because we're the poor members of the family," said the mother.

"But why *are* we, mother?"

"Well—I suppose," she said slowly and bitterly, "it's because your father has no luck."

The boy was silent for some time.

"Is luck money, mother?" he asked, rather timidly.

"No, Paul. Not quite. It's what causes you to have money."

"Oh!" said Paul vaguely. "I thought when Uncle Oscar said *filthy lucker*, it meant money."

"*Filthy lucre* does mean money," said the mother. "But it's lucre, not luck."

"Oh!" said the boy. "Then what *is* luck, mother?"

"It's what causes you to have money. If you're lucky you have money. That's why it's better to be born lucky than rich. If you're rich, you may lose your money. But if you're lucky, you will always get more money."

"Oh! Will you? And is father not lucky?"

"Very unlucky, I should say," she said bitterly.

The boy watched her with unsure eyes.

"Why?" he asked.

"I don't know. Nobody ever knows why one person is lucky and another unlucky."

"Don't they? Nobody at all? Does *nobody* know?"

"Perhaps God. But He never tells."

"He ought to, then. And aren't you lucky either, mother?"

"I can't be, if I married an unlucky husband."

"But by yourself, aren't you?"

"I used to think I was, before I married. Now I think I am very unlucky indeed."

"Why?"

"Well—never mind! Perhaps I'm not really," she said.

The child looked at her to see if she meant it. But he saw, by the lines of her mouth, that she was only trying to hide something from him.

"Well, anyhow," he said stoutly, "I'm a lucky person."

"Why?" said his mother, with a sudden laugh.

He stared at her. He didn't even know why he had said it.

"God told me," he asserted, brazening it out.

"I hope He did, dear!" she said, again with a laugh, but rather bitter.

"He did, mother!"

"Excellent!" said the mother, using one of her husband's exclamations.

The boy saw she did not believe him; or rather, that she paid no attention to his assertion. This angered him somewhere, and made him want to compel her attention.

He went off by himself, vaguely, in a childish way, seeking for the clue to 'luck'. Absorbed, taking no heed of other people, he went about with a sort of stealth, seeking inwardly for luck. He wanted luck, he wanted it, he wanted it. When the two girls were playing dolls in the nursery, he would sit on his big rocking-horse, charging madly into space, with a frenzy that made the little girls peer at him uneasily. Wildly the horse careered, the waving dark hair of the boy tossed, his eyes had a strange glare in them. The little girls dared not speak to him.

When he had ridden to the end of his mad little journey, he climbed down and stood in front of his rocking-horse, staring fixedly into its lowered face. Its red mouth was slightly open, its big eye was wide and glassy-bright.

"Now!" he would silently command the snorting steed. "Now, take me to where there is luck! Now take me!"

And he would slash the horse on the neck with the little whip he had asked Uncle Oscar for. He *knew* the horse could take him to where there was luck, if only he forced it. So he would mount again and start on his furious ride, hoping at last to get there. He knew he could get there.

"You'll break your horse, Paul!" said the nurse.

"He's always riding like that! I wish he'd leave off!" said his elder sister Joan.

But he only glared down on them in silence. Nurse gave him up. She could make nothing of him. Anyhow, he was growing beyond her.

One day his mother and his Uncle Oscar came in when he was on one of his furious rides. He did not speak to them.

"Hallo, you young jockey! Riding a winner?" said his uncle.

"Aren't you growing too big for a rocking-horse? You're not a very little boy any longer, you know," said his mother.

But Paul only gave a blue glare from his big, rather close-set eyes. He would speak to nobody when he was in full tilt. His mother watched him with an anxious expression on her face.

At last he suddenly stopped forcing his horse into the mechanical gallop and slid down.

"Well, I got there!" he announced fiercely, his blue eyes still flaring, and his sturdy long legs straddling apart.

"Where did you get to?" asked his mother.

"Where I wanted to go," he flared back at her.

"That's right, son!" said Uncle Oscar. "Don't you stop till you get there. What's the horse's name?"

"He doesn't have a name," said the boy.

"Gets on without all right?" asked the uncle.

"Well, he has different names. He was called Sansovino last week."

"Sansovino, eh? Won the Ascot. How did you know this name?"

"He always talks about horse-races with Bassett," said Joan.

The uncle was delighted to find that his small nephew was posted with all the racing news. Bassett, the young gardener, who had been wounded in the left foot in the war and had got his present job through Oscar Cresswell, whose batman he had been, was a perfect blade of the 'turf'. He lived in the racing events, and the small boy lived with him.

Oscar Cresswell got it all from Bassett.

"Master Paul comes and asks me, so I can't do more than tell him, sir," said Bassett, his face terribly serious, as if he were speaking of religious matters.

"And does he ever put anything on a horse he fancies?"

"Well—I don't want to give him away—he's a young sport, a fine sport, sir. Would you mind asking him himself? He sort of takes a pleasure in it, and perhaps he'd feel I was giving him away, sir, if you don't mind."

Bassett was serious as a church.

The uncle went back to his nephew and took him off for a ride in the car.

"Say, Paul, old man, do you ever put anything on a horse?" the uncle asked.

The boy watched the handsome man closely.

"Why, do you think I oughtn't to?" he parried.

"Not a bit of it! I thought perhaps you might give me a tip for the Lincoln."

The car sped on into the country, going down to Uncle Oscar's place in Hampshire.

"Honour bright?" said the nephew.

"Honour bright, son!" said the uncle.

"Well, then, Daffodil."

"Daffodil! I doubt it, sonny. What about Mirza?"

"I only know the winner," said the boy. "That's Daffodil."

"Daffodil, eh?"

There was a pause. Daffodil was an obscure horse comparatively.

"Uncle!"

"Yes, son?"

"You won't let it go any further, will you? I promised Bassett."

"Bassett be damned, old man! What's he got to do with it?"

"We're partners. We've been partners from the first. Uncle, he lent me my first five shillings, which I lost. I promised him, honour bright, it was only between me and him; only you gave me that ten-shilling note I started winning with, so I thought you were lucky. You won't let it go any further, will you?"

The boy gazed at his uncle from those big, hot, blue eyes, set rather close together. The uncle stirred and laughed uneasily.

"Right you are, son! I'll keep your tip private. Daffodil, eh? How much are you putting on him?"

"All except twenty pounds," said the boy. "I keep that in reserve."

The uncle thought it a good joke.

"You keep twenty pounds in reserve, do you, you young romancer? What are you betting, then?"

"I'm betting three hundred," said the boy gravely. "But it's between you and me, Uncle Oscar! Honour bright?"

The uncle burst into a roar of laughter.

"It's between you and me all right, you young Nat Gould," he said, laughing. "But where's your three hundred?"

"Bassett keeps it for me. We're partners."

"You are, are you! And what is Bassett putting on Daffodil?"

"He won't go quite as high as I do, I expect. Perhaps he'll go a hundred and fifty."

"What, pennies?" laughed the uncle.

"Pounds," said the child, with a surprised look at his uncle. "Bassett keeps a bigger reserve than I do."

Between wonder and amusement Uncle Oscar was silent. He pursued the matter no further, but he determined to take his nephew with him to the Lincoln races.

"Now, son," he said, "I'm putting twenty on Mirza, and I'll put five on for you on any horse you fancy. What's your pick?"

"Daffodil, uncle."

"No, not the fiver on Daffodil!"

"I should if it was my own fiver," said the child.

"Good! Good! Right you are! A fiver for me and a fiver for you on Daffodil."

The child had never been to a race-meeting before, and his eyes were blue fire. He pursed his mouth tight and watched. A Frenchman just in front had put his money on Lancelot. Wild with excitement, he flayed his arms up and down, yelling *"Lancelot! Lancelot!"* in his French accent.

Daffodil came in first, Lancelot second, Mirza third. The child, flushed and with eyes blazing, was curiously serene. His uncle brought him four five-pound notes, four to one.

"What am I to do with these?" he cried, waving them before the boy's eyes.

"I suppose we'll talk to Bassett," said the boy. "I expect I have fifteen hundred now; and twenty in reserve; and this twenty."

His uncle studied him for some moments.

"Look here, son!" he said. "You're not serious about Bassett and that fifteen hundred, are you?"

"Yes, I am. But it's between you and me, uncle. Honour bright?"

"Honour bright all right, son! But I must talk to Bassett."

"If you'd like to be a partner, uncle, with Bassett and me, we could all be partners. Only, you'd have to promise, honour bright, uncle, not to let it go beyond us three. Bassett and I are lucky, and you must be lucky, because it was your ten shillings I started winning with. . . ."

Uncle Oscar took both Bassett and Paul into Richmond Park for an afternoon, and there they talked.

"It's like this, you see, sir," Bassett said. "Master Paul would get me talking about racing events, spinning yarns, you know, sir. And he was always keen on knowing if I'd made or if I'd lost. It's about a year since, now, that I put five shillings on Blush of Dawn for him: and we lost. Then the luck turned, with that ten shillings he had from you: that we put on Singhalese. And since that time, it's been pretty steady, all things considering. What do you say, Master Paul?"

"We're all right when we're sure," said Paul. "It's when we're not quite sure that we go down."

"Oh, but we're careful then," said Bassett.

"But when are you *sure?*" smiled Uncle Oscar.

"It's Master Paul, sir," said Bassett in a secret, religious voice. "It's as if he had it from heaven. Like Daffodil, now, for the Lincoln. That was as sure as eggs."

"Did you put anything on Daffodil?" asked Oscar Cresswell.

"Yes, sir. I made my bit."

"And my nephew?"

Bassett was obstinately silent, looking at Paul.

"I made twelve hundred, didn't I, Bassett? I told uncle I was putting three hundred on Daffodil."

"That's right," said Bassett, nodding.

"But where's the money?" asked the uncle.

"I keep it safe locked up, sir. Master Paul he can have it any minute he likes to ask for it."

"What, fifteen hundred pounds?"

"And twenty! And *forty*, that is, with the twenty he made on the course."

"It's amazing!" said the uncle.

"If Master Paul offers you to be partners, sir, I would, if I were you: if you'll excuse me," said Bassett.

Oscar Cresswell thought about it.

"I'll see the money," he said.

They drove home again, and, sure enough, Bassett came round to the garden-house with fifteen hundred pounds in notes. The twenty pounds reserve was left with Joe Glee, in the Turf Commission deposit.

"You see, it's all right, uncle, when I'm *sure!* Then we go strong, for all we're worth. Don't we, Bassett?"

"We do that, Master Paul."

"And when are you sure?" said the uncle, laughing.

"Oh, well, sometimes I'm *absolutely* sure, like about Daffodil," said the boy; "and sometimes I have an idea; and sometimes I haven't even an idea, have I, Bassett? Then we're careful, because we mostly go down."

"You do, do you! And when you're sure, like about Daffodil, what makes you sure, sonny?"

"Oh, well, I don't know," said the boy uneasily. "I'm sure, you know, uncle; that's all."

"It's as if he had it from heaven, sir," Bassett reiterated.

"I should say so!" said the uncle.

But he became a partner. And when the Leger was coming on Paul was 'sure' about Lively Spark, which was a quite inconsiderable horse. The boy insisted on putting a thousand on the horse, Bassett went for five hundred, and Oscar Cresswell two hundred. Lively Spark came in first, and the betting had been ten to one against him. Paul had made ten thousand.

"You see," he said, "I was absolutely sure of him."

Even Oscar Cresswell had cleared two thousand.

"Look here, son," he said, "this sort of thing makes me nervous."

"It needn't, uncle! Perhaps I shan't be sure again for a long time."

"But what are you going to do with your money?" asked the uncle.

"Of course," said the boy, "I started it for mother. She said she had no luck, because father is unlucky, so I thought if *I* was lucky, it might stop whispering."

"What might stop whispering?"

"Our house. I *hate* our house for whispering."

"What does it whisper?"

"Why—why"—the boy fidgeted—"why, I don't know. But it's always short of money, you know, uncle."

"I know it, son, I know it."

"You know people send mother writs, don't you, uncle?"

"I'm afraid I do," said the uncle.

"And then the house whispers, like people laughing at you behind your back. It's awful, that is! I thought if I was lucky——"

"You might stop it," added the uncle.

The boy watched him with big blue eyes, that had an uncanny cold fire in them, and he said never a word.

"Well, then!" said the uncle. "What are we doing?"

"I shouldn't like mother to know I was lucky," said the boy.

"Why not, son?"

"She'd stop me."

"I don't think she would."

"Oh!"—and the boy writhed in an odd way—"I *don't* want her to know, uncle."

"All right, son! We'll manage it without her knowing."

They managed it very easily. Paul, at the other's suggestion, handed over five thousand pounds to his uncle, who deposited it with the family lawyer, who was then to inform Paul's mother that a relative had put five thousand pounds into his hands, which sum was to be paid out a thousand pounds at a time, on the mother's birthday, for the next five years.

"So she'll have a birthday present of a thousand pounds for five successive years," said Uncle Oscar. "I hope it won't make it all the harder for her later."

Paul's mother had her birthday in November. The house had been 'whispering' worse than ever lately, and, even in spite of his luck, Paul could not bear up against it. He was very anxious to see the effect of the birthday letter, telling his mother about the thousand pounds.

When there were no visitors, Paul now took his meals with his parents, as he was beyond the nursery control. His mother went into town nearly every day. She had discovered that she had an odd knack of sketching furs and dress materials, so she worked secretly in the studio of a friend who was the chief 'artist' for the leading drapers. She drew the figures of ladies in furs and ladies in silk and sequins for the newspaper advertisements. This young woman artist earned several thousand pounds a year, but Paul's mother only made several hundreds, and she was again dissatisfied. She so wanted to be first in something, and she did not succeed, even in making sketches for drapery advertisements.

She was down to breakfast on the morning of her birthday. Paul watched her face as she read her letters. He knew the lawyer's letter. As his mother read it, her face hardened and became more expressionless. Then a cold, determined look came on her mouth. She hid the letter under the pile of others, and said not a word about it.

"Didn't you have anything nice in the post for your birthday, mother?" said Paul.

"Quite moderately nice," she said, her voice cold and absent.

She went away to town without saying more.

But in the afternoon Uncle Oscar appeared. He said Paul's mother had had a long interview with the lawyer, asking if the whole five thousand could not be advanced at once, as she was in debt.

"What do you think, uncle?" said the boy.

"I leave it to you, son."

"Oh, let her have it, then! We can get some more with the other," said the boy.

"A bird in the hand is worth two in the bush, laddie!" said Uncle Oscar.

"But I'm sure to *know* for the Grand National; or the Lincolnshire; or else the Derby. I'm sure to know for *one* of them," said Paul.

So Uncle Oscar signed the agreement, and Paul's mother touched the whole five thousand. Then something very curious happened. The voices in the house suddenly went mad, like a chorus of frogs on a spring evening. There were certain new furnishings, and Paul had a tutor. He was *really* going to Eton, his father's school, in the following autumn. There were flowers in the winter, and a blossoming of the luxury Paul's mother had been used to. And yet the voices in the house, behind the sprays of mimosa and almond-blossom, and from under the piles of iridescent cushions, simply trilled and screamed in a sort of ecstasy: "There *must* be more money! Oh-h-h; there *must* be more money. Oh, now, now-w! Now-w-w—there *must* be more money!— more than ever! More than ever!"

It frightened Paul terribly. He studied away at his Latin and Greek with his tutor. But his intense hours were spent with Bassett. The Grand National had gone by: he had not 'known', and had lost a hundred pounds. Summer was at hand. He was in agony for the Lincoln. But even for the Lincoln he didn't 'know', and he lost fifty pounds. He became wild-eyed and strange, as if something were going to explode in him.

"Let it alone, son! Don't you bother about it!" urged Uncle Oscar. But it was as if the boy couldn't really hear what his uncle was saying.

"I've got to know for the Derby! I've got to know for the Derby!" the child reiterated, his big blue eyes blazing with a sort of madness.

His mother noticed how overwrought he was.

"You'd better go to the seaside. Wouldn't you like to go now to the seaside, instead of waiting? I think you'd better," she said, looking down at him anxiously, her heart curiously heavy because of him.

But the child lifted his uncanny blue eyes.

"I couldn't possibly go before the Derby, mother!" he said. "I couldn't possibly!"

"Why not?" she said, her voice becoming heavy when she

was opposed. "Why not? You can still go from the sea-side to see the Derby with your Uncle Oscar, if that's what you wish. No need for you to wait here. Besides, I think you care too much about these races. It's a bad sign. My family has been a gambling family, and you won't know till you grow up how much damage it has done. But it has done damage. I shall have to send Bassett away, and ask Uncle Oscar not to talk racing to you, unless you promise to be reasonable about it: go away to the seaside and forget it. You're all nerves!"

"I'll do what you like, mother, so long as you don't send me away till after the Derby," the boy said.

"Send you away from where? Just from this house?"

"Yes," he said, gazing at her.

"Why, you curious child, what makes you care about this house so much, suddenly? I never knew you loved it."

He gazed at her without speaking. He had a secret within a secret, something he had not divulged, even to Bassett or to his Uncle Oscar.

But his mother, after standing undecided and a little bit sullen for some moments, said:

"Very well, then! Don't go to the seaside till after the Derby, if you don't wish it. But promise me you won't let your nerves go to pieces. Promise you won't think so much about horse-racing and *events*, as you call them!"

"Oh no," said the boy casually. "I won't think much about them, mother. You needn't worry. I wouldn't worry, mother, if I were you."

"If you were me and I were you," said his mother, "I wonder what we *should* do!"

"But you know you needn't worry, mother, don't you?" the boy repeated.

"I should be awfully glad to know it," she said wearily.

"Oh, well, you *can*, you know. I mean, you *ought* to know you needn't worry," he insisted.

"Ought I? Then I'll see about it," she said.

Paul's secret of secrets was his wooden horse, that which had no name. Since he was emancipated from a nurse and a nursery-governess, he had had his rocking-horse removed to his own bedroom at the top of the house.

"Surely you're too big for a rocking-horse!" his mother had remonstrated.

"Well, you see, mother, till I can have a *real* horse, I like to have *some* sort of animal about," had been his quaint answer.

"Do you feel he keeps you company?" she laughed.

"Oh yes! He's very good, he always keeps me company, when I'm there," said Paul.

So the horse, rather shabby, stood in an arrested prance in the boy's bedroom.

The Derby was drawing near, and the boy grew more and more tense. He hardly heard what was spoken to him, he was very frail, and his eyes were really uncanny. His mother had sudden strange seizures of uneasiness about him. Sometimes, for half an hour, she would feel a sudden anxiety about him that was almost anguish. She wanted to rush to him at once, and know he was safe.

Two nights before the Derby, she was at a big party in town, when one of her rushes of anxiety about her boy, her first-born, gripped her heart till she could hardly speak. She fought with the feeling, might and main, for she believed in common sense. But it was too strong. She had to leave the dance and go downstairs to telephone to the country. The children's nursery-governess was terribly surprised and startled at being rung up in the night.

"Are the children all right, Miss Wilmot?"

"Oh yes, they are quite all right."

"Master Paul? Is he all right?"

"He went to bed as right as a trivet. Shall I run up and look at him?"

"No," said Paul's mother reluctantly. "No! Don't trouble. It's all right. Don't sit up. We shall be home fairly soon." She did not want her son's privacy intruded upon.

"Very good," said the governess.

It was about one o'clock when Paul's mother and father drove up to their house. All was still. Paul's mother went to her room and slipped off her white fur cloak. She had told her maid not to wait up for her. She heard her husband downstairs, mixing a whisky and soda.

And then, because of the strange anxiety at her heart, she stole upstairs to her son's room. Noiselessly she went along the upper corridor. Was there a faint noise? What was it?

She stood, with arrested muscles, outside his door, listening. There was a strange, heavy, and yet not loud noise. Her heart stood still. It was a soundless noise, yet rushing and powerful. Something huge, in violent, hushed motion. What was it? What in God's name was it? She ought to know. She felt that she knew the noise. She knew what it was.

Yet she could not place it. She couldn't say what it was. And on and on it went, like a madness.

Softly, frozen with anxiety and fear, she turned the door-handle.

The room was dark. Yet in the space near the window, she heard and saw something plunging to and fro. She gazed in fear and amazement.

Then suddenly she switched on the light, and saw her son, in his green pyjamas, madly surging on the rocking-horse. The blaze of light suddenly lit him up, as he urged the wooden horse, and lit her up, as she stood, blonde, in her dress of pale green and crystal, in the doorway.

"Paul!" she cried. "Whatever are you doing?"

"It's Malabar!" he screamed in a powerful, strange voice. "It's Malabar!"

His eyes blazed at her for one strange and senseless second, as he ceased urging his wooden horse. Then he fell with a crash to the ground, and she, all her tormented motherhood flooding upon her, rushed to gather him up.

But he was unconscious, and unconscious he remained, with some brain-fever. He talked and tossed, and his mother sat stonily by his side.

"Malabar! It's Malabar! Bassett, Bassett, I *know!* It's Malabar!"

So the child cried, trying to get up and urge the rocking-horse that gave him his inspiration.

"What does he mean by Malabar?" asked the heart-frozen mother.

"I don't know," said the father stonily.

"What does he mean by Malabar?" she asked her brother Oscar.

"It's one of the horses running for the Derby," was the answer.

And, in spite of himself, Oscar Cresswell spoke to Bassett, and himself put a thousand on Malabar: at fourteen to one.

The third day of the illness was critical: they were waiting for a change. The boy, with his rather long, curly hair, was tossing ceaselessly on the pillow. He neither slept nor regained consciousness, and his eyes were like blue stones. His mother sat, feeling her heart had gone, turned actually into a stone.

In the evening, Oscar Cresswell did not come, but Bassett sent a message, saying could he come up for one moment, just one moment? Paul's mother was very angry at the intrusion, but on second thoughts she agreed. The boy was the same. Perhaps Bassett might bring him to consciousness.

The gardener, a shortish fellow with a little brown moustache and sharp little brown eyes, tiptoed into the room, touched his imaginary cap to Paul's mother, and stole to the bedside, staring with glittering, smallish eyes at the tossing, dying child.

"Master Paul!" he whispered. "Master Paul! Malabar came in first all right, a clean win. I did as you told me. You've made over seventy thousand pounds, you have; you've got over eighty thousand. Malabar came in all right, Master Paul."

"Malabar! Malabar! Did I say Malabar, mother? Did I say Malabar? Do you think I'm lucky, mother? I knew Malabar, didn't I? Over eighty thousand pounds! I call that lucky, don't you, mother? Over eighty thousand pounds! I knew, didn't I know I knew? Malabar came in all right. If I ride my horse till I'm sure, then I tell you, Bassett, you can go as high as you like. Did you go for all you were worth, Bassett?"

"I went a thousand on it, Master Paul."

"I never told you, mother, that if I can ride my horse, and *get there*, then I'm absolutely sure—oh, absolutely! Mother, did I ever tell you? I *am* lucky!"

"No, you never did," said his mother.

But the boy died in the night.

And even as he lay dead, his mother heard her brother's voice saying to her: "My God, Hester, you're eighty-odd thousand to the good, and a poor devil of a son to the bad. But, poor devil, poor devil, he's best gone out of a life where he rides his rocking-horse to find a winner."

MOTHER AND DAUGHTER

VIRGINIA BODOIN had a good job: she was head of a department in a certain government office, held a responsible position, and earned, to imitate Balzac and be precise about it, seven hundred and fifty pounds a year. That is already something. Rachel Bodoin, her mother, had an income of about six hundred a year, on which she had lived in the capitals of Europe since the effacement of a never very important husband.

Now, after some years of virtual separation and 'freedom', mother and daughter once more thought of settling down. They had become, in course of time, more like a married couple than mother and daughter. They knew one another very well indeed, and each was a little 'nervous' of the other. They had lived together and parted several times. Virginia was now thirty, and she didn't look like marrying. For four years she had been as good as married to Henry Lubbock, a rather spoilt young man who was musical. Then Henry let her down: for two reasons. He couldn't stand her mother. Her mother couldn't stand him. And anybody whom Mrs. Bodoin could not stand she managed to sit on, disastrously. So Henry had writhed horribly, feeling his mother-in-law sitting on him tight, and Virginia after all, in a helpless sort of family loyalty, sitting alongside her mother. Virginia didn't really want to sit on Henry. But when her mother egged her on, she couldn't help it. For ultimately her mother had power over her; a strange *female* power, nothing to do with parental authority. Virginia had long thrown parental authority to the winds. But her mother had another, much subtler form of domination, female and thrilling, so that when Rachel said: "Let's squash him!" Virginia had to rush wickedly and gleefully to the sport. And Henry knew quite well when he was being squashed. So that was one of his reasons for going back on Vinny. He called her Vinny, to the superlative disgust of Mrs. Bodoin, who always corrected him: "My daughter *Virginia*——"

The second reason was, again to be Balzacian, that Virginia

hadn't a sou of her own. Henry had a sorry two hundred and fifty. Virginia, at the age of twenty-four, was already earning four hundred and fifty. But she was earning them. Whereas Henry managed to earn about twelve pounds per annum, by his precious music. He had realised that he would find it hard to earn more. So that marrying, except with a wife who could keep him, was rather out of the question. Vinny would inherit her mother's money. But then Mrs. Bodoin had the health and muscular equipment of the Sphinx. She would live for ever, seeking whom she might devour, and devouring him. Henry lived with Vinny for two years, in the married sense of the words: and Vinny felt they *were* married, minus a mere ceremony. But Vinny had her mother always in the background; often as far back as Paris or Biarritz, but still, within letter reach. And she never realised the funny little grin that came on her own elvish face when her mother, even in a letter, spread her skirts and calmly sat on Henry. She never realised that in spirit she promptly and mischievously sat on him too: she could no more have helped it than the tide can help turning to the moon. And she did not dream that he felt it, and was utterly mortified in his masculine vanity. Women, very often, hypnotise one another, and then, hypnotised, they proceed gently to wring the neck of the man they think they are loving with all their hearts. Then they call it utter perversity on his part, that he doesn't like having his neck wrung. They think he is repudiating a heart-felt love. For they are hypnotised. Women hypnotise one another, without knowing it.

In the end, Henry backed out. He saw himself being simply reduced to nothingness by two women, an old witch with muscles like the Sphinx, and a young, spell-bound witch, lavish, elvish and weak, who utterly spoilt him but who ate his marrow.

Rachel would write from Paris: "My Dear Virginia, as I had a windfall in the way of an investment, I am sharing it with you. You will find enclosed my cheque for twenty pounds. No doubt you will be needing it to buy Henry a suit of clothes, since the spring is apparently come, and the sunlight may be tempted to show him up for what he is worth. I don't want my daughter going around with what is presumably a street-corner musician, but please pay the tailor's bill yourself, or you may have to do it over again later." Henry got a suit of clothes, but it was as good as a shirt of Nessus, eating him away with subtle poison.

So he backed out. He didn't jump out, or bolt, or carve his way out at the sword's point. He sort of faded out, distributing his departure over a year or more. He was fond of Vinny, and he could hardly do without her, and he was sorry for her. But at length he couldn't see her apart from her mother. She was a young, weak, spendthrift witch, accomplice of her tough-clawed witch of a mother.

Henry made other alliances, got a good hold on elsewhere, and gradually extricated himself. He saved his life, but he had lost, he felt, a good deal of his youth and marrow. He tended now to go fat, a little puffy, somewhat insignificant. And he had been handsome and striking-looking.

The two witches howled when he was lost to them. Poor Virginia was really half-crazy, she didn't know what to do with herself. She had a violent recoil from her mother. Mrs. Bodoin was filled with furious contempt for her daughter: that she should let such a hooked fish slip out of her hands! That she should allow such a person to turn her down! "I don't quite see my daughter seduced and thrown over by a sponging individual such as Henry Lubbock," she wrote. "But if it has happened, I suppose it is somebody's fault——"

There was a mutual recoil, which lasted nearly five years. But the spell was not broken. Mrs. Bodoin's mind never left her daughter, and Virginia was ceaselessly aware of her mother, somewhere in the universe. They wrote, and met at intervals, but they kept apart in recoil.

The spell, however, was between them, and gradually it worked. They felt more friendly. Mrs. Bodoin came to London. She stayed in the same quiet hotel with her daughter: Virginia had had two rooms in an hotel for the past three years. And, at last, they thought of taking an apartment together.

Virginia was now over thirty. She was still thin and odd and elvish, with a very slight and piquant cast in one of her brown eyes, and she still had her odd, twisted smile, and her slow, rather deep-toned voice, that caressed a man like the stroking of subtle fingertips. Her hair was still a natural tangle of curls, a bit dishevelled. She still dressed with a natural elegance which tended to go wrong and a tiny bit sluttish. She still might have a hole in her expensive and perfectly

new stockings, and still she might have to take off her shoes
in the drawing-room, if she came to tea, and sit there in
her stockinged-feet. True, she had elegant feet: she was
altogether elegantly shaped. But it wasn't that. It was neither
coquetry nor vanity. It was simply that, after having gone
to a good shoemaker and paid five guineas for a pair of
perfectly simple and natural shoes, made to her feet, the said
shoes would hurt her excruciatingly, when she had walked
half a mile in them, and she would simply have to take them
off, even if she sat on the kerb to do it. It was a fatality.
There was a touch of the *gamin* in her very feet, a certain
sluttishness that wouldn't let them stay properly in nice
proper shoes. She practically always wore her mother's old
shoes. "Of course, I go through life in mother's old shoes. If
she died and left me without a supply, I suppose I should
have to go in a bath-chair," she would say, with her odd
twisted little grin. She was so elegant, and yet a slut. It was
her charm, really.

Just the opposite of her mother. They could wear each
other's shoes and each other's clothes, which seemed remarkable, for Mrs. Bodoin seemed so much the bigger of the two.
But Virginia's shoulders were broad; if she was thin, she had
a strong frame, even when she looked a frail rag.

Mrs. Bodoin was one of those women of sixty or so, with
a terrible inward energy and a violent sort of vitality. But
she managed to hide it. She sat with perfect repose, and
folded hands. One thought: What a calm woman! Just as
one may look at the snowy summit of a quiescent volcano, in
the evening light, and think: What peace!

It was strange *muscular* energy which possessed Mrs.
Bodoin, as it possesses, curiously enough, many women over
fifty, and is usually distasteful in its manifestations. Perhaps
it accounts for the lassitude of the young.

But Mrs. Bodoin recognised the bad taste in her energetic
coevals, so she cultivated repose. Her very way of pronounc-
ing the word, in two syllables: re-pòse, making the second
syllable run on into the twilight, showed how much
suppressed energy she had. Faced with the problem of iron-
grey hair and black eyebrows, she was too clever to try
dyeing herself back into youth. She studied her face, her
whole figure, and decided that it was *positive*. There was no
denying it. There was no wispiness, no hollowness, no limp

frail blossom-on-a-bending-stalk about her. Her figure, though not stout, was full, strange, and *cambré*. Her face had an aristocratic arched nose, aristocratic, who-the-devil-are-you grey eyes, and cheeks rather long but also rather full. Nothing appealing or youthfully skittish here.

Like an independent woman, she used her wits, and decided most emphatically not to be youthful or skittish or appealing. She would keep her dignity, for she was fond of it. She was positive. She liked to be positive. She was used to her positivity. So she would just *be* positive.

She turned to the positive period; to the eighteenth century, to Voltaire, to Ninon de l'Enclos and the Pompadour, to Madame la Duchesse and Monsieur le Marquis. She decided that she was not much in the line of la Pompadour or la Duchesse, but almost exactly in the line of Monsieur le Marquis. And she was right. With hair silvering to white, brushed back clean from her positive brow and temples, cut short, but sticking out a little behind, with her rather full, pink face and thin black eyebrows plucked to two fine, superficial crescents, her arching nose and her rather full insolent eyes she was perfectly eighteenth century, the early half. That she was Monsieur le Marquis rather than Madame la Marquise made her really modern.

Her appearance was perfect. She wore delicate combinations of grey and pink, maybe with a darkening iron-grey touch, and her jewels were of soft old coloured paste. Her bearing was a sort of alert repose, very calm, but very assured. There was, to use a vulgarism, no getting past her.

She had a couple of thousand pounds she could lay hands on. Virginia, of course, was always in debt. But, after all, Virginia was not to be sniffed at. She made seven hundred and fifty a year.

Virginia was oddly clever, and not clever. She didn't *really* know anything, because anything and everything was interesting to her for the moment, and she picked it up at once. She picked up languages with extraordinary ease, she was fluent in a fortnight. This helped her enormously with her job. She could prattle away with heads of industry, let them come from where they liked. But she didn't *know* any language, not even her own. She picked things up in her sleep, so to speak, without knowing anything about them.

And this made her popular with men. With all her curious

facility, they didn't feel small in front of her, because she was like an instrument. She had to be prompted. Some man had to set her in motion, and then she worked, really cleverly. She could collect the most valuable information. She was very useful. She worked with men, spent most of her time with men, her friends were practically all men. She didn't feel easy with women.

Yet she had no lover, nobody seemed eager to marry her, nobody seemed eager to come close to her at all. Mrs. Bodoin said: "I'm afraid Virginia is a one-man woman. I am a one-man woman. So was my mother, and so was my grand-mother. Virginia's father was the only man in my life, the only one. And I'm afraid Virginia is the same, tenacious. Unfortunately, the man was what he was, and her life is just left there."

Henry had said, in the past, that Mrs. Bodoin wasn't a one-man woman, she was a no-man woman, and that if she could have had her way, everything male would have been wiped off the face of the earth, and only the female element left.

However, Mrs. Bodoin thought that it was now time to make a move. So she and Virginia took a quite handsome apartment in one of the old Bloomsbury squares, fitted it up and furnished it with extreme care, and with some quite lovely things, got in a very good man, an Austrian, to cook, and they set up married life together, mother and daughter.

At first it was rather thrilling. The two reception-rooms, looking down on the dirty old trees of the Square gardens, were of splendid proportions, and each with three great windows coming down low, almost to the level of the knees. The chimney-piece was late eighteenth century. Mrs. Bodoin furnished the rooms with a gentle suggestion of Louis-Seize merged with Empire, without keeping to any particular style. But she had, saved from her own home, a really remarkable Aubusson carpet. It looked almost new, as if it had been woven two years ago, and was startling, yet somehow rather splendid, as it spread its rose-red borders and wonderful florid array of silver-grey and gold-grey roses, lilies and gorgeous swans and trumpeting volutes away over the floor. Very æsthetic people found it rather loud, they preferred the worn, dim yellowish Aubusson in the big bedroom. But Mrs. Bodoin loved her drawing-room carpet. It was positive, but it was not vulgar. It had a certain grand air in its floridity. She felt it gave her a proper footing. And it behaved very well with her painted cabinets and grey-and-gold brocade chairs and big Chinese vases, which she liked to fill with big flowers: single Chinese peonies, big roses, great tulips, orange lilies. The dim room of London, with all its atmospheric colour, would stand the big, free, fisticuffing flowers.

Virginia, for the first time in her life, had the pleasure of making a home. She was again entirely under her mother's spell, and swept away, thrilled to her marrow. She had had no idea that her mother had got such treasures as the carpets and painted cabinets and brocade chairs up her sleeve: many of them the débris of the Fitzpatrick home in Ireland, Mrs. Bodoin being a Fitzpatrick. Almost like a child, like a bride, Virginia threw herself into the business of fixing up the rooms. "Of course, Virginia, I consider this is *your* apartment," said Mrs. Bodoin. "I am nothing but your *dame de compagnie*, and shall carry out your wishes entirely, if you will only express them."

Of course Virginia expressed a few, but not many. She introduced some wild pictures bought from impecunious artists whom she patronised. Mrs. Bodoin thought the pictures positive about the wrong things, but as far as possible, she let them stay: looking on them as the necessary element of modern ugliness. But by that element of modern ugliness, wilfully so, it was easy to see the things that Virginia had introduced into the apartment.

Perhaps nothing goes to the head like setting up house. You can get drunk on it. You feel you are creating something. Nowadays it is no longer the 'home', the domestic nest. It is 'my rooms', or 'my house', the great garment which reveals and clothes 'my personality'. Mrs. Bodoin, deliberately scheming for Virginia, kept moderately cool over it, but even she was thrilled to the marrow, and of an intensity and ferocity with the decorators and furnishers, astonishing. But Virginia was just all the time tipsy with it, as if she had touched some magic button on the grey wall of life, and with an Open Sesame! her lovely and coloured rooms had begun to assemble out of fairyland. It was far more vivid and wonderful to her than if she had inherited a duchy.

The mother and daughter, the mother in a sort of faded russet crimson and the daughter in silver, began to entertain.

They had, of course, mostly men. It filled Mrs. Bodoin with a sort of savage impatience to entertain women. Besides, most of Virginia's acquaintances were men. So there were dinners and well-arranged evenings.

It went well, but something was missing. Mrs. Bodoin wanted to be gracious, so she held herself rather back. She stayed a little distant, was calm, reposed, eighteenth-century, and determined to be a foil to the clever and slightly-elvish Virginia. It was a pose, and alas, it stopped something. She was very nice with the men, no matter what her contempt of them. But the men were uneasy with her: afraid.

What they all felt, all the men guests, was that *for them*, nothing really happened. Everything that happened was between mother and daughter. All the flow was between mother and daughter. A subtle, hypnotic spell encompassed the two women, and, try as they might, the men were shut out. More than one young man, a little dazzled, *began* to fall in love with Virginia. But it was impossible. Not only was he shut out, he was, in some way, annihilated. The spontaneity was killed in his bosom. While the two women sat, brilliant and rather wonderful, in magnetic connection at opposite ends of the table, like two witches, a double Circe turning the men not into swine—the men would have liked that well enough—but into lumps.

It was tragic. Because Mrs. Bodoin wanted Virginia to fall in love and marry. She really wanted it, and she attributed Virginia's lack of forthcoming to the delinquent Henry. She never realised the hypnotic spell, which of course encompassed her as well as Virginia, and made men just an impossibility to both women, mother and daughter alike.

At this time, Mrs. Bodoin hid her humour. She had a really marvellous faculty of humorous imitation. She could imitate the Irish servants from her old home, or the American women who called on her, or the modern ladylike young men, the asphodels, as she called them: "Of course, you know the asphodel is a kind of onion! Oh yes, just an over-bred onion": who wanted, with their murmuring voices and peeping under their brows, to make her feel very small and very bourgeois. She could imitate them all with a humour that was really touched with genius. But it was devastating. It demolished the objects of her humour so absolutely, smashed them to bits with a ruthless hammer, pounded them to

nothing so terribly, that it frightened people, particularly
men. It frightened men off.

So she hid it. She hid it. But there it was, up her sleeve,
her merciless, hammer-like humour, which just smashed its
object on the head and left him brained. She tried to disown
it. She tried to pretend, even to Virginia, that she had the
gift no more. But in vain; the hammer hidden up her sleeve
hovered over the head of every guest, and every guest felt his
scalp creep, and Virginia felt her inside creep with a little,
mischievous, slightly idiotic grin, as still another fool male
was mystically knocked on the head. It was a sort of uncanny sport.

No, the plan was not going to work: the plan of having
Virginia fall in love and marry. Of course the men *were* such
lumps, such *œufs farcies*. There was one, at least, that Mrs.
Bodoin had real hopes of. He was a healthy and normal and
very good-looking boy of good family, with no money, alas,
but clerking to the House of Lords and very hopeful, and not
very clever, but simply in love with Virginia's cleverness. He
was just the one Mrs. Bodoin would have married for herself.
True, he was only twenty-six, to Virginia's thirty-one. But he
had rowed in the Oxford eight, and adored horses, talked
horses adorably, and was simply infatuated by Virginia's
cleverness. To him Virginia had the finest mind on earth.
She was as wonderful as Plato, but infinitely more attractive,
because she was a woman, and winsome with it. Imagine a
winsome Plato with untidy curls and the tiniest little brown-
eyed squint and just a hint of woman's pathetic need for a
protector, and you may imagine Adrian's feeling for Virginia.
He adored her on his knees, but he felt he could protect
her.

"Of course, he's just a very nice *boy!*" said Mrs. Bodoin.
"He's a boy, and that's all you can say. And he always will
be a boy. But that's the very nicest kind of man, the only
kind you can live with: the eternal boy. Virginia, aren't you
attracted to him?"

"Yes, mother! I think he's an awfully nice *boy*, as you
say," replied Virginia, in her rather low, musical, whimsical
voice. But the mocking little curl in the intonation put the
lid on Adrian. Virginia was not marrying a nice *boy!* She
could be malicious too, against her mother's taste. And Mrs.
Bodoin let escape her a faint gesture of impatience.

For she had been planning her own retreat, planning to give Virginia the apartment outright, and half of her own income, if she would marry Adrian. Yes, the mother was already scheming how best she could live with dignity on three hundred a year, once Virginia was happily married to that most attractive if slightly brainless *boy*.

A year later, when Virginia was thirty-two, Adrian, who had married a wealthy American girl and been transferred to a job in the legation at Washington in the meantime, faithfully came to see Virginia as soon as he was in London, faithfully kneeled at her feet, faithfully thought her the most wonderful spiritual being, and faithfully felt that she, Virginia, could have done wonders with him, which wonders would now never be done, for he had married in the meantime.

Virginia was looking haggard and worn. The scheme of a *ménage à deux* with her mother had not succeeded. And now, work was telling on the younger woman. It is true, she was amazingly facile. But facility wouldn't get her all the way. She had to earn her money, and earn it hard. She had to slog, and she had to concentrate. While she could work by quick intuition and without much responsibility, work thrilled her. But as soon as she had to get down to it, as they say, grip and slog and concentrate, in a really responsible position, it wore her out terribly. She had to do it all off her nerves. She hadn't the same sort of fighting power as a man. Where a man can summon his old Adam in him to fight through his work, a woman has to draw on her nerves, and on her nerves alone. For the old Eve in her will have nothing to do with such work. So that mental responsibility, mental concentration, mental slogging wear out a woman terribly, especially if she is head of a department, and not working *for* somebody.

So poor Virginia was worn out. She was thin as a rail. Her nerves were frayed to bits. And she could never forget her beastly work. She would come home at tea-time speechless and done for. Her mother, tortured by the sight of her, longed to say: "Has anything gone wrong, Virginia? Have you had anything particularly trying at the office to-day?" But she learned to hold her tongue, and say nothing. The question would be the last straw to Virginia's poor overwrought nerves, and there would be a little scene which, despite Mrs. Bodoin's calm and forbearance, offended the elder woman to the quick. She had learned, by bitter experience, to leave her child alone, as one would leave a frail tube of vitriol alone. But, of course, she could not keep her *mind* off Virginia. That was impossible. And poor Virginia, under the strain of work and the strain of her mother's awful ceaseless mind, was at the very end of her strength and resources.

Mrs. Bodoin had always disliked the fact of Virginia's doing a job. But now she hated it. She hated the whole government office with violent and virulent hate. Not only was it undignified for Virginia to be tied up there, but it was turning her, Mrs. Bodoin's daughter, into a thin, nagging, fearsome old maid. Could anything be more utterly English and humiliating to a well-born Irishwoman?

After a long day attending to the apartment, skilfully darning one of the brocade chairs, polishing the Venetian mirrors to her satisfaction, selecting flowers, doing certain shopping and housekeeping, attending perfectly to everything, then receiving callers in the afternoon, with never-ending energy, Mrs. Bodoin would go up from the drawing-room after tea and write a few letters, take her bath, dress with great care— she enjoyed attending to her person—and come down to dinner as fresh as a daisy, but far more energetic than that quiet flower. She was ready now for a full evening.

She was conscious, with gnawing anxiety, of Virginia's presence in the house, but she did not see her daughter till dinner was announced. Virginia slipped in, and away to her room unseen, never going into the drawing-room to tea. If Mrs. Bodoin heard her daughter's key in the latch, she quickly retired into one of the rooms till Virginia was safely through. It was too much for poor Virginia's nerves even to catch sight of anybody in the house, when she came in from the office. Bad enough to hear the murmur of visitors' voices behind the drawing-room door.

And Mrs. Bodoin would wonder: How is she? How is she to-night? I wonder what sort of a day she's had? And this thought would roam prowling through the house, to where Virginia was lying on her back in her room. But the mother would have to consume her anxiety till dinner-time. And then Virginia would appear, with black lines under her eyes, thin, tense, a young woman out of an office, the stigma upon her: badly dressed, a little acid in humour, with an impaired digestion, not interested in anything, blighted by her work.

And Mrs. Bodoin, humiliated at the very sight of her, would control herself perfectly, say nothing but the mere smooth nothings of casual speech, and sit in perfect form presiding at a carefully-cooked dinner thought out entirely to please Virginia. Then Virginia hardly noticed what she ate.

Mrs. Bodoin was pining for an evening with life in it. But Virginia would lie on the couch and put on the loud-speaker. Or she would put a humorous record on the gramophone, and be amused, and hear it again, and be amused, and hear it again, six times, and six times be amused by a mildly funny record that Mrs. Bodoin now knew off by heart. "Why, Virginia, I could repeat that record over to you, if you wished it, without your troubling to wind up that gramophone." And Virginia, after a pause in which she seemed not to have heard what her mother said, would reply: "I'm sure you could, mother." And that simple speech would convey such volumes of contempt for all that Rachel Bodoin was or ever could be or ever had been, contempt for her energy, her vitality, her mind, her body, her very existence, that the elder woman would curl. It seemed as if the ghost of Robert Bodoin spoke out of the mouth of the daughter, in deadly venom. Then Virginia would put on the record for the seventh time.

During the second ghastly year, Mrs. Bodoin realised that the game was up. She was a beaten woman, a woman without object or meaning any more. The hammer of her awful female humour, which had knocked so many people on the head, all the people, in fact, that she had come into contact with, had at last flown backwards and hit herself on the head. For her daughter was her other self, her *alter ego*. The secret and the meaning and the power of Mrs. Bodoin's whole life lay in the hammer, that hammer of her living humour which knocked everything on the head. That had been her lust and her passion, knocking everybody and everything humorously on the head. She had felt inspired in it: it was a sort of mission. And she had hoped to hand on the hammer to Virginia, her clever, unsolid but still actual daughter, Virginia. Virginia was the continuation of Rachel's own self. Virginia was Rachel's *alter ego*, her other self.

But, alas, it was a half-truth. Virginia had had a father. This fact, which had been utterly ignored by the mother, was gradually brought home to her by the curious recoil of the hammer. Virginia was her father's daughter. Could anything

be more unseemly, horrid, more perverse in the natural
scheme of things? For Robert Bodoin had been fully and
deservedly knocked on the head by Rachel's hammer. Could
anything, then, be more disgusting than that he should
resurrect again in the person of Mrs. Bodoin's own daughter,
her own *alter ego* Virginia, and start hitting back with a little
spiteful hammer that was David's pebble against Goliath's
battle-axe!

But the little pebble was mortal. Mrs. Bodoin felt it sink
into her brow, her temple, and she was finished. The hammer
fell nerveless from her hand.

The two women were now mostly alone. Virginia was too
tired to have company in the evening. So there was the
gramophone or loud-speaker, or else silence. Both women
had come to loathe the apartment. Virginia felt it was the
last grand act of bullying on her mother's part, she felt bullied
by the assertive Aubusson carpet, by the beastly Venetian
mirrors, by the big over-cultured flowers. She even felt
bullied by the excellent food, and longed again for a Soho
restaurant and her two poky, shabby rooms in the hotel. She
loathed the apartment: she loathed everything. But she had
not the energy to move. She had not the energy to do anything. She crawled to her work, and for the rest, she lay flat,
gone.

It was Virginia's worn-out inertia that really finished Mrs.
Bodoin. That was the pebble that broke the bone of her
temple: "To have to attend my daughter's funeral, and
accept the sympathy of all her fellow-clerks in her office, no,
that is a final humiliation which I must spare myself. No!
If Virginia must be a lady-clerk, she must be it henceforth on
her own responsibility. I will retire from her existence."

Mrs. Bodoin had tried hard to persuade Virginia to give up
her work and come and live with her. She had offered her
half her income. In vain. Virginia stuck to her office.

Very well! So be it! The apartment was a fiasco, Mrs.
Bodoin was longing, longing to tear it to pieces again. One
last and final blow of the hammer! "Virginia, don't you
think we'd better get rid of this apartment, and live around
as we used to do? Don't you think we'll do that?"—"But all
the money you've put into it? and the lease for ten years!"
cried Virginia, in a kind of inertia.—"Never mind! We had
the pleasure of making it. And we've had as much pleasure

out of living in it as we shall ever have. Now we'd better
get rid of it—quickly—don't you think?"

Mrs. Bodoin's arms were twitching to snatch the pictures
off the walls, roll up the Aubusson carpet, take the china out
of the ivory-inlaid cabinet there and then, at that very
moment.

"Let us wait till Sunday before we decide," said Virginia.

"Till Sunday! Four days! As long as that? Haven't we
already decided in our own minds?" said Mrs. Bodoin.

"We'll wait till Sunday, anyhow," said Virginia.

The next evening, the Armenian came to dinner. Virginia
called him Arnold, with the French pronunciation, Arnault.
Mrs. Bodoin, who barely tolerated him, and could never get
his name, which seemed to have a lot of bouyoums in it,
called him either the Armenian or the Rahat Lakoum, after
the name of the sweetmeat, or simply the Turkish Delight.

"Arnault is coming to dinner to-night, mother."

"Really! The Turkish Delight is coming here to dinner?
Shall I provide anything special?" Her voice sounded as if
she would suggest snails in aspic.

"I don't think so."

Virginia had seen a good deal of the Armenian at the office
when she had to negotiate with him on behalf of the Board
of Trade. He was a man of about sixty, a merchant, had
been a millionaire, was ruined during the war, but was now
coming on again, and represented trade in Bulgaria. He
wanted to negotiate with the British Government, and the
British Government sensibly negotiated with him: at first
through the medium of Virginia. Now things were going
satisfactorily between Monsieur Arnault, as Virginia called
him, and the Board of Trade, so that a sort of friendship had
followed the official relations.

The Turkish Delight was sixty, grey-haired and fat. He had
numerous grandchildren growing up in Bulgaria, but he was
a widower. He had a grey moustache cut like a brush, and
glazed brown eyes over which hung heavy lids with white
lashes. His manner was humble, but in his bearing there was
a certain dogged conceit. One notices the combination sometimes in Jews. He had been very wealthy and kow-towed to,
he had been ruined and humiliated, terribly humiliated, and
now, doggedly, he was rising up again, his sons backing him,
away in Bulgaria. One felt he was not alone. He had his

sons, his family, his tribe behind him, away in the Near East.

He spoke bad English, but fairly fluent guttural French. He did not speak much, but he sat. He sat, with his short, fat thighs, as if for eternity, *there*. There was a strange potency in his fat immobile sitting, as if his posterior were connected with the very centre of the earth. And his brain, spinning away at the one point in question, business, was very agile. Business absorbed him. But not in a nervous, personal way. Somehow the family, the tribe was always felt behind him. It was business for the family, the tribe.

With the English he was humble, for the English like such aliens to be humble, and he had had a long schooling from the Turks. And he was always an outsider. Nobody would ever take any notice of him in society. He would just be an outsider, *sitting*.

"I hope, Virginia, you won't ask that Turkish-carpet gentleman when we have other people. I can bear it," said Mrs. Bodoin. "Some people might mind."

"Isn't it hard when you can't choose your own company in your own house," mocked Virginia.

"No! *I* don't care. I can meet anything; and I'm sure, in the way of selling Turkish carpets, your acquaintance is very good. But I don't suppose you look on him as a personal friend——?"

"I do. I like him quite a lot."

"Well——! As you will. But consider your *other* friends."

Mrs. Bodoin was really mortified this time. She looked on the Armenian as one looks on the fat Levantine in a fez who tries to sell one hideous tapestries at Port Said, or on the seafront at Nice, as being outside the class of human beings, and in the class of insects. That he had been a millionaire, and might be a millionaire again, only added venom to her feeling of disgust at being forced into contact with such scum. She could not even squash him, or annihilate him. In scum there is nothing to squash, for scum is only the unpleasant residue of that which was never anything but squashed.

However, she was not quite just. True, he was fat, and he sat, with short thighs, like a toad, as if seated for a toad's eternity. His colour was of a dirty sort of paste, his brown eyes were glazed under heavy lids. And he never spoke until spoken to, waiting in his toad's silence, like a slave.

But his thick, fine white hair, which stood up on his head

like a soft brush, was curiously virile. And his curious small
hands, of the same soft dull paste, had a peculiar, fat, soft
masculine breeding of their own. And his dull brown eye
could glint with the subtlety of serpents, under the white
brush of eyelash. He was tired, but he was not defeated. He
had fought, and won, and lost, and was fighting again, always
at a disadvantage. He belonged to a defeated race which
accepts defeat, but which gets its own back by cunning. He
was the father of sons, the head of a family, one of the heads
of a defeated but indestructible tribe. He was not alone, and
so you could not lay your finger on him. His whole consciousness was patriarchal and tribal. And somehow, he was
humble, but he was indestructible.

At dinner he sat half-effaced, humble, yet with the conceit
of the humble. His manners were perfectly good, rather
French. Virginia chattered to him in French, and he replied
with that peculiar nonchalance of the boulevards, which was
the only manner he could command when speaking French.
Mrs. Bodoin understood, but she was what one would call a
heavy-footed linguist, so when she said anything, it was
intensely in English. And the Turkish Delight replied in his
clumsy English, hastily. It was not his fault that French was
being spoken. It was Virginia's.

He was very humble, conciliatory, with Mrs. Bodoin. But
he cast at her sometimes that rapid glint of a reptilian glance
as if to say: "Yes! I see you! You are a handsome figure.
As an *objet de vertu* you are almost perfect." Thus his con-
noisseur's, antique-dealer's eye would appraise her. But then
his thick white eyebrows would seem to add: "But what,
under holy Heaven, are you as a woman? You are neither
wife nor mother nor mistress, you have no perfume of sex,
you are more dreadful than a Turkish soldier or an English
official. No man on earth could embrace you. You are a
ghoul, you are a strange genie from the underworld!" And
he would secretly invoke the holy names to shield him.

Yet he was in love with Virginia. He saw, first and fore-
most, the child in her, as if she were a lost child in the gutter,
a waif with a faint, fascinating cast in her brown eyes, waiting till someone would pick her up. A fatherless waif! And
he was tribal father, father through all the ages.

Then, on the other hand, he knew her peculiar disinterested
cleverness in affairs. That, too, fascinated him: that odd,

almost second-sight cleverness about business, and entirely impersonal, entirely in the air. It seemed to him very strange. But it would be an immense help to him in his schemes. He did not really understand the English. He was at sea with them. But with her, he would have a clue to everything. For she was, finally, quite a somebody among these English, these English officials.

He was about sixty. His family was established in the East, his grandsons were growing up. It was necessary for him to live in London for some years. This girl would be useful. She had no money, save what she would inherit from her mother. But he would risk that: she would be an investment in his business. And then the apartment. He liked the apartment extremely. He recognised the *cachet*, and the lilies and swans of the Aubusson carpet really did something to him. Virginia said to him: "Mother gave me the apartment." So he looked on that as safe. And finally, Virginia was almost a virgin, probably quite a virgin, and, as far as the paternal Oriental male like himself was concerned, entirely virgin. He had a very small idea of the silly puppy-sexuality of the English, so different from the prolonged male voluptuousness of his own pleasures. And last of all, he was physically lonely, getting old and tired.

Virginia, of course, did not know why she liked being with Arnault. Her cleverness was amazingly stupid when it came to life, to living. She said he was 'quaint'. She said his nonchalant French of the boulevards was 'amusing'. She found his business cunning 'intriguing', and the glint in his dark glazed eyes, under the white, thick lashes, 'sheiky'. She saw him quite often, had tea with him in his hotel, and motored with him one day down to the sea.

When he took her hand in his own soft still hands, there was something so caressing, so possessive in his touch, so strange and positive in his leaning towards her, that though she trembled with fear, she was helpless.—"But you are so thin, dear little thin thing, you need repose, repose, for the blossom to open, poor little blossom, to become a little fat!" he said in his French.

She quivered, and was helpless. It certainly was quaint! He was so strange and positive, he seemed to have all the power. The moment he realised that she would succumb into his power, he took full charge of the situation, he lost all his hesitation and his humility. He did not want just to make love to her: he wanted to marry her, for all his multifarious reasons. And he must make himself master of her.

He put her hand to his lips, and seemed to draw her life to his in kissing her thin hand. "The poor child is tired, she needs repose, she needs to be caressed and cared for," he said in his French. And he drew nearer to her.

She looked up in dread at his glinting, tired dark eyes under the white lashes. But he used all his will, looking back at her heavily and calculating that she must submit. And he brought his body quite near to her, and put his hand softly on her face, and made her lay her face against his breast, as he soothingly stroked her arm with his other hand. "Dear little thing! Dear little thing! Arnault loves her so dearly! Arnault loves her! Perhaps she will marry her Arnault. Dear little girl, Arnault will put flowers in her life, and make her life perfumed with sweetness and content."

She leaned against his breast and let him caress her. She gave a fleeting, half poignant, half vindictive thought to her mother. Then she felt in the air the sense of destiny, destiny Oh, so nice, not to have to struggle. To give way to destiny.

"Will she marry her old Arnault? Eh? Will she marry him?" he asked in a soothing, caressing voice, at the same time compulsive.

She lifted her head and looked at him: the thick white brows, the glinting, tired dark eyes. How queer and comic! How comic to be in his power! And he was looking a little baffled.

"Shall I?" she said, with her mischievous twist of a grin.

"*Mais oui!*" he said, with all the sang-foid of his old eyes. "*Mais oui! Je te contenterai, tu le verras.*"

"*Tu me contenteras!*" she said, with a flickering smile of real amusement at his assurance. "Will you really content me?"

"But surely! I assure it you. And you will marry me?"

"You must tell mother," she said, and hid wickedly against his waistcoat again, while the male pride triumphed in him.

Mrs. Bodoin had no idea that Virginia was intimate with the Turkish Delight: she did not inquire into her daughter's movements. During the famous dinner, she was calm and a little aloof, but entirely self-possessed. When, after coffee, Virginia left her alone with the Turkish Delight, she made no effort at conversation, only glanced at the rather short, stout man in correct dinner-jacket, and thought how his sort of fatness called for a fez and the full muslin breeches of a bazaar merchant in *The Thief of Baghdad.*

"Do you really prefer to smoke a hookah?" she asked him, with a slow drawl.

"What is a hookah, please?"

"One of those water-pipes. Don't you all smoke them in the East?"

He only looked mystified and humble, and silence resumed. She little knew what was simmering inside his stillness.

"Madame," he said, "I want to ask you something."

"You do? Then why not ask it?" came her slightly melancholy drawl.

"Yes! It is this. I wish I may have the honour to marry your daughter. She is willing."

There was a moment's blank pause. Then Mrs. Bodoin leaned towards him from her distance with curious portentousness.

"What was that you said?" she asked. "Repeat it!"

"I wish I may have the honour to marry your daughter. She is willing to take me."

His dark, glazed eyes looked at her, then glanced away again. Still leaning forward, she gazed fixedly on him, as if spellbound, turned to stone. She was wearing pink topaz ornaments, but he judged they were paste, moderately good.

"Did I hear you say she is willing to take you?" came the slow, melancholy, remote voice.

"Madame, I think so," he said, with a bow.

"I think we'll wait till she comes," she said, leaning back.

There was silence. She stared at the ceiling. He looked closely round the room, at the furniture, at the china in the ivory-inlaid cabinet.

"I can settle five thousand pounds on Mademoiselle Virginia, madame," came his voice. "Am I correct to assume that she will bring this apartment and its appointments into the marriage settlement?"

Absolute silence. He might as well have been on the moon. But he was a good sitter. He just sat until Virginia came in.

Mrs. Bodoin was still staring at the ceiling. The iron had entered her soul finally and fully. Virginia glanced at her, but said:

"Have a whisky-and-soda, Arnault?"

He rose and came towards the decanters, and stood beside her: a rather squat, stout man with white head, silent with misgiving. There was the fizz of the syphon: then they came to their chairs.

"Arnault has spoken to you, mother?" said Virginia.

Mrs. Bodoin sat up straight and gazed at Virginia with big, owlish eyes, haggard. Virginia was terrified, yet a little thrilled. Her mother was beaten.

"Is it true, Virginia, that you are *willing* to marry this— Oriental gentleman?" asked Mrs. Bodoin slowly.

"Yes, mother, quite true," said Virginia, in her teasing soft voice.

Mrs. Bodoin looked owlish and dazed.

"May I be excused from having any part in it, or from having anything to do with your future *husband*—I mean having any business to transact with him?" she asked dazedly, in her slow, distinct voice.

"Why, of course!" said Virginia, frightened, smiling oddly.

There was a pause. Then Mrs. Bodoin, feeling old and haggard, pulled herself together again.

"Am I to understand that your future husband would like to possess this apartment?" came her voice.

Virginia smiled quickly and crookedly. Arnault just sat, planted on his posterior, and heard. She reposed on him.

"Well—perhaps!" said Virginia. "Perhaps he would like to know that I possessed it." She looked at him.

Arnault nodded gravely.

"And do you *wish* to possess it?" came Mrs. Bodoin's slow voice. "Is it your intention to *inhabit* it, with your *husband?*" She put eternities into her long, stressed words.

"Yes, I think it is," said Virginia. "You know you *said* the apartment was mine, mother."

"Very well! It shall be so. I shall send my lawyer to this— Oriental gentleman, if you will leave written instructions on my writing-table. May I ask when you think of getting— *married?*"

"When do you think, Arnault?" said Virginia.

"Shall it be in two weeks?" he said, sitting erect, with his fists on his knees.

"In about a fortnight, mother," said Virginia.

"I have heard? In two weeks! Very well! In two weeks

everything shall be at your disposal. And now, please excuse me." She rose, made a slight general bow, and moved calmly and dimly from the room. It was killing her, that she could not shriek aloud and beat that Levantine out of the house. But she couldn't. She had imposed the restraint on herself.

Arnault stood and looked with glistening eyes round the room. It would be his. When his sons came to England, here he would receive them.

He looked at Virginia. She, too, was white and haggard now. And she flung away from him, as if in resentment. She resented the defeat of her mother. She was still capable of dismissing him for ever, and going back to her mother.

"Your mother is a wonderful lady," he said, going to Virginia and taking her hand. "But she has no husband to shelter her, she is unfortunate. I am sorry she will be alone. I should be happy if she would like to stay here with us."

The sly old fox knew what he was about.

"I'm afraid there's no hope of that," said Virginia, with a return of her old irony.

She sat on the couch, and he caressed her softly and paternally, and the very incongruity of it, there in her mother's drawing-room, amused her. And because he saw that the things in the drawing-room were handsome and valuable, and now they were his, his blood flushed and he caressed the thin girl at his side with passion, because she represented these valuable surroundings, and brought them to his possession. And he said: "And with me you will be very comfortable, very content, oh, I shall make you content, not like madame your mother. And you will get fatter, and bloom like the rose. I shall make you bloom like the rose. And shall we say next week, hein? Shall it be next week, next Wednesday, that we marry? Wednesday is a good day. Shall it be then?"

"Very well!" said Virginia, caressed again into a luxurious sense of destiny, reposing on fate, having to make no effort, no more effort, all her life.

Mrs. Bodoin moved into an hotel next day, and came into the apartment to pack up and extricate herself and her immediate personal belongings only when Virginia was necessarily absent. She and her daughter communicated by letter, as far as was necessary.

And in five days' time Mrs. Bodoin was clear. All business

that could be settled was settled, all her trunks were removed. She had five trunks, and that was all. Denuded and outcast, she would depart to Paris, to live out the rest of her days.

The last day she waited in the drawing-room till Virginia should come home. She sat there in her hat and street things, like a stranger.

"I just waited to say good-bye," she said. "I leave in the morning for Paris. This is my address. I think everything is settled; if not, let me know and I'll attend to it. Well, good-bye!—and I hope you'll be *very happy!*"

She dragged out the last words sinisterly; which restored Virginia, who was beginning to lose her head.

"Why, I think I may be," said Virginia, with the twist of a smile.

"I shouldn't wonder," said Mrs. Bodoin pointedly and grimly. "I think the Armenian grandpapa knows very well what he's about. You're just the harem type, after all." The words came slowly, dropping, each with a plop! of deep contempt.

"I suppose I am! Rather fun!" said Virginia. "But I wonder where I got it? Not from you, mother——" she drawled mischievously.

"I should say *not.*"

"Perhaps daughters go by contraries, like dreams," mused Virginia wickedly. "All the harem was left out of you, so perhaps it all had to be put back into me."

Mrs. Bodoin flashed a look at her.

"You have *all* my *pity!*" she said.

"Thank you, dear. You have just a bit of mine."

THE BLUE MOCCASINS

THE fashion in women changes nowadays even faster than
women's fashions. At twenty, Lina M'Leod was almost pain-
fully modern. At sixty, almost obsolete!

She started off in life to be really independent. In that remote day, forty years ago, when a woman said she was going
to be independent, it meant she was having no nonsense with
men. She was kicking over the masculine traces. and living
her own life, manless.

To-day, when a girl says she is going to be independent, it
means she is going to devote her attentions almost exclusively
to men; though not necessarily to 'a man'.

Miss M'Leod had an income from her mother. Therefore,
at the age of twenty, she turned her back on that image of
tyranny, her father, and went to Paris to study art. Art
having been studied, she turned her attention to the globe
of earth. Being terribly independent, she soon made Africa
look small: she dallied energetically with vast hinterlands of
China: and she knew the Rocky Mountains and the deserts
of Arizona as if she had been married to them. All this, to
escape mere man.

It was in New Mexico she purchased the blue moccasins,
blue bead moccasins, from an Indian who was her guide and
her subordinate. In her independence she made use of men,
of course, but merely as servants, subordinates.

When the war broke out she came home. She was then
forty-five, and already going grey. Her brother, two years
older than herself, but a bachelor, went off to the war; she
stayed at home in the small family mansion in the country,
and did what she could. She was small and erect and brief
in her speech, her face was like pale ivory, her skin like a
very delicate parchment, and her eyes were very blue. There
was no nonsense about her, though she did paint pictures.
She never even touched her delicately parchment face with
pigment. She was good enough as she was, honest-to-God,
and the country town had a tremendous respect for her.

In her various activities she came pretty often into contact
with Percy Barlow, the clerk at the bank. He was only

twenty-two when she first set eyes on him in 1914, and she immediately liked him. He was a stranger in the town, his father being a poor country vicar in Yorkshire. But he was of the confiding sort. He soon confided in Miss M'Leod, for whom he had a towering respect, how he disliked his step-mother, how he feared his father, was but as wax in the hands of that downright woman, and how, in consequence, he was homeless. Wrath shone in his pleasant features, but some-how it was an amusing wrath; at least to Miss M'Leod.

He was distinctly a good-looking boy, with stiff dark hair and odd, twinkling grey eyes under thick dark brows, and a rather full mouth and a queer, deep voice that had a caress-ing touch of hoarseness. It was his voice that somehow got behind Miss M'Leod's reserve. Not that he had the faintest intention of so doing. He looked up to her immensely: "She's miles above me."

When she watched him playing tennis, letting himself go a bit too much, hitting too hard, running too fast, being too nice to his partner, her heart yearned over him. The orphan in him! Why should he go and be shot? She kept him at home as long as possible, working with her at all kinds of war-work. He was so absolutely willing to do everything she wanted: devoted to her.

But at last the time came when he must go. He was now twenty-four and she forty-seven. He came to say good-bye, in his awkward fashion. She suddenly turned away, leaned her forehead against the wall, and burst into bitter tears. He was frightened out of his wits. Before he knew what was happening he had his arm in front of his face and was sob-bing too.

She came to comfort him. "Don't cry, dear, don't! It will all be all right."

At last he wiped his face on his sleeve and looked at her sheepishly. "It was you crying as did me in," he said. Her blue eyes were brilliant with tears. She suddenly kissed him.

"You are such a dear!" she said wistfully. Then she added, flushing suddenly vivid pink under her transparent parch-ment skin: "It wouldn't be right for you to marry an old thing like me, would it?"

He looked at her dumbfounded.

"No, I'm too old," she added hastily.

"Don't talk about old! You're not old!" he said hotly.

"At least I'm too old for *that*," she said sadly.

"Not as far as I'm concerned," he said. "You're younger than me, in most ways, I'm hanged if you're not!"

"Are you hanged if I'm not?" she teased wistfully.

"I am," he said. "And if I thought you wanted me, I'd be jolly proud if you married me. I would, I assure you."

"Would you?" she said, still teasing him.

Nevertheless, the next time he was home on leave she married him, very quietly, but very definitely. He was a young lieutenant. They stayed in her family home, Twybit Hall, for the honeymoon. It was her house now, her brother being dead. And they had a strangely happy month. She had made a strange discovery: a man.

He went off to Gallipoli, and became a captain. He came home in 1919, still green with malaria, but otherwise sound. She was in her fiftieth year. And she was almost white-haired; long, thick, white hair, done perfectly, and perfectly creamy, colourless face, with very blue eyes.

He had been true to her, not being very forward with women. But he was a bit startled by her white hair. However, he shut his eyes to it, and loved her. And she, though frightened and somewhat bewildered, was happy. But she was bewildered. It always seemed awkward to her, that he should come wandering into her room in his pyjamas when she was half dressed, and brushing her hair. And he would sit there silent, watching her brush the long swinging river of silver, of her white hair, the bare, ivory-white, slender arm working with a strange mechanical motion, sharp and forcible, brushing down the long silvery stream of hair. He would sit as if mesmerised, just gazing. And she would at last glance round sharply, and he would rise, saying some little casual thing to her and smiling to her oddly with his eyes. Then he would go out, his thin cotton pyjamas hitching up over his hips, for he was a rather big-built fellow. And she would feel dazed, as if she did not quite know her own self any more. And the queer, ducking motion of his silently going out of her door impressed her ominously, his curious cat head, his big hips and limbs.

They were alone in the house, save for the servants. He had no work. They lived modestly, for a good deal of her money had been lost during the war. But she still painted pictures. Marriage had only stimulated her to this. She painted canvases of flowers, beautiful flowers that thrilled her soul. And he would sit, pipe in fist, silent, and watch her. He had nothing to do. He just sat and watched her small, neat figure and her concentrated movements as she painted. Then he knocked out his pipe and filled it again.

She said that at last she was perfectly happy. And he said that he was perfectly happy. They were always together. He hardly went out, save riding in the lanes. And practically nobody came to the house.

But still, they were very silent with one another. The old chatter had died out. And he did not read much. He just sat still, and smoked, and was silent. It got on her nerves sometimes, and she would think as she had thought in the past, that the highest bliss a human being can experience is perhaps the bliss of being quite alone, quite, quite alone.

His bank firm offered to make him manager of the local branch, and, at her advice, he accepted. Now he went out of the house every morning and came home every evening. which was much more agreeable. The rector begged him to sing again in the church choir: and again she advised him to accept. These were the old grooves in which his bachelor life had run. He felt more like himself.

He was popular: a nice, harmless fellow, everyone said of him. Some of the men secretly pitied him. They made rather much of him, took him home to luncheon, and let him loose with their daughters. He was popular among the daughters too: naturally, for if a girl expressed a wish, he would instinctively say: "What! Would you like it? I'll get it for you." And if he were not in a position to satisfy the desire, he would say: "I only wish I could do it for you. I'd do it like a shot." All of which he meant.

At the same time, though he got on so well with the maidens of the town, there was no coming forward about him. He was, in some way, not wakened up. Good-looking, and big, and serviceable, he was inwardly remote, without self-confidence, almost without a self at all.

The rector's daughter took upon herself to wake him up. She was exactly as old as he was, a smallish, rather sharp-faced young woman who had lost her husband in the war, and it had been a grief to her. But she took the stoic attitude of the young: You've got to live, so you may as well do it! She was a kindly soul, in spite of her sharpness. And she had handsome little fellow. Miss M'Leod looked down a bit on Alice Howells and her pom, so Mrs. Howells felt no special love for Miss M'Leod—"Mrs. Barlow, that is!" she would add sharply. "For it's quite impossible to think of her as anything but Miss M'Leod!"

Percy was really more at ease at the rectory, where the pom yapped and Mrs. Howells changed her dress three or four times a day, and looked it, than in the semi-cloisteral atmosphere of Twybit Hall, where Miss M'Leod wore tweeds and a natural knitted jumper, her skirts rather long, her hair done up pure silver, and painted her wonderful flower pictures in the deepening silence of the daytime. At evening she would go up to change, after he came home. And though it thrilled her to have a man coming into her room as he dressed, snapping his collar-stud, to tell her something trivial as she stood bare-armed in her silk slip, rapidly coiling up the rope of silver hair behind her head, still, it worried her. When he was there, he couldn't keep away from her. And he would watch her, watch her, watch her as if she was the ultimate revelation. Sometimes it made her irritable. She was so absolutely used to her own privacy. What was he looking at? She never watched *him*. Rather she looked the other way. His watching tried her nerves. She was turned fifty. And his great silent body loomed almost dreadful.

He was quite happy playing tennis or croquet with Alice Howells and the rest. Alice was choir-mistress, a bossy little person outwardly, inwardly rather forlorn and affectionate, and not very sure that life hadn't let her down for good. She was now over thirty—and had no one but the pom and her father and the parish—nothing in her really intimate life. But she was very cheerful, busy, even gay, with her choir and school work, her dancing, and flirting, and dressmaking.

She was intrigued by Percy Barlow. "How *can* a man be so nice to *everybody*?" she asked him, a litle exasperated. "Well, why not?" he replied, with the odd smile of his eyes. "It's not why he shouldn't, but how he manages to do it! How can you have so much good-nature? I *have* to be catty to some people, but you're nice to *everybody*."

"Oh, am I!" he said ominously.

He was like a man in a dream, or in a cloud. He was quite a very perky little red-brown Pomeranian dog that she had bought in Florence in the street, but which had turned out a a good bank-manager, in fact very intelligent. Even in appearance, his great charm was his beautifully-shaped head. He had plenty of brains, really. But in his will, in his body, he was asleep. And sometimes this lethargy, or coma, made him look haggard. And sometimes it made his body seem inert and despicable, meaningless.

Alice Howells longed to ask him about his wife. "*Do* you love her? *Can* you really care for her?" But she daren't. She daren't ask him one word about his wife. Another thing she couldn't do, she couldn't persuade him to dance. Never, not once. But in everything else he was pliable as wax.

Mrs. Barlow—Miss M'Leod—stayed out at Twybit all the time. She did not even come in to church on Sunday. She had shaken off church, among other things. And she watched Percy depart, and felt just a little humiliated. He was going to sing in the choir! Yes, marriage was also a humiliation to her. She had distinctly married beneath her.

The years had gone by: she was now fifty-seven, Percy was thirty-four. He was still, in many ways, a boy. But in his curious silence, he was ageless. She managed him with perfect ease. If she expressed a wish, he acquiesced at once. So now it was agreed he should not come to her room any more. And he never did. But sometimes she went to him in his room, and was winsome in a pathetic, heart-breaking way.

She twisted him round her little finger, as the saying goes. And yet secretly she was afraid of him. In the early years he had displayed a clumsy but violent sort of passion, from which she had shrunk away. She felt it had nothing to do with her. It was just his indiscriminating desire for Woman, and for his own satisfaction. Whereas she was not just un-identified Woman, to give him his general satisfaction. So she had recoiled, and withdrawn herself. She had put him off. She had regained the absolute privacy of her room.

He was perfectly sweet about it. Yet she was uneasy with him now. She was afraid of him; or rather, not of him, but of a mysterious something in him. She was not a bit afraid of *him*, oh no! And when she went to him now, to be nice to him, in her pathetic winsomeness of an unused woman of fifty-seven, she found him sweet-natured as ever, but really indifferent. He saw her pathos and her winsomeness. In some way, the mystery of her, her thick white hair, her vivid blue eyes, her ladylike refinement still fascinated him. But his bodily desire for her had gone, utterly gone. And secretly, she was rather glad. But as he looked at her, looked at her, as he lay there so silent, she was afraid, as if some finger were pointed at her. Yet she knew, the moment she spoke to him, he would twist his eyes to that good-natured and 'kindly' smile of his.

It was in the late, dark months of this year that she missed the blue moccasins. She had hung them on a nail in his room. Not that he ever wore them: they were too small. Nor did she: they were too big. Moccasins are male footwear, among the Indians, not female. But they were of a lovely turquoise-blue colour, made all of little turquoise beads, with little forked flames of dead-white and dark-green. When, at the beginning of their marriage, he had exclaimed over them, she had said: "Yes! Aren't they a lovely colour! So blue!" And he had replied: "Not as blue as your eyes, even then."

So, naturally, she had hung them up on the wall in his room, and there they had stayed. Till, one November day, when there were no flowers, and she was pining to paint a still-life with something blue in it—oh, so blue, like delphiniums!—she had gone to his room for the moccasins. And they were not there. And though she hunted, she could not find them. Nor did the maids know anything of them.

So she asked him: "Percy, do you know where those blue moccasins are, which hung in your room?" There was a moment's dead silence. Then he looked at her with his good-naturedly twinkling eyes, and said: "No, I know nothing of them." There was another dead pause. She did not believe him. But being a perfect lady, she only said, as she turned away: "Well then, how curious it is!" And there was another dead pause. Out of which he asked her what she wanted them for, and she told him. Whereon the matter lapsed.

It was November, and Percy was out in the evening fairly often now. He was rehearsing for a 'play' which was to be given in the church schoolroom at Christmas. He had asked her about it. "Do you think it's a bit *infra dig*, if I play one of the characters?" She had looked at him mildly, disguising her real feeling. "If you don't feel *personally* humiliated," she said, "then there's nothing else to consider." And he had answered: "Oh, it doesn't upset *me* at all." So she mildly said: "Then do it, by all means." Adding at the back of her mind: If it amuses you, child!—but she thought, a change had indeed come over the world, when the master of Twybit Hall, or even, for that matter, the manager of the dignified Stubbs' Bank, should perform in public on a schoolroom stage in amateur theatricals. And she kept calmly aloof, preferring not to know any details. She had a world of her own.

When he had said to Alice Howells: "You don't think other folk'll mind—clients of the bank and so forth—think it beneath my dignity?" she had cried, looking up into his twinkling eyes: "Oh, you don't have to keep *your* dignity on ice, Percy—any more than I do mine."

The play was to be performed for the first time on Christmas Eve: and after the play, there was the midnight service in church. Percy therefore told his wife not to expect him home till the small hours, at least. So he drove himself off in the car.

As night fell, and rain, Miss M'Leod felt a little forlorn. She was left out of everything. Life was slipping past her. It was Christmas Eve, and she was more alone than she had ever been. Percy only seemed to intensify her aloneness, leaving her in this fashion.

She decided not to be left out. She would go to the play too. It was past six o'clock, and she had worked herself into a highly nervous state. Outside was darkness and rain: inside was silence, forlornness. She went to the telephone and rang up the garage in Shewbury. It was with great difficulty she got them to promise to send a car for her: Mr. Slater would have to fetch her himself in the two-seater runabout: everything else was out.

She dressed nervously, in a dark-green dress with a few modest jewels. Looking at herself in the mirror, she still thought herself slim, young looking and distinguished. She did not see how old-fashioned she was, with her uncompromising erectness, her glistening knob of silver hair sticking out behind, and her long dress.

It was a three-mile drive in the rain, to the small country town. She sat next to old Slater, who was used to driving horses and was nervous and clumsy with a car, without saying a word. He thankfully deposited her at the gate of St. Barnabas' School.

It was almost half-past seven. The schoolroom was packed

and buzzing with excitement. "I'm afraid we haven't a seat left, Mrs. Barlow!" said Jackson, one of the church sidesmen, who was standing guard in the school porch, where people were still fighting to get in. He faced her in consternation. She faced him in consternation. "Well, I shall have to stay somewhere, till Mr. Barlow can drive me home," she said. "Couldn't you put me a chair somewhere?"

Worried and flustered, he went worrying and flustering the other people in charge. The schoolroom was simply packed solid. But Mr. Simmons, the leading grocer, gave up his chair in the front row to Mrs. Barlow, whilst he sat in a chair right under the stage, where he couldn't see a thing. But he could see Mrs. Barlow seated between his wife and daughter, speaking a word or two to them occasionally, and that was enough.

The lights went down: *The Shoes of Shagput* was about to begin. The amateur curtains were drawn back, disclosing the little amateur stage with a white amateur back-cloth daubed to represent a Moorish courtyard. In stalked Percy, dressed as a Moor, his face darkened. He looked quite handsome, his pale grey eyes queer and startling in his dark face. But he was afraid of the audience—he spoke away from them, stalking around clumsily. After a certain amount of would-be funny dialogue, in tripped the heroine, Alice Howells, of course. She was an Eastern houri, in white gauze Turkish trousers, silver veil, and—the blue moccasins. The whole stage was white, save for her blue moccasins, Percy's dark-green sash, and a negro boy's red fez.

When Mrs. Barlow saw the blue moccasins, a little bomb of rage exploded in her. This, of all places! The blue moccasins that she had bought in the western deserts! The blue moccasins that were not so blue as her own eyes! *Her* blue moccasins! On the feet of that creature, Mrs. Howells.

Alice Howells was not afraid of the audience. She looked full at them, lifting her silver veil. And of course she saw Mrs. Barlow, sitting there like the Ancient of Days in judgment, in the front row. And a bomb of rage exploded in *her* breast too.

In the play, Alice was the wife of the grey-bearded old Caliph, but she captured the love of the young Ali, otherwise Percy, and the whole business was the attempt of these two to evade Caliph and negro-eunuchs and ancient crones, and get into each other's arms. The blue shoes were very important: for while the sweet Leila wore them, the gallant Ali was to know there was danger. But when she took them off, he might approach her.

It was all quite childish, and everybody loved it, and Miss M'Leod might have been quite complacent about it all, had not Alice Howells got her monkey up, so to speak. Alice with a lot of make-up, looked boldly handsome. And suddenly bold she was, bold as the devil. All these years the poor young widow had been 'good', slaving in the parish, and only even flirting just to cheer things up, never going very far and knowing she could never get anything out of it, but determined never to mope.

Now the sight of Miss M'Leod sitting there so erect, so coolly 'higher plane', and calmly superior, suddenly let loose a devil in Alice Howells. All her limbs went suave and molten, as her young sex, long pent up, flooded even to her finger-tips. Her voice was strange, even to herself, with its long, plaintive notes. She felt all her movements soft and fluid, she felt herself like living liquid. And it was lovely. Underneath it all was the sting of malice against Miss M'Leod, sitting there so erect, with her great knob of white hair.

Alice's business, as the lovely Leila, was to be seductive to the rather heavy Percy. And seductive she was. In two minutes, she had him spellbound. He saw nothing of the audience. A faint, fascinated grin came on to his face, as he acted up to the young woman in the Turkish trousers. His rather full, hoarse voice changed and became clear, with a new, naked clang in it. When the two sang together, in the simple banal duets of the play, it was with a most fascinating intimacy. And when, at the end of Act One, the lovely Leila kicked off the blue moccasins, saying: "Away, shoes of bondage, shoes of sorrow!" and danced a little dance all alone, barefoot, in her Turkish trousers, in front of her fascinated hero, his smile was so spellbound that everybody else was spellbound too.

Miss M'Leod's indignation knew no bounds. When the blue moccasins were kicked across the stage by the brazen Alice, with the words: "Away, shoes of bondage, shoes of sorrow!" the elder woman grew pink with fury, and it was all she could do not to rise and snatch the moccasins from the stage, and bear them away. She sat in speechless indignation during the brief curtain between Act One and Act Two. Her mocca-

sins! Her blue moccasins! Of the sacred blue colour, the
turquoise of heaven.

But there they were, in Act Two, on the feet of the bold
Alice. It was becoming too much. And the love-scenes
between Percy and the young woman were becoming nakedly
shameful. Alice grew worse and worse. She was worked up
now, caught in her own spell, and unconscious of everything
save of him, and the sting of that other woman, who presumed
to own him. Own him? Ha-ha! For he was fascinated. The
queer smile on his face, the concentrated gleam of his eyes,
the queer way he leaned forward from his loins towards her,
the new, reckless, throaty twang in his voice—the audience
had before their eyes a man spellbound and lost in passion.

Miss M'Leod sat in shame and torment, as if her chair was
red-hot. She too was fast losing her normal consciousness,
in the spell of rage. She was outraged. The second Act was
working to its climax. The climax came. The lovely Leila
kicked off the blue shoes: "Away, shoes of bondage, away!"
and flew barefoot to the enraptured Ali, flinging herself into
his arms. And if ever a man was gone in sheer desire, it was
Percy, as he pressed the woman's lithe form against his body,
and seemed unconsciously to envelop her, unaware of everything else. While she, blissful in his spell, but still aware of
the audience and of the superior Miss M'Leod, let herself be
wrapped closer and closer.

Miss M'Leod rose to her feet and looked towards the door.
But the way out was packed with people standing holding
their breath as the two on the stage remained wrapped in
each other's arms, and the three fiddles and the flute softly
woke up. Miss M'Leod could not bear it. She was on her
feet, and beside herself. She could not get out. She could not
sit down again.

"Percy!" she said, in a low clear voice. "Will you hand
me my moccasins?"

He lifted his face like a man startled in a dream, lifted his
face from the shoulder of his Leila. His gold-grey eyes were
like softly-startled flames. He looked in sheer horrified
wonder at the little white-haired woman standing below.

"Eh!" he said, purely dazed.

"Will you please hand me my moccasins!"—and she
pointed to where they lay on the stage.

Alice had stepped away from him, and was gazing at the

risen viper of the little elderly woman on the tip of the audience. Then she watched him move across the stage, bending forward from the loins in his queer mesmerized way, pick up the blue moccasins, and stoop down to hand them over the edge of the stage to his wife, who reached up for them.

"Thank you!" said Miss M'Leod, seating herself, with the blue moccasins in her lap.

Alice recovered her composure, gave a sign to the little orchestra, and began to sing at once, strong and assured, to sing her part in the duet that closed the Act. She knew she could command public opinion in her favour.

He too recovered at once, the little smile came back on his face, he calmly forgot his wife again as he sang his share in the duet. It was finished. The curtains were pulled to. There was immense cheering. The curtains opened, and Alice and Percy bowed to the audience, smiling both of them their peculiar secret smile, while Miss M'Leod sat with the blue moccasins in her lap.

The curtains were closed, it was the long interval. After a few moments of hesitation, Mrs. Barlow rose with dignity, gathered her wrap over her arm, and with the blue moccasins in her hand, moved towards the door. Way was respectfully made for her.

"I should like to speak to Mr. Barlow," she said to Jackson, who had anxiously ushered her in, and now would anxiously usher her out.

"Yes, Mrs. Barlow."

He led her round to the smaller class-room at the back, that acted as dressing-room. The amateur actors were drinking lemonade, and chattering freely. Mrs. Howells came forward, and Jackson whispered the news to her. She turned to Percy.

"Percy, Mrs. Barlow wants to speak to you. Shall I come with you?"

"Speak to me? Aye, come on with me."

The two followed the anxious Jackson into the other half-lighted class-room, where Mrs. Barlow stood in her wrap, holding the moccasins. She was very pale, and she watched the two butter-muslin Turkish figures enter, as if they could not possibly be real. She ignored Mrs. Howells entirely.

"Percy," she said, "I want you to drive me home."

"Drive you home!" he echoed.

"Yes, please!"

"Why—when?" he said, with vague bluntness.

"Now—if you don't mind——"

"What—in this get-up?" He looked at himself.

"I could wait while you changed."

There was a pause. He turned and looked at Alice Howells, and Alice Howells looked at him. The two women saw each other out of the corners of their eyes: but it was beneath notice. He turned to his wife, his black face ludicrously blank, his eyebrows cocked.

"Well, you see," he said, "it's rather awkward. I can hardly hold up the third Act while I've taken you home and got back here again, can I?"

"So you intend to play in the third Act?" she asked with cold ferocity.

"Why, I must, mustn't I?" he said blankly.

"Do you *wish* to?" she said, in all her intensity.

"I do, naturally. I want to finish the thing up properly," he replied, in the utter innocence of his head; about his heart he knew nothing.

She turned sharply away.

"Very well!" she said. And she called to Jackson, who was standing dejectedly by the door: "Mr. Jackson, will you please find some car or conveyance to take me home?"

"Aye! I say, Mr. Jackson," called Percy in his strong, democratic voice, going forward to the man. "Ask Tom Lomas if he'll do me a good turn and get my car out of the rectory garage, to drive Mrs. Barlow home. Aye, ask Tom Lomas! And if not him, ask Mr. Pilkington—Leonard. The key's there. You don't mind, do you? I'm ever so much obliged——"

The three were left awkwardly alone again.

"I expect you've had enough with two acts," said Percy soothingly to his wife. "These things aren't up to your mark. I know it. They're only child's play. But, you see, they please the people. We've got a packed house, haven't we?"

His wife had nothing to answer. He looked so ludicrous, with his dark-brown face and butter-muslin bloomers. And his mind was so ludicrously innocent. His body, however, was not so ridiculously innocent as his mind, as she knew when he turned to the other woman.

"You and I, we're more on the nonsense level, aren't we?"

he said, with the new, throaty clang of naked intimacy in his voice. His wife shivered.

"Absolutely on the nonsense level," said Alice, with easy assurance.

She looked into his eyes, then she looked at the blue moccasins in the hand of the other woman. He gave a little start, as if realising something for himself.

At that moment Tom Lomas looked in, saying heartily: "Right you are, Percy! I'll have my car here in half a tick. I'm more handy with it than yours."

"Thanks, old man! You're a Christian."

"Try to be—especially when you turn Turk! Well——" He disappeared.

"I say, Lina," said Percy in his most amiable democratic way, "would you mind leaving the moccasins for the next act? We s'll be in a bit of a hole without them."

Miss M'Leod faced him and stared at him with the full blast of her forget-me-not blue eyes, from her white face.

"Will you pardon me if I don't?" she said.

"What!" he exclaimed. "Why? Why not? It's nothing but play, to amuse the people. I can't see how it can hurt the *moccasins*. I understand you don't quite like seeing me make a fool of myself. But, anyhow, I'm a bit of a born fool. What?"—and his blackened face laughed with a Turkish laugh. "Oh, yes, you have to realise I rather enjoy playing the fool," he resumed. "And, after all, it doesn't really hurt *you*, now does it? Shan't you leave us those moccasins for the last act?"

She looked at him, then at the moccasins in her hand. No, it was useless to yield to so ludicrous a person. The vulgarity of his wheedling, the commonness of the whole performance! It was useless to yield even the moccasins. It would be treachery to herself.

"I'm sorry," she said. "But I'd so much rather they weren't used for this kind of thing. I never intended them to be." She stood with her face averted from the ridiculous couple.

He changed as if she had slapped his face. He sat down on top of the low pupils' desk and gazed with glazed interest round the class-room. Alice sat beside him, in her white gauze and her bedizened face. They were like two rebuked sparrows on one twig, he with his great, easy, intimate limbs, she so light and alert. And as he sat he sank into an unconscious physical sympathy with her. Miss M'Leod walked towards the door.

"You'll have to think of something as'll do instead," he muttered to Alice in a low voice, meaning the blue moccasins. And leaning down, he drew off one of the grey shoes she had on, caressing her foot with the slip of his hand over its slim, bare shape. She hastily put the bare foot behind her other, shod foot.

Tom Lomas poked in his head, his overcoat collar turned up to his ears.

"Car's here," he said.

"Right-o! Tom! I'll chalk it up to thee, lad!" said Percy with heavy breeziness. Then, making a great effort with himself, he rose heavily and went across to the door, to his wife, saying to her, in the same stiff voice of false heartiness:

"You'll be as right as rain with Tom. You won't mind if I don't come out? No! I'd better not show myself to the audience. Well—I'm glad you came, if only for a while. Good-bye then! I'll be home after the service—but I shan't disturb you. Good-bye! Don't get wet now——" And his voice, falsely cheerful, stiff with anger, ended in a clang of indignation.

Alice Howells sat on the infants' bench in silence. She was ignored. And she was unhappy, uneasy, because of the scene.

Percy closed the door after his wife. Then he turned with a looming slowness to Alice, and said in a hoarse whisper: "Think o' that, now!"

She looked up at him anxiously. His face, in its dark pigment, was transfigured with indignant anger. His yellow-grey eyes blazed, and a great rush of anger seemed to be surging up volcanic in him. For a second his eyes rested on her upturned, troubled, dark-blue eyes, then glanced away, as if he didn't want to look at her in his anger. Even so, she felt a touch of tenderness in his glance.

"And that's all she's ever cared about—her own things and her own way," he said, in the same hoarse whisper, hoarse with suddenly-released rage. Alice Howells hung her head in silence.

"Not another damned thing, but what's her own, her own—and her own holy way—damned holy-holy-holy, all to herself." His voice shook with hoarse, whispering rage, burst out at last.

Alice Howells looked up at him in distress.

"Oh, don't say it!" she said. "I'm sure she's fond of you."

"Fond of me! Fond of *me!"* he blazed, with a grin of transcendent irony. "It makes her sick to look at me. I am a hairy brute, I own it. Why, she's never once touched me to be fond of me—never once—though she pretends sometimes. But a man knows——" and he made a grimace of contempt. "He knows when a woman's just stroking him, good doggie!—and when she's really a bit woman-fond of him. That woman's never been real fond of anybody or anything, all her life— she couldn't, for all her show of kindness. She's limited to herself, that woman is; and I've looked up to her as if she was God. More fool me! If God's not good-natured and good-hearted, then what is He——?"

Alice sat with her head dropped, realising once more that men aren't really fooled. She was upset, shaken by his rage, and frightened, as if she too were guilty. He had sat down blankly beside her. She glanced up at him.

"Never mind!" she said soothingly. "You'll like her again to-morrow."

He looked down at her with a grin, a grey sort of grin. "Are you going to stroke me 'good doggie!' as well?" he said.

"Why?" she asked, blank.

But he did not answer. Then after a while he resumed: "Wouldn't even leave the moccasins! And she's hung them up in my room, left them there for years—any man'd consider they were his. And I did want this show to-night to be a success! What are you going to do about it?"

"I've sent over for a pair of pale-blue satin bed-slippers of mine—they'll do just as well," she replied.

"Aye! For all that, it's done me in."

"You'll get over it."

"Happen so! She's curdled my inside, for all that. I don't know how I'm going to be civil to her."

"Perhaps you'd better stay at the rectory to-night," she said softly.

He looked into her eyes. And in that look, he transferred his allegiance.

"You don't want to be drawn in, do you?" he asked, with troubled tenderness.

But she only gazed with wide, darkened eyes into his eyes, so she was like an open, dark doorway to him. His heart beat thick, and the faint, breathless smile of passion came into his eyes again.

"You'll have to go on, Mrs. Howells. We can't keep them waiting any longer."

It was Jim Stokes, who was directing the show. They heard the clapping and stamping of the impatient audience.

"Goodness!" cried Alice Howells, darting to the door.

THINGS

THEY were true idealists from New England. But that is some time ago: before the war. Several years before the war, they met and married; he a tall, keen-eyed young man from Connecticut, she a smallish, demure, Puritan-looking young woman from Massachusetts. They both had a little money. Not much, however. Even added together, it didn't make three thousand dollars a year. Still—they were free. Free!

Ah! Freedom! To be free to live one's own life! To be twenty-five and twenty-seven, a pair of true idealists with a mutual love of beauty, and an inclination towards 'Indian thought'—meaning, alas, Mrs. Besant—and an income a little under three thousand dollars a year! But what is money? All one wishes to do is to live a full and beautiful life. In Europe, of course, right at the fountain-head of tradition. It might possibly be done in America: in New England, for example. But at a forfeiture of a certain amount of 'beauty'. True beauty takes a long time to mature. The baroque is only half-beautiful, half-matured. No, the real silver bloom, the real golden-sweet bouquet of beauty had its roots in the Renaissance, not in any later or shallower period.

Therefore the two idealists, who were married in New Haven, sailed at once to Paris: Paris of the old days. They had a studio apartment on the Boulevard Montparnasse, and they became real Parisians, in the old, delightful sense, not in the modern, vulgar. It was the shimmer of the pure impressionists, Monet and his followers, the world seen in terms of pure light, light broken and unbroken. How lovely! How lovely the nights, the river, the mornings in the old streets and by the flower-stalls and the book-stalls, the afternoons up on Montmartre or in the Tuileries, the evenings on the boulevards!

They both painted, but not desperately. Art had not taken them by the throat, and they did not take Art by the throat. They painted: that's all. They knew people—nice people, if possible, though one had to take them mixed. And they were happy.

Yet it seems as if human beings must set their claws in

something. To be 'free', to be 'living a full and beautiful life', you must, alas, be attached to something. A 'full and beautiful life' means a tight attachment to *something*—at least, it is so for all idealists—or else a certain boredom supervenes; there is a certain waving of loose ends upon the air, like the waving, yearning tendrils of the vine that spread and rotate, seeking something to clutch, something up which to climb towards the necessary sun. Finding nothing, the vine can only trail, half-fulfilled, upon the ground. Such is freedom!—a clutching of the right pole. And human beings are all vines. But especially the idealist. He is a vine, and he needs to clutch and climb. And he despises the man who is a mere *potato*, or turnip, or lump of wood.

Our idealists were frightfully happy, but they were all the time reaching out for something to cotton on to. At first, Paris was enough. They explored Paris *thoroughly*. And they learned French till they almost felt like French people, they could speak it so glibly.

Still, you know, you never talk French with your *soul*. It can't be done. And though it's very thrilling, at first, talking in French to clever Frenchmen—they seem *so* much cleverer than oneself—still, in the long run, it is not satisfying. The endlessly clever *materialism* of the French leaves you cold, in the end, gives a sense of barrenness and incompatibility with true New England depth. So our two idealists felt.

They turned away from France—but ever so gently. France had disappointed them. "We've loved it, and we've got a great deal out of it. But after a while, after a considerable while, several years, in fact, Paris leaves one feeling disappointed. It hasn't quite got what one wants."

"But Paris isn't France."

"No, perhaps not. France is quite different from Paris. And France is lovely—quite lovely. But *to us*, though we love it, it doesn't say a great deal."

So, when the war came, the idealists moved to Italy. And they loved Italy. They found it beautiful, and more poignant than France. It seemed much nearer to the New England conception of beauty: something pure, and full of sympathy, without the *materialism* and the *cynicism* of the French. The two idealists seemed to breathe their own true air in Italy.

And in Italy, much more than in Paris, they felt they could thrill to the teachings of the Buddha. They entered the swell-

ing stream of modern Buddhistic emotion, and they read the
books, and they practised meditation, and they deliberately
set themselves to eliminate from their own souls greed, pain,
and sorrow. They did not realise—yet—that Buddha's very
eagerness to free himself from pain and sorrow is in itself a
sort of greed. No, they dreamed of a perfect world, from
which all greed, and nearly all pain, and a great deal of
sorrow, were eliminated.

But America entered the war, so the two idealists had to
help. They did hospital work. And though their experience
made them realise more than ever that greed, pain, and
sorrow *should* be eliminated from the world, nevertheless the
Buddhism, or the theosophy, didn't emerge very triumphant
from the long crisis. Somehow, somewhere, in some part of
themselves, they felt that greed, pain, and sorrow would never
be eliminated, because most people don't care about eliminating them, and never will care. Our idealists were far too
Western to think of abandoning all the world to damnation,
while they saved their two selves. They were far too un-
selfish to sit tight under a bho tree and reach Nirvana in a
mere couple.

It was more than that, though. They simply hadn't enough
Seitzfleisch to squat under a bho tree and get to Nirvana by
contemplating anything, least of all their own navel. If the
whole wide world was not going to be saved, they, personally,
were not so very keen on being saved just by themselves. No,
it would be so lonesome. They were New Englanders, so it
must be all or nothing. Greed, pain, and sorrow must either
be eliminated from *all the world*, or else, what was the use
of eliminating them from oneself? No use at all! One was
just a victim.

And so, although they still *loved* 'Indian thought', and felt
very tender about it: well, to go back to our metaphor, the
pole up which the green and anxious vines had clambered so
far now proved dry-rotten. It snapped, and the vines came
slowly subsiding to earth again. There was no crack and
crash. The vines held themselves up by their own foliage,
for a while. But they subsided. The beanstalk of 'Indian
thought' had given way before Jack and Jill had climbed off
the tip of it to a further world.

They subsided with a slow rustle back to earth again. But
they made no outcry. They were again 'disappointed'. But

they never admitted it. 'Indian thought' had let them down. But they never complained. Even to one another, they never said a word. They were disappointed, faintly but deeply disillusioned, and they both knew it. But the knowledge was tacit.

And they still had so much in their lives. They still had Italy—dear Italy. And they still had freedom, the priceless treasure. And they still had so much 'beauty'. About the fullness of their lives they were not quite so sure. They had one little boy, whom they loved as parents should love their children, but whom they wisely refrained from fastening upon, to build their lives on him. No, no, they must live their own lives! They still had strength of mind to know that.

But they were now no longer very young. Twenty-five and twenty-seven had become thirty-five and thirty-seven. And though they had had a very wonderful time in Europe, and though they still loved Italy—dear Italy!—yet: they were disappointed. They had got a lot out of it: oh, a very great deal indeed! Still, it hadn't given them quite, not *quite*, what they had expected. Europe was lovely, but it was dead. Living in Europe, you were living on the past. And Europeans, with all their superficial charm, were not *really* charming. They were materialistic, they had no *real* soul. They just did not understand the inner urge of the spirit, because the inner urge was dead in them, they were all survivals. There, that was the truth about Europeans: they were survivals, with no more getting ahead in them.

It was another bean-pole, another vine-support crumbled under the green life of the vine. And very bitter it was, this time. For up the old tree-trunk of Europe the green vine had been clambering silently for more than ten years, ten hugely important years, the years of real living. The two idealists had *lived* in Europe, lived on Europe and on European life and European things as vines in an everlasting vineyard.

They had made their home here: a home such as you could never make in America. Their watchword had been 'beauty'. They had rented, the last four years, the second floor of an old palazzo on the Arno, and here they had all their 'things'. And they derived a profound, profound satisfaction from their apartment: the lofty, silent, ancient rooms with windows on the river, with glistening, dark-red floors, and the beautiful furniture that the idealists had 'picked up'.

Yes, unknown to themselves, the lives of the idealists had been running with a fierce swiftness horizontally, all the time. They had become tense, fierce, hunters of 'things' for their home. While their souls were climbing up to the sun of old European culture or old Indian thought, their passions were running horizontally, clutching at 'things'. Of course they did not buy the things for the things' sakes, but for the sake of 'beauty'. They looked upon their home as a place entirely furnished by loveliness, not by 'things' at all. Valerie had some very lovely curtains at the windows of the long *salotto*, looking on the river: curtains of queer ancient material that looked like finely-knitted silk, most beautifully faded down from vermilion and orange, and gold, and black, down to a sheer soft glow. Valerie hardly ever came into the *salotto* without mentally falling on her knees before the curtains. "Chartres!" she said. "To me they are Chartres!" And Melville never turned and looked at his sixteenth-century Venetian bookcase, with its two or three dozen of choice books, without feeling his marrow stir in his bones. The holy of holies!

The child silently, almost sinisterly, avoided any rude contact with these ancient monuments of furniture, as if they had been nests of sleeping cobras, or that 'thing' most perilous to the touch, the Ark of the Covenant. His childish awe was silent and cold, but final.

Still, a couple of New England idealists cannot live merely on the bygone glory of their furniture. At least, one couple could not. They got used to the marvellous Bologna cupboard, they got used to the wonderful Venetian bookcase, and the books, and the Siena curtains and bronzes, and the lovely sofas and side-tables and chairs they had 'picked up' in Paris. Oh, they had been picking things up since the first day they landed in Europe. And they were still at it. It is the last interest Europe can offer to an outsider: or to an insider either.

When people came, and were thrilled by the Melville interior, then Valerie and Erasmus felt they had not lived in vain: that they still were living. But in the long mornings, when Erasmus was desultorily working at Renaissance Florentine literature, and Valerie was attending to the apartment: and in the long hours after lunch; and in the long, usually very

cold and oppressive evenings in the ancient palazzo: then
the halo died from around the furniture, and the things became things, lumps of matter that just stood there or hung
there, *ad infinitum*, and said nothing; and Valerie and Erasmus
almost hated them. The glow of beauty, like every other
glow, dies down unless it is fed. The idealists still dearly
loved their things. But they had got them. And the sad fact
is, things that glow vividly while you're getting them, go
almost quite cold after a year or two. Unless, of course,
people envy them very much, and the museums are pining
for them. And the Melvilles' 'things', though very good, were
not quite so good as that.

So, the glow gradually went out of everything, out of
Europe, out of Italy—"the Italians are *dears*"—even out of
that marvellous apartment on the Arno. "Why, if I had this
apartment, I'd never, never even want to go out of doors!
It's too lovely and perfect." That was something, of course
—to hear that.

And yet Valerie and Erasmus went out of doors: they even
went out to get away from its ancient, cold-floored, stone-
heavy silence and dead dignity. "We're living on the past,
you know, Dick," said Valerie to her husband. She called
him Dick.

They were grimly hanging on. They did not like to give
in. They did not like to own up that they were through. For
twelve years, now, they had been 'free' people living a 'full
and beautiful life'. And America for twelve years had been
their anathema, the Sodom and Gomorrah of industrial
materialism.

It wasn't easy to own that you were 'through'. They hated
to admit that they wanted to go back. But at last, reluctantly,
they decided to go, "for the boy's sake".—"We can't *bear* to
leave Europe. But Peter is an American, so he had better look
at America while he's young." The Melvilles had an entirely
English accent and manner; almost; a little Italian and French
here and there.

They left Europe behind, but they took as much of it along
with them as possible. Several van-loads, as a matter of fact.
All those adorable and irreplaceable 'things'. And all arrived
in New York, idealists, child, and the huge bulk of Europe
they had lugged along.

Valerie had dreamed of a pleasant apartment, perhaps on

Riverside Drive, where it was not so expensive as east of Fifth Avenue, and where all their wonderful things would look marvellous. She and Erasmus house-hunted. But alas! their income was quite under three thousand dollars a year. They found—well, everybody knows what they found. Two small rooms and a kitchenette, and don't let us unpack a *thing!*

The chunk of Europe which they had bitten off went into a warehouse, at fifty dollars a month. And they sat in two small rooms and a kitchenette, and wondered why they'd done it.

Erasmus, of course, ought to get a job. This was what was written on the wall, and what they both pretended not to see. But it had been the strange, vague threat that the Statue of Liberty had always held over them: "Thou shalt get a job!" Erasmus had the tickets, as they say. A scholastic career was still possible for him. He had taken his exams brilliantly at Yale, and had kept up his 'researches' all the time he had been in Europe.

But both he and Valerie shuddered. A scholastic career! The scholastic world! The *American* scholastic world! Shudder upon shudder! Give up their freedom, their full and beautiful life? Never! Never! Erasmus would be forty next birthday.

The 'things' remained in warehouse. Valerie went to look at them. It cost her a dollar an hour, and horrid pangs. The 'things', poor things, looked a bit shabby and wretched, in that warehouse.

However, New York was not all America. There was the great clean West. So the Melvilles went West, with Peter, but without the things. They tried living the simple life, in the mountains. But doing their own chores became almost a nightmare. 'Things' are all very well to look at, but it's awful handling them, even when they're beautiful. To be the slave of hideous things, to keep a stove going, cook meals, wash dishes, carry water and clean floors: pure horror of sordid anti-life!   ·

In the cabin on the mountains, Valerie dreamed of Florence, the lost apartment; and her Bologna cupboard and Louis-Quinze chairs, above all, her 'Chartres' curtains, stood in New York and costing fifty dollars a month.

A millionaire friend came to the rescue, offering them a cottage on the Californian coast—California! Where the new soul is to be born in man. With joy the idealists moved a little farther west, catching at new vine-props of hope.

And finding them straws! The millionaire cottage was perfectly equipped. It was perhaps as labour-savingly perfect as is possible: electric heating and cooking, a white-and-pearl-enamelled kitchen, nothing to make dirt except the human being himself. In an hour or so the idealists had got through their chores. They were 'free'—free to hear the great Pacific pounding the coast, and to feel a new soul filling their bodies.

Alas! the Pacific pounded the coast with hideous brutality, brute force itself! And the new soul, instead of sweetly stealing into their bodies, seemed only meanly to gnaw the old soul out of their bodies. To feel you are under the fist of the most blind and crunching brute force: to feel that your cherished idealist's soul is being gnawed out of you, and only irritation left in place of it: well, it isn't good enough.

After about nine months, the idealists departed from the Californian west. It had been a great experience, they were glad to have had it. But, in the long run, the West was not the place for them, and they knew it. No, the people who wanted new souls had better get them. They, Valerie and Erasmus Melville, would like to develop the old soul a little further. Anyway, they had not felt any influx of new soul on the Californian coast. On the contrary.

So, with a slight hole in their material capital, they returned to Massachusetts and paid a visit to Valerie's parents, taking the boy along. The grandparents welcomed the child— poor expatriated boy—and were rather cold to Valerie, but really cold to Erasmus. Valerie's mother definitely said to Valerie, one day, that Erasmus ought to take a job, so that Valerie could live decently. Valerie haughtily reminded her mother of the beautiful apartment on the Arno, and the 'wonderful' things in store in New York, and of the 'marvellous and satisfying life' she and Erasmus had led. Valerie's mother said that she didn't think her daughter's life looked so very marvellous at present: homeless, with a husband idle at the age of forty, a child to educate, and a dwindling capital: looked the reverse of marvellous to *her*. Let Erasmus take some post in one of the universities.

"What post? What university?" interrupted Valerie.

"That could be found, considering your father's connections and Erasmus's qualifications," replied Valerie's mother.

"And you could get all your valuable things out of store, and have a really lovely home, which everybody in America would be proud to visit. As it is, your furniture is eating up your income, and you are living like rats in a hole, with nowhere to go to."

This was very true. Valerie was beginning to pine for a home, with her 'things'. Of course, she could have sold her furniture for a substantial sum. But nothing would have induced her to. Whatever else passed away, religions, cultures, continents, and hopes, Valerie would *never* part from the 'things' which she and Erasmus had collected with such passion. To these she was nailed.

But she and Erasmus still would not give up that freedom, that full and beautiful life they had so believed in. Erasmus cursed America. He did not *want* to earn a living. He panted for Europe.

Leaving the boy in charge of Valerie's parents, the two idealists once more set off for Europe. In New York they paid two dollars and looked for a brief, bitter hour at their 'things'. They sailed 'student class'—that is, third. Their income now was less than two thousand dollars instead of three. And they made straight for Paris—cheap Paris.

They found Europe, this time, a complete failure. "We have returned like dogs to our vomit," said Erasmus; "but the vomit has staled in the meantime." He found he couldn't stand Europe. It irritated every nerve in his body. He hated America too. But America at least was a darn sight better than this miserable, dirt-eating continent; which was by no means cheap any more, either.

Valerie, with her heart on her things—she had really burned to get them out of that warehouse, where they had stood now for three years, eating up two thousand dollars—wrote to her mother she thought Erasmus would come back if he could get some suitable work in America. Erasmus, in a state of frustration bordering on rage and insanity, just went round Italy in a poverty-stricken fashion, his coat-cuffs frayed, hating everything with intensity. And when a post was found for him in Cleveland University, to teach French, Italian, and Spanish literature, his eyes grew more beady, and his long, queer face grew sharper and more rat-like with utter baffled fury. He was forty, and the job was upon him.

"I think you'd better accept, dear. You don't care for

Europe any longer. As you say, it's dead and finished. They offer us a house on the college lot, and mother says there's room in it for all our things. I think we'd better cable 'Accept'."

He glowered at her like a cornered rat. One almost expected to see rat's whiskers twitching at the sides of the sharp nose.

"Shall I send the cablegram?" she asked.

"Send it!" he blurted.

And she went out and sent it.

He was a changed man, quieter, much less irritable. A load was off him. He was inside the cage.

But when he looked at the furnaces of Cleveland, vast and like the greatest of black forests, with red and white-hot cascades of gushing metal, and tiny gnomes of men, and terrific noises, gigantic, he said to Valerie:

"Say what you like, Valerie, this is the biggest thing the modern world has to show."

And when they were in their up-to-date little house on the college lot of Cleveland University, and that woebegone débris of Europe: Bologna cupboard, Venice book-shelves, Ravenna bishop's chair, Louis-Quinze side-tables, 'Chartres' curtains, Siena bronze lamps, all were arrayed, and all looked perfectly out of keeping, and therefore very impressive; and when the idealists had had a bunch of gaping people in, and Erasmus had showed off in his best European manner, but still quite cordial and American; and Valerie had been most ladylike, but for all that, "we prefer America"; then Erasmus said, looking at her with queer, sharp eyes of a rat:

"Europe's the mayonnaise all right, but America supplies the good old lobster—what?"

"Every time!" she said, with satisfaction.

And he peered at her. He was in the cage: but it was safe inside. And she, evidently, was her real self at last. She had got the goods. Yet round his nose was a queer, evil scholastic look of pure scepticism. But he liked lobster.